virtual
light

BANTAM BOOKS

New York   Toronto   London   Sydney   Auckland

virtual

light

WILLIAM GIBSON

virtual light

A Bantam Spectra Book/September 1993

Spectra and the portrayal of a boxed "s" are trademarks of Bantam Books,
a division of Bantam Doubleday Dell Publishing Group, Inc.

Book design by Harakawa Sisco, Inc.

Library of Congress Cataloging-in-Publication Data
Gibson, William, 1948–
Virtual light / William Gibson.
p.   cm. — (A Bantam spectra book)
ISBN 0-553-07499-7
1. Twenty-first century—Fiction.   2. California—Fiction.
I. Title.
PS3557.I2264V57   1993
813'.54—dc20   93-7150   CIP
Published simultaneously in the United States and Canada

Bantam Books are published by Bantam Books, a division of Bantam
Doubleday Dell Publishing Group, Inc. Its trademark, consisting of the
words "Bantam Books" and the portrayal of a rooster, is Registered in
U.S. Patent and Trademark Office and in other countries. Marca
Registrada. Bantam Books, 1540 Broadway, New York, New York 10036.

PRINTED IN THE UNITED STATES OF AMERICA

BVG   0 9 8 7

To

Gary Gaetano Bandiera,

major dude, our friend

virtual
light

1

the
luminous
flesh
of giants

The courier presses his forehead against layers of glass, argon, high-impact plastic. He watches a gunship traverse the city's middle distance like a hunting wasp, death slung beneath its thorax in a smooth black pod.

Hours earlier, missiles have fallen in a northern suburb; seventy-three dead, the kill as yet unclaimed. But here the mirrored ziggurats down Lázaro Cárdenas flow with the luminous flesh of giants, shunting out the night's barrage of dreams to the waiting *avenidas*—business as usual, world without end.

The air beyond the window touches each source of light with a faint hepatic corona, a tint of jaundice edging imperceptibly into brownish translucence. Fine dry flakes of fecal snow, billowing in from the sewage flats, have lodged in the lens of night.

Closing his eyes, he centers himself in the background hiss of climate-control. He imagines himself in Tokyo, this room in some new wing of the old Imperial. He sees himself in the streets of Chiyoda-ku, beneath the sighing trains. Red paper lanterns line a narrow lane.

He opens his eyes.

Mexico City is still there.

The eight empty bottles, plastic miniatures, are carefully aligned with the edge of the coffee table: a Japanese vodka, Come Back Salmon, its name more irritating than its lingering aftertaste.

On the screen above the console, the *ptichka* await him, all in a creamy frieze. When he takes up the remote, their high sharp cheekbones twist in the space behind his eyes. Their young men, invariably entering from behind, wear black leather gloves. Slavic faces, calling up unwanted fragments of a childhood: the reek of a black canal, steel racketing steel beneath a swaying train, the high old ceilings of an apartment overlooking a frozen park.

Twenty-eight peripheral images frame the Russians in their earnest coupling; he glimpses figures carried from the smoke-blackened car-deck of an Asian ferry.

He opens another of the little bottles.

Now the *ptichka*, their heads bobbing like well-oiled ma-chines, swallow their arrogant, self-absorbed boyfriends. The camera angles recall the ardor of Soviet industrial cinema.

His gaze strays to NHK Weather. A low-pressure front is crossing Kansas. Next to it, an eerily calm Islamic downlink cease-lessly reiterates the name of God in a fractal-based calligraphy.

He drinks the vodka.

He watches television.

After midnight, at the intersection of Liverpool and Florencia, he stares out at the Zona Rosa from the back of a white Lada, a nanopore Swiss respirator chafing his freshly shaven chin.

And every passing face is masked, mouths and nostrils con-cealed behind filters. Some, honoring the Day of the Dead, resemble the silver-beaded jaws of grinning sugar-skulls. Whatever form they take, their manufacturers all make the same dubious, obliquely com-forting claims about viroids.

He's thought to escape the sameness, perhaps discover something of beauty or passing interest, but here there are only masked faces, his fear, the lights.

An ancient American car comes creeping through the turn, out of Avenida Chapultepec, gouts of carbon pulsing from beneath a dangling bumper. A dusty rind of cola-colored resin and shattered mirror seals its every surface; only the windshield is exposed, and this is black and glossy, opaque as a blob of ink, reminding him of the gunship's lethal pod. He feels the fear begin to accrete, seamlessly, senselessly, with absolute conviction, around this carnival ghost, the Cadillac, this oil-burning relic in its spectral robe of smudged mosaic silver. Why is it allowed to add its filth to the already impossible air? Who sits inside, behind the black windshield?

Trembling, he watches the thing pass.

"That car..." He finds himself leaning forward, compulsively addressing the broad brown neck of the driver, whose massive earlobes somehow recall reproduction pottery offered on the hotel's shopping channel.

"El coche," says the driver, who wears no mask, and turning, now seems to notice the courier for the first time. The courier sees the mirrored Cadillac flare, once, and briefly, with the reflected ruby of a nightclub's laser, then gone.

The driver is staring at him.

He tells the driver to return to the hotel.

He comes awake from a dream of metal voices, down the vaulted concourses of some European airport, distant figures glimpsed in mute rituals of departure.

Darkness. The hiss of climate-control.

The touch of cotton sheets. His telephone beneath the pillow. Sounds of traffic, muted by the gas-filled windows. All tension, his panic, are gone. He remembers the atrium bar. Music. Faces.

He becomes aware of an inner balance, a rare equilibrium. It is all he knows of peace.

And, yes, the glasses are here, tucked beside his telephone. He draws them out, opening the ear pieces with a guilty pleasure that has somehow endured since Prague.

Very nearly a decade he has loved her, though he doesn't think of it in those terms. But he has never bought another piece of software and the black plastic frames have started to lose their sheen. The label on the cassette is unreadable now, sueded white with his touch in the night. So many rooms like this one.

He has long since come to prefer her in silence. He no longer inserts the yellowing audio beads. He has learned to provide his own, whispering to her as he fast-forwards through the clumsy titles and up the moonlit ragged hillscape of a place that is neither Hollywood nor Rio, but some soft-focus digital approximation of both.

She is waiting for him, always, in the white house up the canyon road. The candles. The wine. The jet-beaded dress against the matte perfection of her skin, such whiteness, the black beads drawn smooth and cool as a snake's belly up her tensed thigh.

Far away, beneath cotton sheets, his hands move.

Later, drifting toward sleep of a different texture, the phone beneath his pillow chimes softly and only once.

"Yes?"

"Confirming your reservation to San Francisco," someone says, either a woman or a machine. He touches a key, recording the flight number, says goodnight, and closes his eyes on the tenuous light sifting from the dark borders of the drapes.

Her white arms enfold him. Her blondness eternal.

He sleeps.

2

cruising

with

gunhead

IntenSecure had their wagons detailed every three shifts. They used this big specially car wash off Colby; twenty coats of hand-rubbed Wet Honey Sienna and you didn't let it get too shabby.

That one November evening the Republic of Desire put an end to his career in armed response, Berry Rydell had arrived there a little early.

He liked the way it smelled inside. They had this pink stuff they put through the power-washers to get the road film off, and the smell reminded him of a summer job he'd had in Knoxville, his last year in school. They'd been putting condos into the shell of this big old Safeway out on Jefferson Davis. The architects wanted the cinder block walls stripped just this one certain way, mostly gray showing through but some old pink Safeway paint left in the little dips and crannies. They were from Memphis and they wore black suits and white cotton shirts. The shirts had obviously cost more than the suits, or at least as much, and they never wore ties or undid the top button. Rydell had figured that that was a way for architects to dress; now he lived in L.A., he knew it was true. He'd overheard one of them explaining to the foreman that what they were doing was *exposing the integrity of the material's passage through time.* He thought that was probably bullshit, but he sort of liked the sound of it anyway; like what happened to old people on television.

But what it really amounted to was getting most of this shitty old paint off thousands and thousands of square feet of equally shitty cinder block, and you did it with an oscillating spray-head on the end of a long stainless handle. If you thought the foreman wasn't looking, you could aim it at another kid, twist out a thirty-foot rooster tail of stinging rainbow, and wash all his sunblock off. Rydell and his friends all wore this Australian stuff that came in serious colors, so you could see where you had and hadn't put it. Had to get your right distance on it, though, 'cause up close those heads could take the chrome off a bumper. Rydell and Buddy Crigger both got fired for doing that, finally, and then they walked across Jeff Davis to a beer joint and Rydell wound up spending the night with this girl from Key West, the first time he'd ever slept beside a woman.

Now here he was in Los Angeles, driving a six-wheeled Hotspur Hussar with twenty coats of hand-rubbed lacquer. The Hussar was an armored Land Rover that could do a hundred and forty on a straightaway, assuming you could find one open and had the time to accelerate. Hernandez, his shift super, said you couldn't trust an Englishman to build anything much bigger than a hat, not if you wanted it to work when you needed it; he said IntenSecure should've bought Israeli or at least Brazilian, and who needed Ralph Lauren to design a tank anyway?

Rydell didn't know about that, but that paint job was definitely trying too hard. He thought they probably wanted people to think of those big brown United Parcel trucks, and at the same time they maybe hoped it would look sort of like something you'd see in an Episcopal church. Not too much gilt on the logo. Sort of restrained.

The people who worked in the car wash were mostly Mongolian immigrants, recent ones who had trouble getting better jobs. They did this crazy throat-singing thing while they worked, and he liked to hear that. He couldn't figure out how they did it; sounded like tree-frogs, but like it was two sounds at once.

Now they were buffing the rows of chromed nubs down the sides. Those had been meant to support electric crowd-control grids and were just chromed for looks. The riot-wagons in Knoxville had been electrified, but with this drip-system that kept them *wet*, which was a lot nastier.

"Sign here," said the crew boss, this quiet black kid named Anderson. He was a medical student, days, and he always looked like he was about two nights short of sleep.

Rydell took the pad and the light-pen and signed the signature-plate. Anderson handed Rydell the keys.

"You ought to get you some rest," Rydell said. Anderson grinned, wanly. Rydell walked over to Gunhead, deactivating the door alarm.

Somebody had written that inside, "GUNHEAD," in green marker on the panel above the windshield. The name stuck, but mostly because Sublett liked it. Sublett was Texan, a refugee from some weird trailer-camp video-sect. He said his mother had been getting ready to deed his ass to the church, whatever that meant.

Sublett wasn't too anxious to talk about it, but Rydell had gotten the idea that these people figured video was the Lord's preferred means of communicating, the screen itself a kind of perpetually burning bush. "He's in the de-tails," Sublett had said once. "You gotta watch for Him *close*." Whatever form this worship had taken, it was evident that Sublett had absorbed more television than anyone Rydell had ever met, mostly old movies on channels that never ran anything but. Sublett said Gunhead was the name of a robot tank in a Japanese monster movie. Hernandez thought Sublett had written the name on there himself. Sublett denied it. Hernandez said take it off. Sublett ignored him. It was still there, but Rydell knew Sublett was too law-abiding to commit any vandalism, and anyway the ink in the marker might've killed him.

Sublett had bad allergies. He went into shock from various kinds of cleaners and solvents, so you couldn't get him to come into the car wash at all, ever. The allergies made him light sensitive, too, so he had to wear these mirrored contacts. What with the black IntenSecure uniform and his dry blond hair, the contacts made him look like some kind of Klan-assed Nazi robot. Which could get kind of complicated in the wrong store on Sunset, say three in the morning and all you really wanted was some mineral water and a Coke. But Rydell was always glad to have him on shift, because he was as determinedly nonviolent a rentacop as you were likely to find. And he probably wasn't even crazy. Both of which were definite pluses for Rydell. As Hernandez was fond of pointing out, SoCal had stricter regulations for who could or couldn't be a hairdresser.

Like Rydell, a lot of IntenSecure's response people were former police officers of some kind, some were even ex-LAPD, and if the company's rules about not carrying personal weapons on duty were any indication, his co-workers were expected to turn up packing all manner of hardware. There were metal detectors on the staffroom doors and Hernandez usually had a drawer full of pushdaggers, nunchuks, stun-guns, knucks, boot-knives, and whatever else the detectors had picked up. Like Friday morning at a South Miami high school. Hernandez gave it all back after the shift, but when they went calling, they were supposed to make do with their Glocks and the chunkers.

The Glocks were standard police issue, at least twenty years old, that IntenSecure bought by the truckload from PDs that could afford to upgrade to caseless ammunition. If you did it by the book, you kept the Glocks in their plastic holsters, and kept the holsters Velcroed to the wagon's central console. When you answered a call, you pulled a holstered pistol off the console and stuck it on the patch provided on your uniform. That was the only time you were supposed to be out of the wagon with a gun on, when you were actually *responding*.

The chunkers weren't even guns, not legally anyway, but a ten-second burst at close range would chew somebody's face off. They were Israeli riot-control devices, air-powered, that fired one-inch cubes of recycled rubber. They looked like the result of a forced union between a bullpup assault rifle and an industrial staple gun, except they were made out of this bright yellow plastic. When you pulled the trigger, those chunks came out in a solid stream. If you got really good with one, you could shoot around corners; just kind of bounce them off a convenient surface. Up close, they'd eventually cut a sheet of plywood in half, if you kept on shooting, and they left major bruises out to about thirty yards. The theory was, you didn't always encounter that many armed intruders, and a chunker was a lot less likely to injure the client or the client's property. If you did encounter an armed intruder, you had the Glock. Although the intruder was probably running caseless through a floating breech— not part of the theory. Nor was it part of the theory that seriously tooled-up intruders tended to be tightened on dancer, and were thereby both inhumanly fast *and* clinically psychotic.

There had been a lot of dancer in Knoxville, and some of it had gotten Rydell suspended. He'd crawled into an apartment where a machinist named Kenneth Turvey was holding his girlfriend, two little kids, and demanding to speak to the president. Turvey was white, skinny, hadn't bathed in a month, and had the Last Supper tattooed on his chest. It was a very fresh tattoo; it hadn't even scabbed over. Through a film of drying blood, Rydell could see that Jesus didn't have any face. Neither did any of the Apostles.

"Damn it," Turvey said, when he saw Rydell. "I just wanna speak to the president." He was sitting cross-legged, naked, on his girlfriend's couch. He had something like a piece of pipe across his lap, all wrapped with tape.

"We're trying to get her for you," Rydell said. "We're sorry it's taking so long, but we have to go through channels."

"God damn it," Turvey said wearily, "doesn't nobody understand I'm on a mission from God?" He didn't sound particularly angry, just tired and put out. Rydell could see the girlfriend through the open door of the apartment's single bedroom. She was on her back, on the floor, and one of her legs looked broken. He couldn't see her face. She wasn't moving at all. Where were the kids?

"What *is* that thing you got there?" Rydell asked, indicating the object across Turvey's lap.

"It's a gun," Turvey said, "and it's why I gotta talk to the president."

"Never seen a gun like that," Rydell allowed. "What's it shoot?"

"Grapefruit cans," Turvey said. "Fulla concrete."

"No shit?"

"Watch," Turvey said, and brought the thing to his shoulder. It had a sort of breech, very intricately machined, a trigger-thing like part of a pair of vise-grip pliers, and a couple of flexible tubes. These latter ran down, Rydell saw, to a great big canister of gas, the kind you'd need a hand truck to move, which lay on the floor beside the couch.

There on his knees, on the girlfriend's dusty polyester carpet, he'd watched that muzzle swing past. It was big enough to put your fist down. He watched as Turvey took aim, back through the open bedroom door, at the closet.

"Turvey," he heard himself say, "where's the goddamn *kids*?"

Turvey moved the vise-grip handle and punched a hole the size of a fruit-juice can through the closet door. The kids were in there. They must've screamed, though Rydell couldn't remember hearing it. Rydell's lawyer later argued that he was not only deaf at this point, but in a state of sonically induced catalepsy. Turvey's invention was only a few decibels short of what you got with a SWAT stun-grenade. But Rydell couldn't remember. He couldn't remember shooting Kenneth Turvey in the head, either, or anything else at all until he woke up in the hospital. There was a woman there from *Cops in Trouble*, which had been Rydell's father's favorite show, but she said she couldn't actually talk to him until she'd spoken with his agent. Rydell said he didn't have one. She said she knew that, but one was going to call him.

Rydell lay there thinking about all the times he and his father had watched *Cops in Trouble*. "What kind of trouble we talking here?" he finally asked.

The woman just smiled. "Whatever, Berry, it'll probably be adequate."

He squinted up at her. She was sort of good-looking. "What's your name?"

"Karen Mendelsohn." She didn't look like she was from Knoxville, or even Memphis.

"You from *Cops in Trouble*?"

"Yes."

"What you do for 'em?"

"I'm a lawyer," she said. Rydell couldn't recall ever actually having met one before, but after that he wound up meeting lots more.

———————— •   •   • ————————

Gunhead's displays were featureless slabs of liquid crystal; they woke when Rydell inserted the key, typed the security code, and ran a basic systems check. The cameras under the rear bumper were his favorites; they made parking really easy; you could see exactly where you were backing up. The downlink from the Death Star wouldn't work while he was still in the car wash, too much steel in the building, but it was Sublett's job to keep track of all that with an ear-bead.

There was a notice posted in the staff room at IntenSecure, telling you it was company policy not to call it that, the Death Star, but everybody did anyway. The LAPD called it that themselves. Officially it was the Southern California Geosynclinical Law Enforcement Satellite.

Watching the dashboard screens, Rydell backed carefully out of the building. Gunhead's twin ceramic engines were new enough to still be relatively quiet; Rydell could hear the tires squish over the wet concrete floor.

Sublett was waiting outside, his silver eyes reflecting the red of passing taillights. Behind him, the sun was setting, the sky's colors bespeaking more than the usual cocktail of additives. He stepped back as Rydell reversed past him, anxious to avoid the least droplet of spray from the tires. Rydell was anxious too; he didn't want to have to haul the Texan to Cedars again if his allergies kicked up.

Rydell waited as Sublett pulled on a pair of disposable surgical gloves.

"Howdy," Sublett said, climbing into his seat. He closed his door and began to remove the gloves, gingerly peeling them into a Ziploc Baggie.

"Don't get any on you," Rydell said, watching the care with which Sublett treated the gloves.

"Go ahead, laugh," Sublett said mildly. He took out a pack of hypo-allergenic gum and popped a piece from its bubble. "How's ol' Gunhead?"

Rydell scanned the displays, satisfied. "Not too shabby."

"Hope we don't have to respond to any damn' stealth houses tonight," Sublett said, chewing.

Stealth houses, so-called, were on Sublett's personal list of bad calls. He said the air in them was toxic. Rydell didn't think it made any sense, but he was tired of arguing about it. Stealth houses were bigger than most regular houses, cost more, and Rydell figured the owners would pay plenty to keep the air clean. Sublett maintained that anybody who built a stealth house was paranoid to begin with, would always keep the place locked up too tight, no air circulation, and you'd get that bad toxic buildup.

If there'd been any stealth houses in Knoxville, Rydell hadn't known about them. He thought it was an L.A. thing. Sublett, who'd worked for IntenSecure for almost two years, mostly on day patrol in Venice, had been the first person to even mention them to Rydell. When Rydell finally got to answer a call to one, he couldn't believe the place; it just went down and down, dug in beneath something that looked almost, but not quite, like a bombed-out drycleaning plant. And it was all peeled logs inside, white plaster, Turkish carpets, *big* paintings, slate floors, furniture like he'd never seen before. But it was some kind of tricky call; domestic violence, Rydell figured. Like the husband hit the wife, the wife hit the button, now they were making out it was all just a glitch. But it couldn't *really* be a glitch, because someone had had to hit the button, and there hadn't been any response to the password call that came back to them three-point-eight seconds later. She must've messed with the phones, Rydell thought, then hit the button. He'd been been riding with "Big George" Kechakmadze that night, and the Georgian (Tbilisi, not Atlanta) hadn't liked it either. "You see these people, they're subscribers, man; nobody bleeding, you get your ass *out*, okay?" Big George had said, after. But Rydell kept remembering a tension around the woman's eyes, how she held the collar of the big white robe folded against her throat. Her husband in a matching robe but with thick hairy legs and expensive glasses. There'd been something wrong there but he'd never know what. Not any more than he'd ever understand how their lives really worked, lives that looked like what you saw on tv but weren't.

L.A. was full of mysteries, when you looked at it that way. No bottom to it.

He'd come to like driving through it, though. Not when he had to get anywhere in particular, but just cruising with Gunhead was okay. Now he was turning onto La Cienega and the little green cursor on the dash was doing the same.

"*Forbidden Zone*," Sublett said. "Herve Villechaize, Susan Tyrell, Marie-Pascal Elfman, Viva."

"Viva?" Rydell asked. "Viva *what*?"

"Viva. Actress."

"When'd they make that?"

"1980."

"I wasn't born yet."

"Time on tv's all the *same* time, Rydell."

"Man, I thought you were trying to get over your upbringing and all." Rydell de-mirrored the door-window to better watch a red-headed girl pass him in a pink Daihatsu Sneaker with the top off. "Anyway, I never saw that one." It was just that hour of evening when women in cars looked about as good, in Los Angeles, as anything ever did. The surgeon general was trying to outlaw convertibles; said they contributed to the skin-cancer rate.

"*Endgame*. Al Cliver, Moira Chen, George Eastman, Gordon Mitchell. 1985."

"Well, I was two," Rydell said, "but I didn't see that one either."

Sublett fell silent. Rydell felt sorry for him; the Texan really didn't know any other way to start a conversation, and his folks back home in the trailer-camp would've seen all those films and more.

"Well," Rydell said, trying to pick up his end, "I was watching this one old movie last night—"

Sublett perked up. "Which one?"

"Dunno," Rydell said. "This guy's in L.A. and he's just met this girl. Then he picks up a pay phone, 'cause it's ringing. Late at night. It's some guy in a missile silo somewhere who knows they've just launched theirs at the Russians. He's trying to phone his dad, or his brother, or something. Says the world's gonna end in short order. Then the guy who answered the phone hears these soldiers come in and shoot the guy. The guy on the phone, I mean."

Sublett closed his eyes, scanning his inner trivia-banks. "Yeah? How's it end?"

"Dunno," Rydell said. "I went to sleep."

Sublett opened his eyes. "Who was *in* it?"

"Got me."

Sublett's blank silver eyes widened in disbelief. "Jesus, Berry, you shouldn't oughta *watch* tv, not unless you're gonna pay it attention."

He wasn't in the hospital very long, after he shot Kenneth Turvey; barely two days. His lawyer, Aaron Pursley himself, made the case that they should've kept him in there longer, the better to assess the extent of his post-traumatic shock. But Rydell hated hospitals and anyway he didn't feel too bad; he just couldn't recall exactly what had happened. And he had Karen Mendelsohn to help him out with things, and his new agent, Wellington Ma, to deal with the other people from *Cops in Trouble*, not one of them as nice as Karen, who had long brown hair. Wellington Ma was Chinese, lived in Los Angeles, and Karen said his father had been in the Big Circle gang— though she advised Rydell not to bring it up.

Wellington Ma's business card was a rectangular slice of pink synthetic quartz, laser-engraved with his name, "The Ma-

Mariano Agency," an address on Beverly Boulevard, and all kinds of numbers and e-mail addresses. It arrived by GlobEx in its own little gray suede envelope while Rydell was still in the hospital.

"Looks like you could cut yourself on it," Rydell said.

"You could, many no doubt have," said Karen Mendelsohn, "and if you put it in your wallet and sit down, it shatters."

"Then what's the *point* of it?"

"You're supposed to take very good *care* of it. You won't get another."

Rydell never actually did meet Wellington Ma, at least not 'til quite a while later, but Karen would bring in a little briefcase with a pair of eyephones on a wire and Rydell could talk with him in his office in L.A. It was the sharpest telepresence rig Rydell had ever used, and it really did look just like he was right there. He could see out the window to where there was this lopsided pyramid the color of a Noxzema jar. He asked Wellington Ma what that was and Ma said it was the old Design Center, but currently it was a discount mall, and Rydell could go there when he came to L.A., which was going to be soon.

Turvey's girlfriend, Jenni-Rae Cline, was bringing an intricately interlocking set of separate actions against Rydell, the Department, the City of Knoxville, and the company in Singapore that owned her apartment building. About twenty million in total.

Rydell, having become a cop in trouble, was glad to find that *Cops in Trouble* was right there for him. They'd hired Aaron Pursley, for starters, and of course Rydell knew who *he* was from the show. He had that gray hair, those blue eyes, that nose you could split kindling with, and wore jeans, Tony Lama boots, and plain white oxford-cloth pima cotton cowboy business shirts with Navajo-silver bolo-ties. He was famous and he defended cops like Rydell from people like Turvey's girlfriend and *her* lawyer.

Jenni-Rae Cline's lawyer maintained that Rydell shouldn't have been in her apartment at all, that he'd endangered her life and her children's by so doing, and that he'd killed Kenneth Turvey in the process, Mr. Turvey being described as a skilled craftsman, a steady worker, a loving father-figure for little Rambo and Kelly, a born-again Christian, a recovering addict to 4-Thiobuscaline, and the family's sole means of support.

"Recovering?" Rydell asked Karen Mendelsohn in his room in the airport Executive Suites. She'd just shown him the fax from Jenni-Rae's lawyer.

"Apparently he'd been to a meeting that very day," Karen said.

"What did he *do* there?" Rydell asked, remembering the Last Supper in drying blood.

"According to *our* witnesses, he openly horned a tablespoon of his substance of choice, took the podium by force, and delivered a thirty-minute rant on President Millbank's pantyhose and the assumed current state of her genitalia. He then exposed himself, masturbated but did not ejaculate, and left the basement of the First Baptist Church."

"Jesus," Rydell said. "And this was at one of those drug meetings, like A.A.?"

"It was," Karen Mendelsohn said, "though apparently Turvey's performance has triggered an unfortunate sequence of relapses. We'll send in a team of counselors, of course, to work with those who were at the meeting."

"That's nice," Rydell said.

"Look good in court," she said, "in the unlikely event we ever get there."

"He wasn't 'recovering,'" Rydell said. "Hadn't even recovered from the last bunch he jammed up his nose."

"Apparently true," she said. "But he was also a member of Adult Survivors of Satanism, and *they* are starting to take an interest in this case. Therefore, both Mr. Pursley and Mr. Ma feel it best we coast it but soon, Berry. You and me."

"But what about the court stuff?"

"You're on suspension from the Department, you haven't been charged with anything yet, and your lawyer's name is Aaron-with-two-a's Pursley. You're *out* of here, Berry."

"To L.A.?"

"None other."

Rydell looked at her. He thought about Los Angeles on television. "Will I like it?"

"At first," she said. "At first, it'll probably like *you*. I know *I* do."

Which was how he wound up going to bed with a lawyer—one who smelled like a million dollars, talked dirty, slid all around, and wore underwear from Milan, which was in Italy.

"*The Kill-Fix.* Cyrinda Burdette, Gudrun Weaver, Dean Mitchell, Shinobu Sakamaki. 1997."

"Never saw it," Rydell said, sucking the last of his grande decaf cold capp-with-an-extra-shot from the milky ice at the bottom of his plastic thermos cup.

"Mama saw Cyrinda Burdette. In this mall over by Waco. Got her autograph, too. Kept it up on the set with the prayer-hankies and her hologram of the Reverend Wayne Fallon. She had a prayer-hanky for every damn thing. One for the rent, one to keep the AIDS off, the TB..."

"Yeah? How'd she use 'em?"

"Kept 'em on *top* of the *set*," Sublett explained, and finished the inch of quadruple-distilled water left in the skinny translucent bottle. There was only one place along this part of Sunset sold the stuff, but Rydell didn't mind; it was next to a take-out coffee-bar, and they could park in the lot on the corner. Fellow who ran the lot always seemed kind of glad to see them.

"Prayer-hanky won't keep any AIDS off," Rydell said. "Get yourself vaccinated, like anybody else. Get your momma vaccinated, too." Through the de-mirrored window, Rydell could see a street-shrine to J. D. Shapely, up against the concrete wall that was all that was left of the building that had stood there once. You saw a lot of them in West Hollywood. Somebody had sprayed SHAPELY WAS A COCK-SUCKING FAGGOT in bright pink paint, the letters three feet high, and then a big pink heart. Below that, stuck to the wall, were postcards of Shapely and photographs of people who must've died. God only knew how many millions had. On the pavement at the base of the wall were dead flowers, stubs of candles, other stuff. Something about the postcards gave Rydell the creeps; they made the guy look like a cross between Elvis and some kind of Catholic saint, skinny and with his eyes too big.

He turned to Sublett. "Man, *you* still haven't got your ass vaccinated yet, you got nothin' but stone white-trash ignorance to thank for it."

Sublett cringed. "That's worse than a *live* vaccine, man; that's a whole *'nother* disease right there!"

"Sure is," Rydell said, "but it doesn't *do* anything to you. And there's still plenty of the old kind walking around here. They oughta make it compulsory, you ask me."

Sublett shuddered. "Reverend Fallon always said—"

"Screw Reverend Fallon," Rydell said, hitting the ignition. "Son of a bitch just makes money selling prayer-hankies to people like your momma. You knew that was all bullshit anyway, didn't you, otherwise why'd you come out here?" He put Gunhead into gear and eased over into the Sunset traffic. One thing about driving a Hotspur Hussar, people almost always let you cut in.

Sublett's head seemed to draw down between his high shoulders, giving him the look of a worried, steel-eyed buzzard. "Ain't all *that* simple," he said. "It's everything I been brought up to *be*. Can't *all* be bullshit, can it?"

Rydell, glancing over at him, took pity. "Naw," he said, "I guess it wouldn't have to be, necessarily, all of it, but it's just—"

"What they bring *you* all up to be, Berry?"

Rydell had to think about it. "Republican," he said, finally.

———————— • ———— • ———— • ————————

Karen Mendelsohn had seemed like the best of a whole string of things Rydell felt he could get used to just fine. Like flying business-class or having a SoCal MexAmeriBank card from *Cops in Trouble.*

That first time with her, in the Executive Suites in Knoxville, not having anything with him, he'd tried to show her his certificates of vaccination (required by the Department, else they couldn't get you insured). She'd just laughed and said German nanotech would take care of all of that. Then she showed Rydell this thing through the transparent top of a gadget like a little battery-powered pressure-cooker. Rydell had heard about them, but he hadn't ever seen one; he'd also heard they cost about as much as a small car. He'd read somewhere how they always had to be kept at body temperature.

It looked like it might be moving a little in there. Pale, sort of jellyfish thing. He asked her if it was true they were alive. She told him it wasn't, exactly, but it was *almost,* and the rest of it was Bucky balls and subcellular automata. And he wouldn't even know it was there, but no way was she going to put it in in front of him.

She'd gone into the bathroom to do that. When she came back out in that underwear, he got to learn where Milan was. And while it was true he wouldn't have known the thing was there, he *did* know it was there, but pretty soon he forgot about it, almost.

They chartered a tilt-rotor to Memphis the next morning and got on Air Magellan to LAX. Business-class mostly meant better gizmos in the seatback in front of you, and Rydell's immediate favorite was a telepresence set you could tune to servo-mounted mollies on the outside of the plane. Karen hated to use the little VirtuFax she carried around in her purse, so she'd gotten on to her office in L.A. and had them download her morning's mail into her seatback display. She got down to that fast, talking on the phone, sending faxes, and leaving Rydell to *ooh* and *ah* at the views from the mollies.

The seats were bigger than when he used to fly down to Florida to see his father, the food was better, and the drinks were free. Rydell had three or four of those, fell asleep, and didn't wake up until somewhere over Arizona.

The air was funny, at LAX, and the light was different. California was a lot more crowded than he'd expected, and louder. There was a man there from *Cops in Trouble,* holding up a piece of wrinkled white cardboard that said MENDELSOHN in red marker, only the *S* was backward. Rydell smiled, introduced himself, and shook hands with him. He seemed to like that; said his name was Sergei. When Karen asked him where the fucking car was, he turned bright red and said it would just take him a minute to get it. Karen said no thanks, they'd walk to the lot with him as soon as their bags turned up, no way was she waiting around in a zoo like this. Sergei nodded. He kept trying to fold up the sign and put it into his jacket pocket, but it was too big. Rydell wondered why she'd suddenly gotten bitchy like that. Tired from the trip, maybe. He winked at Sergei, but that just seemed to make the guy more nervous.

After their bags came, Karen's two black leather ones and the softside blue Samsonite Rydell had bought with his new debit-card, he and Sergei carried them out and across a kind of traffic-loop. The air outside was about the same, but hotter. This recording kept saying that the white spaces were for loading and unloading only. There were all kinds of cars jockeying around, babies crying, people leaning on piles of luggage, but Sergei knew where they were going—over to this garage across the way.

Sergei's car was long, black, German, and looked like some-body had just cleaned it all over with warm spit and Q-Tips. When Rydell offered to ride shotgun, Sergei got rattled again and hustled him into the back seat with Karen. Which made her laugh, so Rydell felt better.

As they were pulling out of the garage, Rydell spotted two cops over by these big stainless-steel letters that said METRO. They wore air-conditioned helmets with clear plastic visors. They were poking at an old man with their sticks, though it didn't look like they had them turned on. The old man's jeans were out at the knees and he had big patches of tape on both cheekbones, which almost always means can-cer. He was so burned, it was hard to tell if he was white or what. A crowd of people was streaming up the stairs behind the old man and the cops, under the METRO sign, and stepping around them.

"Welcome to Los Angeles," she said. "Be glad you aren't taking the subway."

They had dinner that night in what Karen said was Hollywood, with Aaron Pursley himself, in a Tex-Mex restaurant on North Flores Street. It was the best Tex-Mex food Rydell had ever had. About a month later, he tried to take Sublett there for his birthday, maybe cheer him up with a down-home meal, but the man out front just wouldn't let them in.

"Full up," he said.

Rydell could see plenty of empty tables through the window. It was early and there was hardly anybody in there. "How 'bout those," Rydell said, pointing at all the empty tables.

"Reserved," the man said.

Sublett said spicy foods weren't really such a good idea for him anyway.

What he'd come to like best, cruising with Gunhead, was getting back up in the hills and canyons, particularly on a night with a good moon.

Sometimes you saw things up there and couldn't quite be sure you'd seen them or not. One full-moon night Rydell had slung Gunhead around a curve and frozen a naked woman in the headlights, the way a deer'll stop, trembling, on a country road. Just a second she was there, long enough for Rydell to think he'd seen that she either wore silver horns or some kind of hat with an upturned crescent, and that she might've been Japanese, which struck him right then as the weirdest thing about any of it. Then she saw him—he *saw* her see him—and smiled. Then she was gone.

Sublett had seen her, too, but it only kicked him into some kind of motormouthed ecstasy of religious dread, every horror-movie he'd ever seen tumbling over into Reverend Fallon's rants about witches, devil-worshippers, and the living power of Satan. He'd gone through his week's supply of gum, talking nonstop, until Rydell had finally told him to shut the fuck up.

Because now she was gone, he wanted to think about her. How she'd looked, what she might have been doing there, and how it was she'd vanished. With Sublett sulking in the shotgun seat, Rydell had tried to remember just exactly how it was she'd managed to so perfectly and suddenly *not* be there. And the funny thing was, he sort of remembered it two ways, which was nothing at all like the way he still didn't really remember shooting Kenneth Turvey, even though he'd heard production assistants and network lawyers go over it so many times he felt like he'd seen it, or at least the *Cops in Trouble* version (which never aired). One way he remembered it, she'd just sort of gone down the slope beside the road, though whether she was running or floating, he couldn't say. The other way he remembered, she'd jumped—though that was such a poor word for it—*up* the slope above the other side of the road, somehow clearing all that dust-silvered moonlit vegetation, and just flat-out impossible *gone*, forty feet if it was five.

And did Japanese women ever have that kind of long curly hair? And hadn't it looked like the shadowed darkness of her bush had been shaved into something like an exclamation point?

He'd wound up buying Sublett four packs of the special gum at an all-night Russian pharmacy on Wilshire, amazed at what the stuff cost him.

He'd seen other things, too, up the canyons, particularly when he'd drawn a shift on deep graveyard. Mostly fires, small ones, where fires couldn't be. And lights in the sky, sometimes, but Sublett was so full of trailer-camp contactee shit that if Rydell saw a light now, driving, he knew better than to mention it.

But sometimes, when he was up there, he'd think about her. He knew he didn't know what she was, and in some funny way he didn't even care if she'd been human or not. But he hadn't ever felt like she was bad, just different.

So now he just drove, shooting the shit with Sublett, on the night that would turn out to be his very last night on patrol with IntenSecure. No moon, but a rare clear sky with a few stars showing.

Five minutes to their first house check, then they'd be swinging back toward Beverly Hills.

They were talking about this chain of Japanese gyms called Body Hammer. Body Hammer didn't offer much in the way of traditional gym culture; in fact they went as far as possible in the opposite direction, catering mostly to kids who liked the idea of being injected with Brazilian fetal tissue and having their skeletons reinforced with what the ads called "performance materials."

Sublett said it was the Devil's work.

Rydell said it was a Tokyo franchise operation.

Gunhead said: "Multiple homicide, hostage-taking in progress, may involve subscriber's minor children. Benedict Canyon. You have IntenSecure authorization to employ deadly, repeat, deadly force."

And the dash lit up like an old-time video arcade.

The way it had worked out, Rydell hadn't actually had time to get used to Karen Mendelsohn, business-class seats, or any of that stuff.

Karen lived, umpteen floors up, in Century City II, aka the Blob, which looked sort of like a streamlined, semi-transparent green tit and was the third-tallest structure in the L.A. Basin. When the light was right, you could see almost clear through it, and make out the three giant struts that held it up, each one so big around you could stuff an ordinary skyscraper up it with room to spare. There were elevators up through these tripod-things, and they ran at an angle; Rydell hadn't had time to get used to that either.

The tit had a carefully corroded copper nipple, like one of those Chinese hats, that could've covered a couple of football fields. That was where Karen's apartment was, under there, along with an equally pricey hundred others, a tennis club, bars and restaurants, and a mall you had to pay to join before you could shop there. She was right out on the edge, with big curved windows set into the green wall.

Everything in there was different shades of white, except for her clothes, which were always black, her suitcases, which were black, too, and the big terry robes she liked to wear, which were the color of dry oatmeal.

Karen said it was Aggressive Retro Seventies and she was getting a little tired of it. Rydell saw how she could be, but figured it might not be polite to say so.

The network had gotten him a room in a West Hollywood hotel that looked more like a regular condo-building, but he never did spend much time there. Until the Pooky Bear thing broke in Ohio, he'd mostly been up at Karen's.

The discovery of the first thirty-five Pooky Bear victims pretty much put paid to Rydell's career as a cop in trouble. It hadn't helped that the officers who'd first reached the scene, Sgt. China Valdez and Cpl. Norma Pierce, were easily the two best-looking women on the whole Cincinnati force ("balls-out telegenic," one of the production assistants had said, though Rydell thought it sounded weird under the circumstances). Then the count began to rise, ultimately going right off any known or established serial-killing scale. Then it was revealed that all the victims were children. Then Sgt. Valdez went post-traumatic in stone bugfuck fashion, walking into a downtown tavern and clipping both kneecaps off a known pedophile—this amazingly repulsive character, nickname of Jellybeans, who had absolutely no connection with the Pooky Bear murders.

Aaron Pursley was already Learing it back to Cincinnati in a plane that had no metal in it whatsoever, Karen had locked the goggles across her eyes and was talking nonstop to at least six people at once, and Rydell was sitting on the edge of her big white bed, starting to get the idea that something had changed.

When she finally took the goggles off, she just sat there, staring at a white painting on a white wall.

"They got suspects?" Rydell asked.

Karen looked over at him like she'd never seen him before.

"Suspects? They've got *confessions* already . . ." It struck

Rydell how old she looked right then, and he wondered how old she actually was. She got up and walked out of the room.

She came back five minutes later in a fresh black outfit. "Pack. I can't have you here now." Then she was gone, no kiss, no goodbye, and that was that.

He got up, put a television on, and saw the Pooky Bear killers for the first time. All three of them. They looked, he thought, pretty much like everybody else, which is how people who do that kind of shit usually do look on television.

He was sitting there in one of her oatmeal robes when a pair of rentacops let themselves in without knocking. Their uniforms were black and they were wearing the same kind of black high-top SWAT-trainers that Rydell had worn on patrol in Knoxville, the ones with the Kevlar insoles in case somebody snuck up and tried to shoot you in the bottom of the foot.

One of them was eating an apple. The other one had a stun-stick in his hand.

"Hey, pal," the first one said, around a mouthful of apple, "we gotta show you out."

"I had a pair of shoes like that," Rydell said. "Made in Portland, Oregon. Two hundred ninety-nine dollars out at CostCo."

The one with the stick grinned. "You gonna get packing now?"

So Rydell did, picking up anything that wasn't black, white, or oatmeal and tossing it into his blue Samsonite.

The rentacop with the stick watched him, while the other one wandered around, finishing his apple.

"Who you guys with?" Rydell asked.

"IntenSecure," said the one with the stick.

"Good outfit?" Rydell was zipping up his bag.

The man shrugged.

"Outa Singapore," the other one said, wrapping the core of his apple in a crumpled Kleenex he'd taken from his pants pocket. "We got all the big buildings, gated communities, like that." He carefully tucked the apple-core into the breast-pocket of his crisp black uniform shirt, behind the bronze badge.

"You got money for the Metro?" Mr. Stick asked Rydell.

"Sure," Rydell said, thinking of his debit-card.

"Then you're better off than the majority of assholes we get to escort out of here," the man said.

A day later, the network pulled the plug on his Mex-AmeriBank card.

Hernandez might be wrong about English SWAT-wagons, Rydell found himself thinking, punching the Hotspur Hussar into six-wheel overdrive and feeling Gunhead suck down on pavement like a twin-engined, three-ton leech. He'd never really stomped on that thing before.

Sublett yelped as the crash-harnesses tightened automatically, yanking him up out of his usual slouch.

Rydell slung Gunhead up onto a verge covered in dusty ice-plant, doing seventy past a museum-grade Bentley, and on the wrong side at that. Eyeblink of a woman passenger's horrified face, then Sublett must have managed to slap the red plastic plate that activated the strobes and the siren.

Straight stretch now. No cars at all. Rydell straddled the centerline and floored it. Sublett was making a weird keening sound that synched eerily with the rising ceramic whine of the twin Kyoceras, and it came to Rydell that the Texan had snapped completely under the pressure of the thing, and was singing in some trailer-camp tongue known only to the benighted followers of the Rev. Fallon.

But, no, when he glanced that way, he saw Sublett, lips moving, frantically scanning the client-data as it seethed on the dash-screens, his eyes bugging like the silver contacts might pop right out. But while he read, Rydell saw, he was actually loading his worn-out, secondhand Glock, his long white fingers moving in the most matter-of-fact way imaginable, as though he were making a sandwich or folding a newspaper.

And *that* was scary.

"Death Star!" Rydell yelled. It was Sublett's job to keep the bead in his ear at all times, listening for the satellite-relayed, instantly overriding Word of the Real Cops.

Sublett turned, snapping the magazine into his Glock, his face so pale that it seemed to reflect the colors of the dash-display as readily as did the blank steel rounds of his eyes.

"The help's all *dead*," he said, "an' they got the three *kids* in the *nursery*." He sounded like he was talking about something mildly baffling he was seeing on television, say a badly altered version of some old, favorite film, drastically recast for some obscure ethnic market-niche. "Say they're gonna kill 'em, Berry."

"What do the fucking *cops* say about it?" Rydell shouted, pounding on the padded figure-eight steering wheel in the purest rage of frustration he'd ever felt.

Sublett touched a finger to his right ear. He looked like he was about to scream. "Down," he said.

Gunhead's right front fender clipped off somebody's circa-1943 fully-galvanized Sears rural-route mailbox, no doubt acquired at great cost on Melrose Avenue.

"They *can't* be fucking *down*," Rydell said, "they're the *police*."

Sublett tugged the bead from his ear and offered it to Rydell. "Static's all..."

Rydell looked down at his dash-display. Gunhead's cursor was a green spear of destiny, whipping along a paler-green canyon road toward a chaste white circle the size of a wedding-ring. In the window immediately to the right, he could read the vital-signs data on the subscriber's three kids. Their pulse rates were up. In the window below, there was a ridiculously peaceful-looking infrared frame of the subscriber's front gate. It looked solid. The read-out said it was locked and armed.

Right then, probably, was when he decided just to go for it.

A week or so later, when it had all been sorted out, Hernandez was basically sympathetic about the whole thing. Not happy, mind you, because it had happened over his shift, but he did say he couldn't much blame Rydell under the circumstances.

IntenSecure had brought in a whole planeload of people from the head office in Singapore, Rydell had heard, to keep it all out of the media and work out some kind of settlement with the subscribers, the Schonbrunns. He had no idea what that settlement might have finally amounted to, but he was just as happy not to know; there was no such program as *RentaCops in Trouble*, and the Schonbrunn's front gate alone had probably been worth a couple of dozen of his paychecks.

IntenSecure could replace that gate, sure, because they'd installed it in the first place. It had been quite a gate, too, some kind of Japanese fiber-reinforced sheeting, thermoset to concrete, and it sure as hell had managed to get most of that Wet Honey Sienna off Gunhead's front end.

Then there was the damage to the house itself, mostly to the living-room windows (which he'd driven through) and the furniture (which he'd driven over).

But there had to be something for the Schonbrunns on top of that, Hernandez explained. Something for emotional pain, he said, pumping Rydell a cup of old nasty coffee from the big stainless thermos behind his desk. There was a fridge-magnet on the thermos that said I'M NOT OKAY, YOU'RE NOT OKAY—BUT, HEY, THAT'S OKAY.

It was two weeks since the night in question, ten in the morning, and Rydell was wearing a five-day beard, a fine-weave panama Stetson, a pair of baggy, faded orange trunks, a KNOXVILLE POLICE DEPARTMENT t-shirt that was starting to disintegrate at the shoulder-seams, the black SWAT-trainers from his IntenSecure uniform, and an inflated transparent cast on his left arm. " 'Emotional pain,' " Rydell said.

Hernandez, who was very nearly as wide as his desk, passed Rydell the coffee. "You *way* lucky, all I can say."

"I'm out a job, arm in a cast, I'm 'way lucky'?"

"Seriously, man," Hernandez said, "you coulda killed yourself. LAPD, they coulda greased your ass down *dead.* Mr. and Mrs. Schonbrunn, they been *very* nice about this, considering Mrs. Schonbrunn's embarrassment and everything. Your arm got hassled, hey, I'm sorry..." Hernandez shrugged, enormously. "Anyway, you not *fired,* man. We just can't let you *drive* now. You want us put you on gated residential, no problem."

"No thanks."

"Retail properties? You wanna work evenings, Encino Fashion Mall?"

"No."

Hernandez narrowed his eyes. "You seen the pussy over there?"

"Nope."

Hernandez sighed. "Man, what happen with all that shit coming down on you in Nashville?"

"Knoxville. Department came down for permanent suspension. Going in without authorization or proper back-up."

"And that bitch, one's suing your ass?"

"She and her son got caught sticking up a muffler shop in Johnson City, last I heard..." Now it was Rydell's turn to shrug, except it made his shoulder hurt.

"See," Hernandez said, beaming, "you lucky."

———————————— • ———— • ———— • ————————————

In the instant of putting Gunhead through the Schonbrunn's locked-and-armed Benedict Canyon gate, Rydell had experienced a fleeting awareness of something very high, very pure, and quite clinically *empty;* the *doing* of the thing, the not-thinking; that weird adrenal exultation and the losing of every more troublesome aspect of self.

And that—he later recalled remembering, as he'd fought the

wheel, slashing through a Japanese garden, across a patio, and through a membrane of armored glass that gave way like something in a dream—had been a lot like what he'd felt as he'd drawn his gun and pulled the trigger, emptying Kenneth Turvey's brain-pan, and most copiously, across a seemingly infinite expanse of white-primered wallboard that nobody had ever bothered to paint.

Rydell went over to Cedars to see Sublett.

IntenSecure had sprung for a private cubicle, the better to keep Sublett away from any cruising minions of the media. The Texan was sitting up in bed, chewing gum, and watching a little liquid-crystal disk-player propped on his chest.

"*Warlords of the 21st Century*," he said, when Rydell edged in, "James Wainwright, Annie McEnroe, Michael Beck."

Rydell grinned. "When'd they make it?"

"1982." Sublett muted the audio and looked up. "But I've seen it a couple times already."

"I been over at the shop seein' Hernandez, man. He says you don't have to worry any about your job."

Sublett looked at Rydell with his blank silver eyes. "How 'bout yours, Berry?"

Rydell's arm started to itch, inside the inflated cast. He bent over and fished a plastic drinking-straw from the little white waste-basket beside the bed. He poked the straw down inside the cast and wiggled it around. It helped some. "I'm history, over there. They won't let me drive anymore."

Sublett was looking at the straw. "You shouldn't ought to touch *used* stuff, not in a hospital."

"You don't have nothin' contagious, Sublett. You're one of the cleanest motherfuckers ever lived."

"But what you gonna *do*, Berry? You gotta make a living, man."

Rydell dropped the straw back into the basket. "Well, I don't

know. But I know I don't wanna do gated residential and I know I
don't wanna do any malls."

"What about those hackers, Berry? You figure they'll get the
ones set us up?"

"Nope. Too many of 'em. Republic of Desire's been around
a while. The Feds have a list of maybe three hundred 'affiliates,' but
there's no way to haul 'em all in and figure out who actually did it.
Not unless one of 'em rats on somebody, which they do tend to do
on a pretty regular basis."

"But how come they'd want to do that to us anyway?"

"Hell, Sublett, how should I know?"

"Just *mean*," Sublett said.

"Well, that, for sure, and Hernandez says the LAPD told him
they figured somebody wanted *Mrs.* Schonbrunn caught more or less
with her pants down." Neither Sublett nor Rydell had actually seen
Mrs. Schonbrunn, because she was, as it turned out, in the nursery.
Although her kids weren't, having gone up to Washington State with
their daddy to fly over the three newest volcanoes.

Nothing that Gunhead had logged that night, since leaving the
car wash, had been real. Someone had gotten into the Hotspur Hussar's on-board computer and plugged a bunch of intricately crafted
and utterly spurious data into the communications bundle, cutting Rydell and Sublett off from IntenSecure *and* the Death Star (which
hadn't, of course, been down). Rydell figured a few of those good ol'
Mongol boys over at the car wash might know a little bit about that.

And maybe, in that instant of weird clarity, with Gunhead's
crumpled front end still trying to climb the shredded remains of a
pair of big leather sofas, and with the memory of Kenneth Turvey's
death finally real before him, Rydell had come to the conclusion that
that high crazy thing, that rush of Going For It, was maybe something
that wasn't always quite entirely to be trusted.

"But, man," Sublett had said, as if to himself, "they gonna

kill those little *babies."* And, with that, he'd snapped his harness open and was out of there, Glock in hand, before Rydell could do anything at all. Rydell had had him shut the siren and the strobes off a block away, but surely anybody in the house was now aware that Inten-Secure had arrived.

"Responding," Rydell heard himself say, slapping a hol-stered Glock onto his uniform and grabbing his chunker, which aside from its rate of fire was probably the best thing for a shoot-out in a nursery full of kids. He kicked the door open and jumped out, his trainers going straight through the inch-thick glass top of a coffee-table. (Needed twelve stitches, but it wasn't deep.) He couldn't see Sublett. He stumbled forward, cradling the yellow bulk of the chunker, vaguely aware that there was something wrong with his arm.

"*Freeze, cocksucker!"* said the biggest voice in the world, "*LAPD! Drop that shit or we blow your ass* away!" Rydell found him-self the focus of an abrupt and extraordinarily painful radiance, a light so bright that it fell into his uncomprehending eyes like hot metal. "*You* hear *me, cocksucker?"* Wincing, fingers across his eyes, Rydell turned and saw the bulbous armored nacelles of the descend-ing gunship. The downdraft was flattening everything in the Japanese garden that Gunhead hadn't already taken care of.

Rydell dropped the chunker.

"*The pistol, too, asshole!"*

Rydell grasped the Glock's handle between thumb and fore-finger. It came away, in its plastic holster, with a tiny but distinct *skritch* of Velcro, somehow audible through the drumming of the helicopter's combat-muffled engine.

He dropped the Glock and raised his arms. Or tried to. The left one was broken.

They found Sublett fifteen feet from Gunhead. His face and hands were swelling like bright pink toy balloons and he seemed to be suffocating, Schonbrunn's Bosnian housekeeper having employed a product that contained xylene and chlorinated hydrocarbons to clean some crayon-marks off a bleached-oak end table.

"What the fuck's wrong with *him*?" asked one of the cops.

"He's got allergies," Rydell said through gritted teeth; they'd cuffed his hands behind his back and it hurt like hell. "You gotta get him to Emergency."

Sublett opened his eyes, or tried to.

"Berry..."

Rydell remembered the name of the movie he'd seen on television. "*Miracle Mile*," he said.

Sublett squinted up at him. "Never seen it," Sublett said, and fainted.

Mrs. Schonbrunn had been entertaining her Polish landscape gardener that evening. The cops found her in the nursery. Angered beyond speech, she was cinched quite interestingly up in a couple of thousand dollars worth of English latex, North Beach leather, and a pair of vintage Smith & Wesson handcuffs that someone had paid to have lovingly buffed and redone in black chrome—the gardener evidently having headed for the hills when he heard Rydell parking Gunhead in the living room.

3

not

a nice

party

Chevette never stole things, or anyway not from other people, and definitely not when she was pulling tags. Except this one bad Monday when she took this total asshole's sunglasses, but that was because she just didn't like him.

How it was, she was standing up there by this ninth-floor window, just looking out at the bridge, past the gray shells of the big stores, when he'd come up behind her. She'd almost managed to make out Skinner's room, there, high up in the old cables, when the tip of a finger found her bare back. Under Skinner's jacket, under her t-shirt, touching her.

She wore that jacket everywhere, like some kind of armor. She knew that nanopore was the only thing to wear, riding this time of year, but she wore Skinner's old horsehide anyway, with her bar-coded Allied badges on the lapels. The little ball-chains on the zippers swinging as she spun to knock that finger aside.

Bloodshot eyes. A face that looked as though it were about to melt. He had a short little greenish cigar in his mouth but it wasn't lit. He took it out, swirled its wet end in a small glass of clear liquor, then took a long suck on it. Grinning at her around it. Like he knew she didn't belong here, not at a party like this and not in any old but seriously expensive hotel up over Geary.

But it had been the last tag of the day, a package for a lawyer, with Tenderloin's trash-fires burning so close by, and around them, huddled, all those so terminally luckless, utterly and chemically lost. Faces aglow in the fairy illumination of the tiny glass pipes. Eyes canceled in that terrible and fleeting satisfaction. Shivers, that gave her, always.

Locking and arming her bike in the hollow sound of the Morrisey's underground lot, she'd taken a service elevator to the lobby, where the security grunts tried to brace her for the package, but there was no way. She wouldn't deliver to anyone at all except this one very specific Mr. Garreau in 808, as stated right here on the tag. They ran a scanner across the bar-code on her Allied badge, x-rayed the package, put her through a metal-detector, and waved her into an elevator lined with pink mirrors and trimmed in bank-vault bronze.

So up she'd gone, to eight, to a corridor quiet as the floor of some forest in a dream. She found Mr. Garreau there, his shirtsleeves white and his tie the color of freshly poured lead. He signed the tab without making eye-contact; package in hand, he'd closed the door's three brass digits in her face. She'd checked her hair in the mirror-polished italic zero. Her tail was sticking up okay, in back, but she wasn't sure they'd got the front right. The spikes were still too long. Wispy, sort of. She headed back down the hall, the hardware jingling on Skinner's jacket, her new SWAT-trainers sinking into freshly vacuumed pile the color of rain-wet terracotta.

But when the elevator doors opened, this Japanese girl fell out. Or near enough, Chevette grabbing her beneath both arms and propping her against the edge of the door.

"Where party?"

"What folks gonna ask *you*," Chevette said.

"Floor nine! *Big* party!"

The girl's eyes were all pupil, her bangs glossy as plastic.

So Chevette, with a real glass wine-glass full of real French wine in one hand, and the smallest sandwich she'd ever seen in the other, came to find herself wondering how long she still had before the hotel's computer noticed she hadn't yet left the premises. Not that they were likely to come looking for her here, because someone had obviously put down good money to have this kind of party.

Some really private kind, because she could see these people in a darkened bathroom, smoking ice through a blown-glass dolphin, its smooth curves illuminated by the fluttering bluish tongue of an industrial-strength lighter.

Not just one room, either, but lots of them, all connected up. And lots of people, too, the men mostly gotten up in those suits with the four-button jackets, stiff shirts with those choker collars, and no tie but a little jeweled stud. The women wore clothes Chevette had only seen in magazines. Rich people, had to be, and foreign, too. Though maybe rich was foreign enough.

She'd managed to get the Japanese girl horizontal on a long green couch, where she was snoring now, and safe enough unless somebody sat on her.

Looking around, Chevette had seen that she wasn't the only underdressed local to have somehow scammed entry. The guy in the bathroom working the big yellow Bic, for starters, but he was an extreme case. Then there were a couple of pretty obvious Tenderloin working-girls, too, but maybe that was no more than the accepted amount of local color for whatever this was supposed to be.

But then this asshole's right in her face, grinning his mean-ass drunken grin, and she's got her hand on a little folding-knife, something else she's borrowed from Skinner. It has a hole in the blade that you can press the tip of your thumb into and snap it open, one-handed. That blade's under three inches, broad as a soup-spoon, wickedly serrated, and ceramic. Skinner says it's a *fractal* knife, its actual edge more than twice as long as the blade itself.

"You're not enjoying yourself, I think," he says. European, but she's not sure which flavor. Not French or German. His jacket's leather, too, but nothing like Skinner's. Some thin-skinned animal whose hide drapes like heavy silk, the color of tobacco. She thinks of the smell of the yellow-spined magazines up in Skinner's room, some so old the pictures are only shades of gray, the way the city looks, sometimes, from the bridge.

"Doing fine 'til *you* showed up," Chevette says, thinking it's probably time to go, this guy's bad news.

"Tell me," he says, looking appraisingly at the jacket and the t-shirt and the bike-pants, "what *services* you offer."

"The fuck's *that* supposed to mean?"

"Clearly," he says, pointing at the Tenderloin girls across the room, "you offer something more *interesting*," and he rolls his tongue wetly around the word, "than these two."

"Fuck *that*," Chevette says, "I'm a messenger."

And a funny pause crosses his face, like something's gotten past his drunk, nudged him. Then he throws back his head and laughs like it's the biggest joke in the world. She gets a look at a lot of very white, very expensive-looking teeth. Rich people never have any metal in their teeth, Skinner's told her.

"I say something funny?"

The asshole wipes his eyes. "But we have something in common, you and I . . ."

"I doubt it."

"*I* am a messenger," he says, though he looks to Chevette like a moderate hill would put him in line for a pig-valve.

"A courier," he says, like he's reminding himself.

"So proj *on*," she says, and steps around him, but just then the lights go out, the music starts, and its the intro to Chrome Koran's "She God's Girlfriend." Chevette, who has kind of a major thing for Chrome Koran, and cranks them on her bike whenever she needs a boost to proj on, just moves with it now, everybody dancing, even the icers from the bathroom.

With the asshole gone, or anyway forgotten, she notices how much better these people look dancing. She finds herself opposite this girl in a leather skirt, little black boots with jingling silver spurs. Chevette grins; the girl grins back.

"You're from the city?" the girl asks, as "She God's Girlfriend" ends, and for a second Chevette thinks she's being asked if she's a municipal messenger. The girl—woman—is older than she'd thought; late twenties maybe, but definitely older than Chevette. Good-looking without looking like it came out of a kit; dark eyes, dark hair cut short. "San Francisco?"

Chevette nods.

The next tune's older than she is; that black guy who turned white, and then his face fell in, she guesses. She looks down for her drink but they all look alike. Her Japanese doll dances past, bangs swinging, no recognition in her eyes as she sees Chevette.

"Cody can usually find all he needs, in San Francisco," the woman says, a tiredness behind her voice but at the same time you can tell she thinks its all pretty funny. German, Chevette thinks by her accent.

"Who?"

The woman raises her eyebrows. "Our host." But she's still got her wide easy grin.

"Just sort of walked in..."

"Could I only say the same!" The woman laughs.

"Why?"

"Then I could walk out again."

"You don't like it?" Up close, she smells expensive. Chevette's suddenly worried about how she must smell herself, after a day on the bike and no shower. But the woman takes her elbow and leads her aside.

"You *don't* know Cody?"

"No." Chevette sees the drunk, the asshole, through the doorway into the next room, where the lights are still on. He's looking right at her. "And I think maybe I should leave now, okay?"

"You don't have to. Please. I only envy you the option."

"You German?"

"Padanian."

Chevette knows that's part of what used to be Italy. The northern part, she thinks. "Who's this Cody?"

"Cody *likes* a party. Cody likes *this* party. This party's been going on for several *years* now. When it isn't here, it's in London, Prague, Macau..." A boy is moving through the crowd with a tray of drinks. He doesn't look to Chevette like he works for the hotel. His stiff white shirt's not so stiff anymore; it's open all the way, wrinkled tails hanging loose, and she sees he has one of those things like a little steel barbell through one nipple. His stiff collar's popped off at the front and sticks up behind his neck like a slipped halo. The woman takes a glass of white wine when he offers the tray. Chevette shakes her head. There's a white saucer on the tray, with pills and what look like twists of dancer.

The boy winks at Chevette and moves on.

"You find this strange?" The woman drinks her wine off and tosses the empty glass over her shoulder. Chevette hears it break.

"Huh?"

"Cody's party."

"Yeah. I guess. I mean, I just walked in..."

"Where do you live?"

"The bridge." Watching for the reaction.

The grin widens. "Really? It looks so...mysterious. I'd like to go there, but there are no tours, and they say it's dangerous..."

"It's not," Chevette says, then hesitates. "Just don't...dress *up* so much, right? But it's not *dangerous*, not even as much as the neighborhood around here." Thinking of the ones around the trash-fires. "Just don't go out on Treasure Island. Don't try to go all the way to Oakland. Stay over on the suspension side."

"You *like* it, living there?"

"Shit, yes. I wouldn't live anywhere else."

The woman smiles. "You're very lucky then, I think."

"Well," Chevette says, feeling clumsy, "I gotta go."

"My name is Maria..."

"Chevette," offering her hand. Almost like her own other name. Chevette-Marie.

They shake.

"Goodbye, Chevette."

"You have a nice party, okay?"

"This is *not* a nice party."

Settling the wide shoulders of Skinner's jacket, Chevette nods to the woman Maria and begins to work her way through the crowd. Which is tighter now by several degrees, like maybe this Cody's friends are still arriving. More Japanese here now, she notices, all of them serious suits; their wives or secretaries or whatever are all wearing pearls. But evidently this doesn't prevent them getting into the spirit of the thing. It's gotten noisier, too, as people have gotten more whacked. There's that loud constant burr of party-noise you get when the drinks kick in, and now she wants to be out of there all that much faster.

She finds herself stuck near the door to the bathroom where she'd seen the icers, but it's closed now. A bunch of French people are talking French and laughing and waving their hands around, but Chevette can hear somebody vomiting in there. "Coming *through*," she says to a man with a bowtie and a gray crewcut, and just pushes past him, spilling part of his drink. He says something after her in French.

She feels really claustro now, like she does up in offices sometimes when a receptionist makes her wait to pick something up, and she sees the office people walking back and forth, and wonders whether it all means anything or if they're just walking back and forth. Or maybe the wine's gotten to her, a little, because drinking isn't something she does much, and now she doesn't like the taste of it in the back of her throat.

And suddenly there's her drunk, her Euro with his unlit cigar, sweaty brow too close to the dull-eyed, vaguely worried face of one of the Tenderloin girls. He's got her backed into a corner. And everyone's jammed so tight, this close to the door and the corridor and freedom, that Chevette finds herself pressed up against his back for a second, not that that interrupts whatever infinitely dreary shit he's laying down for the girl, no, though he does jam his elbow, hard, back into Chevette's ribs to get himself more space.

And Chevette, glancing down, sees something sticking out of a pocket in the tobacco-colored leather.

Then it's in her hand, down the front of her bike-pants, she's out the door, and the asshole hasn't even noticed.

In the sudden quiet of the corridor, party sounds receding as she heads for the elevator, she wants to run. She wants to laugh, too, but now she's starting to feel scared.

Walk.

Past the party's build-up of trays, dirty glasses, plates.

Remembering the security grunts in the lobby.

The thing stuck down her pants.

Down a corridor that opens off this one, she sees the doors of a service elevator spread wide now and welcoming. A Central Asian kid with a paint-splattered steel cart stacked up with flat rectangles that are television screens. He gives her a careful look as she edges in beside him. His face is all cheekbones, bright hooded eyes, his hair shaved up high in one of those near-vertical dos all these guys favor. He has a security badge clipped to the front of his clean gray workshirt and a VirtuFax slung around his neck on a red nylon cord.

"Basement," Chevette says.

His fax buzzes. He raises it, pushes the button, peers into the eyepiece. The thing in her bike-pants starts to feel huge. Then he drops the fax back to his chest, blinks at her, and pushes a button marked B-6. The doors rumble shut and Chevette closes her eyes.

She leans back against the big quilted pads hung on the walls and wishes she were up in Skinner's room, listening to the cables creak. The floor there's a layer of two-by-fours laid on edge; the very top of the hump of the cable, riding its steel saddle, sticks up through the middle, and Skinner says there are 17,464 strands of wire in that cable. Each one is about as thick as a pencil. You can press your ear against it and hear the whole bridge sing, when the wind's just right.

The elevator stops at four for no reason at all. Nobody there when the door opens. Chevette wants to press B-6 again but she makes herself wait for the kid with the fax to do it. He does.

And B-6 is not the garage she so thoroughly wants now, but this maze of hundred-year-old concrete tunnels, floored in cracked asphalt tile, with big old pipes slung in iron brackets along the ceiling. She slips out while he's fiddling with one of the wheels on his cart.

A century's-worth of padlocked walk-in freezers, fifty vacuum cleaners charging themselves at a row of numbered stations, rolls of broadloom stacked like logs. More people in work clothes, some in kitchen whites, but she's trying for tag-pulling attitude and looks, she hopes, like she's making a delivery.

She finds a narrow stairway and climbs. The air is hot and dead. Motion-sensors click the lights for her at the start of each flight. She feels the whole weight of this old building pressing down on her.

But her bike is there, on B-2, behind a column of nicked concrete.

"Back *off,*" it says when she's five feet away. Not loud, like a car, but it sounds like it means it.

Under its coat of spray-on imitation rust and an artful bandaging of silver duct-tape, the geometry of the paper-cored, carbon-wrapped frame makes Chevette's thighs tremble. She slips her left hand through the recognition-loop behind the seat. There's a little double *zik* as the particle-brakes let go, then she's up and on it.

It's never felt better, as she pumps up the oil-stained ramp and out of there.

career
opportunities

Rydell's roommate, Kevin Tarkovsky, wore a bone through his nose and worked in a wind-surfing boutique called Just Blow Me.

Monday morning, when Rydell told him he'd quit his job with IntenSecure, Kevin offered to try to find him something in sales, in the beach-culture line.

"You got an okay build, basically," Kevin said, looking at Rydell's bare chest and shoulders. Rydell was still wearing the orange trunks he'd worn when he'd gone to see Hernandez. He'd borrowed them from Kevin. He'd just taken his cast off, deflating it and crumpling it into the five-gallon plastic paint bucket that served as a wastebasket. The bucket had a big self-adhesive daisy on the side. "You *could* work out a little more regularly. And maybe get some tats. Tribal black-work."

"Kevin, I don't know how to surf, windsurf, anything. Hardly been in the ocean in my life. Couple of times down Tampa Bay." It was about ten in the morning. Kevin had the day off work.

"Sales is about providing an *experience*, Berry. The customer needs *information*, you provide it. But you give 'em an *experience*, too." Kevin tapped his two-inch spindle of smooth white beef-bone by way of illustration. "Then you sell them a new outfit."

"But I don't have a tan."

Kevin was the approximate color and sheen of a pair of mid-brown Cole-Haan loafers that Rydell's aunt had given him for his fifteenth birthday. This had nothing to do with either genetics or exposure to unfiltered sunlight, but was the result of regular injections and a complicated regimen of pills and lotions.

"Well," Kevin admitted, "you *would* need a tan."

Rydell knew that Kevin didn't wind surf, and never had, but that he did bring home disks from the shop and play them on a goggle-set, going over the various moves involved, and Rydell had no doubt that Kevin could provide every bit of information a prospective buyer might desire. *And* that all-important experience; with his cordovan tan, gym-tuned physique, and that bone through his nose, he got a lot of attention. Mainly from women, though it didn't actually seem to do that much for him.

What Kevin sold, primarily, was clothing. Expensive kind that supposedly kept the UV *and* the pollutants in the water off you. He had two whole cartons full of the stuff, stacked in their room's one closet. Rydell, who currently didn't have much in the way of a wardrobe, was welcome to paw through there and borrow whatever took his fancy. Which wasn't a lot, as it turned out, because wind-surfing gear tended to be Day-Glo, black nanopore, or mirrorflex. A few of the jazzier items had UV-sensitive JUST BLOW ME logos that appeared on days when the ozone was in particularly shabby shape, as Rydell had discovered the last time he'd gone to the farmers market.

He and Kevin were sharing one of two bedrooms in a sixties house in Mar Vista, which meant Sea View but there wasn't any. Someone had rigged up a couple of sheets of drywall down the middle of the room. On Rydell's side, the drywall was covered with those same big self-adhesive daisies and a collection of souvenir bumperstickers from places like Magic Mountain, Nissan County, Disneyland, and Skywalker Park. There were two other people sharing the house, three if you counted the Chinese girl out in the garage (but she had her own bathroom in there).

Rydell had bought a futon with most of his first month's pay from IntenSecure. He'd bought it at this stall in the market; they were cheaper there, and the stall was called Futon Mouth, which Rydell thought was pretty funny. The Futon Mouth girl had explained how you could slip the Metro guy on the platform a twenty, then he'd let you get on the train with the rolled-up futon, which came in a big green plastic sack that reminded Rydell of a bodybag.

Lately, waiting to take the cast off, he'd spent a lot of time on that futon, staring up at those bumper-stickers. He wondered if whoever had put them there had actually bothered to go to all those places. Hernandez had once offered him work at Nissan County. IntenSecure had the rentacop franchise there. His parents had honeymooned at Disneyland. Skywalker Park was up in San Francisco; it had been called Golden Gate, before, and he remembered a couple of fairly low-key riots on television when they'd privatized it.

"You on line to any of the job-search nets, Berry?"

Rydell shook his head.

"This one's on me," Kevin said, passing Rydell the helmet. It wasn't anything like Karen's slick little goggles; just a white plastic rig like kids used for games. "Put it on. I'll dial for you."

"Well," Rydell said, "this is nice, Kevin, but you don't have to go to all this trouble."

Kevin touched the bone in his nose. "Well, there's the rent."

There was that. Rydell put the helmet on.

"Now," Sonya said, just as perky as could be, "we're showing that you did graduate from this post-secondary training program—"

"Academy," Rydell corrected. "Police."

"Yes, Berry, but we're showing that you were then employed for a total of eighteen days, before being placed on suspension." Sonya looked like a cartoon of a pretty girl. No pores. No texture anywhere. Her teeth were very white and looked like a single unit, something that could be snapped out intact for closer inspection. But not for cleaning, because there was no need; cartoons didn't eat. She had wonderful tits, though; she had the tits Rydell would have drawn for her if he'd been a talented cartoonist.

"Well," Rydell said, thinking of Turvey, "I got into some trouble after they assigned me to Patrol."

Sonya nodded brightly. "I see, Berry." Rydell wondered what she did see. Or what the expert system that used her as a hand-puppet could see. Or *how* it saw. What did someone like Rydell look like to an employment agency's computer system? Not like much, he decided.

"Then you moved to Los Angeles, Berry, and we show ten weeks of employment with the IntenSecure Corporation's residential armed-response branch. Driver with experience of weapons."

Rydell thought of the rocket-pods slung under the LAPD chopper. Probably they'd had one of those CHAIN guns in there, too. "Yep," he agreed.

"And you've resigned your position with IntenSecure."

"Guess so."

Sonya beamed at Rydell as though he'd just admitted, shyly, to a congressional appointment or a post-doctoral degree. "Well, Berry," she said, "let me put my *thinking cap* on for just a second!" She winked, then closed her big cartoon eyes.

Jesus, Rydell thought. He tried to glance sideways, but Kevin's helmet didn't have any peripherals, so there was nothing there. Just Sonya, the empty rectangle of her desk, sketchy details suggesting an office, and the employment agency's logo behind her on the wall. The logo made her look like the anchorwoman on a channel that only reported *very* good news.

Sonya opened her eyes. Her smile became incandescent. "You're from the *South*," she said.

"Uh-huh."

"Plantations, Berry. Magnolias. Tradition. But a certain *darkness* as well. A Gothic quality. Faulkner."

Fawk—? "Huh?"

"*Nightmare Folk Art*, Berry. Ventura Boulevard, Sherman Oaks."

Kevin watched as Rydell removed the helmet and wrote an address and telephone number on the back of last week's *People.* The magazine belonged to Monica, the Chinese girl in the garage; she always got hers printed out so there was never any mention of scandal or disaster, but with a triple helping of celebrity romance, particularly anything to do with the British royal family.

"Something for you, Berry?" Kevin looked hopeful.

"Maybe," Rydell said. "This place in Sherman Oaks. I'll call 'em up, check it out."

Kevin fiddled with his nose-bone. "I can give you a lift," he said.

There was a big painting of the Rapture in the window of Nightmare Folk Art. Rydell knew paintings like that from the sides of Christian vans parked beside shopping centers. Lots of bloody car-wrecks and disasters, with all the Saved souls flying up to meet Jesus, whose eyes were a little too bright for comfort. This one was a lot more detailed than the ones he remembered. Each one of those Saved souls had its own individual face, like it actually represented somebody, and a few of them reminded him of famous people. But it still looked like it had been painted by either a fifteen-year-old or an old lady.

Kevin had let him off at the corner of Sepulveda and he'd walked back two blocks, looking for the place, past a crew in wide-brim hardhats who were pouring the foundations for a palm tree. Rydell wondered if Ventura had had real ones before the virus; the replacements were so popular now, people wanted them put in everywhere.

Ventura was one of those Los Angeles streets that just went on forever. He knew he must've driven Gunhead past Night-mare Folk Art more times than he could count, but these streets looked completely different when you walked them. For one thing, you were pretty much alone; for another, you could see how cracked and dusty a lot of the buildings were. Empty spaces behind dirty glass, with a yellowing pile of junk-mail on the floor inside and maybe a puddle of what couldn't be rainwater, so you sort of wondered what it was. You'd pass a couple of those, then a place selling sunglasses for six times the rent Rydell paid for his half of the room in Mar Vista. The sunglasses place would have some kind of rentacop inside, to buzz you in.

Nightmare Folk Art was like that, sandwiched between a dead hair-extension franchise and some kind of failing real estate place that sold insurance on the side. NIGHTMARE FOLK ART—SOUTHERN GOTHIC, the letters hand-painted all lumpy and hairy, like mosquito legs in a cartoon, white on black. But with a couple of expensive cars parked out front: a silver-gray Range Rover, looking like Gunhead dressed up for the prom, and one of those little antique Porsche two-seaters that always looked to Rydell like the wind-up key had fallen off. He gave the Porsche a wide berth; cars like that tended to have hypersensitive anti-theft systems, not to mention hyper-aggressive.

There was a rentacop looking at him through the armored glass of the door; not IntenSecure, but some off brand. Rydell had borrowed a pair of pressed chinos from Kevin. They were a little tight in the waist, but they beat hell out of the orange trunks. He had on a black IntenSecure uniform-shirt with the patches ripped off, his Stetson, and his SWAT shoes. He wasn't sure black really made it with khaki. He pushed the button. The rentacop buzzed him in.

"Got an appointment with Justine Cooper," he said, taking his sunglasses off.

"With a client," the rentacop said. He looked about thirty, and like he should've been out on a farm in Kansas or somewhere. Rydell looked over and saw a skinny woman with black hair. She was talking to a fat man who had no hair at all. Trying to sell him something, it looked like.

"I'll wait," Rydell said.

The farmer didn't answer. State law said he couldn't have a gun, just the industrial-strength stunner he wore in a beat-up plastic holster, but he probably did anyway. One of those little Russian hold-outs that chambered some godawful overheated caliber originally in-tended for killing the engine blocks of tanks. The Russians, never too safety-minded, had the market in Saturday-night specials.

Rydell looked around. That ol' Rapture was big at Nightmare Folk Art, he decided. Those kind of Christians, his father had always maintained, were just pathetic. There the Millennium had up, come, and gone, no Rapture to speak of, and here they were, still beating that same drum. Sublett and his folks down in their trailer-camp in Texas, watching old movies for Reverend Fallon—at least that had some kind of spin on it.

He tried to sneak a look, see what the lady was trying to sell to the fat man, but she caught his eye and that wasn't good. So he worked his way deeper into the shop, pretending to check out the merchan-dise. There was a whole section of these nasty-looking spidery wreath-things, behind glass in faded gilt frames. The wreaths looked to Rydell like they were made of frizzy old hair. There were tiny little baby coffins, all corroded, and one of them had been planted with ivy. There were coffee tables made out of what Rydell supposed were tombstones, old ones, the lettering worn down so faint you couldn't read it. He paused beside a bedstead welded together from a bunch of those pickaninny jockey-boys it had been against the law to have on your lawn in Knoxville. The jockey-boys had all been freshly-painted with big, red-lipped, watermelon-eating grins. The bed was spread with a hand-stitched quilt patterned like a Confederate flag. When he looked for a price tag, all he found was a yellow SOLD sticker.

"Mr. Rydell? May I call you Berry?" Justine Cooper's jaw was so narrow that it looked like she wouldn't have room for the ordinary complement of teeth in there. Her hair was cut short, a polished brown helmet. She wore a couple of dark, flowing things that Rydell supposed were meant to conceal the fact that she was built more or less like a stick-insect. She didn't sound like she was from anywhere south of anywhere, much, and there was a visible tension strung through her, like wires.

Rydell saw the fat man walk out, pausing on the sidewalk to deactivate the Range Rover's defenses.

"Sure."

"You're from Knoxville?" He noticed she was breathing deliberately, like she was trying not to hyperventilate.

"That's right."

"You don't have much of an accent."

"Well, I wish everybody felt that way." He smiled, but she didn't smile back.

"Is your *family* from Knoxville, Mr. Rydell?"

Shit, he thought, go ahead, call me Berry. "My father was, I guess. My mother's people are from up around Bristol, mostly."

Justine Cooper's dark eyes, not showing much white, were looking right at him, but they didn't seem to be registering anything. He guessed she was somewhere in her forties.

"Ms. Cooper?"

She gave a violent start, as though he'd goosed her.

"Ms. Cooper, what are those wreath-sort-of-things in those old frames there?" Pointing at them.

"Memorial wreaths. Southwestern Virginia, late nineteenth, early twentieth century."

Good, Rydell thought, get her talking about the stock. He walked over to the framed wreaths for a closer look. "Looks like hair," he said.

"It *is*," she said. "What else would it be?"

"Human hair?"

"Of course."

"You mean like *dead* people's hair?" He saw now the minute braiding, the hair twisted up into tiny flowerlike knots. It was lusterless and no particular color.

"Mr. Rydell, I'm afraid that I may have wasted your time." She moved tentatively in his direction. "When I spoke with you on the phone, I was under the impression that you might be, well, much more *of* the South . . ."

"How do you mean, Ms. Cooper?"

"What we offer people here is a certain *vision*, Mr. Rydell. A certain *darkness* as well. A Gothic quality."

Damn. That talking head in the agency display had been playing this shit back word for word.

"I don't suppose you've read Faulkner?" She raised one hand to brush at something invisible, something hanging in front of her face.

There it was again. "Nope."

"No, I didn't think so. I'm hoping to find someone who can help to *convey* that very darkness, Mr. Rydell. The *mind* of the South. A *fever dream* of sensuality."

Rydell blinked.

"But you *don't* convey that to me. I'm sorry." It looked like the invisible cobweb had come back.

Rydell looked at the rentacop, but he didn't seem to be listening to any of this. Hell, he seemed to be asleep.

"Lady," Rydell said carefully, "I think you're crazier than a sack full of assholes."

Her eyebrows shot up. "There," she said.

"There what?"

"Color, Mr. Rydell. Fire. The brooding verbal polychromes of an almost unthinkably advanced decay."

Rydell had to think about that. He found himself looking at the jockey-boy bed. "Don't you ever get any black people in here, complaining about stuff like this?"

"On the contrary," she said, a new edge in her tone, "we do quite a good business with the more affluent residents of South Central. They, at least, have a sense of irony. I suppose they have to."

Now he'd have to walk to whatever the nearest station was, take the subway home, and tell Kevin Tarkovsky he hadn't been Southern enough.

The rentacop was letting him out.

"Where exactly you from, Ms. Cooper?" he asked her.

"New Hampshire," she said.

He was on the sidewalk, the door closing behind him.

"Fucking Yankees," he said to the Porsche roadster. It was what his father would have said, but he had a hard time now connecting it to anything.

One of those big articulated German cargo-rigs went by, the kind that burned canola oil. Rydell hated those things. The exhaust smelled like fried chicken.

hay

problemas

3

The courier's dreams are made of hot metal, shadows that scream and run, mountains the color of concrete. They are burying the orphans on a hillside. Plastic coffins, pale blue. Clouds in the sky. The priest's tall hat. They do not see the first shell coming in from the concrete mountains. It punches a hole in *everything*: the hillside, the sky, a blue coffin, the woman's face.

A sound too vast to be any sound at all, but through it, somehow, they hear, arriving only now, the distant festive *pop-popping* of the mortars, tidy little clouds of smoke rising on the gray mountainside.

He comes upright, alone in the wide bed, trying to scream, and the words are in a language he no longer allows himself to speak.

His head throbs. He drinks flat water from the stainless carafe on the nightstand. The room sways, blurs, comes back into focus. He forces himself from the bed, pads naked to the tall, old-fashioned windows. Fumbles the heavy drapes aside. San Francisco. Dawn like tarnished silver. It is Tuesday. Not Mexico.

In the white bathroom, wincing in the sudden light, scrubbing cold water into his numb face. The dream recedes, but leaves a residue. He shivers, cold tile unpleasant beneath his bare feet. The whores at the party. This Harwood. Decadent. The courier disapproves of decadence. His work brings him into contact with real wealth, genuine power. He meets people of substance. Harwood is wealth without substance.

He puts out the bathroom light and gingerly returns to his bed, favoring the ache in his head.

With the striped duvet drawn up to his chin, he begins to sort through the previous evening. There are gaps. Overindulgence. He disapproves of overindulgence. Harwood's party. The voice on the phone, instructing him to attend. He'd already had several drinks. He sees a young girl's face. Anger, contempt. Her short dark hair twisted up in spikes.

His eyes feel as if they are too large for their sockets. When he rubs them, bright sick flashes of light surround him. The cold weight of the water moves in his stomach.

He remembers sitting at the broad mahogany desk, drinking. Before the call, before the party. He remembers the two cases open, in front of him, identical. He keeps her in one. The other is for that with which he has been entrusted. Expensive, but then he has no doubt that the information it contains is very valuable. He folds the thing's graphite earpieces and snaps the case shut. Then he touches the case that holds all her mystery, the white house on the hillside, the release she offers. He puts the cases in the pockets of his jacket—

But now he tenses, beneath the duvet, his stomach twisted with a surge of anxiety.

He wore the jacket to that party, much of which he cannot remember.

Ignoring the pounding of his head, he claws his way out of the bed and finds the jacket crumpled on the floor beside a chair.

His heart is pounding.

Here. That which he must deliver. Zipped into the inner pocket. But the outer pockets are empty.

She is gone. He roots through his other clothing. On his hands and knees, a pulsing agony behind his eyes, he peers under the chair. Gone.

But she, at least, can be replaced, he reminds himself, still on his knees, the jacket in his hands. He will find a dealer in that sort of software. Recently, he now admits, he had started to suspect that she was losing resolution.

Thinking this, he is watching his hands unzip the inner pocket, drawing out the case that contains his charge, their property, that which must be delivered. He opens it.

The scuffed black plastic frames, the label on the cassette worn and unreadable, the yellowed translucence of the audio-beads.

He hears a thin high sound emerge from the back of his throat. Very much as he must have done, years ago, when the first shell arrived.

the

bridge

Careful to correctly calculate the thirty-percent tip, Yamazaki paid the fare and struggled out of the cab's spavined rear seat. The driver, who knew that all Japanese were wealthy, sullenly counted the torn, filthy bills, then tossed the three five-dollar coins into a cracked Nissan County thermos-mug taped to the faded dashboard. Yamazaki, who was not wealthy, shouldered his bag, turned, and walked toward the bridge. As ever, it stirred his heart to see it there, morning light aslant through all the intricacy of its secondary construction.

The integrity of its span was rigorous as the modern program itself, yet around this had grown another reality, intent upon its own agenda. This had occurred piecemeal, to no set plan, employing every imaginable technique and material. The result was something amorphous, startlingly organic. At night, illuminated by Christmas bulbs, by recycled neon, by torchlight, it possessed a queer medieval energy. By day, seen from a distance, it reminded him of the ruin of England's Brighton Pier, as though viewed through some cracked kaleidoscope of vernacular style.

Its steel bones, its stranded tendons, were lost within an accretion of dreams: tattoo parlors, gaming arcades, dimly lit stalls stacked with decaying magazines, sellers of fireworks, of cut bait, betting shops, sushi bars, unlicensed pawnbrokers, herbalists, barbers, bars. Dreams of commerce, their locations generally corresponding with the decks that had once carried vehicular traffic; while above them, rising to the very peaks of the cable towers, lifted the intricately suspended barrio, with its unnumbered population and its zones of more private fantasy.

He'd first seen it by night, three weeks before. He'd stood in fog, amid sellers of fruit and vegetables, their goods spread out on blankets. He'd stared back into the cavern-mouth, heart pounding. Steam was rising from the pots of soup-vendors, beneath a jagged arc of scavenged neon. Everything ran together, blurring, melting in the fog. Telepresence had only hinted at the magic and singularity of the thing, and he'd walked slowly forward, into that neon maw and all that patchwork carnival of scavenged surfaces, in perfect awe. Fairyland. Rain-silvered plywood, broken marble from the walls of forgotten banks, corrugated plastic, polished brass, sequins, painted canvas, mirrors, chrome gone dull and peeling in the salt air. So many things, too much for his reeling eye, and he'd known that his journey had not been in vain.

In all the world, surely, there was no more magnificent a Thomasson.

He entered it now, Tuesday morning, amid a now-familiar stir—the carts of ice and fish, the clatter of a machine that made tortillas—and found his way to a coffee shop whose interior had the texture of an ancient ferry, dark dented varnish over plain heavy wood, as if someone had sawn it, entire, from some tired public vessel. Which was entirely possible, he thought, seating himself at the long counter; toward Oakland, past the haunted island, the wingless carcass of a 747 housed the kitchens of nine Thai restaurants.

The young woman behind the counter wore tattooed bracelets in the form of stylized indigo lizards. He asked for coffee. It arrived in thick heavy porcelain. No two cups here were alike. He took his notebook from his bag, flicked it on, and jotted down a brief description of the cup, of the minute pattern of cracks in its glazed surface, like a white tile mosaic in miniature. Sipping his coffee, he scrolled back to the previous day's notes. The man Skinner's mind was remarkably like the bridge. Things had accumulated there, around some armature of original purpose, until a point of crisis had been attained and a new program had emerged. But what was that program?

He had asked Skinner to explain the mode of accretion resulting in the current state of the secondary structure. What were the motivations of a given builder, an individual builder? His notebook had recorded the man's rambling, oblique response, transcribing and translating it.

> There was this man, fishing. Snagged his tackle. Hauled up a bicycle. All covered in barnacles. Everybody laughed. Took that bike and he built a place to eat. Clam broth, cold cooked mussels, Mexican beer. Hung that bike over the counter. Just three stools in there and he slung his box out about eight feet, used Super Glue and shackles. Covered the walls inside with postcards. Like shingles. Nights, he'd curl up behind the counter. Just gone, one morning. Broken shackle, some splinters still stuck to the wall of a barber shop. You could look down, see the water between your toes. See, he slung it out too far.

Yamazaki watched steam rise from his coffee, imagining a bicycle covered in barnacles, itself a Thomasson of considerable potency. Skinner had seemed curious about the term, and the notebook had recorded Yamazaki's attempt to explain its origin and the meaning of its current usage.

> Thomasson was an American baseball player, very handsome, very powerful. He went to the Yomiyuri Giants in 1982, for a large sum of money. Then it was discovered that he could not hit the ball. The writer and artisan Gempei Akasegawa appropriated his name to describe certain useless and inexplicable monuments, pointless yet curiously artlike features of the urban landscape. But the term has subsequently taken on other shades of meaning. If you wish, I can

access and translate today's definitions in our *Gendai Yogo Kisochi-shiki*, that is, *The Basic Knowledge of Modern Terms.*

But Skinner—gray, unshaven, the whites of his blue eyes yellowed, blotched with broken veins, had merely shrugged. Three of the residents who had previously agreed to be interviewed had cited Skinner as an original, one of the first on the bridge. The location of his room indicated a certain status as well, though Yamazaki wondered how many would have welcomed a chance to build atop one of the cable towers. Before the electric lift had been installed, the climb would have been daunting for anyone. Today, with his bad hip, the old man was in effect an invalid, relying on his neighbors and the girl. They brought him food, water, kept his chemical toilet in operation. The girl, Yamazaki assumed, received shelter in return, though the relationship struck him as deeper somehow, more complex.

But if Skinner was difficult to read because of age, personality, or both, the girl who shared his room was opaque in that ordinary, sullen way Yamazaki associated with young Americans. Though perhaps that was only because he, Yamazaki, was a stranger, Japanese, and one who asked too many questions.

He looked down the counter, taking in the early-morning profiles of the other customers. Americans. The fact that he was actually here, drinking coffee beside these people, still struck a chord of wonder. How extraordinary. He wrote in his notebook, the pen ticking against the screen.

> The apartment is in a tall Victorian house, built of wood and very elaborately painted, in a district where the names of streets honor nineteenth-century American politicians: Clay, Scott, Pierce, Jackson. This morning, Tuesday, leaving the apartment, I noticed, on the side of the topmost newel, indications of a vanished hinge. I suspect that this must once have supported an infant-gate. Going along Scott in search of a cab, I came upon a sodden postcard, face up on the sidewalk. The narrow features of the martyr Shapely, the AIDS saint, blistered with rain. Very melancholy.

"They shouldn't oughta said that. About Godzilla, I mean."

Yamazaki found himself blinking up at the earnest face of the girl behind the counter.

"I'm sorry?"

"They shouldn't oughta *said* that. About Godzilla. They shouldn't oughta laughed. We had our earthquakes here, you didn't laugh at us."

see you

do okay

Hernandez followed Rydell into the kitchen of the house in Mar Vista. He wore a sleeveless powder-blue jumpsuit and a pair of those creepy German shower-sandals, the kind with about a thousand little nubs to massage the soles of your feet. Rydell had never seen him out of uniform before and it was kind of a shock. He had these big old tattoos on his upper arms; roman numerals; gang stuff. His feet were brown and compact and sort of bearlike.

It was Tuesday morning. There was nobody else in the house. Kevin was at Just Blow Me, and the others were out doing whatever it was they did. Monica might've been in her place in the garage, but you never saw too much of her anyway.

Rydell got his bag of cornflakes out of the cupboard and carefully unrolled it. About enough for a bowl. He opened the fridge and took out a plastic, snap-top, liter container with a strip of masking-tape across the side. He'd written MILK EXPERIMENT on the masking-tape with a heavy marker.

"What's that?" Hernandez asked.

"Milk."

"Why's it say 'experiment'?"

"So nobody'll drink it. I figured it out in the dorm at the Academy." He dumped the cornflakes in a bowl, covered them with milk, found a spoon, and carried his breakfast to the kitchen table.

The table had a trick leg, so you had to eat without putting your elbows down.

"How's the arm?"

"Fine." Rydell forgot about not putting his elbow down. Milk and cornflakes slopped across the scarred white plastic of the tabletop.

"Here." Hernandez went to the counter and tore off a fat wad of beige paper towels.

"Those are whatsisname's," Rydell said, "and he seriously doesn't like us to use them."

"Towel experiment," Hernandez said, tossing Rydell the wad.

Rydell blotted up the milk and most of the flakes. He couldn't imagine what Hernandez was doing here, but then he'd never have imagined that Hernandez drove a white Daihatsu Sneaker with an animated hologram of a waterfall on the hood.

"That's a nice car out there," Rydell said, nodding in the direction of the carport and spooning cornflakes into his mouth.

"My daughter Rosa's car. Been in the shop, man."

Rydell chewed, swallowed. "Brakes or something?"

"The fucking waterfall. Supposed to be these little animals, they come out of the bushes and sort of *look* at it, the waterfall, you know?" Hernandez leaned back against the counter, flexing his toes into the nubby sandals. "Some kind of, like, Costa Rican *animals*, you know? Ecology theme. She's real green. Made us take out what was left of the lawn, put in all these ground-cover things look like gray spiders. But the shop can't get those fucking *animals* to show, man. We got a warranty and everything, but it's, you know, been a pain in the ass." He shook his head.

Rydell finished his cornflakes.

"You ever been to Costa Rica, Rydell?"

"No."

"It's fucking beautiful, man. Like Switzerland."

"Never been there."

"No, I mean what they do with data. Like the Swiss, what they did with money."

"You mean the havens?"

"You got it. Those people smart. No army, navy, air force, just neutral. And they take care of everybody's data."

"Regardless what it is."

"Hey, fucking 'A.' Smart people. And spend that money on *ecology*, man."

Rydell carried the bowl, the spoon, the damp wad of towels, to the sink. He rinsed the bowl and spoon, wiped them with the towels, then stuck the towels as far down as possible behind the rest of the garbage in the bag under the sink. Straightening up, he looked at Hernandez. "Something I can do for you, super?"

"Other way around." Hernandez smiled. Somehow it wasn't reassuring. "I been thinking about you. Your situation. Not good. Not good, man. You never get to be a cop now. Now you resign, I can't even hire you back on IntenSecure to work gated residential. Maybe you get on with a regular square-badge outfit, sit in that little pillbox in a liquor store. You wanna do that?"

"No."

"That's good, 'cause you get your ass *killed*, doing that. Somebody come in there, take your little pillbox *out*, man."

"Right now I'm looking at something in retail sales."

"No shit? Sales? What you sell?"

"Bedsteads made out of cast-iron jockey-boys. These pictures made out of hundred-year-old human hair."

Hernandez narrowed his eyes and shoved off the counter, headed for the living room. Rydell thought he might be leaving, but he was only starting to pace. Rydell had seen him do this a couple of times in his office at IntenSecure. Now he turned, just as he was about to enter the living room, and paced back to Rydell.

"You got this hard-assed *attitude* sometimes, man, I dunno. You oughta stop and think maybe I'm trying to help you a little, right?" Back toward the living room again.

"Just tell me what you want, okay?"

Hernandez stopped, turned, sighed. "Never been up to NoCal, right? San Francisco? Anybody know you up there?"

"No."

"IntenSecure's licensed in NoCal, too, right? Different state, different laws, whole different attitude, they might as well be a different fucking country, but we've got our shit up there. More office buildings, lot of hotels. Gated residential's not so big up there, not 'til you get out to the edge-cities. Concord, Hacienda Business Center, like that. We got a good piece of that, too."

"But it's the same company. They won't hire me here, they won't hire me there."

"Fucking 'A.' Nobody talking about *hiring* you. What this is, there's maybe something there for you with a guy. Works freelance. Company has certain kinds of *problems*, sometime they bring *in* somebody. But the *guy*, he's not IntenSecure. Freelance. Office up there, they got that kind of situation now."

"Wait a second. What are we talking about here? We're talking about freelance armed-response?"

"Guy's a skip-tracer. You know what that is?"

"Finds people when they try to get out from under debt, blow off the rent, like that?"

"Or take off with your kid in a custody case, whatever. But, you know, those kinds of skips, they can mostly be handled through the net, these days. Just keep plugging their stats into DatAmerica, eventually you gonna find 'em. Or even," he shrugged, "you can go to the cops."

"So what a skip-tracer mostly does—" Rydell suggested, remembering one particular episode of *Cops in Trouble* he'd seen with his father.

"Is keep you from having to go to the cops."

"Or to a licensed private detective agency."

"You got it." Hernandez was watching him.

Rydell walked past him, into the living room, hearing the German shower-sandals come squishing after him across the kitchen's dull tile floor. Someone had been smoking tobacco in there the night before. He could smell it. It was in violation of the lease. The landlord would give them hell about it. The landlord was a Serb immigrant who drove a fifteen-year-old BMW, wore these weird furry Tyrolean hats, and insisted on being called Wally. Because Wally knew that Rydell worked for IntenSecure, he'd wanted to show him the flashlight he kept clipped under the dash in his BMW. It was about a foot long and had a button that triggered a big shot of capsicum gas. He'd asked Rydell if Rydell thought it was "enough."

Rydell had lied. Had told him that people who did, for instance, a whole *lot* of dancer, they actually *liked* a blast or two of good capsicum. Like it cleared their sinuses. Got their juices flowing. They got *off* on it.

Now Rydell looked down and saw for the first time that the living room carpet in the house in Mar Vista was exactly the same stuff he'd crawled across in Turvey's girlfriend's apartment in Knoxville. Maybe a little cleaner, but the same stuff. He'd never noticed that before.

"Listen, Rydell, you don't want to take this, fine. My day off, I drive over here, you appreciate that? You get tweaked by some hackers, you fall for it, you push the response too hard, I can understand. But it happened, man, it's on your file, and this is the best I can do. But listen up. You do right by the company, maybe that gets back to Singapore."

"Hernandez..."

"My day *off*..."

"Man, I don't know anything about finding people—"

"You can *drive*. All they want. Just drive. You drive the tracer, see? He's got his leg hassled, he can't drive. And this is, like, delicate, this thing. Requires some smarts. I told them I thought you could *do* it, man. I *did* that. I told them."

Monica's copy of *People* was on the couch, open to a story about Gudrun Weaver, this actress in her forties who'd just found the Lord, courtesy of the Reverend Wayne Fallon, in time to get her picture in *People*. There was a full-page picture of her on a couch in her living room, gazing raptly at a bank of monitors, each one showing the same old movie.

Rydell saw himself on the futon from Futon Mouth, staring up at those big stick-on flowers and bumper-stickers. "Is it legal?"

Hernandez slapped his powder-blue thigh. It sounded like a pistol shot. "Legal? We are talking IntenSecure Corporation here. We are talking *major shit.* I am trying to *help* you, man. You think I would ask you to do something fucking illegal?"

"But what's the *deal*, Hernandez? I just go up there and drive?"

"Fucking 'A'! Drive! Mr. Warbaby say drive, you drive."

"Who?"

"Warbaby. This Lucius Warbaby."

Rydell picked up Monica's copy of *People* and found a picture of Gudrun Weaver and the Reverend Wayne Fallon. Gudrun Weaver looked like an actress in her forties. Fallon looked like a possum with hair-implants and a ten-thousand-dollar tuxedo.

"This Warbaby, Berry, he's right on top of this shit. He's a fucking *star*, man. Otherwise why they hire him? You do this, you *learn* shit. You still young, man. You can *learn* shit."

Rydell tossed the *People* back onto the couch. "Who they trying to find?"

"Hotel theft. Somebody took something. We got the security there. Singapore, man, they're in some kind of serious twist about it. All I know."

Rydell stood in the warm shade of the carport, gazing down into the shimmering depths of the animated waterfall on the hood of Hernandez's daughter's Sneaker, mist rising through green boughs of rain forest. He'd once seen a Harley done up so that everything that wasn't triple-chromed was crawling, fast forward, with life-sized bugs. Scorpions, centipedes, you name it.

"See," Hernandez said, "see there, where it blurs? That's supposed to be some kind of fucking *sloth*, man. Some *lemur*, you know? Factory warranty."

"When do they want me to go?"

"I give you this number." Hernandez handed Rydell a torn scrap of yellow paper. "Call them."

"Thanks."

"Hey," Hernandez said, "I like to see you do okay. I do. I like that." He touched the Sneaker's hood. "Look at this shit. Factory fucking *warranty.*"

morning

after

Chevette dreamed she was riding Folsom, a stiff sidewind threatening to push her into oncoming. Took a left on Sixth, caught that wind at her back, ran a red at Howard and Mission, a stale green at Market, bopped the brakes and bunnied both sets of tracks.

Coming down in a hard lean, she headed up Nob on Taylor.

"Make it this time," she said.

Legs pumping, the wind a strong hand in the small of her back, sky clear and beckoning at the top of the hill, she thumbed her chain up onto some huge-ass custom ring, too big for her derailleur, too big to fit any frame at all, and felt the shining teeth catch, her hammering slowing to a steady spin—but then she was losing it.

She stood up and started pounding, screaming, lactic acid slamming through her veins. She was at the crest, lifting off—

Colored light slanted into Skinner's room through the tinted pie-wedge panes of the round window. Tuesday morning.

Two of the smaller sections of glass had fallen out; the gaps were stuffed with pieces of rag, throwing shadows on the tattered yellow wall of *National Geographic*s. Skinner was sitting up in bed, wearing an old plaid shirt, blankets and sleeping-bag pulled high up his chest. His bed was an eight-panel oak door up on four rusty Volkswagen hubs, with a slab of foam on top of that. Chevette slept on the floor, on a narrower piece of foam she rolled up every morning and stuck behind a long wooden crate full of greasy hand tools. The smell of tool grease worked its way into her sleep, sometimes, but she didn't mind it.

She snaked her arm out into the November chill and snagged a sweater off the seat of a paint-caked wooden stool. She pulled the sweater into her bag and twisted into it, tugging it down over her knees. It hung to her knees when she stood up, the neckband so stretched that she had to keep pushing it back up on her shoulder. Skinner didn't say anything; he hardly ever did, first thing.

She rubbed her eyes, went to the ladder bolted to the wall and climbed the five rungs, undoing the catch on the roof-hatch without bothering to look at it. She came up here most mornings now, started her day with the water and then the city. Unless it was raining, or too foggy, and then it was her turn to pump the ancient Coleman, its red-painted tank like a toy submarine. Skinner did that, on good days, but he stayed in bed a lot when it rained. Said it got to his hip.

She climbed out of the square hole and sat on its edge, dangling her bare legs down into the room. Sun struggling to burn off the silvery gray. On hot days it heated the tar on the roof's flat rectangle and you could smell it.

Skinner had showed her pictures of the La Brea pits in *National Geographic*, big sad animals going down forever, down in L.A. a long time ago. That was what tar was, asphalt, not just something they made in a factory somewhere. He liked to know where things came from.

His jacket, the one she always wore, that had come from D. Lewis, Great Portland Street. That was in London. Skinner liked maps. Some of the *National Geographics* had maps folded into them, and all the countries were big, single blobs of color from one side to the other. And there hadn't been nearly as many of them. There'd been countries big as anything: Canada, USSR, Brazil. Now there were lots of little ones where those had been. Skinner said America had gone that route without admitting it. Even California had all been one big state, once.

Skinner's roof was eighteen feet by twelve. Somehow it looked smaller than the room below, even though the walls of the room were packed solid with Skinner's stuff. Nothing on the roof but a rusty metal wagon, a kid's toy, with a couple of rolls of faded tarpaper stacked in it.

She looked past three cable-towers to Treasure Island. Smoke rose, there, from a fire on the shore, where the low cantilever, cottoned down in fog, shot off to Oakland. There was a dome-thing, up on the farthest suspension tower, honeycombed into sections like new copper, but Skinner said it was just Mylar, stretched over two-by-twos. They had an uplink in that, something that talked to satellites. She thought she'd go and see it one day.

A gray gull slid by, level with her eyes.

The city looked the same as ever, the hills like sleeping animals behind the office towers she knew by their numbers. She ought to be able to see that hotel.

The night before grabbed her by the back of the neck.

She couldn't believe she'd done that, been that stupid. The case she'd pulled out of that dickhead's pocket was hanging up in Skinner's jacket, on the iron hook shaped like an elephant's head. Nothing in it but a pair of sunglasses, expensive-looking but so dark she hadn't even been able to see through them last night. The security grunts in the lobby had scanned her badges when she'd gone in; as far as they knew, she'd never come back down. Their computer would've started looking for her, eventually. If they queried Allied, she'd say she forgot, blew the checkout off, took the service elevator down after she'd pulled her tag at 808. No way had she been at any party, and who'd seen her there anyway? The asshole. And maybe he'd figure she'd done him for his glasses. Maybe he'd felt it. Maybe he'd remember, when he sobered up.

Skinner yelled there was coffee, but they were out of eggs. Chevette shoved off the edge of the hole, swung down and in, catching the top rung.

"Want any, you're gonna get 'em," Skinner said, looking up from the Coleman.

"Save me coffee." She pulled on a pair of black cotton leggings and got into her trainers without bothering to lace them. She

opened the hatch in the floor and climbed through, still worrying
about the asshole, his glasses, her job. Down ten steel rungs off the
side of an old crane. The cherry-picker basket waiting where she'd
left it when she'd gotten back. Her bike cabled to an upright with a
couple of Radio Shack screamers for good measure. She climbed
into the waist-high yellow plastic basket and hit the switch.

The motor whined and the big-toothed cog on the bottom let
her down the slope. Skinner called the cherry-picker his *funicular.*
He hadn't built it, though; a black guy named Fontaine had built it for
him, when Skinner had started to have trouble with the climb. Fontaine lived on the Oakland end, with a couple of women and a lot of
children. He took care of a lot of the bridge's electrical stuff. He'd
show up once in a while in a long tweed overcoat, a toolbag in each
hand, and he'd grease the thing and check it. And Chevette had a
number to call him at if it ever broke down completely, but that hadn't
happened yet.

It shook when it hit the bottom. She climbed out onto the
wooden walkway and went along the wall of taut milky plastic, hal-
ogen-shadows of plants behind it and the gurgle of hydroponics.
Turned the corner and down the stairs to the noise and morning
hustle of the bridge. Nigel coming toward her with one of his carts,
a new one. Making a delivery.

" 'Vette," with his big goofy grin. He called her that.

"Seen the egg lady?"

"City side," he said, meaning S.F. always, Oakland being always only 'Land. "Good one, huh?" with a gesture of builder's pride
for his cart. Chevette saw the braised aluminum frame, the Taiwan-
ese hubs and rims beefed up with fat new spokes. Nigel did work
for some of the other riders at Allied, ones who still rode metal. He
hadn't liked it when Chevette had gone for a paper frame. Now she
bent to run her thumb along a specially smooth braise. "Good one,"
she agreed.

"That Jap shit delaminate on you yet?"

"No way."

" 'S gonna. Bunny down too hard, it's glass."

"Come see you when it does."

Nigel shook his hair at her. The faded wooden fishing-plug that hung from his left ear rattled and spun. "Too late then." He shoved his cart toward Oakland.

Chevette found the egg lady and bought three, twisted up that way in two big dry blades of grass. Magic. You hated to take it apart, it was so perfect, and you could never get it back together or figure out how she did it. The egg lady took the five-piece and dropped it into the little bag around her scrawny lizard neck. She had no teeth at all, her face a nest of wrinkles that centered into that wet slit of a mouth.

Skinner was sitting at the table when she got back. More like a shelf than a table. He was drinking coffee out of a dented steel thermos-mug. If you just came in and saw him like that, it didn't strike you right away how old he was; just big, his hands, shoulders, all his bones, big. Gray hair slicked back from his forehead's lifetime collection of scars, little dents, a couple of black dots like tattoos, where some kind of grit had gotten into a cut.

She undid the eggs, the egg lady's magic, and put them in a plastic bowl. Skinner heaved himself up from his creaking chair, wincing as he took the weight with his hip. She handed him the bowl and he swung over to the Coleman. The way he scrambled eggs, he didn't use any butter, just a little water. Said he'd learned it from a cook on a ship. It made good eggs but the pan was hard to clean, and that was Chevette's job. While he broke the eggs, she went to the jacket on its hook, and took that case out.

You couldn't tell what it was made of, and that meant expensive. Something dark gray, like the lead in a pencil, thin as the shell of one of those eggs, but you could probably drive a truck over it. Like her bike. She'd figured out how you opened it the night before; finger here, thumb there, it opened. No catch or anything, no spring. No trademark, either; no patent numbers. Inside was like black suede, but it gave like foam under your finger.

Those glasses, nested there. Big and black. Like that Orbison in the poster stuck to Skinner's wall, black and white. Skinner said the way to put a poster up forever was use condensed milk for the glue. Kind that came in a can. Nothing much came in cans, anymore, but Chevette knew what he meant, and the weird big-faced guy with the black glasses was laminated solid to the white-painted ply of Skinner's wall.

She pulled them from the black suede, the stuff springing instantly back to a smooth flat surface.

They bothered her. Not just that she'd stolen them, but they weighed too much. Way too heavy for what they were, even with the big earpieces. The frames looked as though they'd been carved from slabs of graphite. Maybe they had, she thought; there was graphite around the paper cores in her bike's frame, and it was Asahi Engineering.

Rattle of the spatula as Skinner swirled the eggs.

She put them on. Black. Solid black.

"Katharine Hepburn," Skinner said.

She pulled them off. "Huh?"

"Big glasses like that."

She picked up the lighter he kept beside the Coleman, clicked It, held the flame behind one lens. Nothing.

"What're they for, welding?" He put her share of the eggs in an aluminum mess-tray stamped 1952. Set it down beside a fork and her mug of black coffee.

She put the glasses on the table. "Can't see through 'em. Just black." She pulled up the backless maple chair and sat, picking up the fork. She ate her eggs. Skinner sat, eating his, looking at her. "Soviet," he said, after a swallow from his thermos-mug.

"Huh?"

"How they made sunglasses in the ol' Soviet. Had two factories for sunglasses, one of 'em always made 'em like that. Kept right on puttin' 'em out in the stores, nobody'd buy 'em, buy the ones from the other factory. How the place packed it in."

"The factory made the black glasses?"

"Soviet Union."

"They stupid, or what?"

"Not that simple . . . Where'd you get 'em?"

She looked at her coffee. "Found 'em." She picked it up and drank.

"You working, today?" He pulled himself up, stuffed the front of his shirt down into his jeans, the rusted buckle on his old leather belt held with twisted paper clips.

"Noon to five." She picked up the glasses, turning them. They weighed too much for how big they were.

"Gotta get somebody up here, check the fuel cell . . ."

"Fontaine?"

He didn't answer. She bedded the glasses in black suede, closed the case, got up, took the dishes to the wash-basin. Looked back at the case on the table.

She'd better toss them, she thought.

9

when

diplomacy

fails

ydell took a CalAir tilt-rotor out of Burbank into Tuesday's early evening. The guy in San Francisco had paid for it from the other end; said call him Freddie. No seatback fun on CalAir, and the passengers definitely down-scale. Babies crying. Had a window seat. Down there the spread of lights through the faint glaze of some previous passenger's hair-oil: the Valley. Turquoise voids of a few surviving pools, lit subsurface. A dull ache in his arm.

He closed his eyes. Saw his father at the kitchen sink of his mobile home in Florida, washing out a glass. At that precise moment the death no doubt already growing in him, established fact, some line crossed. Talking about his brother, Rydell's uncle, three years younger and five years dead, who'd once sent Rydell a t-shirt from Africa. Army stamps on the bubblepack envelope. One of those old-timey bombers, B-52, and WHEN DIPLOMACY FAILS.

"Is that the Coast Highway, do you think?"

Opened his eyes to the lady leaning across him to peer through the film of hair-oil. Like Mrs. Armbruster in fifth grade; older than his father would be now.

"I don't know," Rydell said. "Might be. All just looks like streets to me. I mean," he added, "I'm not *from* here."

She smiled at him, settling back into the grip of the narrow seat. Completely like Mrs. Armbruster. Same weird combination of tweed, oxford-cloth, Santa Fe blanket coat. These old ladies with their bouncy thick-soled shoes.

"None of us *are.*" Reaching out to pat his khaki knee. "Not these days." Kevin had said it was okay to keep the pants.

"Uh-huh," Rydell said, his hand feeling desperately for the recliner button, the little dimpled steel circle waiting to tilt him back into the semblance of sleep. He closed his eyes.

"I'm on my way to San Francisco to assist in my late husband's transfer to a smaller cryogenic unit," she said. "One that offers *individual* storage modules. The trade magazines call them 'boutique operations,' grotesque as that may seem."

Rydell found the button and discovered that CalAir's seats allowed a maximum recline of ten centimeters.

"He's been in cryo, oh, nine years now, but I've never liked to think of his brain tumbling around in there like that. Wrapped in foil. Don't they always make you think of baked potatoes?"

Rydell's eyes opened. He tried to think of something to say.

"Or like tennis shoes in a dryer," she said. "I know they're frozen solid, but there's nothing about it that seems like any kind of *rest,* is there?"

Rydell concentrated on the seatback in front of him. A plastic blank. Gray. Not even a phone.

"These smaller places can't promise anything new in the way of an eventual awakening, of course. But it seems to me that there's an added degree of dignity. *I* think of it as dignity, in any case."

Rydell glanced sideways. Found his gaze caught in hers: hazel eyes, mazed there in the finest web of wrinkles.

"And I certainly won't be there if he's ever thawed, or, well, *whatever* they might eventually intend to do with them. I don't believe in it. We argued about it constantly. I thought of all those billions dead, the annual toll in all the *poor* places. 'David,' I said, 'how can you *contemplate* this when the bulk of humanity lives without air-conditioning?' "

Rydell opened his mouth. Closed it.

"Myself, I'm a card-carrying member of Cease Upon the Midnight."

Rydell wasn't sure what "card-carrying" meant, but Cease Upon the Midnight was mutual self-help euthanasia, and illegal in Tennessee. Though they did it there anyway, and someone on the force had told him that they left milk and cookies out for the ambulance crews. Did it eight or nine at a time, mostly. CUTM. "Cut'em," the paramedics called it. Offed themselves with cocktails of legally prescribed drugs. No muss, no fuss. Tidiest suicides around.

"Excuse me, ma'am," Rydell said, "but I've got to try to catch a little sleep here."

"You go right ahead, young man. You do look rather tired."

Rydell closed his eyes, put his head back, and stayed that way until he felt the rotors tilting over into descent-mode.

⎯⎯⎯⎯⎯⎯ • ⎯⎯⎯ • ⎯⎯⎯ • ⎯⎯⎯⎯⎯⎯

"Tommy Lee Jones," the black man said. His hair was shaped like an upside-down flowerpot with a spiral path sculpted into the side of it. Sort of like a Shriner's fez, but without the tassel. He was about five feet tall and his triple-oversized shirt made him look nearly as wide. The shirt was lemon-yellow and printed with life-size handguns, in full color, all different kinds. He wore a huge pair of navy blue shorts that came to way below his knees, Raiders socks, sneakers with little red lights embedded in the edges of the soles, and a pair of round mirrored glasses with lenses the size of five-dollar coins.

"You got the wrong guy," Rydell said.

"No, man, you *look* like him."

"Like who?"

"Tommy Lee Jones."

"Who?"

"Was an *actor*, man." For a second Rydell thought this guy had to be with Reverend Fallon. Even had those shades, like Sublett's contacts. "You Rydell. Ran you on Separated at Birth."

"You Freddie?" Separated at Birth was a police program you

used in missing persons cases. You scanned a photo of the person you wanted, got back the names of half a dozen celebrities who looked vaguely like the subject, then went around asking people if they'd seen anybody lately who reminded them of A, B, C...The weird thing was, it worked better than just showing them a picture of the subject. The instructor at the Academy in Knoxville had told Rydell's class that that was because it tapped into the part of the brain that kept track of celebrities. Rydell had imagined that as some kind of movie-star lobe. Did people really have those? Maybe Sublett had a great big one. But when they'd run the program on Rydell in the Academy, he'd come up a dead ringer for Howie Clacton, the Atlanta pitcher; he'd didn't remember any Tommy Lee Jones. But then he hadn't thought he looked all that much like Howie Clacton, either.

This Freddie extended a very soft hand and Rydell shook it. "You got luggage?" Freddie asked.

"Just this." Hefting his Samsonite.

"That's Mr. Warbaby right over there," Freddie said, nodding in the direction of an exit-gate, where a uniformed *chilanga* was checking people's seat-stubs before letting them out. Another black man loomed behind her, huge, broad as this Freddie, looking twice his height.

"Big guy."

"Uh-huh," Freddie said, "and best we not keep him waiting. Leg's hurting him today and he just *insisted* on walking in here from the lot to meet you."

Rydell took the man in as he approached the gate, handing his stub to the guard. He was enormous, over six feet, but the thing that struck Rydell most was a *stillness* about him, that and some kind of sorrow in his face. It was a look he'd seen on the face of a black minister his father had taken to watching, toward the end there. You looked at that minister's face and you felt like he'd seen every sad-ass thing there was, so maybe you could even believe what he was saying. Or anyway Rydell's father had, maybe, at least a little bit.

"Lucius Warbaby," taking the biggest hands Rydell had ever seen from the deep pockets of a long olive overcoat stitched from diamond-quilted silk, his voice pitched so far into the bass that it suggested subsonics. Rydell looked at the proffered hand and saw he wore one of those old-fashioned gold knuckle-duster rings, WAR-BABY across it in diamond-chip sans-serif capitals.

Rydell shook it, fingers curled over diamond and bullion. "Pleased to meet you, Mr. Warbaby."

Warbaby wore a black Stetson set dead level on his head, the brim turned up all the way around, and glasses with heavy black frames. Clear lenses, windowpane plain. The eyes behind those lenses were Chinese or something; catlike, slanted, a weird goldy brown. He was leaning on one of those adjustable canes you get at the hospital. There was a carbon brace clamped around his left leg, big midnight-blue nylon cushions padding it. Skinny black jeans, brand new and never washed, were tucked into spit-shined Texas dogger boots in three shades of black.

"Juanito *says* you're a decent driver," Warbaby said, as though it was about the saddest thing he'd ever heard. Rydell hadn't ever heard anybody call Hernandez that. "Says you don't know the area up here..."

"That's right."

"Up-side of *that*," Warbaby said, "is nobody here knows *you*. Carry the man's bag, Freddie."

Freddie took Rydell's soft-side with obvious reluctance, as though it wasn't something he'd ordinarily care to be seen with.

The hand with the knuckle-duster came down on Rydell's shoulder. Like the ring weighed twenty pounds. "Juanito tell you any-thing with regard to what we're doing up here?"

"Said a hotel theft. Said IntenSecure was bringing you in on a kind of contract basis—"

"Theft, yes." Warbaby looked like he had the moral gravity of the universe pressing down on him and was determined to bear the brunt. "Something missing. And all more ... *complicated,* now."

"How's that?"

Warbaby sighed. "Man who's missing it, he's dead now."

Something else in those eyes. "Dead *how*?" Rydell asked, as the weight at last was taken from his shoulder.

"*Hom*-icide," Warbaby said, low and doleful but very clear.

"You're wondering about my name," Warbaby said from the backseat of his black Ford Patriot.

"I'm wondering where to put the key, Mr. Warbaby," Rydell said, behind the wheel, surveying the option-laden dash. American cars were the only cars in the world that still bothered to physically display the instrumentation. Maybe that was why there weren't very many of them. Like those Harleys with chain-drives.

"My grandmother," Warbaby rumbled, like a tectonic plate giving up and diving for China, "was Vietnamese. Grandaddy, a De-troit boy. *Army* man. Brought her home from Saigon, but then he didn't stick around. *My* daddy, his son, he changed *his* name to War-baby, see? A gesture. Sentiment."

"Uh-huh," Rydell said, starting the big Ford and checking out the transmission. Saigon was where rich people went on vacation.

Four-wheel drive. Ceramic armor. Goodyear Streetsweepers you'd need a serious gun to puncture. There was a cardboard air-freshener, shaped like a pine-tree, hanging in front of the heater-vent.

"Now the Lucius part, well, I couldn't tell you."

"Mr. Warbaby," Rydell said, looking back over his shoulder, "where you want me to drive you to?"

A modem-bleep from the dash.

Freddie, in the plush bucket beside Rydell, whistled. "Moth-er*fuck*," he said, "that's nasty."

Rydell swung back to watch as the fax emerged: a fat man, naked on sheets solid with blood. Pools of it, where the brilliance of the photographer's strobes lay frozen like faint mirages of the sun.

"What's that under his chin?" Rydell asked.

"Cuban necktie," Freddie said.

"*No*, man," Rydell's voice up an octave, "what *is* that?"

"Man's tongue," Freddie said, tearing the image from the slit and passing it back to Warbaby.

Rydell heard the fax rattle in his hand.

"These people," Warbaby said. "Terrible."

10

the

modern

dance

Yamazaki sat on a low wooden stool, watching Skinner shave.

Skinner sat on the edge of his bed, scraping his face pink with a disposable razor, rinsing the blade in a dented aluminum basin that he cradled between his thighs.

"The razor is old," Yamazaki said. "You do not throw it away?"

Skinner looked at him, over the plastic razor. "Thing is, Scooter, they just don't *get* any duller, after a while." He lathered and shaved his upper lip, then paused. Yamazaki had been "Kawasaki" for the first several visits. Now he was "Scooter." The pale old eyes regarded him neutrally, hooded under reddish lids. Yamazaki sensed Skinner's inward laughter.

"I make you laugh?"

"Not today," Skinner said, dropping the razor into the basin of water, suds and gray whiskers recoiling in a display of surface tension. "Not like the other day, watching you chase those turds around."

Yamazaki had spent one entire morning attempting to diagram the sewage-collection arrangements for the group of dwellings he thought of as comprising Skinner's "neighborhood." Widespread use of transparent five-inch hose had made this quite exciting, like some game devised for children, as he'd tried to follow the course of a given bolus of waste from one dwelling down past the next. The hoses swooped down through the superstructure in graceful random arcs, bundled like ganglia, to meet below the lower deck in a thousand-gallon holding tank. When this was full to capacity, Skinner had explained, a mercury-switch in a float-ball triggered a jet-pump, forcing the accumulated sewage into a three-foot pipe that carried it into the municipal system.

He'd made a note to consider this junction as an interface between the bridge's program and the program of the city, but extracting Skinner's story of the bridge was obviously more important. Convinced that Skinner somehow held the key to the bridge's existential meaning, Yamazaki had abandoned his physical survey of secondary construction in order to spend as much time as possible in the old man's company. Each night, in his borrowed apartment, he would send the day's accumulation of material to Osaka University's Department of Sociology.

Today, climbing to the lift that would carry him to Skinner's room, he had met the girl on her way to work, descending, her shoulder through the frame of her bicycle. She was a courier in the city.

Was it significant that Skinner shared his dwelling with one who earned her living at the archaic intersection of information and geography? The offices the girl rode between were electronically conterminous—in effect, a single desktop, the map of distances obliterated by the seamless and instantaneous nature of communication. Yet this very seamlessness, which had rendered physical mail an expensive novelty, might as easily be viewed as porosity, and as such created the need for the service the girl provided. Physically transporting bits of information about a grid that consisted of little else, she provided a degree of absolute security in the fluid universe of data. With your memo in the girl's bag, you knew precisely where it was; otherwise, your memo was nowhere, perhaps everywhere, in that instant of transit.

He found her attractive, Skinner's girl, in an odd, foreign way, with her hard white legs and her militant, upthrust tail of dark hair.

"Dreamin', Scooter?" Skinner set the basin aside, his hands

trembling slightly, and settled his shoulders against musty-looking pillows. The white-painted plywood wall creaked faintly.

"No, Skinner-san. But you promised you would tell me about the first night, when you decided to take the bridge..." His tone was mild, his words deliberately chosen to irritate, to spur his subject to speech. He activated the notebook's recording function.

"We didn't *decide* anything. I told you that..."

"But somehow it happened."

"Shit *happens.* Happened that night. No signals, no leader, no architects. You think it was politics. That particular dance, boy, that's over."

"But you have said that the people were 'ready.'"

"But not *for* anything. That's what you can't seem to get, can you? Like the bridge was here, but I'm not saying it was *waiting.* See the difference?"

"I think—"

"You think shit." The notebook sometimes had trouble with Skinner's idioms. In addition, he tended to slur. An expert system in Osaka had suggested he might have sustained a degree of neural damage, perhaps as the result of using street drugs, or of one or more minor strokes. But Yamazaki believed Skinner had simply been too long in proximity to whatever strange attractor had permitted the bridge to become what it had become. "Nobody," Skinner said, speaking slowly and deliberately at first, as if for emphasis, "was *using* this bridge for anything. After the Little Grande came through, understand?"

Yamazaki nodded, watching the characters of Skinner's translated speech scroll down the notebook.

"Earthquake fucked it *good,* Scooter. The tunnel on Treasure caved in. Always been unstable there ... First they were gonna re-build, they said, bottom up, but they flat-out didn't have the money. So they put chain link, razor-wire, concrete up at both ends. Then the Germans came in, maybe two years later, sold 'em on nanomech, how to build the new tunnel. Be cheap, carry cars *and* a mag-lev. And nobody believed how fast they could do it, once they got it legislated past the Greens. Sure, those Green biotech lobbies, they made 'em actually grow the sections out in Nevada. Like pumpkins, Scooter. Then they hauled 'em out here under bulk-lifters and sank 'em in the Bay. Hooked 'em up. Little tiny machines crawling around in there, hard as diamonds; tied it all together tight, and bam, there's your tunnel. Bridge just sat there."

Yamazaki held his breath, expecting Skinner to lose the thread, as he so often had before—often, Yamazaki suspected, deliberately.

"This one woman, she kept saying plant the whole thing with ivy, Virginia creeper . . . Somebody else, they said tear it down before another quake did it for 'em. But there it was. In the cities, lot of people, no place to go. Cardboard towns in the park, if you were lucky, and they'd brought those drip-pipes down from Portland, put 'em around the buildings. Leaks enough water on the ground, you don't want to lay there. That's a *mean* town, Portland. Invented that there . . ." He coughed. "But that one night, people just *came*. All kinds of stories, after, how it happened. Pissing down rain, too. Nobody's idea of riot weather."

Yamazaki imagined the two spans of the deserted bridge in the downpour, the crowds accumulating. He watched as they climbed the wire fences, the barricades, in such numbers that the chain link twisted, fell. They had climbed the towers, then, more than thirty falling to their deaths. But when the dawn came, survivors clung there, news helicopters circling them in the gray light like patient dragonflies. He had seen this many times, watching the tapes in Osaka. But Skinner had been there.

"Maybe a thousand people, this end. Another thousand in Oakland. And we just started running. Cops falling back, and what were they protecting, anyway? Mainly the crowd-orders they had, keep people from getting together in the street. They had their choppers up in the rain, shining lights on us. Just made it easier. I had this pair of pointy boots on. Ran up to that 'link, it was maybe fifteen feet tall. Just kicked my toes in there and started climbing. Climb a fence like that easy, boots got a point. Up, man, I was up that thing like I was flying. Coils of razor at the top, but people behind me were pushing up anything; hunks of two-by-four, coats, sleeping-bags. To lay across the wire. And I felt like . . . weightless . . ."

Yamazaki felt that he was somehow close, very close, to the heart of the thing.

"I jumped. Don't know who jumped *first,* but I just jumped. Out. Hit pavement. People yelling. They'd crashed the barriers on the Oakland side, by then. Those were lower. We could see their lights as they ran out on the cantilever. The police 'copters and these red highway flares some of the people had. They ran toward Treasure. Nobody out there since the Navy people left . . . We ran too. Met up somewhere in the middle and this *cheer* went up . . ." Skinner's eyes were unfocused, distant. "After that, they were singing, hymns and shit. Just milling around, singing. Crazy. Me and some others, we were stoked. And we could see the cops, too, coming from both ends. Fuck that."

Yamazaki swallowed. "And then?"

"We started climbing. The towers. Rungs they welded on those suckers, see, so painters could get up there. We were climbing. Television had their own 'copters out by then, Scooter. We were making it to world news and we didn't know it. Guess you don't. Wouldn't've give a shit anyway. Just climbing. But that was going out live. Was gonna make it hard for the cops, later. And, man, people were falling off. Guy in front of me had black tape wrapped 'round his shoes, kept the soles on. Tape all wet, coming loose, his feet kept slipping. Right in front of my face. His foot kept coming back off the rung and I'd get his heel in my eye. I didn't watch it . . . Near to the top and both of 'em come off at once." Skinner fell silent, as if listening to some distant sound. Yamazaki held his breath.

"How you learn to climb, up here," Skinner said, "the first thing is, you don't look down. Second thing is, you keep one hand and one foot on the bridge *all the time.* This guy, he didn't know that. And those shoes of his . . . He just went off, backward. Never made a sound. Sort of . . . graceful."

Yamazaki shivered.

"But I kept climbing. Rain had quit, light was coming. Stayed."

"How did you feel?" Yamazaki asked.

Skinner blinked. "Feel?"

"What did you do then?"

"I saw the city."

Yamazaki rode Skinner's lift down to where stairs began, its yellow upright cup like a piece of picnicware discarded by a giant. All around him, now, the rattle of an evening's commerce, and from a darkened doorway came the slap of cards, a woman's laughter, voices raised in Spanish. Sunset pink as wine, through sheets of plastic that snapped like sails in a breeze scented with frying foods, woodsmoke, a sweet oily drift of cannabis. Boys in ragged leather crouched above a game whose counters were painted pebbles.

Yamazaki stopped. He stood very still, one hand on a wooden railing daubed with hyphens of aerosol silver. Skinner's story seemed to radiate out, through the thousand things, the unwashed smiles and the smoke of cooking, like concentric rings of sound from some secret bell, pitched too low for the foreign, wishful ear.

We are come not only past the century's closing, he thought, *the millennium's turning, but to the end of something else. Era? Paradigm? Everywhere, the signs of closure.*

Modernity was ending.

Here, on the bridge, it long since had.

He would walk toward Oakland now, feeling for the new thing's strange heart.

11

pulling

tags

Tuesday, she just wasn't on. Couldn't proj. No focus. Bunny Malatesta, the dispatcher, could feel it, his voice a buzz in her ear.

"Chev, don't take this the wrong way, but you got like the monthlies or something?"

"Fuck off, Bunny."

"Hey, I just mean you're not your usual ball of fire today. All I mean."

"Gimme a tag."

"655 Mo, fifteenth, reception."

Picked up, made it to 555 Cali, fifty-first floor. Pulled her tag and back down. The day gone gray after morning's promise.

"456 Montgomery, thirty-third, reception, go freight."

Pausing, her hand in the bike's recognition-loop. "How come?"

"Says messengers carvin' graffiti in the passenger elevators. Go freight or they'll toss you, be denied access, at which point Allied terminates your employment."

She remembered seeing Ringer's emblem carved into the inspection plate in one of 456's passenger elevators. Fucking Ringer. He'd defaced more elevators than anyone in history. Carried around a regular toolkit to do it with.

456 sent her to 1 EC with a carton wider than she was

supposed to accept, but that was what racks and bungies were for, and why give the cage-drivers the trade? Bunny buzzed her on her way out and gave her 50 Beale, the cafeteria on the second floor. She guessed that would be a woman's purse, done up in a plastic bag from the kitchen, and she was right. Brown, sort of lizardskin, with a couple of green sprouts stuck in the corners of the bag. Women left their purses, remembered, called up, got the manager to send for a messenger. Good for a tip, usually. Ringer and some of the others would open them up, go through the contents, find drugs sometimes. She wouldn't do that. She thought about the sunglasses...

She couldn't get a run today. There was no routing in effect at Allied, but sometimes you'd get a run by accident; pick up here, drop off there, then something here. But it was rare. When you worked for Allied you rode harder. Her record was sixteen tags in a day; like doing forty at a different company.

She took the purse to Fulton at Masonic, got two fivers after the owner checked to see everything was there.

"Restaurant's supposed to take it to the cops," Chevette said. "*We* don't like to be responsible." Blank look from the purse-lady, some kind of secretary. Chevette pocketed the fives.

"298 Alabama," Bunny said, as if offering her some pearl of great price. "Tone those thighs..."

Bust her ass out there to get there, then she'd pick up and do it. But she couldn't get on top of it, today.

The asshole's sunglasses...

"For tactical reasons," the blonde said, "we do not currently advocate the use of violence or sorcery against private individuals."

Chevette had just pumped back from Alabama Street, day's last tag. The woman on the little CNN flatscreen over the door to Bunny's pit wore something black and stretchy pulled over her face, three triangular holes cut in it. Blue letters at the bottom of the screen read FIONA X—SPOKESPERSON—SOUTH ISLAND LIBERATION FRONT.

The overlit fluorescent corridor into Allied Messengers smelled of hot styrene, laser printers, abandoned running-shoes, and stale bag lunches, this last tugging Chevette toward memories of some unheated day-care basement in Oregon, winter's colorless light slanting in through high dim windows. But now the street door banged open behind her, a pair of muddy size-eleven neon sneakers came pounding down the stairs, and Samuel Saladin DuPree, his cheeks spackled with crusty gray commas of road-dirt, stood grinning at her, hugely.

"Happy about something, Sammy Sal?"

Allied's best-looking thing on two wheels, no contest whatever, DuPree was six-two of ebon electricity poured over a frame of such elegance and strength that Chevette imagined his bones as polished metal, triple-chromed, a quicksilver armature. Like those old movies with that big guy, the one who went into politics, after he'd get the meat ripped off him. Thinking about Sammy Sal's bones made most girls want him to jump theirs, but not Chevette. He was gay, they were friends, and Chevette wasn't too sure how she felt about all that anyway, lately.

"Fact is," Sammy Sal said, smearing dirt from his cheek with the back of one long hand, "I've decided to kill Ringer. And the truth, y'know, it makes you *free*..."

"Ho," Chevette said, "you musta pulled a tag over 456 today."

"I did, dear, *do* that thing. All the way up, in a dirty freight elevator. A *slow* dirty freight elevator. And why?"

" 'Cause Ringer's 'graved his tag in their brass, Sal, and their rosewood, too?"

"Eggs-ackly, Chevette, honey." Sammy Sal undid the blue and white bandanna around his neck and wiped his face with it. "Therefore, his ass dies screaming."

"...and must begin, now, to systematically sabotage the

workplace," Fiona X said, "or be branded an enemy of the human race."

The door to the dispatch-pit, so thickly stapled with scheds, sub-charts, tattered Muni regs, and faxed complaints that Chevette had no idea what the surface underneath might look like, popped open. Bunny extruded his scarred and unevenly shaven head, turtle-like, blinking in the light of the corridor, and glanced up automatically, his gaze attracted by the tone of Fiona X's sound-bite. His expression blanked at the sight of her mask, the mental channel-zap executed in less time than it had taken him to look her way. "You," he said, eyes back on Chevette, "Chevy. In here."

"Wait for me, Sammy Sal," she said.

Bunny Malatesta had been a San Francisco bike messenger for thirty years. Would be still, if his knees and back hadn't given out on him. He was simultaneously the best and the worst thing about messing for Allied. The best because he had a bike-map of the city hung behind his eyes, better than anything a computer could generate. He knew every building, every door, what the security was like. He had the mess game *down*, Bunny did, and, better still, he knew the lore, all the history, the stories that made you know you were part of something, however crazy it got, that was worth doing. He was a legend himself, Bunny, having Krypto'd the windshields of some seven police cars in the course of his riding career, a record that still stood. But he was the worst for those same reasons and more, because there wasn't any bullshitting him at all. Any other dispatcher, you could cut yourself a little extra slack. But not Bunny. He just *knew*.

Chevette followed him in. He closed the door behind her. The goggles he used for dispatching dangled around his neck, one pad-ded eyepiece patched with cellophane tape. There were no windows in the room and Bunny kept the lights off when he was working. Half a dozen color monitors were arranged in a semicircle in front of a black swivel armchair with Bunny's pink rubber Sacro-saver back-rest strapped to it like some kind of giant bulging larva.

Bunny rubbed his lower back with the heels of his hands. "Disk's killing me," he said, not particularly to Chevette.

"Oughta let Sammy Sal crack it for you," she suggested. "He's real good."

"It's cracked already, sweetheart. What's wrong with it in the first place. Now tell me what were you doin' over the Morrisey last night. And it better be good."

"Pulling a tag," Chevette said, going on automatic, the way she had to if she were going to lie and get away with it. She'd been halfway expecting something like this, but not so soon.

She watched as Bunny took the goggles off, disconnected them, and put them on top of one of the monitors. "So how come you never checked back out? They call us on it, say you went in to make a delivery, they scanned your badges, you never come back out. Look, I tell 'em, I know she's not there *now*, guys, 'cause I got her out Alabama Street on a call, okay?" He was watching her.

"Hey, Bunny," Chevette said, "it was my last tag, my ride was down in the basement, I saw a freight el on its way down, jumped in. I know I'm supposed to clock out at security, but I thought they'd have somebody on the parking exit, you know? I get up the ramp and there's nobody, a car's going out, so I deak under the barrier and I'm in the street. I shoulda gone back around and done the lobby thing?"

"You know it. It's regs."

"It was late, you know?"

Bunny sat down, wincing, in the chair with the Sacro-saver. He cupped each knee in a big-knuckled hand and stared at her. Very un-Bunny. Like something was really bothering him. Not just security grunts pissing because a mess blew the check-out off. "How late?"

"Huh?"

"They wanna know when you left."

"Maybe ten minutes after I went in. Fifteen tops. Basement in there's a rat-maze."

"You went in 6:32:18," he said. "They got that when they scanned you. The tag, this lawyer, they talked to him, so they know you delivered." He still had that look.

"Bunny, what's the deal? Tell 'em I screwed up, is all."

"You didn't go anywhere else? In the hotel?"

"Uh-uh," she said, and felt this funny ripple move through her, like she'd crossed some line and couldn't go back. "I *gave* the guy his package, Bunny."

"I don't think they're worrying about the guy's package," Bunny said.

"So?"

"Lookit, Chev," he said, "security guy calls, that's one thing. Sorry, boss, won't let it happen again. But this was somebody up in the company, IntenSecure it's called, and he called up Wilson *direct.*" Allied's owner. "So I gotta make nice with Wilson *and* Mr. Security, I gotta have Grasso cover for me on the board and naturally he screws everything up…"

"Bunny," she said, "I'm sorry."

"Hey. You're sorry, I'm sorry, but there's some big shit rent-acop sitting behind a desk and he's putting fucking Wilson through about what precisely did *you* do after you gave that lawyer his package. About what kind of *employee* are you exactly, how long you *mess* for Allied, any criminal *record,* any *drug* use, where you *live.*"

Chevette saw the asshole's black glasses, right where she'd left them. In their case, behind Skinner's '97 *Geographic*s. She tried to lift them out of there with mind-power. Right up to the tar-smelling roof and off the edge. Put those bastards in the Bay like she should've done this morning. But no, they were there.

"That ain't *normal,*" Bunny said. "Know what I mean?"

"You tell 'em where I live, Bunny?"

"Out on the bridge," he said, then cracked her a little sliver of grin. "Not like you got much of an address, is it?" Now he spun himself around in the chair and began to shut the monitors down.

"Bunny," she said, "what'll they do now?"

"Come and find you." His back to her. "Here. 'Cause they won't know where else to go. You didn't *do* anything, did you, Chevy?" The back of his skull showing gray stubble.

Automatic. "No. No . . . Thanks, Bunny."

He grunted in reply, neutral, ending it, and Chevette was back in the corridor, her heart pounding under Skinner's jacket. Up the stairs, out the door, plotting the quickest way home, running red lights in her head, gotta get rid of the glasses, gotta—

Sammy Sal had Ringer braced up against a blue recyc bin. Worry was starting to penetrate Ringer's rudimentary view of things. "Didn't *do* nuthin to you, man."

"Been carvin' your name in elevators again, Ringer."

"But I din't do nuthin to *you*!"

"Cause and effect, mofo. We know it's a tough concept for you, but try: you *do* shit, other shit follows. You go scratching your tag in the clients' fancy elevators, we *hassle* you, man." Sammy Sal spread the long brown fingers of his left hand across Ringer's beat-to-shit helmet, palming it like a basketball, and twisted, lifting, the helmet's strap digging into Ringer's chin. "Din't *do* nuthin!" Ringer gurgled.

Chevette ducked past them, heading for the bike-rack beneath the mural portrait of Shapely. Someone had shot him in his soulful martyr's eye with a condomful of powder blue paint, blue running all down his hallowed cheek.

"Hey," Sammy Sal said, "come here and help me torment this shit-heel."

She stuck her hand through the recognition-loop and tried to pull her handlebars out of the rack's tangle of molybdenum steel, graphite, and aramid overwrap. The other bikes' alarms all went off at once, a frantic chorus of ear-splitting bleats, basso digital siren-moans, and one extended high-volume burst of snake-hiss Spanish profanity, cunningly mixed with yelps of animal torment. She swung her bike around, got her toe in the clip, and kicked for the street, almost going over as she mounted. She saw Sammy Sal, out the corner of her eye, drop Ringer.

She saw Sammy Sal straddle his own bike, a pink and black-fleck fat-tube with Fluoro-Rimz that ran off a hub-generator.

Sammy Sal was coming after her. She'd never wanted company less.

She took off.

Proj. Just proj.

Like her morning dream, but scarier.

12

eye

movement

ydell looked at these two San Francisco cops, Svobodov and Orlovsky, and decided that working for Warbaby had a chance of being interesting. These guys were the real, the super-heavy thing. Homicide was colossus, any department anywhere.

And here he'd been in Northern California all of forty-eight minutes and he was sitting at a counter drinking coffee with Homicide. Except they were drinking tea. Hot tea. In glasses. Heavy on the sugar. Rydell was at the far end, on the other side of Freddie, who was drinking milk. Then Warbaby, with his hat still on, then Svobodov, then Orlovsky.

Svobodov was nearly as tall as Warbaby, but it all seemed to be sinew and big knobs of bone. He had long, pale hair, combed straight back from his rocky forehead, eyebrows to match, and skin that was tight and shiny, like he'd stood too long in front of a fire. Orlovsky was thin and dark, with a widow's peak, lots of hair on the backs of his fingers, and those glasses that looked like they'd been sawn in half.

They both had that eye thing, the one that pinned you and held you and sank right in, heavy and inert as lead.

Rydell had had a course in that at the Police Academy, but it hadn't really taken. It was called Eye Movement Desensitization & Response, and was taught by this retired forensic psychologist named Bagley, from Duke University. Bagley's lectures tended to wander off into stories about serial killers he'd processed at Duke, auto-erotic strangulation fatalities, stuff like that. It sure passed the time between High Profile Felony Stops and Firearms Training System Scenarios. But Rydell was usually kind of rattled after Felony Stops, because the instructors kept asking him to take the part of the felon. And he couldn't figure out why. So he'd have trouble concentrating, in Eye Movement. And if he did manage to pick up anything useful from Bagley, a session of FATSS would usually make him forget it. FATSS was like doing Dream Walls, but with guns, real ones.

When FATSS tallied up your score, it would drag you right down the entrance wounds, your own or the other guy's, and make the call on whether the loser had bled to death or copped to hydrostatic shock. There were people who went into full-blown post-traumatic heeb-jeebs after a couple of sessions on FATSS, but Rydell always came out of it with this shit-eating grin. It wasn't that he was violent, or didn't mind the sight of blood; it was just that it was such a rush. And it wasn't real. So he never had learned to throw that official hoodoo on people with his eyes. But this Lt. Svobodov, he had the talent beaucoup, and his partner, Lt. Orlovsky, had his own version going, nearly as effective and he did it over the sawn-off tops of those glasses. Guy looked sort of like a werewolf anyway, which helped.

Rydell continued to check out the San Francisco Homicide look. Which seemed to be old tan raincoats over black flak vests over white shirts and ties. The shirts were button-down oxfords and the ties were the stripey kind, like you were supposed to belong to a club or something. Cuffs on their trousers and great big pebble-grain wingtips with cleated Vibram soles. About the only people who wore shirts and ties and shoes like that were immigrants, people who wanted it as American as it got. But layering it up with a bullet-proof and a worn-out London Fog, he figured that was some kind of statement. The streamlined plastic butt of an H&K didn't exactly hurt, either, and Rydell could see one peeking out of Svobodov's open flak vest. Couldn't remember the model number, but it looked like the one with the magazine down the top of the barrel. Shot that caseless ammo looked like wax crayons, plastic propellant molded around alloy flechettes like big nails.

"If we knew what you *already* know, Warbaby, maybe that makes everything more simple." Svobodov looked around the little diner, took a pack of Marlboros out of his raincoat.

"Illegal in *this* state, buddy," the waitress said, pleased at any opportunity to threaten somebody with the law. She had that big kind of hair. This was one of those places you ate at if you worked graveyard at some truly shit-ass industrial job. If your luck held, Rydell figured, you'd get this particular waitress into the bargain.

Svobodov fixed her with a couple of thousand negative volts of Cop Eye, tugged a black plastic badge-holder out of his flak vest, flipped it open in her direction, and let it fall back on its nylon thong, against his chest. Rydell noticed the click when it hit; some kind of back-up armor under the white shirt.

"Those two Mormon boys from Highway Patrol come in here, you show that to *them*," she said.

Svobodov put the cigarette between his lips.

Warbaby's fist came up, clutching a lump of gold the size of a hand grenade.

He lit the Russian's cigarette with it.

"Why you have this, Warbaby?" Svobodov said, eyeing the lighter. "You smoking something?"

"Anything but those Chinese Marlboros, Arkady." Mournful as ever. "They're fulla fiberglass."

"American brand," Svobodov insisted, "licensed by maker."

"Hasn't been a legal cigarette manufactured in this country in six years," Warbaby said, sounding as sad about that as anything else.

"Marl-bor-*ro*," Svobodov said, taking the cigarette out of his mouth and pointing to the lettering in front of the filter. "When we were kids, Warbaby, Marlboro, she was *money*."

"Arkady," Warbaby said, as though with enormous patience, "when *we* were kids, man, *money* was money."

Orlovsky laughed. Svobodov shrugged. "What you know, Warbaby?" Svobodov said, back to business.

"Mr. Blix has been found dead, at the Morrisey. Murdered."

"Pro job," Orlovsky said, making it one word, *projob*. "They want we assume some bullshit ethnic angle, see?"

Svobodov squinted at Warbaby. "We don't *know* that," he said.

"The *tongue*," Orlovsky said, determined. "That's *color*. To throw us off. They think we think Latin Kings."

Svobodov sucked on his cigarette, blew smoke in the general direction of the waitress. "What you know, Warbaby?"

"Hans Rutger Blix, forty-three, naturalized Costa Rican." Warbaby might have been making the opening remarks at a funeral.

"My hairy ass," Svobodov said, around the Marlboro.

"Warbaby," Orlovsky said, "we know you were working on this *before* this asshole got his throat cut."

"Asshole," Warbaby said, like maybe the dead guy had been a close personal friend, a lodge-brother or something. "Man's dead, is all. That make him an asshole?"

Svobodov sat there, puffing on his Marlboro. Stubbed it out on the plate in front of him, beside his untouched tuna melt. "Asshole. Believe it."

Warbaby sighed. "Man had a jacket, Arkady?"

"You want his jacket," Svobodov said, "you tell us what you were supposed to be doing for him. We know he talked to you."

"We never spoke."

"Okay," Svobodov said. "IntenSecure he talked to. You freelance."

"Strictly," Warbaby said.

"Why did he talk to IntenSecure?"

"Man *lost* something."

"What?"

"Something of a personal nature."

Svobodov sighed. "Lucius. Please."

"A pair of sunglasses."

Svobodov and Orlovsky looked at each other, then back to Warbaby. "IntenSecure brings in Lucius Warbaby because this guy loses his sunglasses?"

"Maybe they were expensive," Freddie offered, softly. He was studying his reflection in the mirror behind the counter.

Orlovsky put his hairy fingers together and cracked his knuckles.

"He thought he might have lost them at a *party*," Warbaby offered, "someone might even have *taken* them."

"What party?" Svobodov shifted on his stool and Rydell heard the hidden armor creak.

"Party at the Morrisey."

"Whose party?" Orlovsky, over those glasses.

"Mr. Cody Harwood's party," Warbaby said.

"Harwood," Svobodov said, "Harwood..."

"Name 'Pavlov' ring a bell?" Freddie said, to no one in particular.

Svobodov grunted. "Money."

"None of it in Marlboros, either," Warbaby said. "Mr. Blix went down to Mr. Harwood's party, had a few drinks—"

"Had a BA level like they won't need to embalm," Orlovsky said.

"Had a few drinks. Had this property in the pocket of his jacket. Next morning, it was gone. Called security at the Morrisey. They called IntenSecure. IntenSecure called me..."

"His phone is gone," Svobodov said. "They took it. Nothing to tie him to anyone. No agenda, notebook, nothing."

"Pro job," Orlovsky intoned.

"The glasses," Svobodov said. "What kind of glasses?"

"Sunglasses," Freddie said.

"We found these." Svobodov took something from the side pocket of his London Fog. A Ziploc evidence bag. He held it up. Rydell saw shards of black plastic. "Cheap VR. Ground into the carpet."

"Do you know what he ran on them?" Warbaby asked.

Now it was Orlovsky's turn for show-and-tell. He produced a second evidence bag, this one from inside his black vest. "Looked for software, couldn't find it. Then we x-ray him. Somebody shoved this down his throat." A black rectangle. The stick-on label worn and stained. "But before they cut him."

"What is it?" Warbaby asked.

"McDonna," Svobodov said.

"Huh?" Freddie was leaning across Warbaby to peer at the thing. "Mc-what?"

"Fuck chip." It sounded to Rydell like *fock cheap,* but then he got it. "McDonna."

"Wonder if they read it all the way *down*?" Freddie said, from the rear of the Patriot. He had his feet up on the back of the front passenger seat and the little red lights around the edges of his sneakers were spelling out the lyrics to some song.

"Read what?" Rydell was watching Warbaby and the Russians, who were standing beside one of the least subtle unmarked cars Rydell had ever seen: a primer-gray whale with a cage of graphite expansion-grating protecting the headlights and radiator. Fine rain was beading up on the Patriot's windshield.

"That porn they found down the guy's esophagus." If Warbaby always sounded sad, Freddie always sounded relaxed. But Warbaby sounded like he really was sad, and Freddie's kind of relaxed sounded like he was just the opposite. "Lotta code in a program like that. Hide all sorta goodies in the wallpaper, y'know? Running fractal to get the skin texture, say, you could mix in a lot of text..."

"You into computer stuff, Freddie?"

"I'm Mr. Warbaby's technical consultant."

"What do you think they're talking about?"

Freddie reached up and touched one of his sneakers. The red words vanished. "They're having the real conversation now."

"What's that?"

"The *deal* conversation. We want what they got on Blix, the dead guy."

"Yeah? So what *we* got?"

"'We'?" Freddie whistled. "You just drivin'." He pulled his feet back and sat up. "But it ain't exactly classified: IntenSecure and DatAmerica more or less the same thing."

"No shit." Svobodov seemed to be doing most of the talking. "What's that mean?"

"Means we tight with a bigger data-base than the police. Next time ol' Rubadub needs him a look-see, he'll be glad he did us a favor. But tonight, man, tonight it just burns his Russian ass."

Rydell remembered the time he'd gone over to "Big George" Kechakmadze's house for a barbecue and the man had tried to sign him up for the National Rifle Association. "You get a lot of Russians on the force, up here?"

"Up here? All over."

"Kinda funny how many of those guys go into police work."

"Think about it, man. Had 'em a whole *police* state, over there. Maybe they just got a feel for it."

Svobodov and Orlovsky climbed into the gray whale. Warbaby walked to the Patriot, using his alloy cane. The police car rose up about six inches on hydraulics and began to moan and shiver, rain dancing on its long hood as Orlovsky revved the engine.

"Jesus," Rydell said, "they don't care who sees 'em comin', do they?"

"They *want* you see 'em coming," Freddie said, obscurely, as Warbaby opened the right rear passenger door and began the process of edging his stiff-legged bulk into the back seat.

"Take off," Warbaby said, slamming the door. "Protocol. We leave first."

"Not that way," Freddie said. "That'll get us Candlestick Park. *That* way."

"Yes," said Warbaby, "we have business downtown." Sad about it.

Downtown San Francisco was really something. With everything hemmed in by hills, built up and down other hills, it gave Rydell a sense of, well, he wasn't sure. *Being* somewhere. Somewhere in particular. Not that he was sure he *liked* being there. Maybe it just felt so much the opposite of L.A. and that feeling like you were cut loose in a grid of light that just spilled out to the edge of everything. Up here he felt like he'd come *in* from somewhere, these old buildings all around and close together, nothing more modern than that one big spikey one with the truss-thing on it (and he knew that one was old, too). Cool damp air, steam billowing from grates in the pavement. People on the streets, too, and not just the usual kind; people with jobs and clothes. Kind of like Knoxville, he tried to tell himself, but it wouldn't stick. Another strange place.

"No, man, a left, a *left*!" Freddie thumping on the back of his seat. And another city-grid to learn. He checked the cursor on the Patriot's dash-map, looking for a left that would get them to this hotel, the Morrisey.

"Don't bang on Mr. Rydell's seat," Warbaby said, a six-foot scroll of fax bunched in his hands, "he's driving." It had come in on their way here. Rydell figured it was the jacket on Blix, the guy who'd gotten his throat cut.

"Fassbinder," Freddie said. "You ever hear of this Rainer Fassbinder?"

"I'm not in a joking mood, Freddie," Warbaby said.

"No joke. I ran Separated at Birth on this Blix, man, scanned this stiff-shot the Russian sent you before? Says he looks like Rainer Fassbinder. And that's when he's dead, with his throat cut. This Fassbinder, he musta been pretty rough-looking, huh?"

Warbaby sighed. "Freddie..."

"Well, German, anyway. Clicked with the nationality—"

"Mr. Blix was not German, Freddie. Says here Mr. Blix wasn't even Mr. Blix. Now let me read. Rydell needs quiet, in order to adjust to driving in the city."

Freddie grunted, then Rydell heard his fingers clicking over the little computer he carried everywhere.

Rydell took the left he thought he was looking for. Combat zone. Ruins. Fires in steel cans. Hunched dark figures, faces vampire white.

"Don't brake," Warbaby said. "Or accelerate."

Something came spinning, end over end, out of the crow-shouldered coven, splat against the windshield; clung, then fell away, leaving a smudge of filthy yellow. Hadn't it been gray and bloody, like a loop of intestine?

Red at the intersection.

"Run the light," Warbaby instructed. Rydell did, amid horns of protest. The yellow stuff still there.

"Pull over. No. Right up on the sidewalk. Yes." The Patriot's Goodyear Streetsweepers bouncing up and over the jagged curb. "In the glove compartment."

A light came on as Rydell opened it. Windex, a roll of gray paper towels, and a box of throwaway surgical gloves.

"Go on," Warbaby said. "Nobody bother us."

Rydell pulled a glove on, took the Windex and the towels, got out. "Don't get any on you," he said, thinking of Sublett. He gave the yellow smear a good shot of Windex, wadded up three of the towels in his gloved hand, wiped until the glass was clean. He skinned the glove down around the wet wad, the way they'd shown him in the Academy, but then he didn't know what to do with it.

"Just toss it," Warbaby said from inside. Rydell did. Then he walked back from the car, five paces, and threw up. Wiped his mouth with a clean towel. He got back in, shut the door, locked it, put the Windex and the towels in the glove compartment.

"You gonna gargle with that, Rydell?"

"Shut up, Freddie," Warbaby said. The Patriot's suspension creaked as Warbaby leaned forward. "Leavings from a slaughterhouse, most likely," he said. "But it's good you know to take precautions." He settled back. "Had us a group here once called Sword of the Pig. You ever hear of that?"

"No," Rydell said, "I never did."

"They'd steal fire-extinguishers out of buildings. Re-charge them with blood. Blood from a slaughterhouse. But they let it out, you understand, that this blood, well, it was human. Then they'd go after the Jesus people, when they marched, with those same extinguishers..."

"Jesus," Rydell said.

"*Exactly,*" Warbaby said.

"You see that door, there?" Freddie said.

"What door?" The lobby of the Morrisey made Rydell want to whisper, like being in church or a funeral home. The carpet was so soft, it made him want to lie down and go to sleep.

"That black one," Freddie said.

Rydell saw a black-lacquered rectangle, perfectly plain, not even a knob. Now that he thought about it, it didn't match anything else in sight. The rest of the place was polished wood, frosted bronze, panels of carved glass. If Freddie hadn't told him it was a door, exactly, he would have taken it for art or something, some kind of painting. "Yeah? What about it?"

"That's a *restaurant,*" Freddie said, "and it's so expensive, you can't even go *in* there."

"Well," Rydell said, "there's lots of those."

"No, man," Freddie insisted, "I mean even if you were *rich,* had money out your ass, you could *not* go in there. Like it's private. Japanese thing."

They were standing around by the security desk while Warbaby talked to somebody on a house phone. The three guys on duty at the desk wore IntenSecure uniforms, but really fancy ones, with bronze logo-buttons on their peaked caps.

Rydell had parked the Patriot in an underground garage, floors down in the roots of the place. He hadn't seen anything like that before: teams of people in chef's whites putting together a hundred plates of some skinny kind of salad, little Sanyo vacuum-cleaners bleeping along in pastel herds, all this back-stage stuff you'd never guess was there if you were just standing here in the lobby.

The Executive Suites, where he'd stayed in Knoxville with Karen Mendelsohn, had had these Korean robot bugs that cleaned up when you weren't looking. They'd even had a special one that ate dust off the wallscreen, but Karen hadn't been impressed. It just meant they couldn't afford people, she said.

Rydell watched as Warbaby turned, handing the phone to one of the guys in the peaked caps. Warbaby gestured for Freddie and Rydell. Leaned on his cane as they walked toward him.

"They'll take us up now," he said. The cap Warbaby had handed the phone to came out from behind the counter. He saw Rydell was wearing an IntenSecure shirt with the patches ripped off, but he didn't say anything. Rydell wondered when he was going to have a chance to buy some clothes, and where he should go to do it. He looked at Freddie's shirt, thinking Freddie probably wasn't the guy to ask.

"This way, sir," the cap said to Warbaby. Freddie and Rydell followed Warbaby across the lobby. Rydell saw how he jabbed his cane, hard, into the carpeting, the brace on his leg ticking like a slow clock.

tweaking

Sometimes, when she rode hard, when she could really proj, Chevette got free of everything: the city, her body, even time. That was the messenger's high, she knew, and though it felt like freedom, it was really the melding-with, the clicking-in, that did it. The bike between her legs was like some hyper-evolved alien *tail* she'd somehow extruded, as though over patient centuries; a sweet and intricate bone-machine, grown Lexan-armored tires, near-frictionless bearings, and gas-filled shocks. She was entirely part of the city, then, one wild-ass little dot of energy and matter, and she made her thousand choices, instant to instant, according to how the traffic flowed, how rain glinted on the streetcar tracks, how a secretary's mahogany hair fell like grace itself, exhausted, to the shoulders of her loden coat.

And she was starting to get that now, in spite of everything; if she just let go, quit thinking, let her mind sink down into the machinery of bone and gear-ring and carbon-wound Japanese paper...

But Sammy Sal swerved in beside her, bass pumping from his bike's bone-conduction beatbox. She had to bunny the curb to keep from going over on a BART grate. Her tires left black streaks as the particle-brakes caught, Sammy Sal braking in tandem, his Fluoro-Rimz strobing, fading.

"Something *eating* you, little honey?" His hand on her arm, rough and angry. "Like maybe some wonder product makes you smarter, faster? Huh?"

"Let me go."

"No way. I *got* you this job. You're gonna blow it, I'm gonna know *why.*" He slammed his other palm on the black foam around his bars, killing the music.

"*Please,* Sammy, I gotta get up to Skinner's—"

He let go of her arm. "Why?"

She started to cough, caught it, took three deep breaths. "You ever steal anything, Sammy Sal? I mean, when you were working?"

Sammy Sal looked at her. "No," he said, finally, "but I been known to fuck the clients."

Chevette shivered. "Not me."

"No," Sammy Sal said, "but you don't pull tags all the places I do. 'Sides, you a girl."

"But I stole something last night. From this guy's pocket, up at this party at the Hotel Morrisey."

Sammy Sal licked his lips. "How come you had your hand in his pocket? He somebody you know?"

"He was some asshole," Chevette said.

"Oh. *Him.* Think I *met* him."

"Gave me a hard time. It was sticking out of his pocket."

"You sure it was his *pocket* this hard time sticking out of?"

"Sammy Sal," she said, "this is serious. I'm scared shitless."

He was looking at her, close. "*That* it? You scared? *Stole* some shit, you scared?"

"Bunny says some security guys called up Allied, even called up Wilson and everything. Looking for me."

"Shit," Sammy Sal said, still studying her, "I thought you *high,* on dancer. Thought Bunny found out. Come after you, gonna chew your little bitch ear off. You just *scared*?"

She looked at him. "That's right."

"Well," he said, digging his fingers into the black foam, "what you scared *of*?"

"Scared they'll come up to Skinner's and find 'em."

"Find what?"

"These glasses."

"*Spy*, baby? *Shot? Looking*, like Alice 'n' all?" He drummed his fingers on the black foam.

"These black glasses. Like sunglasses, but you can't see through 'em."

Sammy Sal tilted his beautiful head to one side. "What's that mean?"

"They're just black."

"Sunglasses?"

"Yeah. But just black."

"Huh," he said, "you *had* been fucking the clients, but only just the cute ones, like me, you'd know what those are. Tell you don't have that many upscale boyfriends, pardon me. You date you some architects, some brain-surgeons, you'd know what those are." His hand came up, forefinger flicking the corroded ball-chain that dangled from the zip-tab at the neck of Skinner's jacket. "Those *VL* glasses. Virtual light."

She'd heard of it, but she wasn't sure what it was. "They expensive, Sammy Sal?"

"Shit, yes. 'Bout as much as a Japanese car. Not all that much more, though. Got these little EMP-drivers around the lenses, work your optic nerves direct. Friend of mine, he'd bring a pair home from the office where he worked. Landscape architects. Put 'em on, you go out walking, everything looks normal, but every plant you see, every tree, there's this little label hanging there, what its name is, Latin under that..."

"But they're solid black."

"Not if you turn 'em *on*, they aren't. Turn 'em on, they don't even look like sunglasses. Just make you look, I dunno, serious." He grinned at her. "You look too damn' serious anyway. That your problem."

She shivered. "Come back up to Skinner's with me, Sammy. Okay?"

"Don't like heights, much," he said. "That little box blow right off the top of that bridge, one night."

"Please, Sammy? This thing's got me tweaking. Be okay, riding with you, but I stop and I start thinking about it, I'm scared I'm gonna freeze up. What'll I *do*? Maybe I get there and it's the cops? What'll Skinner say, the cops come up there? Maybe I go in to work tomorrow and Bunny cans me. What'll I *do*?"

Sammy Sal gave her the look he'd given her the night she'd asked him to get her on at Allied. Then he grinned. Mean and funny. All those sharp white teeth. "Keep it between your legs, then. Come on, you *try* to keep up."

He bongoed off the curb, his Fluoro-Rimz flaring neon-white when he came down pumping. He must have thumbed Play then, because she caught the bass throbbing as she came after him through the traffic.

14

loveless

You want another beer, honey?"

The woman behind the bar had an intricate black tracery along either side of her shaven skull, down to what Yamazaki took to be her natural hairline. The tattoo's style combined Celtic knots and cartoon lightning-bolts. Her hair, above it, was like the pelt of some nocturnal animal that had fed on peroxide and Vaseline. Her left ear had been randomly pierced, perhaps a dozen times, by a single length of fine steel wire. Ordinarily Yamazaki found this sort of display quite interesting, but now he was lost in composition, his notebook open before him.

"No," he said, "thank you."

"Don't wanna get fucked up, or what?" Her tone perfectly cheerful. He looked up from the notebook. She was waiting.

"Yes?"

"You wanna sit here, you gotta buy something."

"Beer, please."

"Same?"

"Yes, please."

She opened a bottle of Mexican beer, fragments of ice sliding down the side as she put it down on the bar in front of him, and moved on to the customer to his left. Yamazaki returned to his notebook.

Skinner has tried repeatedly to convey that there is no agenda here whatever, no underlying structure. Only the bones, the bridge, the Thomasson itself. When the Little Grande came, it was not Godzilla. Indeed, there is no precisely equivalent myth in this place and culture (though this is perhaps not equally true of Los Angeles). The Bomb, so long awaited, is gone. In its place came these plagues, the slowest of cataclysms. But when Godzilla came at last to Tokyo, we were foundering in denial and profound despair. In all truth, we welcomed the most appalling destruction. Sensing, even as we mourned our dead, that we were again presented with the most astonishing of opportunities.

"That's real nice," the man to his left said, placing his left hand on Yamazaki's notebook. "That's gotta be Japanese, it's so nice." Yamazaki looked up, smiling uncertainly, into eyes of a most peculiar emptiness. Bright, focused, yet somehow flat.

"From Japan, yes," Yamazaki said. The hand withdrew slowly, caressingly, from his notebook.

"Loveless," the man said.

"I'm sorry?"

"Loveless. My name."

"Yamazaki."

The eyes, very pale and wide-set, were the eyes of something watching from beneath still water. "Yeah. Figured it was something like that." An easy smile, pointed with archaic gold.

"Yes? Like?"

"Something Japanese. Something 'zaki, something 'zuki. Some shit like that." The smile growing somehow sharper. "Drink up your Corona there, Mr. Yamazuki." The stranger's hand, closing hard around his wrist. "Gettin' warm, huh?"

in 1015

There was a product called Kil'Z that Rydell had gotten to know at the Academy. It smelled, but faintly, of some ancient hair-tonic, flowery and cool, and you used it in situations where considerable bodily fluids had been spilled. It was an anti-viral agent, capable of nuking HIV's 1 through 5, Crimean-Congo, Mokola fever, Tarzana Dengue, and the Kansas City flu.

He smelled it now, as the IntenSecure man used a black-anodyzed passkey to open the door into 1015.

"We'll be sure to lock it up when we go," Warbaby said, touching the brim of his hat with his index finger. The IntenSecure man hesitated, then said, "Yessir. Anything else you want?"

"No," Warbaby said, and went into the room, Freddie on his heels. Rydell decided the thing for him to do was follow them in. He did, closing the door in the IntenSecure man's face. Dark. The curtains drawn. Smell of Kil'Z. The lights came on. Freddie's hand on the switch. Warbaby staring at a lighter patch of the brick-colored carpet, the place where the bed must've been.

Rydell glanced around. Old-fashioned, expensive-looking. Clubby, sort of. The walls covered in some kind of shiny, white-and-green striped stuff like silk. Polished wooden furniture. Chairs upholstered mossy green. A big brass lamp with a dark green shade. A faded old picture in a fat gilt frame. Rydell went over for a closer look. A horse pulling a kind of two-wheeled wagon-thing, just a little seat there, with a bearded man in a hat like Abe Lincoln. "Currier & Ives," it said. Rydell wondered which one was the horse. Then he saw a round, brownish-purple splotch of dried blood on the glass. It had crackled up, the way mud does in a summer creek bed, but tiny. Hadn't had any of that Kil'Z on it, either, by the look of it. He stepped back.

Freddie, in his big shorts and the shirt with the pictures of pistols, had settled into one of the green chairs and was opening his laptop. Rydell watched him reel out a little black cable and pop it into the jack beside the telephone. He wondered if Freddie's legs got cold, wearing shorts up here in November. He'd noticed that some black people were so far into fashion, they'd wear clothes like there wasn't any such thing as weather.

Warbaby just stared at the place where the bed had been, looking sad as ever. "Well?" he said.

"I'm *gettin'* it, I'm gettin' it," Freddie said, twiddling a little ball on his laptop.

Warbaby grunted. Watching him, it looked to Rydell as though the lenses of his black-framed glasses winked black for a second. Trick of the light. Then Rydell got this funny feeling, because Warbaby just looked *right through him*, his traveling gaze fixed on some moving something so keenly that Rydell himself was turning to look—at nothing.

He looked back at Warbaby. Warbaby's cane came up, pointing at the space where the bed would have been, then swung back down to the carpet. Warbaby sighed.

"Want the site-data from SFPD now?" Freddie asked.

Warbaby grunted. His eyes were darting from side to side. Rydell thought of tv documentaries about voodoo, the priests' eyes rolling when the gods got into them.

Freddie twirled the trackball under his finger. "Prints, hair, skin-flakes . . . You know what a hotel room is."

Rydell couldn't stand it. He stepped in front of Warbaby and looked him in the eye. "What the hell you doing?"

Warbaby saw him. Gave him a slow sad smile and removed his glasses. Took a big, navy blue silk handkerchief from the side pocket of his long coat and polished the glasses. He handed them to Rydell. "Put them on."

Rydell looked down at the glasses and saw that the lenses were black now.

"Go on," Warbaby said.

Rydell noticed the weight as he slid them on. Pitch black. Then there was a stutter of soft fuzzy ball-lightning, like what you saw when you rubbed your eyes in the dark, and he was looking at Warbaby. Just behind Warbaby, hung on some invisible wall, were words, numbers, bright yellow. They came into focus as he looked at them, somehow losing Warbaby, and he saw that they were forensic stats.

"Or," Freddie said, "you can just be here *now*—"

And the bed was back, sodden with blood, the man's soft, heavy corpse splayed out like a frog. That thing beneath his chin, blue-black, bulbous.

Rydell's stomach heaved, bile rose in his throat, and then a naked woman rolled up from another bed, in a different room, her hair like silver in some impossible moonlight—

Rydell yanked the glasses off. Freddie lay back in the chair, shaking with silent laughter, his laptop across his knees. "Man," he managed, "you oughta *seen* the look you had! Put parta the guy's porno on there from Arkady's evidence report..."

"Freddie," Warbaby said, "are you all that anxious to be looking for work?"

"Nossir, Mr. Warbaby."

"I can be hard, Freddie. You know that."

"Yessir." Freddie sounded worried now.

"A man died in this room. Someone bent over him on this bed," he gestured at the bed that wasn't there, "cut him a new smile, and pulled his tongue out through it. That isn't a casual homicide. You don't learn those kinds of tricks with anatomy from watching television, Freddie." He held out his hand to Rydell. Rydell gave him the glasses. Their lenses were black again.

Freddie swallowed. "*Yes*sir, Mr. Warbaby. Sorry."

"How'd you do that?" Rydell asked.

Warbaby wiped the glasses again and put them back on. They were clear now. "There are drivers in the frames and lenses. They affect the nerves directly."

"It's a virtual light display," Freddie said, eager to change the subject. "Anything can be digitized, you can see it there."

"Telepresence," Rydell said.

"Naw," Freddie said, "that's *light.* That's photons coming out and hitting on your eye. This doesn't work like that. Mr. Warbaby walks around and looks at stuff, he can see the data-feed at the same time. You put those glasses on a man doesn't *have* eyes, optic nerve's okay, he can *see* the input. That's why they built the first ones. For blind people."

Rydell went to the drapes, pulled them apart, looked down into some night street in this other city. People walking there, a few.

"Freddie," Warbaby said, "flip me that Washington girl off the decrypted IntenSecure feed. The one works for Allied Messenger Service."

Freddy nodded, did something with his computer.

"Yes," Warbaby said, gazing at something only he could see, "it's possible. Entirely possible. Rydell," and he removed the glasses, "you have a look." Rydell let the drapes fall back, went to Warbaby, took the glasses, put them on. Somehow he felt it would be a mistake to hesitate, even if it meant having to look at the dead guy again.

Black into color into full face and profile of this girl. Fingerprints. Image of her right retina blown up to the size of her head. Stats. WASHINGTON, CHEVETTE-MARIE. Big gray eyes, long straight nose, a little grin for the camera. Dark hair cut short and spikey, except for this crazy ponytail stuck up from the crown of her head.

"Well," Warbaby asked, "what do you think?"

Rydell couldn't figure what he was being asked. Finally he just said "Cute."

He heard Freddie snort, like that was a dumb thing to say.

But Warbaby said "Good. That way you remember."

16

sunflower

Sammy Sal lost her, where Bryant stuttered out in that jackstraw tumble of concrete tank-traps. Big as he was, he had no equal when it came to riding tight; he could take turns that just weren't possible; he could bongo and pull a three-sixty if he had to, and Chevette had seen him do it on a bet. But she had a good idea where she'd find him.

She looked up, just as she whipped between the first of the slabs, and the bridge seemed to look down at her, its eyes all torches and neon. She'd seen pictures of what it had looked like, before, when they drove cars back and forth on it all day, but she'd never quite believed them. The bridge was what it was, and somehow always had been. Refuge, weirdness, where she slept, home to however many and all their dreams.

She skidded past a fish-wagon, losing traction in shaved ice, in gray guts the gulls would fight over in the morning. The fish man yelled something after her, but she didn't catch it.

She rode on, between stalls and stands and the evening's commerce, looking for Sammy Sal.

Found him where she thought she would, leaning on his bars beside an espresso wagon, not even breathing hard. A Mongolian girl with cheekbones like honey-coated chisels was running him a cup. Chevette bopped the particle-brakes and slid in beside him.

"Thought I'd have time for a short one," he said, reaching for the tiny cup.

Her legs ached with trying to keep up with him. "You better," she said, with a glance toward the bridge, then she gestured to the girl to run her one. She watched the steaming puck of brown grounds thumped out, the fresh scoop, the quick short tamp. The girl swung the handle up and twisted the basket back into the machine.

"You know," Sammy Sal said, pausing before a first shallow sip, "you shouldn't *have* this kind of problem. You don't need to. There's only but two kinds of people. People can afford hotels like that, they're one kind. We're the other. Used to be, like, a middle class, people in between. But not anymore. How you and I relate to those other people, we proj their messages on. We get *paid* for it. We try not to drip rain on the carpet. And we get by, okay? But what happens on the interface? What happens when we touch?"

Chevette burned her mouth on espresso.

"Crime," Sammy Sal said, "sex. Maybe drugs." He put his cup down on the wagon's plywood counter. "About covers it."

"You fuck them," Chevette said. "You said."

Sammy Sal shrugged. "I *like* to. Trouble comes down from that, I'm up for it. But you just went and *did* something, no reason. Reached through the membrane. Let your fingers do the walking. Bad idea."

Chevette blew on her coffee. "I know."

"So how you going to deal with whatever's coming down?"

"I'm going up to Skinner's room, get those glasses, take 'em up on the roof, and throw 'em over."

"Then what?"

"Then I go on the way I do, 'til somebody turns up."

"Then what?"

" 'Didn't do it. Don't know shit. Never happened.' "

He nodded, slow, but he was studying her. "Uh-huh. Maybe. Maybe not. Somebody wants those glasses back, they can lean on you real hard. Another way to go: we get 'em, ride back over to Allied, tell 'em how it happened."

"We?"

"Uh-huh. I'll go with you."

"I'll lose my job."

"You can get you *another* job."

She drank the little cup off in a gulp. Wiped her mouth with the back of her hand. "Job's all I got, Sammy. *You* know that. You got it for me."

"You got a place to sleep, up there. You got that crazy old motherfucker took you in—"

"I *feed* him, Sammy Sal—"

"You got your *ass* intact, honey. Some rich man decide to screw you over, 'cause you took his data-glasses, maybe that ceases to be the case."

Chevette put her empty cup down on the counter, dug in the pockets of her jacket. Gave the girl fifteen for the two coffees and a two-dollar tip. Squared her shoulders under Skinner's jacket, the ball-chains rattling. "No. Once that shit's in the Bay, nobody can prove I did anything."

Sammy Sal sighed. "You're an innocent."

It sounded funny, like she didn't know you could use the word that way. "You coming, Sammy Sal?"

"What for?"

"Talk to Skinner. Get between him and his magazines. That's where I left them. Behind his magazines. Then he won't see me get them out. I'll go up on the roof and off them."

"Okay," he said, "but I say you'll just be fucking up worse."

"I'll take the chance, okay?" She dismounted and started wheeling her bike toward the bridge.

"I guess you will," Sammy Sal said, but then he was off his bike, too, and pushing it, behind her.

———— • • • ————

There'd only ever been three *really* good, that was to say seriously magic, times in Chevette's life. One was the night Sammy Sal had told her he'd try to get her on at Allied, and he had. One was the day she'd paid cash money for her bike at City Wheels, and rode right on out of there. And there'd been the night she first met Lowell at Cognitive Dissidents—if you could count that now as lucky.

Which was not to say that these were the times she'd been luckiest, because *those* were all times that had been uniformly and life-threateningly shitty, except for the part where the luck cut in.

She'd been lucky the night she'd gone over the razor-wire and out of the Juvenile Center outside Beaverton, but that had been one deeply shitty night. She had scars on both palms to prove it.

And she'd been *very* lucky the time she'd first wandered out onto the bridge, the lower deck, her knees wobbling with a fever she'd picked up on her way down the coast. *Everything* hurt her: the lights, every color, every sound, her mind pressing out into the world like a swollen ghost. She remembered the loose, flapping sole of her sneaker dragging over the littered deck, how that hurt her, too, and how she had to sit down, finally, everything up and turning, around her, the Korean man running out of his little store to yell at her, get up, get up, not here, not here. And Not Here had seemed like such a totally good idea, she'd gone straight there, right over backward, and hadn't even felt her skull slam the pavement.

And that was where Skinner had found her, though he didn't remember or maybe want to talk about it; she was never sure. She didn't think he could've gotten her up to his room on his own; he needed help to get back up there himself, with his hip and everything. But there were still days when an energy got into him and you could see how strong he must've been, once, and then he'd do things you didn't think he could do, so she'd never be sure.

The first thing she'd seen, opening her eyes, was the round church-window with the rags stuck into the gaps, and sun coming through it, little dots and blobs of colors she'd never seen before, all swimming in her fevered eye like bugs in water. Then the bone-crack time, the virus wringing her like the old man had wrung the gray towels he wrapped her head in. When the fever broke and rolled away, out a hundred miles it felt like, back out to *there* and over the rim of sickness, her hair fell out in dry clumps, stuck to the damp towels like some kind of dirty stuffing.

When it grew back, it came in darker, nearly black. So after that she felt sort of like a different person. Or anyway her own person, she'd figured.

And she'd stayed with Skinner, doing what he said to get them food and keep things working up in his room. He'd send her down to the lower deck, where the junk-dealers spread their stuff. Send her down with anything: a wrench that said "BMW" on the side, a crumbling cardboard box of those flat black things that had played music once, a bag of plastic dinosaurs. She never figured any of it would be worth anything, but somehow it always was. The wrench bought a week's food, and two of the round things brought even more. Skinner knew where old things came from, what they'd been for, and could guess when somebody'd want them. At first she was worried that she wouldn't get enough for the things she sold, but he didn't seem to care. If something didn't sell, like the plastic dinosaurs, it just went back into stock, what he called the stuff ranged around the bases of the four walls.

As she'd gotten stronger, and her new hair grew in, she'd started ranging farther from the room on top of the tower. Not into either city, at first, though she'd walked over to Oakland a couple of times, over the cantilever, and looked out at it. Things felt different over there, though she was never sure why. But where she felt best was on the suspension bridge, all wrapped in it, all the people hanging and hustling and doing what they did, and the way the whole thing grew a little, changed a little, every day. There wasn't anything like that, not that she knew of, not up in Oregon.

At first she didn't even know that it made her feel good; it was just this weird thing, maybe the fever had left her a little crazy, but one day she'd decided she was just happy, a little happy, and she'd have to get used to it.

But it turned out you could be sort of happy and restless at the same time, so she started keeping back a little of Skinner's junk-money to use to explore the city. And that was plenty to do, for a while. She found Haight Street and walked it all the way to the wall around Skywalker, with the Temple of Doom and everything sticking up in there, but she didn't try to go in. There was this long skinny park that led up to it, called the Panhandle, and that was still public. Way too public, she thought, with people, mostly old or anyway looking that way, stretched out side by side, wrapped in silvery plastic to keep the rays off, this crinkly stuff that glittered like those Elvis suits in a video they'd showed them sometimes, up in Beaverton. It kind of made her think of maggots, like if somebody rolled each one up in its own little piece of foil. They had a way of moving like that, just a little bit, and it creeped her out.

The Haight sort of creeped her out, too, even though there were stretches that felt almost like you were on the bridge, nobody normal in sight and people doing things right out in public, like the cops were never going to come at all. But she wasn't ever scared, on the bridge, maybe because there were always people around she knew, people who lived there and knew Skinner. But she liked looking around the Haight because there were a lot of little shops, a lot of places that sold cheap food. She knew this bagel place where you could buy them a day old, and Skinner said they were better that way anyway. He said fresh bagels were the next thing to poison, like they'd plug you up or something. He had a lot of ideas like that. Most of the shops, she could actually go into, if she was quiet and smiled a little and kept her hands in her pockets.

One day on Haight she saw this shop called Colored People and she couldn't figure out what it sold. There was a curtain behind the window and a few things set out in front of that: cactus in pots, big rusty hunks of metal, and a bunch of these little steel things, polished and bright. Rings and things. Little rods with round balls on the ends. They were hung on the needles of the cactus and spread out on the rusted metal. She decided she'd open the door and just look in, because she'd seen a couple of people going in and out and knew it wasn't locked. A big fat guy in white coveralls, with his head all shaved, coming out, whistling, and these two tall women, black-haired, like handsome crows, all dressed in black, going in. She just wondered what it was.

She stuck her head in there. There was a woman with short red hair behind a counter, and every wall covered with these bright cartoony pictures, colors that made your eyes jump, all snakes and dragons and everything. So many pictures it was hard to take it in, so it wasn't until the woman said come on, don't just block the door, and Chevette had come in, that she saw this woman wore a sleeveless flannel shirt, open all the way down, and her front and arms all covered, solid, with those same pictures.

Now Chevette had seen tattoos in the Juvenile Center, and on the street before that, but those were the kind you did yourself, with ink and needles, thread and an old ballpoint. She walked over and took a good long look at the colors exploding between the woman's breasts—which, though she was maybe thirty, weren't as big as Chevette's—and there was an octopus there, a rose, bolts of blue lightning, all of it tangling together, no untouched skin at all.

"You want something," the woman said, "or you just looking?"

Chevette blinked. "No," she heard herself say, "but I was sort of wondering what those little metal things are, in the window."

The woman swung a big black book around on the counter, like a school binder except its covers were chrome-studded black leather. Flipped it open and Chevette was looking at this guy's thing, a big one, just hanging there. There were two little steel balls on either side of its wedge-shaped head.

Chevette just sort of grunted.

"Call that an amphalang," the woman said. She started flipping through the album. "Barbells," she said. "Septum spike. Labret stud. That's a chunk ring. This one's called a milkchurn. These are bomb weights. Surgical steel, niobium, white gold, fourteen-carat." She flipped it back to the jim with the bolt, sideways through the end of it. Maybe it was a trick, Chevette thought, a trick picture.

"That's gotta hurt," Chevette said.

"Not as much as you'd think," this big deep voice, "and then it starts to feel jus' *good*..."

Chevette looked up at this black guy, his big white grin, all those teeth, a micropore filtration-mask pulled down under his chin, and that was how she'd met Samuel Saladin DuPree.

Two days later she saw him again in Union Square, hanging with a bunch of bike messengers. She'd already put messengers down as something to watch for in the city. They had clothes and hair like nobody else, and bikes with neon and light-up wheels, handlebars curved up and over like scorpion-tails. Helmets with little radios built in. Either they were going somewhere fast or they were just goofing, hanging, drinking coffee.

He was standing there with his legs over either side of the cross-tube of his bike, eating half a sandwich. Music was coming out of the black-flecked pink frame, mostly bass, and he was sort of bopping to it. She edged up to get a better look at the bike, how it was made, the intricacy of its brakes and shifters pulling her straight in. Beauty.

"Dang," he said, around a mouthful of sandwich, "dang, my *am*-phalang. Where *did* you get those shoes?"

They were Skinner's, old canvas sneakers, too long for her so she'd stuck some paper in the toes.

"Here." He handed her the other half of his sandwich. "I'm full already."

"Your bike," she said, taking the sandwich.

"What about it?"

"It's ... it's ..."

"Like it?"

"Uh-huh!"

He grinned. "Sugawara frame, Sugawara rings 'n' 'railers, Zuni hydraulics. *Clean.*"

"I like the *wheels*," Chevette said.

"Well," he said, "that's just flash. Lets some motherfucker see you 'fore he runs you over, y'know?"

Chevette touched the handlebars. Felt that music.

"Eat that sandwich," he said. "Look like you need it."

She did, and she did, and that was how they got to talking.

Shouldering their bikes up the plywood stairs, Chevette telling him about the Japanese girl, how she fell out of that elevator. How she, Chevette, wouldn't even have been at that party if she hadn't been standing right there, right then. Sammy grunting, his Fluoro-Rimz gone dead opal now they weren't turning.

"Who was it *throwing* this do, Chev? You think to ask anybody that?"

Remembering that Maria. "Cody. Said it was Cody's party..."

Sammy Sal stopped, his brows lifting. "Huh. Cody *Har*wood?"

She shrugged, the paper bike next to weightless on her shoulder. "Dunno."

"You know who that is?"

"No." Reaching the platform, putting the bike down to wheel it.

"That's some serious money. Advertising. Harwood Levine, but that was his father."

"Well, I said it was rich." Not paying him much attention.

"His father's company did Millbank's PR, both elections."

But she was activating the recognition-loop now, not bothering with the screamers from Radio Shack. Sammy's Fluoro-Rimz pulsed as he set his bike down beside hers. "I'll loop it to mine. Be okay here anyway."

"That's what *I* said," Sammy said, "last two I lost." He watched her pull the loop out, twist it around his bike's frame, careful of the pink-and-black enamel, and seal it with her thumbprint.

She headed for the yellow lift, glad to see it there, where she'd left it, and not at the top of the track. "Let's *do* this thing, okay?" Remembering she'd meant to buy Skinner some soup from Thai Johnny's wagon, that sweet-sour lemon one he liked.

———————— ● ● ● ————————

When she'd told Sammy she wanted to mess, wanted her own bike, he'd gotten her this little Mexican headset taught you every street in San Francisco. Three days and she had it down, pretty much, even though he said that wasn't like the map in a messenger's head. You needed to know buildings, how to get into them, how to act, how to keep your wheels from getting stolen. But when he'd taken her in to meet Bunny, that was magic.

Three weeks and she'd earned enough to buy her first serious bike. That was magic, too.

Somewhere around then she started hanging out after work with a couple of the other Allied girls, Tami Two and Alice Maybe, and that was how she'd wound up at Cognitive Dissidents, that night she'd met Lowell.

———————— ● ● ● ————————

"Nobody locks their door here," Sammy said, on the ladder below her, as she lifted the hatch.

Chevette closed her eyes, saw a bunch of cops (whatever that would look like) standing around Skinner's room. Opened her eyes and stuck her head up, eyes level with the floor.

Skinner was on his bed, his little television propped on his chest, big old yellow toenails sticking out of holes in his lumpy gray socks. He looked at her over the television.

"Hey," she said, "I brought Sammy. From work." She climbed up, making room for Sammy Sal's head and shoulders.

"Howdy," Sammy Sal said.

Skinner just stared at him, colors from the little screen flicking across his face.

"How you doin'?" Sammy Sal asked, climbing up.

"Bring anything to eat?" Skinner asked her.

"Thai Johnny'll have soup ready in a while," she said, moving toward the shelves, the magazines. Dumb-ass thing to say and she knew it, because Johnny's soup was always ready; he'd started it years ago and just kept adding to the pot.

"How you doin', Mr. Skinner?" Sammy Sal stood slightly hunched, feet apart, holding his helmet with both hands, like a boy saying hello to his girlfriend's father. He winked at Chevette.

"What you winkin' at, boy?" Skinner shut the set off and snapped its screen shut. Chevette had bought it for him off a container-ship in the Trap. He said he couldn't tell the difference anymore between the "programs" and the "commercials," whatever that meant.

"Somethin' in my eye, Mr. Skinner," Sammy Sal said, his big feet shifting, even more like a nervous boyfriend. Made Chevette want to laugh. She got behind Sammy's back and reached in behind the magazines. It was there. Into her pocket.

"You ever seen the view from up top here, Sammy?" She knew she had this big crazy grin on, and Skinner was staring at it, trying to figure what was happening, but she didn't care. She swung up the ladder to the roof-hatch.

"Gosh, no, Chevette, honey. Must be just breathtaking."

"Hey," Skinner said, as she opened the hatch, "what's got into you?"

Then she was up and out and into one of the weird pockets of stillness you got up there sometimes. Usually the wind made you want to lie down and hang on, but then there were these patches when nothing moved, dead calm. She heard Sammy Sal coming up the ladder behind her. She had the case out, was moving toward the edge.

"Hey," he said, "lemme see."

She raised the thing, winding up to throw.

He plucked it from her fingers.

"Hey!"

"Shush." Opening it, pulling them out. "Huh. Nice ones..."

"Sammy!" Reaching for them. He gave her the case instead.

"See how you do this now?" Opening them, one side-piece in either hand. "Left is *aus*, right's *ein*. Just move 'em a little." She saw how he was doing it, in the light that spilled up through the hatch from Skinner's room. "Here. Check it out." He put them on her.

She was facing the city when he did it. Financial district, the Pyramid with its brace on from the Little Grande, the hills behind that. "Fuck a *duck,*" she said, these towers blooming there, buildings bigger than anything, a stone regular grid of them, marching in from the hills. Each one maybe four blocks at the base, rising straight and featureless to spreading screens like the colander she used to steam vegetables. Then Chinese writing filled the sky. "Sammy..."

She felt him grab her as she lost her balance.

The Chinese writing twisted into English.

SUNFLOWER CORPORATION

"Sammy..."

"Huh?"

"What the fuck *is* this?" Anything she focused on, another label lit the sky, dense patches of technical words she didn't understand.

"How should I know," he said. "Let me see." Reaching for the glasses.

"Hey," she heard Skinner say, his voice carrying up through the hatch, "it's Scooter. What you doin' back here?"

Sammy Sal pulled the glasses off and she was kneeling, looking down through the hatch at that Japanese nerd who came around to see Skinner, the college boy or social worker or whatever he was. But he looked even more lost than usual. He looked scared. And there was somebody with him.

"Hey, Scooter," Skinner said, "how you doing?"

"This Mr. Loveless," Yamazaki said. "He ask to meet you."

Gold flashed up at Chevette from the stranger's grin. "Hi there," he said, taking his hand out of the side pocket of his long black raincoat. The gun wasn't very big, but there was something too easy in the way he held it, like a carpenter with a hammer. He was wearing surgical gloves. "Why don't you come on down here?"

the

trap

17

How this works," Freddie said, handing Rydell a debit-card, "you pay five hundred to get in, then you're credited for five hundred dollars' worth of merchandise."

Rydell looked at the card. Some Dutch bank. If this was how they were going to pay him, up here, maybe it was time he asked them what he'd actually be getting. But maybe he should wait until Freddie was in a better mood.

Freddie said this Container City place was a good quick bet for clothes. Regular clothes, Rydell hoped. They'd left Warbaby drinking herbal tea in some kind of weird coffee joint because he said he needed to think. Rydell had gone out to the Patriot while Warbaby and Freddie held a quick huddle, there.

"What if he wants us, wants the car?"

"He'll beep us," Freddie said. He showed Rydell how to put the debit-card into a machine that gave him a five-hundred-dollar Container City magstrip and validated the parking on the Patriot. "This way." Freddie pointed at a row of turnstiles.

"Aren't you gonna buy one?" Rydell asked.

"Shit, no," Freddie said. "I don't get *my* clothes off boats." He took a card out of his wallet and showed Rydell the IntenSecure logo.

"I thought you guys were strictly freelance."

"Strictly but frequently," Freddie said, feeding the card to a

turnstile. It clicked him through. Rydell fed it the magstrip and followed him.

"Costs people five hundred bucks just to get in here?"

"Why people call it the Trap. But that's just how they make
sure the overhead's covered. You don't come in here unless you know
you're gonna drop that much. Gives 'em a guaranteed per-cap."

Container City turned out to be the biggest semi-roofed mall
Rydell had ever seen, if you could call something a mall that had
ships parked in it, big ones. And the five-hundred-dollar guaranteed
purchase didn't seem to have put anybody off; there were more people in here than out on the street, it looked like. "Hong Kong money,"
Freddie said. "Bought 'em a hunk of the Embarcadero."

"Hey," Rydell said, pointing at a dim, irregular outline that
rose beyond gantries and towers of floodlights, "that's that bridge,
the one people live on."

"Yeah," Freddie said, giving him a funny look, "crazy-ass
people." Steering Rydell onto an escalator that ran up the white-
painted flank of a container ship.

Rydell looked around at Container City as they rose. "Crazier
than anything in L.A.," he said, admiringly.

"No way," Freddie said, "I'm *from* L.A. This just a *mall*, man."

Rydell bought a burgundy nylon bomber, two pairs of black
jeans, socks, underwear, and three black t-shirts. That came out to just
over five hundred. He used the debit-card to make up the difference.

"Hey," he told Freddie, his purchases in a big yellow Container City bag, "that's a pretty good deal. Thanks."

Freddie shrugged. "Where they say those jeans made?"

Rydell checked the tag. "African Union."

"Slave labor," Freddie said, "you shouldn't buy that shit."

"I didn't think about it. They got any food in here?"

"Food Fair, yeah..."

"You ever try this Korean pickled shit? It's hot, man..."

"I got an ulcer." Freddie was methodically spooning plain

white frozen yogurt into his mouth with a marked lack of enthusiasm.

"Stress. That's stress-related, Freddie."

Freddie looked at Rydell over the rim of the pink plastic yogurt cup. "You trying to be funny?"

"No," Rydell said. "I just know about ulcers because they thought my daddy had them."

"Well, didn't he? Your 'daddy'? Did he have 'em or not?"

"No," Rydell said. "He had stomach cancer."

Freddie winced, put his yogurt down, rattled the ice in his paper cup of Evian and drank some. "Hernandez," he said, "he told us you were trainin' to be a cop, some redneck place..."

"Knoxville," Rydell said. "I *was* a cop. Just not for very long."

"I hear you, I hear you," Freddie said, like he wanted Rydell to relax, maybe even to like him. "You got trained and all? Cop stuff?"

"Well, they try to give you a little bit of everything," Rydell said. "Crime scene investigation... Like up in that room today. I could tell they hadn't done the Super Glue thing."

"No?"

"No. There's this chemical in Super Glue sticks to the water in a print, see, and about ninety-eight percent of a print *is* water. So you've got this little heater, for the glue? Screws into a regular light socket? So you tape up the doors and windows with garbage bags and stuff and you leave that little heater turned on. Leave it twenty-four hours, then you come back and purge the room."

"How you do that?"

"Open up the doors, windows. Then you dust. But they hadn't done that, over at the hotel. It leaves this film all over. And a smell..."

Freddie raised his eyebrows. "Shit. You almost kinda *technical*, aren't you, Rydell?"

"Mostly it's just common sense," he said. "Like not going to the bathroom."

"Not going?"

"At a crime scene. Don't ever use the toilet. Don't flush it.

You drop something in a toilet, the way the water goes . . . You ever notice how it goes up, underneath there?"

Freddie nodded.

"Well, maybe your perp flushed it after he dropped something in there. But it doesn't always work like it's meant to, and it might be just floating back there . . . You come in and flush it *again*, then it's gone for sure."

"Damn," Freddie said, "I never knew that."

"Common sense," Rydell said, wiping his lips with a paper napkin.

"I think Mr. Warbaby's right about you, Rydell."

"How's that?"

"He says we're wasting you, just letting you drive that four-by-four. Bein' straight with you, man, I wasn't sure, myself." Freddie waited, like he figured Rydell might take offense.

"Well?"

"You know that brace on Mr. Warbaby's leg?"

"Yeah."

"You know that bridge, the one you noticed when we were coming up here?"

"Yeah."

"And Warbaby, he showed you that picture of that tough-ass messenger kid?"

"Yeah."

"Well," Freddy said, "She's the one Mr. Warbaby figures took that man's property. And she lives out on that bridge, Rydell. And that bridge, man, that's one *evil* motherfucking place. Those people anarchists, antichrists, *cannibal* motherfuckers out there, man . . ."

"I heard it was just a bunch of homeless people," Rydell said, vaguely recollecting some documentary he'd seen in Knoxville, "just sort of making do."

"No, man," Freddie said, "*homeless* fuckers, they're on the *street*. Those *bridge* motherfuckers, they're like king-hell satanists and shit. You think you can just move on out there yourself? No fucking way. They'll just let their *own kind*, see? Like a cult. With 'nitiations and shit."

" 'Nitiations?"

"*Black* 'nitiates," Freddie said, leaving Rydell to decide that he probably didn't mean it racially.

"Okay," Rydell said, "but what's it got to do with that brace on Warbaby's knee?"

"That's where he *got* that knee *hassled*," Freddie said. "He went *out* there, knowing he was takin' his life in his *hands*, to try and recover this little baby. Baby *girl*," Freddie added, like he liked the ring of that. " 'Cause these bridge motherfuckers, they'll *do* that."

"Do what?" Rydell asked, flashing back to the Pooky Bear killings.

"They steal children," Freddie said. "And Mr. Warbaby and me, we can't *either* of us go out there anymore, Rydell, because those motherfuckers are *on* to us, you followin' me?"

"So you want *me* to?" Rydell asked, stuffing his folded napkin into the oily white paper box that had held his two Kim Chee WaWa's.

"I'll let Mr. Warbaby explain it to you," Freddie said.

They found Warbaby where they'd left him, in this dark, high-ceilinged coffee place in what Freddie said was North Beach. He was wearing those glasses again and Rydell wondered what he might be seeing.

Rydell had brought his blue Samsonite in from the Patriot, his bag from Container City. He went into the bathroom to change his clothes. There was just the one, unisex, and it really was a bathroom because it had a bathtub in it. Not like anybody used it, because there was this mermaid painted full-size on the inside, with a brown cigarette butted out on her stomach, just above where the scales started.

Rydell discovered that Kevin's khakis were split up the ass. He wondered how long he'd been walking around like that. But he hadn't noticed it back at Container City, so he hoped it had happened in the car. He took the IntenSecure shirt off, stuffed it into the wastebasket, put on one of the black t-shirts. Then he unlaced his trainers and tried to figure out a way to change pants, socks, and underwear without having to put his feet on the floor, which was wet. He thought about doing it in the tub, but that looked sort of scummy, too. Decided you could manage it, sort of, by standing with your feet on the top of your sneakers, and then sort of half-sitting on the toilet. He put everything he took off into the basket. Wondering how much the debit-card Freddie had given him was still good for, he transferred his wallet to the right back pocket of his new jeans. Put on his new jacket. Washed his hands and face in a gritty trickle of water. Combed his hair. Packed the rest of his new clothes into the Samsonite, saving the Container City bag to keep dirty laundry in.

He wanted a shower, but he didn't know when he'd get one. Clean clothes were the next best thing.

Warbaby looked up when Rydell got back to his table. "Freddie's told you a little about the bridge, has he, Rydell?"

"Says it's all baby-eatin' satanists."

Warbaby glowered at Freddie. "Too colorfully put, perhaps, but all too painfully close to the truth, Mr. Rydell. Not at all a wholesome place. And effectively outside the reach of the law. You won't find our friends Svobodov or Orlovsky out there, for instance. Not in any official capacity."

Rydell caught Freddie start to grin at that, but saw how it was pinched off by Warbaby's glare.

"Freddie gave me the idea you want me to go out there, Mr. Warbaby. Go out there and find that girl."

"Yes," Warbaby said, gravely, "we do. I wish that I could tell you it won't be dangerous, but that is not the case."

"Well . . . How dangerous *is* it, Mr. Warbaby?"

"Very," Warbaby said.

"And that girl, she's dangerous, too?"

"Extremely," Warbaby said, "and all the more because she

doesn't always look it. You *saw* what was done to that man's throat, after all..."

"Jesus," Rydell said, "you think that little girl did *that*?"

Warbaby nodded, sadly. "Terrible," he said, "these people will do terrible things..."

When they got out to the car, he saw that he'd parked it right in front of this mural of J. D. Shapely wearing a black leather biker jacket and no shirt, being carried up to heaven by half a dozen extremely fruity-looking angels with long blond rocker hair. There were these blue, glowing coils of DNA or something spiraling out of Shapely's stomach and attacking what Rydell assumed was supposed to be an AIDS virus, except it looked more like some kind of rusty armored space station with mean robot arms.

It made him think what a weird-ass thing it must've been to be that guy. About as weird as it had ever been to be anybody, ever, he figured. But it would be even weirder to be Shapely, and dead like that, and *then* have to look at that mural.

YET HE *LIVES* IN US NOW, it said under the painting, in foot-high white letters, AND THROUGH HIM DO *WE* LIVE.

Which was, strictly speaking, true, and Rydell had had a vaccination to prove it.

18

capacitor

Chevette's mother had had this boyfriend once named Oakley, who drank part-time and drove logging trucks the rest, or anyway he said he did. He was a long-legged man with his blue eyes set a little too far apart, in a face with those deep seams down each cheek. Which made him look, Chevette's mother said, like a real cowboy. Chevette just thought it made him look kind of dangerous. Which he wasn't, usually, unless he got himself around a bottle or two of whiskey and forgot where he was or who he was with; like particularly if he mistook Chevette for her mother, which he'd done a couple of times, but she'd always gotten away from him and he'd always been sorry about it afterward, bought her Ring-Dings and stuff from the Seven-Eleven. But what Oakley did that she remembered now, looking down through the hatch at this guy with his gun, was take her out in the woods one time and let her shoot a pistol.

And this one had a face kind of like Oakley's, too, those eyes and those grooves in his cheeks. Like you got from smiling a lot, the way he was now. But it sure wasn't a smile that would ever make anybody feel good. Gold at the corners of it.

"Now come on down here," he said, stressing each word just the same.

"Who the fuck are you?" Skinner, sounding more interested than pissed-off.

The gun went off. Not very loud, but sharp, with this blue

flash. She saw the Japanese guy sit down on the floor, like his legs had gone out from under him, and she thought the guy had shot him.

"Shut up." Then up at Chevette, "I *told* you to get down here."

Then Sammy Sal touched her on the back of her neck, his fingertips urging her toward the hatch before they withdrew.

The guy might not even know Sammy Sal was up here at all. Sammy Sal had the glasses. And one thing Chevette was sure of now, this guy was no cop.

"Sorry," the Japanese guy said, "sorry I..."

"I'm going to shoot you in the right eye with a subsonic titanium bullet." Still smiling, the way he might say *I'm going to buy you a sandwich.*

"I'm coming," Chevette said. And he didn't shoot, not her, not the Japanese guy.

She thought she heard Sammy Sal step back across the roof, away from her, but she didn't look back. She wasn't sure whether she should try to close the hatch behind her or not. She decided not to because the guy had only told her to come down. She'd have to reach past the edge of the hole to get hold of the hatch and it might look to him like she was going for a gun or something. Like in a show.

She dropped down from the bottom rung, trying to keep her hands where he could see them.

"What were you doing up there?" Still smiling. His gun wasn't anything like Oakley's big old Brazilian revolver; it was a little stubby square thing made out of dull metal, the color of Skinner's old tools. A thin ring of brighter metal around the narrow hole in the end. Like the pupil of an eye.

"Looking at the city," she said, not feeling scared, particularly. Not really feeling anything, except her legs were trembling.

He glanced up, the gun staying right where it was. She didn't want him to ask her if was she alone up there, because the answer might hang in the air and tell him it was a lie. "You know what I'm here for."

Skinner was sitting up on his bed, back against the wall,

looking as wide awake as she'd ever seen him. The Japanese guy, who didn't look like he'd been shot after all, was sitting on the floor, his skinny legs spread out in front of him in a V.

"Well," Skinner said, "I'd guess money or drugs, but it happens you're shit out of luck. Give you fifty-six dollars and a stale joint of Humbolt, you want it."

"Shut up." When the automatic smile went away, it was like he didn't have any lips. "I'm talking to her."

Skinner looked like he was about to say something, or maybe laugh, but he didn't.

"The glasses." Now the smile was back. He raised the gun, so that she was looking right into the little hole. *If he shoots me,* she thought, *he'll still have to hunt for them.*

"Hepburn," Skinner said, with a crazy little grin, and just then Chevette noticed that the poster of Roy Orbison had a hole in the middle of its gray forehead. "Down there," she said, pointing to the hatch in the floor.

"Where?"

"My bike," hoping Sammy Sal didn't bump into that old rusty wagon in the dark up there, make a noise.

He looked up at the roof-hatch, like he could hear what she was thinking.

"Lean up against the wall there, palms flat." He moved in closer. "Get your feet apart..." The gun touched her neck. His other hand slid under Skinner's jacket, feeling for a weapon. "Stay that way." He'd missed Skinner's knife, the one with the fractal blade. She turned her head a little and saw him wrapping something red and rubbery around one of the Japanese guy's wrists, doing it one-handed. She thought of those gummy-worm candies you bought out of a big plastic jar. He yanked the Japanese guy by the red thing, dragging him across the floor to the shelf-table where she'd eaten breakfast. He stuck one end of the red thing behind the angle-brace that held the table up, then twisted it around the guy's other wrist. He took another one out of his pocket and shook it out, like a toy snake. Reached behind Skinner with it and did something with his hand. "You stay on that bed, old man," touching the gun to Skinner's temple. Skinner just looking at him.

He came back to Chevette. "You're climbing down a ladder. Need yours in front."

The thing was cool and slick and fused into itself as soon as he had it around her wrists. Flowed together. Moved by itself. Plastic ruby bracelets, like a kid's toy. One of those tricks with molecules.

"I'm going to watch you," he said, with another glance up at the open roof-hatch, "so you just go down nice and slow. And if you jump, or run when you get to the bottom, I'll kill you."

And she didn't doubt he would, if he could, but she was remembering something Oakley had told her that day in the woods, how it was hard to hit something if you had to shoot almost straight down at it, even harder straight up. So maybe the thing to do was just proj when she hit the bottom. she'd only have to clear about six feet from the ladder to be where he couldn't see her. But she looked at the gun's black and silver eye and it just didn't seem like a good idea.

So she went to the hole in the floor and got down on her knees. It wasn't easy, with her hands tied that way. He had to steady her, grabbing a handful of Skinner's jacket, but she got her feet down on the third rung and her fingers around the top one, and worked her way down that way. She had to get her feet on a rung, let go of the one she was holding, snatch the next one down before she lost her balance, do it again.

But she got to think while she was doing it, and that helped her decide to go ahead and try to do what she had in mind. It was weird to be thinking that way, how quiet she felt, but it wasn't the first time. She'd felt that way in Beaverton, the night she'd gone over the wire, and that without any more planning. And one time these truckers had tried to drag her into the sleeper in the back; she'd made like she didn't mind, then threw a thermos of hot coffee in one's face, kicked the other in the head, and gotten out of there. They'd looked for her for an hour, with flashlights, while she squatted down in river-mud and let mosquitos eat her alive. Lights searching for her through that brush.

She got to the bottom and backed off a step, holding her bound wrists out where he could see them if he wanted to. He came down fast, no wasted movement, not a sound. His long coat was made of something black, some cloth that didn't throw back the light, and she saw he was wearing black cowboy boots. She knew he could run just fine in those, if he had to; people didn't always think so, but you could.

"Where is it?" Gold flashing at the corners of his smile. His hair, brushed straight back, was somewhere between brown and blond. He moved his hand, keeping her aware of the gun. She saw his hand was starting to sweat, spots of wetness darkening there, inside the white rubber glove.

"We gotta take the—" She stopped. The yellow lift was where she and Sammy Sal had left it, so how had he gotten up?

Extra bits of gold. "We took the stairs."

They'd come up the painter's ladder, bare steel rungs, some of them rusted through. So she wouldn't hear the lift. No wonder the Japanese guy had looked scared. "Well," she said, "you coming?"

He followed her over to the lift. She kept her eyes on the deck, so she wouldn't forget and look up to try and find Sammy, who had to be there, somewhere. He wouldn't have had time to get down, or else they would have heard him.

He held her shoulder again while she swung her leg over and climbed in, then got in after her, watching her the whole time.

"This one's down," she said, pointing at one of the levers.

"Do it."

She moved it a notch, another, and the engine whined beneath their feet, gearing them down the incline. There was a patch of light at the bottom, under a bulb caged in corroded aluminum, and she wondered what he'd do if somebody happened to step into it just then, say Fontaine or one of the other people who came to check the electrical stuff. Anybody. He'd shoot them, she decided. Just pop them and roll them over into the dark. You could see it in his face. It was right there.

He got out first, helped her over. A wind was rising and you could feel the harmonics coming up through your soles, the bridge starting to hum like a muffled harp. She could hear people laughing, somewhere.

"Where?" he said.

She pointed to where her bike stood, cabled to Sammy Sal's. "The pink and black one."

He gestured with the gun.

"Back *off*," her bike said when she was five feet from it.

"What's that?" The gun in her back.

"This other bike. Clunker with a voice-alarm. Keeps people off mine." She bent to thumb the tab that released Sammy Sal's bike, but she didn't touch the recognition-loop behind the seat of her own.

"I fucking *mean* it, shithead," her bike said.

"Shut it off," he said.

"Okay."

She knew she had to do it in one go, flip it sideways and over, just her thumb and forefinger on the nonconductive rubber of the tire.

But it was really just an accident that the frame hit his gun. She saw an inch of lightning arc between her bike and the pistol, hot purple and thick as your finger, the particle-brake capacitors in the up-tube emptying their stored charge into the anti-theft system worked into the fake rust and the carefully frayed silver duct-tape. He went down on his knees, eyes unfocused, a single silver bubble of spit forming and bursting between his half-open lips. She thought she saw steam curl from the gun in his hand.

Proj, she thought, crouching to run, but then the black thing hit him and knocked him flat, flapping down out of the dark above them with a sound like broken wings. A roll of tarpaper. She made out Sammy Sal then, standing up there on a dark carbon cross-brace, his arm around an upright. She thought she saw his white smile.

"Forgot this," he said, and tossed something down. The glasses in their case. Hands tied, she caught them anyway, like they knew where they wanted to go. She'd never know why he did that.

Because the little pistol made a chewing sound then, blue pops like a dozen backfires run together, and Sammy Sal went over backward off the brace, just gone.

And then she was running.

superball

Yamazaki heard gunfire, where he knelt on the floor, his wrists joined by glistening plastic behind the rough metal brace that supported Skinner's wall-table. Or was it only the sound of some hydraulic tool?

There was a smell in the room, high and acrid. He thought it must be the smell of his own fear.

His eyes were level with a chipped white plate, a smear of pulped avocado blackening on its edge.

"Told him what I had," Skinner said, struggling to his feet, his arms fastened behind him. "Didn't want it. Want what they want, don't they?" The little television slid off the edge of the bed and hit the floor, its screen popping out on a rainbow ribbon of flat cable. "Shit." He swayed, wincing as his bad hip took his weight, and Yamazaki thought he would fall. Skinner took one step, another, leaning forward to maintain his balance.

Yamazaki strained at the plastic bonds. Yelped as he felt them tighten. Like something alive.

"You tug, twist 'em," Skinner said, behind him, "bastards'll clinch up on you. Cops used to carry those. Got made unconstitutional." There was a crash that shook the room and made the light flicker. Yamazaki looked over his shoulder and saw Skinner sitting on the floor, his knees drawn half up, leaning forward. "There's a pair of twenty-inch bolt-cutters in here," the old man said, indicating a dented, rust-scarred green toolkit with his left foot. "That'll do it, if I can get 'em out." Yamazaki watched as he began to work his toes through the holes in his ragged gray socks. "Not sure I can do shit with 'em, once I do..." He stopped. Looked at Yamazaki. "Better idea, but you won't like it."

"Skinner-san?"

"Look at that brace there."

Discolored blobs of puddled welding-rod held the thing together, but it looked sturdy enough. He counted the mismatched heads of nine screws. The diagonal brace itself seemed to be made up of thin metal shims, lashed together top and bottom with rusting twists of wire.

"I made that," Skinner said. "Those're three sections of blade off a factory saw. Never did grind the teeth off. On top there."

Yamazaki's fingertips moved over hidden roughness.

"Shot, Scooter. Wouldn't cut for shit. Why I used 'em."

"I saw plastic?" Poising his wrists.

"Wait *up*. You start sawing on that crazy-goo, it isn't gonna like it. Have to get through it quick or it's gonna close up right down to the bone. I said *wait...*"

Yamazaki froze. He looked back.

"You're too close to the center. You cut through there, you'll have a ring around each wrist and the suckers'll *still* close up. You want to go through as close to one side as possible, get over here and get the cutter on the other one before it does you. I'll try to get this open..." He bumped the case with his toes. It rattled.

Yamazaki brought his face close to the red restraint. It had a faint, medicinal smell. He took a breath, set his teeth, and sawed furiously with his wrists. The thing began to shrink. Bands of iron, the pain hot and impossible. He remembered Loveless's hand around his wrist.

"*Do* it," Skinner said.

The plastic parted with an absurdly loud pop, like some sound-effect in a child's cartoon. He was free and, for an instant, the red band around his left wrist loosened, absorbing the rest of the mass.

"Scooter!"

It tightened. He scrambled for the toolkit, amazed to see it open, as Skinner kicked it over with his heel, spilling a hundred pieces of tooled metal.

"Blue handles!"

The bolt-cutter was long, clumsy, its handles wrapped in greasy blue tape. He saw the red band narrowing, starting to sink below the level of his flesh. Fumbled the cutter one-handed from the tangle, sank its jaws blindly into his wrist and brought all his weight down on the uppermost handle. A stab of pain. The detonation.

Skinner blew air out between his lips, a long low sound of relief. "You okay?"

Yamazaki looked at his wrists. There was a deep, bluish gouge in the left one. It was starting to bleed, but no more than he would have expected. The other had been scratched by the saw. He glanced around the floor, looking for the remains of the restraint.

"*Do* me," Skinner said. "But hook it under the plastic, okay? Try not to take a hunk out. And do the second one *fast.*"

Yamazaki tested the action of the cutter, knelt behind Skinner, slid one of the blades beneath the plastic around the old man's right wrist. The skin translucent there, blotched and discolored, the veins swollen and twisted. The plastic parted easily, with that same ridiculous noise, instantly whipping itself around Skinner's other wrist, writhing like a live thing. He severed it before it could tighten, but this time, with the cartoon pop, it simply vanished.

Yamazaki stared at the space where the restraint had been.

"Katey bar the door!" Skinner roared.

"What?"

"Lock the fucking hatch!"

Yamazaki scrambled across the floor on hands and knees, dropped the hatch into place, and bolted it with a flat device of dull bronze, something that might once have been part of a ship. "The girl," he said, looking back at Skinner.

"She can *knock*," Skinner said. "You want that dickhead with the gun back in here?"

Yamazaki didn't. He looked up at the ceiling-hatch, the one that opened onto the roof. Open now.

"Go up there and look for the 'mo."

"Skinner-san? Pardon?"

"Big fag buddy. The black one, right?"

Not knowing what or whom Skinner was talking about, Yamazaki climbed the ladder. A gust of wind threw rain into his face as he thrust his head up through the opening. He had the sudden intense conviction that he was high atop some ancient ship, some black iron schooner drifting derelict on darkened seas, its plastic sails shredded and its crew mad or dead, with Skinner its demented captain, shouting orders from his cell below.

"There is nobody here, Skinner-san!"

The rain came down in an explosive sheet, hiding the lights of the city.

Yamazaki withdrew his head, feeling for the hatch, and closed it above him. He fastened the catch, wishing it were made of stronger stuff.

He descended the ladder.

Skinner was on his feet now, swaying toward his bed. "Shit," he said, "somebody's broken my tv." He toppled forward onto the mattress.

"Skinner?"

Yamazaki knelt beside the bed. Skinner's eyes were closed, his breath shallow and rapid. His left hand came up, fingers spread, and scratched fitfully at the tangled thatch of white hair at the open collar of his threadbare flannel shirt. Yamazaki smelled the sour tang of urine above the acrid edge of whatever explosive had propelled Loveless's bullet. He looked at Skinner's jeans, blue gone gray with wear, wrinkles sculpted permanently, shining faintly with grease, and saw that Skinner had wet himself.

He stood there for several minutes, uncertain of what he should do. Finally he took a seat on the paint-splattered stool beside the little table where he had so recently been a prisoner. He ran his fingertips over the teeth of the saw blades. Looking down, he noticed a neat red sphere. It lay on the floor beside his left foot.

He picked it up. A glossy marble of scarlet plastic, cool and slightly yielding. One of the restraints, either his or Skinner's.

He sat there, watching Skinner and listening to the bridge groan in the storm, a strange music emerging from the bundled cables. He wanted to press his ear against them, but some fear he couldn't name held him from it.

Skinner woke once, or seemed to, and struggled to sit up, calling, Yamazaki thought, for the girl.

"She isn't here," Yamazaki said, his hand on Skinner's shoulder. "Don't you remember?"

"Hasn't been," Skinner said. "Twenty, thirty years. Motherfucker. Time."

"Skinner?"

"Time. That's the *total fucking motherfucker*, isn't it?"

Yamazaki held the red sphere before the old man's eyes. "Look, Skinner. See what it became?"

"Superball," Skinner said.

"Skinner-san?"

"You go and fucking *bounce* it, Scooter." He closed his eyes. "Bounce it *high*..."

20

the
big
empty

S wear to God," Nigel said, "this shit just *moved.*"

Chevette, with her eyes closed, felt the blunt back of the ceramic knife press into her wrist; there was a sound like an inner-tube letting go when you've patched it too many times, and then that wrist was free.

"Shit. *Jesus—*" His hands rough and quick, Chevette's eyes opening to a second pop, a red blur whanging back and forth around the stacked scrap. Nigel's head following it, like the counterweighted head of a plaster dog that Skinner had found once and sent her down to sell.

Every wall in this narrow space racked with metal, debraised sections of old Reynolds tubing, dusty jam jars stuffed with rusting spokes. Nigel's workshop, where he built his carts, did what shade-tree fixes he could to any bike came his way. The salmon-plug that dangled from his left ear ticked in counterpoint to his swiveling head, then jingled as he snatched the thing in mid-bounce. A ball of red plastic.

"Man," he said, impressed, "who *put* this on you?"

Chevette stood up and shivered, this tremor running down through her like a live thing, the way those red bracelets had moved.

How she felt, now, was just the way she'd felt that day she'd come back to the trailer and found her mother all packed up and gone. No message there but a can of ravioli in a pot on the stove,

with the can-opener propped up beside it. She hadn't eaten that ravioli and she hadn't eaten any since and she knew she never would.

But this feeling had come, that day, and swallowed everything up inside it, so big you couldn't really prove it was there except
by an arithmetic of absence and the memory of better days. And
she'd moved around in it, whatever it was, from one point to another,
'til she'd wound up behind that wire in Beaverton, in a place so bad
it was like a piece of broken glass to rub against that big empty. And
thereby growing aware of the thing that had swallowed the world,
though it was only just visible, and then in sidelong glances. Not a
feeling so much as a form of gas, something she could almost smell
in the back of her throat, lying chill and inert in the rooms of her
subsequent passage.

"You okay?" Nigel's greasy hair in his eyes, the red ball in
his hand, a cocktail toothpick with a spray of amber cellophane stuck
in the corner of his mouth.

For a long time she'd wondered if maybe the fever hadn't
burned it out, hadn't accidentally fried whatever circuit in her it fed
back on. But as she'd gotten used to the bridge, to Skinner, to messing at Allied, it had just come to seem like the emptiness was filled
with ordinary things, a whole new world grown up in the socket of
the old, one day rolling into the next—whether she danced in Dissidents, or sat up all night talking with her friends, or slept curled in
her bag up in Skinner's room, where wind scoured the plywood walls
and the cables thrummed down into rock that drifted (Skinner said)
like the slowest sea of all.

Now *that* was broken.

" 'Vette?"

That jumper she'd seen, a girl, hauled up and over the side
of a Zodiac with a pale plastic hook, white and limp, water running
from nose and mouth. Every bone broken or dislocated, Skinner said,
if you hit just right. Ran through the bar naked and took a header off
some tourist's table nearest the railing, out and over, tangled in Ha-
ru's Day-Glo net and imitation Japanese fishing floats. And didn't
Sammy Sal drift that way now, maybe already clear of the dead zone

that chased the fish off the years of toxic lead fallen there from un-counted coats of paint, out into the current that sailed the bridge's dead, people said, past Mission Rock, to wash up at the feet of the micropored wealthy jogging the concrete coast of China Basin?

Chevette bent over and threw up, managing to get most of it into an open, empty paint can, its lip thickly scabbed with the gray primer that Nigel used to even out his dodgier mends.

"Hey, hey," Nigel dancing around her, unwilling in his shy bearish way to touch her, his big hands hovering, anxious that she was sick and worried she'd puke over his work, something that might ultimately require the in-depth, never-before-attempted act of clean-ing out, rather than up, his narrow nest. "Water? Want water?" Of-fering her the old coffee can he kept there to quench hot metal. Oily flux afloat atop it like gas beside a dock, and she nearly heaved again, but sat down instead.

Sammy Sal dead, maybe Skinner, too. Him and that grad student tied up up there with the plastic worms.

"Chev?"

He'd put the coffee can down and was offering her an open can of beer instead. She waved it aside, coughing.

Nigel shifted, foot to foot, then turned and peered through the triangular shard of lucite that served as his one window. It was vibrating with the wind. "Stormin'," he said, like he was glad to note the world outside continuing on any recognizable course at all, how-ever drastic. "Stormin' down rain."

Running from Skinner's and the gun in the killer's hand, from his eyes and the gold in the corners of his smile, bent low for balance over her bound hands and the case that held the asshole's glasses, Chevette had seen all the others running, too, racing, it must have been, against the breaking calm, the first slap of rain almost warm when it came. Skinner would've known it was coming; he'd have watched the barometer in its corny wooden case like the wheel of some old boat; he knew his weather, Skinner, perched in his box on the top of the bridge. Maybe the others knew, too, but it was the style to wait and then race it, holding out for a last sale, another smoke, some bit of business. The hour before a storm was good for that, people making edgy purchases against what was ordinarily a bearable uncertainty. Though a few were lost, if the storm was big enough, and not always the unestablished, the newcomers lashed with their ragged baggage to whatever freehold they might have managed on the outer structure; sometimes a whole patchwork section would just let go, if the wind caught it right; she hadn't seen that but there were stories. There was nothing to stop the new people from coming in to the shelter of the decks, but they seldom did.

She wiped her mouth with the back of her hand and took the beer from Nigel. Took a sip. It was warm. She handed it back to him. He took the toothpick from his mouth, started to raise the can for a swallow, thought better of it, put it down beside his welding-torch.

"Somethin's wrong," he said. "I can *tell*."

She massaged her wrists. Twin rings of rash coming up, pink and moist, where the plastic had gripped her. Picked up the ceramic knife and closed it automatically.

"Yeah," she said, "yeah. Something's wrong..."

"*What's* wrong, Chevette?" He shook hair out of his eyes like a worried dog, fingers running nervously over his tools. His hands were like pale dirty animals, capable in their mute and agile way of solving problems that would have hopelessly baffled the man himself. "That Jap shit delaminated on you," he decided, "and you're pissed..."

"No," she said, not really hearing him.

"Steel's what you want for a messenger bike. Weight. Big basket up front. Not cardboard with some crazy aramid shit wrapped around it, weighs about as much as a sandwich. What if you hit a b-bus? Bang into the back of it? You got more m-mass than the b-bike, you flip over and c-crack open...crack your..." His hands twisting, trying more accurately to frame the physics of the accident he was seeing. Chevette looked up and saw that he was trembling.

"Nigel," she said, standing up, "somebody just put that thing on me for a joke, understand?"

"It *moved,*" he said. "I saw it."

"Well, not a *funny* joke, okay? But I knew where to come. To you, right? And you took it off."

Nigel shook his hair back into his eyes, shy and pleased. "You had that knife. Cuts good." Then he frowned. "You need a *steel* knife..."

"I know," she said. "I gotta go now..." Bending to pick up the paint can. "I'll toss this. Sorry."

"It's a storm," Nigel said. "Don't go out in a storm."

"I've got to," she said. "I'll be okay." Thinking how he'd kill Nigel, too, if he found her here. Hurt him. Scare him.

"I cut them off." Holding up the red ball.

"Get rid of that," she said.

"Why?"

"Look at this rash."

Nigel dropped the ball like it was poison. It bounced out of sight. He wiped his fingers down the filthy front of his t-shirt.

"Nigel, you got a screwdriver you'll give me? A flathead?"

"Mine are all worn down..." The white animals running over a shoal of tools, happy to be hunting, while Nigel gravely watched them. "I throw those flathead screws away as soon as I get 'em off. Hex is how you want to go—"

"I *want* one that's all worn down."

The right hand pounced, came up with its prize, black-handled and slightly bent.

"That's the one," she said, zipping up Skinner's jacket.

Both hands offered it to her, Nigel's eyes hiding behind his hair, watching. "I ... like you, Chevette."

"I know," she said, standing there with a paint can with vomit in it in one hand, a screwdriver in the other. "I know you do."

Baffled by the patchwork of plastic that roofed the upper deck, the rain was following waste-lines and power-cables, emerging overhead at crazy angles, in random cascades, miniature Niagaras rushing off corrugated iron and plywood. From the entrance to Nigel's workshop, Chevette watched an awning collapse, gallons of silver water splashing all at once from what had been a taut concavity, a bulging canvas bathtub that gave way with a sharp crack, instantly becoming several yards of flapping, sodden cloth. Nothing here was ever planned, in any overall sense, and problems of drainage were dealt with as they emerged. Or not, more likely.

Half the lights were out, she saw, but that could be because people had shut them down, had pulled as many plugs as possible. But then she caught the edge of that weird pink flash you got when a transformer blew, and she heard it boom. Out toward Treasure. That took care of most of the remaining lights and suddenly she stood in near darkness. There was nobody in sight, nobody at all. Just a hundred-watt bulb in an orange plastic socket, twirling around in the wind.

She moved out into the center of the deck, trying to watch out for fallen wires. She remembered the can in her hand and flung it sideways, hearing it hit and roll.

She thought of her bike lying there in the rain, its capacitors drained. Somebody was going to take it, for sure, and Sammy Sal's, too. It was the biggest thing, the most valuable thing she'd ever owned, and she'd earned every dollar she'd put down on the counter at City Wheels. She didn't think about it like it was a *thing*, more the way she figured people thought about horses. There were messengers who named their bikes, but Chevette never would have done that, and somehow because she *did* think about it like it was something alive.

Proj, she told herself, *they'll get you if you stay here.* Her back to San Francisco, she set out toward Treasure.

They who? That one with his gun. He'd come for the glasses. Came for the glasses and killed Sammy. Had those people sent him, the ones who called up Bunny and Wilson the owner? Rentacops. Security guys.

The case in her pocket. Smooth. And that weird cartoon of the city, those towers with their spreading tops. Sunflower.

"Jesus," she said, "where? Where'm I *going*?"

To Treasure, where the wolf-men and the death-cookies hung, the bad crazies chased off the bridge to haunt the woods there? Been a Navy base there, Skinner said, but a plague put paid to that just after the Little Grande, something that turned your eyes to mush, then your teeth fell out. Treasure Island fever, like maybe something crawled out of a can at that Navy place, after the earthquake. So nobody went there now, nobody normal. You saw their fires at night, sometimes, and smoke in the daytime, and you walked straight over to the Oakland span, the cantilever, and the people who lived *there* weren't the same, really, as the people over here in the suspension.

Or should she go back, try to get her bike? An hour's riding and the brakes would be charged again. She saw herself just riding, maybe east, riding forever into whatever country that was, deserts like you saw on television, then flat green farms where big machines came marching along in rows, doing whatever it was they did. But she remembered the road down from Oregon, the trucks groaning past in the night like lost mad animals, and she tried to picture herself riding down that. No, there wasn't any *place* out on a road like that, nothing human-sized, and hardly ever even a light, in all the fields of dark. Where you could walk and walk forever and never come to anything, not even a place to sit down. A bike wouldn't get her anywhere out there.

Or she could go back to Skinner's. Go up there and see— No. She shut that down, hard.

The empty rose out of the rain-rattled shadows like a gas, and she held her breath, not to breathe it in.

How it was, when you lost things, it was like you only knew for the first time that you'd ever had them. Took a mother's leaving for you to know she'd ever been there, because otherwise she *was* that place, everything, like weather. And Skinner and the Coleman stove and the oil she had to drop into the little hole to keep its leather gasket soft so the pump would work. You didn't wake up every morning and say *yes* and *yes* to every little thing. But little things were what it was all made of. Or just somebody to see, there, when you woke up. Or Lowell. When she'd had Lowell—if she could say she ever had, and she guessed she hadn't, really—but while he'd *been* there, anyway, he'd been a little like that—

"Chev? That you?"

And there he was. Lowell. Sitting up cross-legged on top of a rusty cooler said SHRIMP across the front, smoking a cigarette and watching rain run off the shrimp man's awning. She hadn't seen him for three weeks now, and the only thing she could think of was how she really must look like total shit. That skinhead boy they called Codes was sitting up beside him, black hood of a sweatshirt pulled up and his hands hidden in the long sleeves. Codes hadn't ever liked her.

But Lowell, he was grinning around the glow of that cigarette. "Well," he said, "you gonna say 'hi' or what?"

"Hi," Chevette said.

21

cognitive
dissidents

Rydell wasn't too sure about this whole bridge thing, and less sure about what Freddie had had to say about it, in Food Fair and on the way back from North Beach. He kept remembering that documentary he'd seen in Knoxville and he was pretty sure there hadn't been anything on that about cannibals or cults. He thought that had to be Freddie wanting him to think that, because he, Rydell, was the one who had to go out there and get this girl, Chevette Washington.

And now he was actually out on it, watching people hurry to get their stuff out of the way of the weather, it looked even less like what Freddie had said it was all about. It looked like a carnival, sort of. Or a state fair midway, except it was roofed over, on the upper level, with crazy little shanties, just boxes, and whole house-trailers winched up and glued into the suspension with big gobs of adhesive, like grasshoppers in a spider-web. You could go up and down, between the two original deck levels, through holes they'd cut in the upper deck, all different kinds of stairs patched in under there, plywood and welded steel, and one had an old airline gangway, just sitting there with its tires flat.

Down on the bottom deck, once you got in past a lot of food-wagons, there were mostly bars, the smallest ones Rydell had ever seen, some with only four stools and not even a door, just a big shutter they could pull down and lock.

But none of it done to any plan, not that he could see. Not like a mall, where they plug a business into a slot and wait to see whether it works or not. This place had just *grown*, it looked like, one thing patched onto the next, until the whole span was wrapped in this formless mass of *stuff*, and no two pieces of it matched. There was a different material anywhere you looked, almost none of it being used for what it had originally been intended for. He passed stalls faced with turquoise Formica, fake brick, fragments of broken tile worked into swirls and sunbursts and flowers. One place, already shuttered, was covered with green-and-copper slabs of desoldered component-board.

He found himself grinning at it all, and at the people, none of them paying him the least attention, cannibalistic or otherwise. They looked to be as mixed a bunch as their building materials: all ages, races, colors, and all of them rushing ahead of the storm that very definitely was coming now, wind stiffening as he threaded his way past carts and old ladies lugging straw suitcases. A little kid, staggering with his arms wrapped around a big red fire-extinguisher, bumped into his legs. Rydell hadn't ever seen a little kid with tattoos like that. The boy said something in some other language and then he was gone.

Rydell stopped and got Warbaby's map out of his jacket pocket. It showed where this girl lived and how to get up there. Right up on the roof of the damned thing, in a little shanty stuck to the top of one of the towers they hung the cables from. Warbaby had beautiful handwriting, really graceful, and he'd drawn this map out in the back of the Patriot, and labelled it for Rydell. Stairs here, then you went along this walkway, took some kind of elevator.

Finding that first set of stairs was going to be a bitch, though, because, now that he looked around, he saw *lots* of narrow little stairways snaking up between stalls and shuttered micro-bars, and no pattern to it at all. He guessed they all led up into the same rats-nest, but there was no guarantee they'd all connect up.

Exhaustion hit him, then, and he just wanted to know where

and when he was supposed to sleep, and what was all this bullshit about, anyway? What had he let Hernandez get him in for?

Then the rain hit, the wind upping its velocity a couple of notches and the locals diving seriously for cover, leaving Rydell to hunch in the angle between a couple of old-fashioned Japanese vending-machines. The overall structure, if you could call it that, was porous enough to let plenty of rain in, but big enough and clumsy enough to tangle seriously with the wind. The whole thing started creaking and popping and sort of groaning. And the lights started going out.

He saw a burst of white sparks and a wire came down, out of that crazy tangle. Somebody yelled, but the words were pulled away into the wind and he couldn't make them out. He looked down and saw water rising around his SWAT shoes. Not good, he thought: puddles, wet shoes, alternating current.

There was a fruitstand next to one of the vending-machines, knocked together from scavenged wood like a kid's fort. But it had a sort of shelf under it, raised up six inches, and it looked dry under there. He hunched himself in, on top of it, with his feet up out of the water. It smelled like overripe tangerines, but it was ninety-percent dry and the vending-machine took most of the wind.

He zipped his jacket as high as it went, balled his fists into the pockets, and thought about a hot bath and a dry bed. He thought about his Futon Mouth futon, down in Mar Vista, and actually felt homesick. Jesus, he thought, be missing those stick-on flowers next.

A canvas awning came down, its wooden braces snapping like toothpicks, spilling maybe twenty gallons of rain. And right then was when he saw her, Chevette Washington, right out in plain sight. Just like he was dreaming. Not twenty feet away. Just standing there.

Rydell had sort of had this girlfriend down in Florida, after his father had moved down there and gotten sick. Her name was Claudia Marsalis and she was from Boston and her mother had her RV in the same park as Rydell's father, right near Tampa Bay. Rydell was in his first year at the Academy, but you got a couple of breaks and his father knew ways to get a deal on plane tickets.

So Rydell would go down there on breaks and stay with his father and sometimes at night he'd go out and ride around with Claudia Marsalis in her mother's '94 Lincoln, which Claudia said had been cherry when they brought it down but now the salt was starting to get to it. Evidently up in Boston she'd only ever taken it out on the road in the summer, so the chemicals wouldn't eat it out. It had these blue-and-white MASS. HERITAGE plates on it because it was a collector's item. They were the old-fashioned kind, stamped metal, and they didn't light up from inside.

It was kind of rough, around that part of Tampa, with the street signs all chewed up for target practice or the late-night demonstration of the choke on somebody's shotgun. There were plenty of shotguns around to be demonstrated, too; a few in the window-rack of every pick-up and 4x4, and usually a couple of big old dogs. Claudia used to give Rydell a hard time about that, about these Florida boys in gimme hats, riding around with their guns and dogs. Rydell told her it didn't have anything to do with him, he was from Knoxville, and people didn't drive around Knoxville with their guns showing. Or shoot holes in street signs either, not if the Department could help it. But Claudia was one of those people thought everything south of D.C. was all just the same, or maybe she just pretended to to tease him.

But at night it smelled like salt and magnolia and swamp, and they'd drive around in that Lincoln with the windows down and listen to the radio. When it got dark you could watch the lights on ships, and on the big bulk-lifters that went drumming past like the world's slowest UFOs. They'd maybe get in a little listless boogy in the back seat, sometimes, but Claudia said it just got you too sweaty in Florida and Rydell tended to agree. It was just they were both down there and alone and there wasn't much else to do.

One night they were listening to a country station out of Georgia and "Me And Jesus'll Whup Your Heathen Ass" came on, this hardshell Pentecostal Metal thing about abortion and ayatollahs and all the rest of it. Claudia hadn't ever heard that one before and she about wet her pants, laughing. She just couldn't believe that song. When she'd gotten hold of herself and wiped the tears out of her eyes, she'd asked Rydell why he wanted to be a policeman anyway? And he'd felt kind of uncomfortable about that, because it was like she thought his going to the Academy was funny, too, as funny as she thought that dumb-ass song was. But also because it wasn't actually something he'd thought about, much.

The truth was, it probably had a lot to do with how he and his father had always watched *Cops in Trouble* together, because that show seriously did teach you respect. You got to see what kind of problems the police were flat up against. Not just tooled-up slime-balls high on shit, either, but the slimeballs' lawyers and the damn courts and everything. But if he told her it was because of a tv show, he knew she'd just laugh at that, too. So he thought about it a while and told her it was because he liked the idea of being in a position to help out people when they were really in trouble. When he'd said that, she just looked at him.

"Berry," she said, "you really mean that, don't you?"

"Sure," he said, "guess I do."

"But Berry, when you're a cop, people are just going to *lie* to you. People will think of you as the enemy. The only time they'll want to talk to you *is* when they're in trouble."

Driving, he glanced sideways at her. "How come you know so much about it, then?"

"Because that's what my father does," she said, end of conversation, and she never did bring it up again.

But he'd thought about that, driving Gunhead for IntenSecure, because that was like being a cop except it wasn't. The people you were there to help didn't even give enough of a shit to lie to you, mostly, because they were the ones paying the bill.

And here he was, out on this bridge, crawling out from under a fruitstand to follow this girl that Warbaby and Freddie—who Rydell was coming to decide he didn't trust worth a rat's ass—claimed had butchered that German or whatever he was up in that hotel. And stolen these glasses Rydell was supposed to get back, ones like War-baby's. But if she'd stolen them before, how come she'd gone back to kill the guy later? But the real question was, what did that have to do with anything, or even with watching *Cops in Trouble* all those times with his father? And the answer, he guessed, was that he, like anybody else in his position, was just trying to make a living.

Solid streams of rain were coming down out of various points in all that jackstraw stuff upstairs, splashing on the deck. There was a pink flash, like lightning, off down the bridge. He thought he saw her fling something to the side, but if he stopped to check it out he might lose her. She was moving now, avoiding the waterfalls.

Street-surveillance technique wasn't something you got much training in, at the Academy, not unless you looked like such good detective material that they streamlined you right into the Advanced CI courses. But Rydell had gone and bought the textbook anyway. Trouble was, because of that he knew you pretty well needed at least one partner to do it with, and that was assuming you had a radio link and some citizens going about their business to give you a little cover. Doing it this way, how he had to do it now, about the best you could hope for was just to sneak along behind her.

He knew it was her because of that crazy hair, that ponytail stuck up in the back like one of those fat Japanese wrestlers. She wasn't fat, though. Her legs, sticking out of a big old biker jacket that might've been hanging in a barn for a couple of years, looked like she must work out a lot. They were covered with some tight shiny black stuff, like Kevin's micropore outfits from Just Blow Me, and they went down into some kind of dark boots or high-top shoes.

Paying that much attention to her, and trying to stay out of sight in case she turned around, he managed to walk right under one of those waterfalls. Right down the back of his neck. Just then he heard somebody call to her, "Chev, that you?" and he went down on one knee in a puddle, behind this stack of salvaged lumber, two-by-fours with soggy plaster sticking to them. ID positive.

The waterfall behind him was making too much noise for him to hear what was said then, but he could see them: a young guy with a black leather jacket, a lot newer than hers, and somebody else in something black, with a hood pulled up. They were sitting up on a cooler or something, and the guy with the leather was dragging on a cigarette. Had his hair combed up in sort of a crest; good trick, in that rain. The cigarette arced out and winked off in the wet, and the guy got down from there and seemed to be talking to the girl. The one with the black hood got down, too, moving like a spider. It was a sweatshirt, Rydell saw, with sleeves that hung down six inches past his hands. He looked like a floppy shadow from some old movie Rydell had seen once, where shadows got separated from people and you had to catch them and sew them back on. Probably Sublett could tell him what that was called.

He worked hard on not moving, kneeling there in that puddle, and then *they* were moving, the two of them on either side of her and the shadow glancing back to check behind them. He caught a fraction of white face and a pair of hard, careful eyes.

He counted: one, two, three. Then he got up and followed them.

He couldn't say how far they'd gone before he saw them drop, it looked like, straight out of sight. He wiped rain from his eyes and tried to figure it, but then he saw that they'd gone down a flight of stairs, this one cut into the lower deck, which was the first time he'd seen that. He could hear music as he came up on it, and see this bluish glow. Which proved to be from this skinny little neon sign that said, in blue capital letters: COGNITIVE DISSIDENTS.

He stood there for a second, hearing water sizzle off the sign's transformer, and then he just took those stairs.

They were plywood, stapled with that sandpapery no-slip stuff, but he almost slipped anyway. By the time he'd gotten halfway to the bottom, he knew it was a bar, because he could smell beer and a couple of different kinds of smoke.

And it was warm, down there. It was like walking into a steam bath. And crowded. Somebody threw a towel at him. It was soaking wet and hit him in the chest, but he grabbed it and rubbed at his hair and face with it, tossed it back in the direction it had come from. Somebody else, a woman by the sound, laughed. He went over to the bar and found an empty space at the end. Fished in his soggy pockets for a couple of fives and clicked them down on the counter. "Beer," he said, and didn't look up when somebody put one down in front of him and swept the coins out of sight. It was one of those brewed-in-America Japanese brands that people in places like Tampa didn't drink much. He closed his eyes and drank about half of it at a go. As he opened his eyes and put it down, somebody beside him said "Tumble?"

He looked over and saw this jawless character with little pink glasses and a little pink mouth, thinning sandy hair combed straight back and shining with something more than the damp in the room.

"What?" Rydell said.

"I said 'tumble.'"

"I heard you," Rydell said.

"So? Need the service?"

"Uh, look," Rydell said, "all I need right now's this beer, okay?"

"Your phone," the pink-mouthed man said. "Or fax. Guaranteed tumble, one month. Thirty days or your next thirty free. Unlimited long, domestic. You need overseas, we can talk overseas. But three hundred for the basic tumble." All of this coming out in a buzz that reminded Rydell of the kind of voice-chip you got in the cheapest possible type of kid's toy.

"Wait a sec," Rydell said.

The man blinked a couple of times, behind his pink glasses.

"You talking about doing that thing to a pocket phone, right? Where you don't have to pay the company?"

The man just looked at him.

"Well, thanks," Rydell said, quickly. "I appreciate it, but I just don't have any phone *on* me. If I did, I'd be happy to take you up on it."

Still looking at him. "Thought I saw you before..." Doubt.

"Naw," Rydell said. "I'm from Knoxville. Just come in out of the rain." He decided it was time to risk turning around and checking the place out, because the mirrors behind the bar were steamed up solid and running with drops. He swung his shoulder around and saw that Japanese woman, the one he'd seen that time up in the hills over Hollywood, when he'd been cruising with Sublett. She was standing up on a little stage, naked, her long curly hair falling around her to her waist. Rydell heard himself grunt.

"Hey," the man was saying, "hey..."

Rydell shook himself, a weird automatic thing, like a wet dog, but she was still there.

"Hey. Credit." The drone again. "Got problems? Maybe just wanna see what they've *got* on you? Anybody else, you got the right numbers—"

"Hey," Rydell said, "wait up. That woman up there?"

The pink glasses tilted.

"Who is that?" Rydell asked.

"That's a hologram," the man said, in a completely different voice, and walked away.

"Damn," said the bartender, behind him. "You just set a record for blowing off Eddie the Shit. Earned yourself a beer, my man."

The bartender was a black guy with copper beads in his hair. He was grinning at Rydell. "Call him Eddie the Shit cause he ain't worth one, don't give another. Hook your phone up to some box doesn't have a battery, push a few buttons, pass a dead chicken over it, take your money. That's Eddie." He uncapped a beer and put it down beside the other one.

Rydell looked back at the Japanese woman. She hadn't moved. "I just came in out of the rain," he said, all he could think to say.

"Good night for it," the bartender said.

"Say," Rydell said, "that lady up there—"

"That's Josie's dancer," the bartender said. "You watch. She'll dance her in a minute, soon as there's a song she likes."

"Josie?"

The bartender pointed. Rydell looked where he was pointing. Saw a very fat woman in a wheelchair, her hair the color and texture of coarse steel wool. She wore brand-new blue denim bib overalls and an XXL white sweatshirt, and both her hands were hidden inside something that sat on her lap like a smooth gray plastic muff. Her eyes were closed, face expressionless. He couldn't have said for sure that she wasn't asleep.

"Hologram?" The Japanese woman hadn't moved at all. Rydell was remembering what he'd seen, that night. The horned crown, all silver. Her pubic hair, shaved like an exclamation point. This one didn't have either of those, but it was her. It was.

"Josie's always projectin'," the bartender said, like it was something that couldn't really be helped.

"From that thing on her lap?"

"That's the interface," the bartender said. "Projector's, well, there." He pointed. "Top of that NEC sign."

Rydell saw a little black gizmo clamped to the top of this old illuminated sign. It looked kind of like an old camera, the optical kind. He didn't know if NEC was a beer or what. The whole wall was covered with these signs, all different brands, and now he recognized a few of the names he decided they were ads for old electronics companies.

He looked at the gizmo, back at the fat woman in the wheel-chair, and felt sad. Angry, too. Like he'd lost something. "Not like I knew what I thought it was," he said to himself.

"Fool anybody," said the bartender.

Rydell thought about somebody sitting out there by that valley road. Waiting for cars. Like he and his friends would lie under the bushes down Jefferson Street and toss cans under people's tires. Sounded like a hubcap had come off. See them get out and look, shake their heads. So what he'd seen had just been a version of that, somebody playing with an expensive toy.

"Shit," he said, and put his mind to looking for Chevette Washington in all this crowd. He didn't notice the beer-smell now, or the smoke, more the wet hair and clothes and just bodies. And there she was, her and her two friends, hunched over a little round table in a corner. The sweatshirt's hood was down now, showing Rydell a white, stubbled head with some kind of bat or bird tattooed on the side, up where it would be hidden if the hair grew in. It was the kind of tattoo somebody had done by hand, not the kind you got done on a computer-driven table. Baldhead had a hard little face, in profile, and he was wasn't talking. Chevette Washington was telling something to the other one and not looking happy.

Then the music changed, these drums coming in, like there were millions of them, ranked backed somehow beyond the walls, and weird waves of static riding in on that, falling back, riding in again, and women's voices, crying like birds, and none of it natural, the voices dopplering past like sirens on a highway, and the drums, when you listened, made up of little snipped bits of sound that weren't drums at all.

The Japanese woman—the hologram, Rydell reminded himself—raised her arms and began to dance, a sort of looping shuffle, timed not to the tempo of the drums but to the waves of static washing back and forth across the sound, and when Rydell thought to look he saw the fat woman's eyes were open, her hands moving inside that plastic muff.

Nobody else in the bar was paying it any attention at all, just Rydell and the woman in the wheelchair. Rydell leaned there on the bar, watching the hologram dance and wondering what he should do next.

Warbaby's shopping list went like this: best he got the glasses and the girl, next best was the glasses, just the girl was definitely third, but a must if that was all that was going.

Josie's music slid out and away for the last time and the hologram's dance ended. There was some drunken applause from a couple of the tables, Josie nodding her head a little like she was thanking them.

The terrible thing about it, Rydell thought, was that there Josie was, shoehorned into that chair, and she just wasn't much good at making that thing dance. It reminded him of this blind man in the

park in Knoxville, who sat there all day strumming an antique National guitar. There he was, blind, had this old guitar, and he just
couldn't chord for shit. Never seemed to get any better at it, either.
Didn't seem fair.

Now some people got up from a table near where Chevette
Washington was sitting. Rydell was in there quick, bringing the beer
he'd won for getting rid of Eddie the Shit. He still wasn't close enough
to pick out what they were saying, but he could try. He tried to think
up ways to maybe start up a conversation, but it seemed pretty hope-
less. Not that he looked particularly out of place, because he had the
impression that most of this crowd weren't regulars here, just a
random sampling, come in out of the rain. But he just didn't have
any idea what this place was about. He couldn't figure out what "Cognitive Dissidents" meant; it wouldn't help him figure out what the
theme, or whatever, was. And besides, whatever Chevette Washington and her guy were discussing, it looked to be getting sort of
heated.

Her guy, he thought. Something there in her body-language
that said Pissed-Off Girlfriend, and something in how hard this boy
was studying to show how little any of it bothered him, like maybe
she was the Ex—

All this abruptly coming to nothing at all as every conversation
died and Rydell looked up from his beer to see Lt. Orlovsky, the vam-
pire-looking cop from SFPD Homicide, stepping in from the stairwell in
his London Fog, some kind of fedora that looked like it was molded
from flesh-colored plastic on his head, and those scary half-frame
glasses. Orlovsky stood there, little streams running off the hem of his
rain-darkened coat and pooling around his wingtips, while he unbut-
toned the coat with one hand. Still had his black flak vest on underneath, and now that hand came up to rest on the smooth,
injection-molded, olive-drab butt of his floating-breech H&K. Rydell
looked for the badge-case on the nylon neck-thong, but didn't see it.

The whole bar was looking at Orlovsky.

Orlovsky looked around the room, over the tops of his
glasses, taking his time, giving them all a good dose of Cop Eye. The

music, some weird hollow techie stuff that sounded like bombs going off in echo-chambers, started to make a different kind of sense.

Rydell saw Josie the wheelchair woman looking at the Russian with an expression Rydell couldn't process.

Spotting Chevette Washington in her corner, Orlovsky walked over to her table, still taking his time, making the rest of the room take that same time. His hand still on that gun.

It seemed to Rydell like the Russian just might be about to haul out and shoot her. Sure looked like it, but what kind of cop would do that?

Now Orlovsky stopped in front of their table, just the right distance, too far for them to reach him and far enough to allow room to pull that big gun if he was going to.

The Boyfriend, Rydell was somehow pleased to see, looked fit to shit himself. Baldhead looked like he'd been cast in plastic, just frozen there, hands on the table. Between his hands, Rydell saw a pocket phone.

Orlovsky locked the girl with his full current of Eye-thing, his face lined, gray in this light, unsmiling. He jerked the brim of the plastic fedora, just this precise little fraction, and said "Get up."

Rydell looked at her and saw her trembling. There was never any question the Russian meant her and not her friends—Boyfriend looking like he might faint any second and Baldhead playing statue.

Chevette Washington stood up, shaky, the rickety little wooden chair going over behind her.

"Out." The hat-brim indicated the stairs. The hairy back of Orlovsky's hand covered the butt of the H&K.

Rydell heard his own knees creak with tension. He was leaning forward, gripping the edges of the table. He could feel old dried pads of gum under there.

The lights went out.

Much later, trying to explain to Sublett what it had been like when Josie whipped her hologram on Orlovsky, Rydell said it looked sort of like the special effect at the end of *Raiders of the Lost Ark,* that part where those angels or whatever they were came swirling out of that box and got all over those Nazis.

But it had all been happening at once, for Rydell. When the lights went, they all went, all those signs on the wall, everything, and Rydell just tossed that table sideways, without even thinking about it, and Went For where she'd been standing. And this ball of light had shot down, expanding, from a point on the wall that must've marked the upper edge of that NEC sign. It was the color of the hologram's skin, kind of honey and ivory, all marbled through with the dark of her hair and eyes, like a fast-forward of a satellite storm-system. All around that Russian, a three-foot sphere around his head and shoulders, and as it spun, her eyes and mouth, open in some silent scream, blinked by, all magnified. Each eye, for a fraction of a second, the size of the ball itself, and the white teeth big, too, each one long as a man's hand.

Orlovsky swatted at it, and that kept him, for some very little while, from getting his gun out.

But it also gave off enough light to let Rydell see he was grabbing the girl and not Boyfriend. Just sort of picking her up, forgetting everything he'd ever been taught about come-alongs and restraints, and running, best he could, for the stairs.

Orlovsky yelled something, but it must've been in Russian.

His uncle, the one who'd gone off to Africa in the Army, used to say, if he liked how a woman's ass moved when she walked, that it looked like two baby bobcats in a croker sack. And that was the expression that popped into Rydell's mind as he ran up those stairs with Chevette Washington held out in front of him like a big bunch of groceries. But it didn't have anything to do with sexy.

He was just lucky she didn't get an eye or break any of his ribs.

rub-a-dub

Whoever had grabbed her, she just kept kicking and punching, right up the stairs, backward. But he had her held out so far in front of him that he almost fell on top of her.

Then she was out on the deck, in what light there was, and looking at some kind of plastic machine gun, the color of a kid's army toy, in the hands of another one of these big ugly raincoat guys, this one with no hat and his wet hair slicked back from a face with the skin on too tight.

"You drop her now, fuckhead," this one with the gun said. Had an accent out of an old monster movie. She barely kept to her feet when the one who was holding her let go.

"Fuckhead," the gun-guy said, like *Fock Ed*, "you try to make move or what?"

"War," the one who'd grabbed her said, then doubled over, coughing. "Baby," he said, straightening, then winced, hugging his ribs, looking at her. "Jesus *fuck*, you got a kick on you." Sounded American, but not West Coast. In a cheap nylon jacket with one sleeve half ripped off at the shoulder, white fuzzy stuff hanging out.

"You try to make a move..." And the plastic gun was pointing right at the guy's face.

"*War*-baby, *war*-baby," the guy said, or anyway it sounded like that, "*war*-baby sent me to get her. He's parked back out there past those tank-trap things, waiting for me to bring her out."

"Arkady..." It was the one in the plastic hat, coming up the stairs behind the guy who'd grabbed her. He had a pair of night-vision glasses on, that funny-looking center-tube poking out from beneath the brim of his hat. He was holding up something that looked like a miniature aerosol can. He said something in this language. Russian? He gestured with the little can, back down the stairs.

"You use capsicum in an enclosed space like that," said the one who'd grabbed her, "people'll get hurt. Get you some permanent sinus problems."

The tight-faced man looked at him like he was something crawled out from under a rock. "You drive, yes?" he said, gesturing for the hat-man to put the thing away, whatever it was.

"We had a coffee. Well, you had tea. Svobodov, right?"

Chevette caught the tight-faced man's glance at her, like he hadn't liked her hearing his name. She wanted to tell him she'd heard it *Rub-a-Dub*, how this other guy talked, so that couldn't really be it, could it?

"Why you grab her?" asked the tight-faced man, Rub-a-Dub.

"She coulda got away in the dark, couldn't she? Didn't know your partner here had night vision. Besides, he sent me to get her. Didn't mention *you*. In fact, they said you didn't come out here."

The one with the hat was behind her now, jerking her arm up in a hold. "Lemme *go*—"

"Hey," the one who'd grabbed her said, like it made things okay, "these men are *police* officers. SFPD Homicide, right?"

Rub-a-Dub whistled softly. "*Fuck*head."

"Cops?" she asked.

"Sure are."

Which produced a little snort of exasperation from Rub-a-Dub.

"Arkady, now we go. These dirtbags try to spy us from below..." The hat-man pulling off his night-glasses and dancing like he had to pee.

"Hey," she said, "somebody's *killed* Sammy. If you're cops, listen, he *killed* Sammy Sal!"

"Who's Sammy?" the one in the torn jacket said.

"I *work* with him! At Allied. Sammy DuPree. Sammy. He got shot."

"Who shot him?"

"Ry-dell. Shut fuck up." *Shot, Fock, Op.*

"She's tellin' us she's got-information-regarding-a-possible-homicide, and you're telling me to shut up?"

"Yes, I tell you shut *fuck* up. War-baby. He will explain."

And her arm twisted up so she'd go with them.

23

gone

and

done it

vobodov had insisted on cuffing him to Chevette Washington. They were Beretta cuffs, just like he'd carried on patrol in Knoxville. Svobodov said he and Orlovsky needed their hands free in case any of these bridge people caught on they were taking the girl off.

But if they were taking her in, how come they hadn't read her any Miranda, or even told her she was under arrest? Rydell had already decided that if it got to court and he was called to witness, no way was he going to perjure himself and say he'd heard any fucking Miranda. These Russians were balls-out cowboys as far as he could see, just exactly the kind of officers the Academy had tried hard to train Rydell not to be.

In a way, though, what they were reflected what a lot of people more or less unconsciously expected cops to be and do, and that, this one lecturer at the Academy had said, was because of mythology. Like what they called the Father Mulcahy Syndrome, in barricaded hostage situations. Where somebody took a hostage and the cops tried to decide what to do. And they'd all seen this movie about Father Mulcahy once, so'd they'd say, yeah, I got it, I'll get a priest, I'll get the guy's parents, I'll lay down my gun and I'll go in there and talk him out. And he'd go in there and get his ass drilled out real good. Because he forgot, and let himself think a movie was how you really did it. And it could work the other way, too, so you gradually *became* how you saw cops were in movies and on television. They'd all been warned about that. But people like Svobodov and Orlovsky, people who'd come here from other countries, maybe that media stuff worked even stronger on them. Check how they dressed, for one thing.

Man, he was going to have him a shower. Hot shower. He was going to stay in there until he couldn't stand it anymore, or until the hot ran out. Then he was going to get out and towel off and put on all brand-new, totally *dry* clothes, in whatever hotel room Warbaby had got for him. He was going to send down for a couple of club sandwiches and an ice-bucket with about four-five of those long-neck Mexican beers like they drank in L.A. And he'd sit there with a remote and watch some television. Maybe see *Cops in Trouble.* Maybe he'd even call up Sublett, shoot the shit, tell him about this wild-ass time up in Northern California. Sublett always worked deep graveyard because he was light-sensitive, so if it happened to be his night off, he'd be up watching his movies.

"Watch where you're *walking*—" Yanking his cuffed hand so hard he nearly fell over. He'd been about to go one side of an upright as she was about to go the other. "Hey. Sorry," he said.

She wouldn't look at him. But she just didn't look to Rydell like she'd sit down on some guy's chest with a razor and haul his tongue out the hard way. Well, she did have that ceramic knife, when Svobodov shook her down, plus a pocket phone and the damn glasses everybody was after. Those looked just like Warbaby's, and had this case. The Russians were real happy about that, and now they were tucked away safe in the inside pocket of Svobodov's flak vest.

She wasn't the right *kind* of scared, either, something kept telling him. She wasn't giving off that vibe of perp fear that you got to know by about your third day on the job. It was like *victim* fear, what it was, even though she'd already flat-out admitted to Orlovsky that she'd stolen those glasses. Said she'd done that up at a party in that hotel, the night before. But neither of the Russians had said shit about any homicide beef, or any Blix or whatever the victim's name had been. Or even larceny. And she'd said that about somebody kill-ing Sammy, whoever Sammy was. Maybe Sammy was the German. But the Russians had just dropped it, and shut Rydell up, and now she'd clammed up except to bitch at him if he started to fall asleep on his feet.

The place was coming back to life, sort of, now that the storm had quit, but it was God knows when in the morning and there weren't exactly a lot of people swarming out yet to check the damage. Lights kept coming back on, here and there, and there were a few people sweeping water off decks and things, and a few drunks, and this guy who looked like he was on dancer, talking to himself a mile a minute, who kept following them until Svobodov pulled out his H&K and spun around and said he'd grease him to fucking catfood if he didn't get his dancer ass to Oakland like yesterday, fuckhead, and the guy did, naturally, his eyes about to bug right out of his head, and Orlovsky laughing at him.

They came out into some more lights, about where Rydell had first laid eyes on Chevette Washington. Looking down to keep track of his footing, Rydell saw she was wearing black SWAT trainers just like his. Lexan insoles.

"Hey," he said, "major footwear."

And she just looked up at him like he was crazy, and he saw tears running down her face.

And Svobodov jammed the muzzle of that H&K, hard, into the joint of Rydell's jaw, just in front of his right ear, and said: "*Fuck-*head. You don't *talk* to her."

Rydell looked at Svobodov, edgewise, down the top of the barrel. Waited until he thought it was safe to say okay.

After that, he didn't try to say anything to her, or even look at her. When he thought he could get away with it, he looked at Svobodov. When they took that cuff off, he just might deck that son of a bitch.

But just after the Russian had pulled the gun out of his ear, Rydell had registered something behind him. Not registered big-time, but it clicked for him later: this big bear of a longhair, blinking out at them, where they stood in the light, from this little doorway looked like it wasn't more than a foot wide.

———————•———•———•———————

Rydell didn't have anything special going about black people or immigrants or anything, not like a lot of people did. In fact, that had been one of the things that had gotten him into the Academy when he hadn't exactly had great grades from high school. They'd run all these tests on him and decided he wasn't racist. He wasn't, either, but not because he thought about it particularly. He just couldn't see the point. It just made for a lot of hassle, being that way, so why be that way? Nobody was going to go back and live where they lived before, were they, and if they did (he vaguely suspected) there wouldn't be any Mongolian barbecue and maybe we'd all be listening to Pentecostal Metal and anyway the President was black.

He had to admit, though, as he and Chevette Washington walked out between those tank-trap slabs, their cuffed wrists swinging in that stupid prom-night unison that you get with handcuffs, that currently he was feeling a little put upon by a few very specific blacks and immigrants. Warbaby's tv-preacher melancholy had worn thin on him; he thought Freddie was, as his father would have put it, a jive-ass motherfucker; Svobodov and Orlovsky, they must be what his uncle, the one who went in the army, had meant by stone pigs.

And here he could see Freddie with his butt propped against the front fender of the Patriot, bobbing his head to something on earphones, the lyrics or whatever sliding around the edges of his sneakers, animated in red LEDs. Must've sat out the rain in the car, because his pistol-print shirt and his big shorts weren't even wet.

And Warbaby there in his long quilted coat, his hat jammed down level with those VL glasses. Looked like a refrigerator, if a refrigerator could lean on a cane.

And the Russians' gray tanker of an unmarked, pulled up nose to nose with the Patriot, armored tires and that graphite mesh rhino-chaser screaming Cop Car at anybody who was interested. As indeed some were, Rydell saw, a thin crowd of bridge-people watching from various perches on the concrete slabs and battened food-wagons. Little kids, a couple of Mexican-looking women with hairnets like they worked in food-preparation, some rough-looking boys in muddy workclothes and leaning on shovels and push-brooms there. Just looking, their faces carefully neutral, the way people's faces got when they saw cops working and were curious.

And somebody in the Russians' car, hunched down knees-up in the shotgun seat.

The Russians closing in tight on either side of Rydell and the girl, walking them out. Rydell could feel them responding to the presence of the crowd. Shouldn't've left the car out there like that.

Svobodov, this close, sort of creaked when he walked, and that was the armor under his shirt that Rydell had noticed before, back in that greasy spoon. Svobodov was smoking one of his Marlboro cigarettes, hissing out clouds of blue smoke. Had the gun out of sight now.

And right up to Warbaby, Freddie shining the whole scene on with a grin that made Rydell want to kick him, but Warbaby looking sad as ever.

"Get this fucking cuff off," Rydell said to Warbaby, raising his wrist, Chevette Washington's coming up with it. The crowd saw the cuffs then; there was a ripple of reaction, voices.

Warbaby looked at Svobodov. "You get it?"

"Here." Svobodov touched the front of his London Fog.

Warbaby nodded, looked at Chevette Washington, then at Rydell. "Good then." To Orlovsky: "Take the cuffs off."

Orlovsky took Rydell's wrist, slid a mag-strip into the slot in the cuff.

"Get in the car," Warbaby said to Rydell.

"They haven't read her any Miranda," Rydell said.

"Get in the car. You're driving, remember?"

"She under arrest, Mr. Warbaby?"

Freddie giggled.

Chevette Washington was holding her wrist up for Orlovsky, but he was putting the mag-strip away.

"Rydell," Warbaby said, "get in the car now. We've done our part here."

The passenger-side door of the gray car opened. A man got out. Black cowboy boots and a long black waterproof. Sandy hair, no particular length. He had those deep smile-creases down his cheeks, like somebody had carved them there. Light-colored eyes. Then he did smile, and it was about two-thirds gum and a third teeth, with gold at the corners.

"That's him," Chevette Washington said, in this hoarse voice, "he killed Sammy."

And that was when the big longhair, the one in the dirty shirt, the one Rydell had noticed back on the bridge, plowed this bicycle square into Svobodov's back. Not any regular bicycle, either, but this big old rusty coaster-brake number with a heavy steel basket welded in front of the bars. The bike and the basket probably weighed a hundred pounds between them, and there must've been another hundred pounds of scrap metal piled up in the basket when Svobodov got nailed. Put him face-down across the hood of the Patriot, Freddie jumping like a scalded cat.

The longhair landed on top of Svobodov and all that junk like a bear with rabies, grabbed him by the ears, and starting slamming his face into the hood. Orlovsky was pulling out his H&K and Rydell saw Chevette Washington bend down, tug something out of the top of one SWAT shoe. Jab it into Orlovsky's back. Looked like a screwdriver. Hit whatever armor he was wearing, but it put him off-balance as he pulled the trigger.

Nothing in the world ever sounded like caseless ammunition, at full-auto, out of a floating breech. It wasn't the sound of a machine gun, but a kind of ear-shattering, extended whoop.

The first burst didn't seem to hit anything, but with Chevette Washington clawing at his gun arm, Orlovsky tried to turn it on her. Second burst went in the general direction of the crowd. People screaming, grabbing up kids.

Warbaby's mouth was just open, like he couldn't believe it.

Rydell was behind Orlovsky when he tried to bring the gun up again, and, well, it was just one of those times.

He side-kicked the Russian about three inches below the back of his knee, that third burst whooping almost straight up as Orlovsky went down.

Freddie tried to grab Chevette Washington, seemed to see the screwdriver for the first time, and just managed to bring his laptop up with both hands. That screwdriver went right through it. Freddie yelped and dropped it.

Rydell grabbed the loose cuff, the one that had been around his wrist, and just pulled.

Opened the passenger-side door of the Patriot and hauled her right in after him. Getting into the driver's seat, he had a grand-stand view of the longhair pounding Svobodov's bloody face into the hood, all these pieces of rusty junk jumping each time he did it.

Key. Ignition.

Rydell saw Chevette Washington's phone and the case with the VL glasses fall out of Svobodov's flak vest. Powered down the window and reached around. Somebody shot the longhair off Svobodov, pop, pop, pop, and Rydell, stomping it in reverse, saw the man from the cop car swinging a little gun around, two-handed. Just like they taught you in FATSS. The back of the Patriot slammed into something and Svobodov flew off the hood in a cloud of rusty chain and odd lengths of pipe. Chevette Washington was trying to get out the passenger door, so he had to hang on to the cuff and spin the wheel one-handed, let go of her long enough to shove it into forward and tromp on it, then grab her again.

The passenger door slammed shut as he took it straight for the man with the big smile, who maybe got off one more before he had to get out of the way, fast.

The Patriot was fishtailing in about an inch of water, and he barely missed clipping the back of a big orange waste-hauler pulled up beside a building there.

He caught this one crazy glimpse in the dash-mirror, out the back window: the bridge towering up like something wrapped in sea-weed, sky graying now behind it, and Warbaby taking one stiff-legged step, another, raising the cane straight out from his shoulder, pointing it at the Patriot like it was a magic wand or something.

Then whatever came out of the end of Warbaby's cane took out the Patriot's back window, and Rydell hung a right so tight it almost tipped them over.

"Jesus," said Chevette Washington, like somebody talking in their sleep, "what are you *doing*?"

He didn't know, but hadn't he just gone and done it?

24

song

of the

central

pier

Whenthe lights went out, Yamazaki fumbled in the dark for his bag. Finding it, he felt through it for his flashlight.

In the white beam, Skinner slept slack-jawed beneath the blankets and a ragged sleeping-bag.

Yamazaki searched the several shelves above the table-ledge: small glass jars of spices, identical jars containing steel screws, an ancient Bakelite telephone reminding him of the origin of the verb "to dial," rolls of many different kinds and colors of adhesive tape, twists of heavy copper wire, pieces of what he took to be salt-water tackle, and, finally, a bundle of dusty candle-stubs secured with a rotting rubber band. Selecting the longest of these, he found a lighter beside the green camp-stove. Standing the candle upright on a white saucer, he lit it. The flame fluttered and went out.

Flashlight in hand, he moved to the window and tugged it more tightly into its deep circular frame.

Now the candle stayed lit, though the flame pulsed and swelled in drafts he could never hope to locate. Returning to the window, he looked out. The darkened bridge was invisible. Rain was driving almost horizontally against the window, tiny droplets reaching his face through cracks in the glass and corroded segments of the supporting lead.

It occurred to him that Skinner's room might be made to

function as a camera obscura. If the church window's tiny central bull's-eye pane were removed, and the other panes covered, an inverted image would be cast on the opposite wall.

Yamazaki knew that the central pier, the bridge's center anchorage, had once qualified as one of the world's largest pinhole cameras. In the structure's pitch-black interior, light shining in through a single tiny hole had projected a huge image of the underside of the lower deck, the nearest tower, and the surrounding bay. Now the heart of the anchorage housed some uncounted number of the bridge's more secretive inhabitants, and Skinner had advised him against attempting to go there. "Nothin' like those Mansons out in the bushes on Treasure, Scooter, but you don't want to bother 'em anyway. Okay people but they just aren't looking for anybody to drop in, know what I mean?"

Yamazaki crossed to the smooth curve of cable that interrupted the room's floor. Only an oval segment of it was visible, like some mathematical formula barely breaking a topological surface in a computer representation. He bent to touch it, the visible segment polished by other hands. Each of the thirty-seven cables, containing four hundred and seventy-two wires, had withstood, and withstood now, a force of some million pounds. Yamazaki felt something, some message of vast, obscure moment, shiver up through the relic-smooth dorsal hump. The storm, surely; the bridge itself was capable of considerable mobility; it expanded and contracted with heat and cold; the great steel teeth of the piers were sunk into bedrock beneath the Bay mud, bedrock that had scarcely moved even in the Little Grande.

Godzilla. Yamazaki shivered, recalling television images of Tokyo's fall. He had been in Paris, with his parents. Now a new city rose there, its buildings grown, literally, floor by floor.

The candlelight showed him Skinner's little television, forgotten on the floor. Taking it to the table, he sat on the stool and examined it. There was no visible damage to the screen. It had simply come away from its frame, on a short length of multicolored ribbon. He folded the ribbon into the frame and pressed with his thumbs on either side of the screen. It popped back into place, but would it still function? He bent to examine the tiny controls. ON.

Lime-and-purple diagonals chased themselves across the screen, then faded, revealing some steadycam fragment, the NHK logo displayed in the lower left corner. "—heir-apparent to the Harwood Levine public relations and advertising fortune, departed San Francisco this afternoon after a rumored stay of several days, declining comment on the purpose of his visit." A long face, horselike yet handsome, above a raincoat's upturned collar. A large white smile. "Accompanying him," mid-distance shot down an airport corridor, the slender, dark-haired woman wrapped in something luxurious and black, silver gleaming at the heels of her shining boots, "was Maria Paz, the Padanian media personality, daughter of film director Carlo Paz—." The woman, who looked unhappy, vanished, to be replaced by infrared footage from New Zealand, as Japanese peace-keeping forces in armored vehicles advanced on a rural airport. "—losses attributed to the outlawed South Island Liberation Front, while in Wellington—" Yamazaki attempted to change the channel, but the screen only strobed its lime-and-purple, then framed a portrait of Shapely. A BBC docu-drama. Calm, serious, mildly hypnotic. After two more unsuccessful attempts at locating another channel, Yamazaki let the British voiceover blot out the wind, the groaning of the cables, the creaking of the plywood walls. He focused his attention on the familiar story, its outcome fixed, comforting—if only in its certainty.

James Delmore Shapely had come to the attention of the AIDS industry in the early months of the new century. He was thirty-one years old, a prostitute, and had been HIV-positive for twelve years. At the time of his "discovery," by Dr. Kim Kutnik of Atlanta, Georgia, Shapely was serving a two hundred and fifty day prison term for soliciting. (His status as HIV-positive, which would automatically have warranted more serious charges, had apparently been "glitched.") Kutnik, a researcher with the Sharman Group, an American subsidiary of Shibata Pharmaceuticals, was sifting prison medical data in search of individuals who had been HIV-positive for a decade or more, were asymptomatic, and had entirely normal (or, as in Shapely's case, above the norm) T-cell counts.

One of the Sharman Group's research initiatives centered around the possibility of isolating mutant strains of HIV. Arguing that viruses obey the laws of natural selection, several Sharman biologists had proposed that the HIV virus, in its then-current genetic format, was excessively lethal. Allowed to range unchecked, argued the Sharman team, a virus demonstrating 100 percent lethality must eventually bring about the extinction of the host organism. (Other Sharman researchers countered by citing the long incubation period as contributing to the survival of the host population.) As the BBC writers were careful to make clear, the idea of locating nonpathogenic strains of HIV, with a view of overpowering and neutralizing lethal strains, had been put forward almost a decade earlier, though the "ethical" implications of experimentation with human subjects had impeded research. The core observation of the Sharman researchers dated from this earlier work: The virus wishes to survive, and cannot if it kills its host. The Sharman team, of which Dr. Kutnik was a part, intended to inject HIV-positive patients with blood extracted from individuals they believed to be infected with nonpathogenic strains of the virus. It was possible, they believed, that the nonpathogenic strain would overpower the lethal strain. Kim Kutnik was one of seven researchers given the task of locating HIV-positive individuals who might be harboring a nonpathogenic strain. She elected to begin her search through a sector of data concerned with current inmates of state prisons who were (a) in apparent good health, and (b) had tested HIV-positive at least a decade before. Her initial search turned up sixty-six possibles—among them, J. D. Shapely.

Yamazaki watched as Kutnik, played by a young British actress, recalled, from a patio in Rio, her first meeting with Shapely. "I'd been struck by the fact that his T-cell count that day was over 1,200, and that his responses to the questionnaire seemed to indicated that 'safe sex,' as we thought of it then, was, well, not exactly a priority. He was a very open, very outgoing, really a very *innocent* character, and when I asked him, there in the prison visiting room, about oral sex, he actually blushed. Then he laughed, and said, well, he said he 'sucked cock like it was going out of style'..." The actress-Kutnik looked as though she were about to blush herself. "Of course," she said, "in those days we didn't really understand the disease's exact vectors of infection, because, grotesque as it now seems, there had been no real research into the precise modes of transmission..."

Yamazaki cut the set off. Dr. Kutnik would arrange Shapely's release from prison as an AIDS research volunteer under Federal law. The Sharman Group's project would be hindered by fundamentalist Christians objecting to the injection of "HIV-tainted" blood into the systems of terminally ill AIDS patients. As the project foundered, Kutnik would uncover clinical data suggesting that unprotected sex with Shapely had apparently reversed the symptoms of several of her patients. There would be Kutnik's impassioned resignation, the flight to Brazil with the baffled Shapely, lavish funding against a backdrop of impending civil war, and what could only be described as an extremely pragmatic climate for research.

But it was such a sad story.

Better to sit here by candlelight, elbows on the edge of Skinner's table, listening for the song of the central pier.

25

without

a paddle

He kept saying he was from Tennessee and he didn't *need* this shit. She kept thinking she was going to die, the way he was driving, or anyway those cops would be after them, or the one who shot Sammy. She still didn't know what had happened, and wasn't that Nigel who'd plowed into that tight-faced one?

But he'd hung this right off Bryant, so she told him left on Folsom, because if the assholes were coming, she figured she wanted the Haight, best place she knew to get lost, and that was definitely what she intended to do, earliest opportunity. And this Ford was just like the one Mr. Matthews drove, ran the holding facility up in Beaverton. And she'd tried to stab somebody with a screwdriver. She'd never done anything like that in her life before. And she'd wrecked that black guy's computer, the one with the haircut. And this bracelet on her left wrist, the other half flipping around, open, on three links of chain—

He reached over and grabbed the loose cuff. Did something to it without taking his eyes off the street. He let go. Now it was locked shut.

"Why'd you do that?"

"So you don't snag it on something, wind up cuffed to the door-handle or a street sign—"

"Take it off."

"No key."

She rattled it at him. "Take it off."

"Stick it up the sleeve of your jacket. Those are Beretta cuffs. Real good cuffs." He sounded like he was sort of happy to have something to talk about, and his driving had evened out. Brown eyes. Not old; twenties, maybe. Cheap clothes like K-Mart stuff, all wet. Light brown hair cut too short but not short enough. She watched a muscle in his jaw work, like he was chewing gum, but he wasn't.

"Where we going?" she asked him.

"Fuck if I know," he said, gunning the engine a little. "You the one said 'left'..."

"Who are you?"

He glanced over at her. "Rydell. Berry Rydell."

"Barry?"

"Berry. Like straw. Like dingle. Hey, this a *big* fucking street, lights and everything—"

"Right."

"So where should I—"

"Right!"

"Okay," he said, and hung it. "Why?"

"The Haight. Lots of people up late, cops don't like to go there..."

"Ditch this car there?"

"Turn your back on it two seconds, it's history."

"They got ATM's there?"

"Uh-uh."

"Well, here's one..." Up over a curb, hunks of crazed safety-glass falling out of the frame where the back window had been. She hadn't even noticed that.

He dug a soggy-looking wallet out of his back pocket and started pulling cards out of it. Three of them. "I have to try to get some cash," he said. He looked at her. "You wanna jump out of this car and run," he shrugged, "then you just go for it." Then he reached in his jacket pocket and pulled out the glasses and Codes's phone that she'd scooped when the lights went out in Dissidents. Because she knew from Lowell that people in trouble need a phone, most times worse than anything. He dropped them in her lap, the asshole's glasses and the phone. "Yours."

Then he got out, walked over to the ATM, and started feeding it cards. She sat there, watching it emerge from its armor, the way they do, shy and cautious, its cameras coming out, too, to monitor the transaction. He stood there, drumming his fingers on the side, his mouth like he was whistling but he wasn't making any noise. She looked down at the case and the phone and wondered why she didn't just jump out and run, like he said.

Finally he came back, thumb-counting a fold of bills, stuck it down in his front jeans pocket, and got in. He sailed the first of his cards out the open window at the ATM, which was pulling back into its shell like a crab. "Don't know how they cancelled that one so quick, after you put that thing through Freddie's laptop." Flicked another. Then the last one. They lay in front of the ATM as its lexan shield came trundling down, their little holograms winking up in the machine's halogen floods.

"Somebody'll get those," she said.

"Hope so," he said, "hope they get 'em and go to Mars." Then he did something in reverse with all four wheels and the Ford sort of jumped up and backward, into the street, some other car swerving past them all brakes and horn and the driver's mouth a black O, and the part of her that was still a messenger sort of liked it. All the times they'd cut her off. "Shit," he said, jamming the gear-thing around until he got what he needed and they took off.

The handcuff was rubbing on the rash where the red worm had been. "You a cop?"

"No."

"Security? Like from the hotel?"

"Uh-uh."

"Well," she said, "what are you?"

Streetlight sliding across his face. Seemed like he was thinking about it. "Up shit creek. Without a paddle."

colored

people

The first thing Rydell saw when he got out of the Patriot, in the alley off Haight Street, was a one-armed, one-legged man on a skateboard. This man lay on his stomach, on the board, and propelled himself along with a curious hitching motion that reminded Rydell of the limbs of a gigged frog. He had his right arm and his left leg, which at least allowed for some kind of symmetry, but there was no foot on the leg. His face, as if by some weird osmosis, was the color of dirty concrete, and Rydell couldn't have said what race he was. His hair, if he had any, was covered by a black knit cap, and the rest of him was sheathed in a black, one-piece garment apparently stitched from sections of heavy-duty rubber inner-tube. He looked up, as he hitched past Rydell, through puddles left by the storm, headed for the mouth of the alley, and said, or Rydell thought he said: "You wanna *talk* to me? You wanna *talk* to me, you better shut your fuckin' *mouth*..."

Rydell stood there, Samsonite dangling, and watched him go.

Then something rattled beside him. The hardware on Chevette Washington's leather jacket. "Come on," she said, "don't wanna hang around back in here."

"You see that?" Rydell asked, gesturing with his suitcase.

"You hang around back in here, you'll see worse than that," she said.

Rydell looked back at the Patriot. He'd locked it and left the key under the driver's seat, because he hadn't wanted to make it look too easy, but he'd forgotten about that back window. He'd never been in the position before of actively wanting a car to be stolen.

"You sure somebody'll take that?" he asked her.

"We don't get out of here, they'll take us with it." She started walking. Rydell followed. There was stuff painted on the brick walls as high as anyone could reach, but it didn't look like any language he'd ever seen, except maybe the way they wrote cuss-words in a printed cartoon.

They'd just rounded the corner, onto the sidewalk, when Rydell heard the Patriot's engine start to rev. It gave him goosebumps, like something in a ghost story, because there hadn't been anybody back in there at all, and now he couldn't see the skateboard man anywhere.

"Look at the ground," Chevette Washington said. "Don't look up when they go by or they'll kill us..."

Rydell concentrated on the toes of his black SWATs. "You hang out with car-thieves much?"

"Just *walk*. Don't talk. Don't look."

He heard the Patriot wheel out of the alley and draw up beside them, pacing them. His toes were making little squelching noises, each time he took a step, and what if the last thing you knew before you died was just some pathetic discomfort like that, like your shoes were soaked and your socks were wet, and you weren't ever going to get to change them?

Rydell heard the Patriot take off, the driver fighting the unfamiliar American shift-pattern. He started to look up.

"Don't," she said.

"Those friends of yours or what?"

"Alley pirates, Lowell calls 'em."

"Who's Lowell?"

"You saw him in Dissidents."

"That bar?"

"Not a bar. A chill."

"Serves alcohol," Rydell said.

"A chill. Where you hang."

" 'You' who? This Lowell, he hang there?"

"Yeah."

"You too?"

"No," she said, angry.

"He your friend, Lowell? Your boyfriend?"

"You said you weren't a cop. You *talk* like one."

"I'm not," he said. "You can ask 'em."

"He's just somebody I used to know," she said.

"Fine."

She looked at the Samsonite. "You got a gun or something, in there?"

"Dry socks. Underwear."

She looked up at him. "I don't get you."

"Don't have to," he said. "We just walking, or you maybe know somewhere to go? Like off this street?"

"We want to look at some flash," she said to the fat man. He had a couple of things through each nipple, looked like Yale locks. Kind of pulled him down, there, and Rydell just couldn't look at them. Had on some kind of baggy white pants with the crotch down about where the knees should've been, and this little blue velvet vest all embroidered with gold. He was big and soft and fat and covered with tattoos.

Rydell's uncle, the one who'd gone to Africa with the army and hadn't come back, had had a couple of tattoos. The best one went right across his back, this big swirly dragon with horns and sort of a goofy grin. He'd gotten that one in Korea, eight colors and it had all been done by a computer. He'd told Rydell how the computer had mapped his back and showed him exactly what it was going to look like when it was done. Then he had to lie down on this table while this robot put the tattoo on. Rydell had imagined a robot kind of like a vacuum-cleaner, but with twisty chrome arms had needles on the end. But his uncle said it was more like being fed through a dot-matrix printer, and he'd had to go back eight times, one time for each color. It was a great dragon, though, and lots brighter than the tattoos on his uncle's arms, which were American eagles and a Harley trademark. When his uncle worked out in the backyard with Rydell's set of Sears weights, Rydell would watch the dragon ripple.

This fat bald guy with the weights through his nipples had tattoos everywhere except his hands and his head. Looked like he was wearing a suit of them. They were all different, no American eagles or Harley trademarks either, and they sort of ran together. They made Rydell feel kind of dizzy, so he looked up at the walls, which were covered with more tattoos, like samples for you to pick from.

"You've been here *before*," the man said.

"Yeah," Chevette Washington said, "with Lowell. You remember Lowell?"

The fat man shrugged.

"My friend and I," she said, "we wanna pick something out..."

"I haven't seen your *friend* before," the fat man said, perfectly nice about it but Rydell could hear the question in his voice. He was looking at Rydell's suitcase.

"It's okay," she said. "He knows Lowell. He's a 'Land boy, too."

"You *bridge* people," the fat man said, like he liked bridge people. "That storm was just *terrible*, wasn't it? I hope it didn't do you people too much *damage*... We had a client last month brought in a wide-angle Cibachrome he wanted done as a *back-piece*. Your whole suspension span and *everything* on it. *Beautiful* shot but he wanted it inked just that size, and he just wasn't *broad* enough..." He looked up at Rydell. "Would've *fit*, on your friend here..."

"Couldn't he get it?" she asked, and Rydell caught that instinct to keep people talking, keep them involved.

"We're a *full-service* shop here at Colored People," the fat man said. "Lloyd put it on a graphics engine, *rotated* it thirty degrees, *heightened* the perspective, and it's *gorgeous*...Now, were you interested in seeing some flash for *yourself*, or for your big *friend* here?"

"Uh, actually," Chevette said, "we're looking for something for both of us. Like, uh, matching, you know?"

The fat man smiled. "That's *romantic*..."

Rydell looked at her.

"Just come *this* way." The fat man sort of jingled when he walked, and it made Rydell wince. "May I bring you some complimentary *tea*?"

"Coffee?" Rydell asked hopefully.

"I'm *sorry*," the fat man said, "but Butch *left* at twelve and I don't know how to operate the *machine*. But I can bring you some nice *tea*."

"Yeah," Chevette said, urging Rydell along with little elbow-jabs, "tea."

The fat man took them down a hallway and into a little room with a couple of wallscreens and a leather sofa. "I'll just get your *tea*," he said, and shuffled out, jingling.

"Why'd you say that, about matching tattoos?" Rydell was looking around the room. Clean. Blank walls. Soft light but no shadows.

"Because he'll leave us alone while we're trying to pick one, and 'cause it'll take us so long to make up our minds."

Rydell put his Samsonite down and sat on the couch. "So we can stay here?"

"Yeah, as long as we keep calling up flash."

"What's that?"

She picked up a little remote and turned one of the wallscreens on. Started blipping through menus. Hi-rez close-ups of tattooed skin. The fat man came back with a couple of big rough mugs of steaming tea on a little tray. "Yours is *green*," he said to Chevette Washington, "and *yours* is Mormon," he said to Rydell, "because you *did* ask for coffee..."

"Um, thanks," Rydell said, taking the mug he was offered.

"Now you two take plenty of *time*," the fat man said, "and you *want* anything, just call." He went out, tray tucked under his arm, and closed the door behind him.

"Mormon?" Rydell sniffed at the tea. It didn't smell much of anything.

"Aren't supposed to drink coffee. That kind of tea's got ephedrine in it."

"Got drugs in it?"

"It's made from a plant with something that'll keep you awake. Like coffee."

Rydell decided it was too hot to drink now anyway. Put it down on the floor beside the couch. The girl on the wallscreen had a dragon sort of like his uncle's, but on her left hip. Little tiny silver ring through the top edge of her belly button. Chevette Washington flipped it to a big sweaty biker-arm with President Millbank's face looking out from it in shades of gray.

Rydell struggled out of his damp jacket, noticing the ripped shoulder, the cheap white stuffing popping out. He dropped it behind the couch. "You got any tattoos?"

"No," she said.

"So how come you know about this?"

"Lowell," she said, flipping through half a dozen more images, "he's got a Giger."

" 'Giger'?" Rydell opened his Samsonite, got out a pair of socks, and started unlacing his SWAT shoes.

"This painter. Like nineteenth-century or something. Real classical. Bio-mech. Lowell's got this Giger back-piece done off a painting called 'N.Y.C. XXIV.' " She said it *x, x, i, v.* "It's like this city. Shaded black-work. But he wants sleeves to go with it, so we'd come in here to look for more Gigers to match it."

"Why don't you sit down," Rydell said, "you're making my neck hurt." She was pacing back and forth in front of the screens. He took his wet socks off, put them in the Container City bag, and put the dry ones on. Thought about leaving his shoes off for a while, but what if he had to leave in a hurry? He put them back on. He was lacing them up when she sat down beside him.

She unzipped her jacket and shrugged it off, the loose Beretta cuff rattling. The sleeves of her plain black t-shirt had been scissored off and her upper arms were smooth and pale. She reached over the end of the couch and put the jacket down, sort of propped against the wall, the leather stiff enough that it just stayed there, its arms slumped down, like it was asleep. Like Rydell wished he could be. Now she had the remote in her hand.

"Hey," Rydell said, "that guy in the raincoat back there, the one shot—" He was about to say the big longhair on the bicycle, but she grabbed his wrist, the handcuff rattling.

"Sammy. He shot Sammy, up at Skinner's. He . . . He was after the glasses, and Sammy had them, and—"

"Wait. Wait a sec. The glasses. Everybody wants the glasses. That guy wants 'em, Warbaby wants 'em . . ."

"Who's Warbaby?"

"The big black man shot the back window out of his car I was stealing. That Warbaby."

"You think *I* know what they are?"

"You don't know why people are *after* them?"

She gave him a look like you might give a dog that had just told you it was a good day to spend all your money on one particular kind of lottery ticket.

"Let's start over," Rydell suggested. "You tell me where you *got* the glasses."

"Why should I?"

He thought about it. "Because you'd be dead by now if I hadn't done the kind of dirt-stupid *shit* I just did, back there."

She thought about that. "Okay," she said.

Maybe there really was something in the fat man's Mormon tea, or maybe Rydell had just crossed over into that point of tiredness where it all flipped around for a while and you started to feel like you were more awake, some ways, than you usually ever were. But he wound up sipping that tea and listening to her, and when she'd get too deep into her story to remember to keep flipping the tattoo-pictures on the wallscreen, he'd do it for her.

When you worked it around to sequential order, she was this girl from Oregon, didn't have any family, who'd come down here and moved out on that bridge with this old man, crazy by the sound of it, had a bad hip and needed somebody around to help him. Then she'd gotten her a job riding a bicycle around San Francisco, delivering messages. Rydell knew about messengers from his foot-patrol period in downtown Knoxville, because you had to keep ticketing them for riding on the sidewalk, traffic violation, and they'd give you a hard time about it. But they made pretty good money if they worked at it. This Sammy she'd said was shot, murdered, he was another messenger, a black guy who'd gotten her on at Allied, where she worked.

And her story of how she'd taken the glasses out of the guy's pocket at this big drunk party she'd wandered into up in the Morrisey, that made as much sense to him as anything. And it wasn't the kind of story people made up. Not like the glasses crawled into her hand or anything, she just flat-out stole them, impulse, just because the guy was in her face and obnoxious. Nuisance crime, except they'd turned out to be valuable.

But from her description he knew her asshole up in the Morrisey had been the same one got himself the Cuban necktie, your German-born Costa Rican citizen who maybe wasn't either, star of that X-rated fax of Warbaby's and the one Svobodov and Orlovsky had been investigating. If they had been.

"Shit," he said, in the middle of something she was trying to tell him.

"What?"

"Nothing. Keep talking..."

The Russians were bent, and he knew that. They were Homicide, they were bent, and he'd bet dollars to donuts they weren't even investigating the case. They could talk Warbaby's way onto the crime-scene, tap their department's computer, but the rest of it had just been window-dressing, for him, for Rydell, the hired help. And what was that that Freddie had said, about DatAmerica and IntenSecure being basically your same company?

But Chevette Washington was on a roll of her own now, like sometimes when people get started talking they just let it all hang out, and she was saying how Lowell, who was the one with the hair and not the skinhead, and who actually had, sort of, been her boyfriend for a while, was a guy who could (you know?) get things done with computers, if you had the money, and that sort of scared her because he was always talking about the cops and how he didn't have to worry about them.

Rydell nodded, automatically flipping through a couple more pictures of tattoos—lady there with these pink carnations sort of followed her bikini-line—but really he was listening to something going around in his own head. Like Hernandez was IntenSecure, the Morisey was IntenSecure, Warbaby was IntenSecure, Freddie said DatAmerica and IntenSecure were like the same thing—

"—Desire . . ."

Rydell blinked. Skinny guy there with J. D. Shapely all mournful on his chest. But you'd be mournful, too, you had chest hair growing out your eyes. "What?"

"Republic. Republic of Desire."

"What is?"

"Why Lowell says the cops won't ever bother him, but I told him he was full of shit."

"Hackers," Rydell said.

"You haven't heard a word I said."

"No," Rydell said, "no, that's not true. Desire. Republic of. Run that one by again, okay?"

She took the remote, blipped through a shaven head with a sun at the very top, planets orbiting down to the top of the ears, a hand with a screaming mouth on the palm, feet covered with blue-green creature-scales. "I *said*," she said, "Lowell bullshits about that, how he's connected up with this Republic of Desire, how they can do anything they feel like with computers, so anybody messes with him is gonna get it."

"No shit," Rydell said. "You ever see these guys?"

"You don't *see* them," she said, "not like *live*. You *talk* to them, on the phone. Or like with goggles, and that's the wildest."

"Why?"

" 'Cause they look like *lobsters* and shit. Or some tv star. Anything. But I don't know why I'm telling you."

"Because I'll nod out otherwise, then how're we gonna decide if we're getting the creature-feet or the crotch-carnations?"

"It's your turn," she said, and just sat there until he started talking.

He told her how he was from Knoxville and about getting into the Academy, about how he'd always watched *Cops in Trouble* and then when he'd been a cop and gotten in trouble, it had looked like he was going to be on the show. How they'd brought him out to Los Angeles because they didn't want Adult Survivors of Satanism stealing their momentum, but then the Pookey Bear murders had come along and they'd sort of lost interest, and he'd had to get on with IntenSecure and drive Gunhead. He told her about Sublett and living with Kevin Tarkovsky in the house in Mar Vista, and sort of skipped over the Republic of Desire and the night he'd driven Gunhead into the Schonbrunn's place in Benedict Canyon. About how Hernandez had come over, just the other morning but it seemed like years, to tell him he could come up here and drive for this Mr. Warbaby. Then she wanted to know what it was that skip tracers did, so he explained what it was they were supposed to do, and what it was he figured they probably *did* do, and she said they sounded like bad news.

When he was done, she just looked at him. "That's it? That's how you got here and what you're doing?"

"Yeah," he said, "guess it is."

"Jesus," she said. Sort of shook her head. They both watched a couple of full body-suits blip past, one of them all circuit-patterns, like they stenciled on old-fashioned circuit-boards. "You got eyes," she said, and yawned in the middle of it, "like two piss-holes in a snowbank."

There was a knock at the door. It opened a crack, and somebody, not the man who jingled when he walked, said: "You having any luck picking a design? Henry's gone home..."

"Well it's just so hard to decide," Chevette Washington said, "there's so many of them and we want to get just the right one."

"That's fine," said the voice, bored. "You just go right on looking." The door closed.

"Let me see those glasses," Rydell said.

She reached over and got her jacket. Got out the case with the glasses, the phone. Handed him the glasses. The case was made out of some dark stuff, thin as eggshell, rigid as steel. He opened it. The glasses looked exactly like Warbaby's. Big black frames, the lenses black now. They had a funny heft to them, weighed more than you thought they would.

Chevette Washington had flipped open the phone's keypad.

"Hey," Rydell said, touching her hand, "they'll have your number for sure. You dial out on that, or even take a call, they'll be in here in about ten minutes."

"Won't have this number," she said. "It's one of Codes's phones. I took it off the table when the lights went out."

"Thought you said you didn't just steal things."

"Well," she said, "if Codes had it, it's stolen already. Codes trades 'em off people in the city, then Lowell gets somebody to tumble 'em, change the numbers." She tapped the pad, held the little phone to her ear. "Dead," she said, shrugging.

"Here," Rydell said, putting the glasses down on his lap and taking the phone. "Maybe it got wet, or the battery's knocked loose. What's old Codes trade for these, anyway?" He ran his thumbnail around the back of the phone, looking for the place where you could pry it open.

"Well," she said, "stuff."

He popped the case. Saw a tightly rolled mini-Ziploc wedged

in there beside the battery. It had pushed the contacts out of align-
ment. He took it out and unrolled it. "Stuff?"

"Uh-huh."

"This type of stuff."

"Uh-huh."

He looked at her. "If this is 4-Thiobuscaline, it's a controlled
substance."

She looked at the bag of grayish powder, then at him. "But
you aren't a cop anymore."

"You don't do this stuff, do you?"

"No. Well, once or twice. Lowell did, sometimes."

"Well, just don't do any around me, because I've seen what
it does. Nice normal people do a couple of hits of this, they go snake-
shit crazy." He tapped the bag. "Enough in this to get half a dozen
people fucked up like you wouldn't believe." He handed it to her and
picked up the phone, trying to get the battery back where it belonged.

"I'd believe it," she said. "I saw what it did to Lowell . . . "

"Dial tone," he said. "Who you want to call?"

Thought about it, then she took the phone and flipped it shut.
"Guess there isn't anybody."

"That old man have a phone?"

"No," she said, and her shoulders hunched. "I'm scared they
killed him, too. 'Cause of me . . ."

Rydell couldn't think of anything to say to that. He was too
tired to flick the remote. Some guy's arm with a furled Confederate
flag on it. Just like home. He looked at her. She sure didn't look
anywhere near as tired as he was. That could just be being young,
he thought. He sure hoped she wasn't on any ice or dancer or anything. Maybe she was in some kind of shock, still. Said this Sammy
had been killed, two others she was worried about. Evidently she'd
known the guy plowed in Svobodov on that bicycle, but she didn't
know yet that he'd been shot. Funny what you miss seeing in a fight.
Well, he didn't see any reason to tell her, not right now.

"I'll try Fontaine," she said, opening the phone again.

"Who?"

"He does Skinner's electricity and stuff." She dialled a number, put the phone to her ear.

His eyes closed and his head hit the back of the couch so hard it almost woke him up.

27

after

the storm

S mells like piss," Skinner said, accusingly, waking Yamazaki from a dream in which he stood beside J. D. Shapely on a
great dark plane, before a black and endless wall inscribed with the
names of the dead.

Yamazaki raised his head from the table. The room in darkness. Light through the church window.

"What are you doing here, Scooter?"

Yamazaki's buttocks and lower back ached. "The storm," he
said, still half in his dream.

"What storm? Where's the girl?"

"Gone," Yamazaki said. "Don't you remember? Loveless?"

"What are you talking about?" Skinner struggled up on one
elbow, kicking off the blankets and the sleeping-bag back, his gray-
stubbled face twisted with disgust. "Need a bath. Dry clothes."

"Loveless. He found me in a bar. He made me bring him
here. I think he must have followed me, earlier, when I left you—"

"Sure. Shut up, Scooter, okay?"

Yamazaki closed his mouth.

"Now we need a bunch of water. Hot. First for coffee, then
some so I can wash off. You know how to work a Coleman stove?"

"A what?"

"Green thing over there, red tank on the front. You go jiggle
that tank off, I'll tell you how to pump it up."

Yamazaki stood up, wincing at the pain in his back, and stumbled toward the green-painted metal box Skinner was pointing at.

"Gone off fucking that no-ass greaseball boyfriend of hers again. Useless, Scooter..."

He stood on Skinner's roof, pantlegs flapping in a breeze that gave no hint of last night's storm, looking out at the city washed in a strange iron light, shreds of his dream still circling dimly... Shapely had spoken to him, his voice the voice of the young Elvis Presley. He said that he had forgiven his killers.

Yamazaki stared at Transamerica's upright thorn, bandaged with the brace they'd applied after the Little Grande, half-hearing the dreamed voice. *They just didn't know any better, Scooter.*

Skinner cursing, below, as he sponged himself with water Yamazaki had warmed on the Coleman stove.

Yamazaki thought of his thesis advisor in Osaka.

"I don't care," Yamasaki said, in English, San Francisco his witness.

The whole city was a Thomasson. Perhaps America itself was a Thomasson.

How could they understand this in Osaka, in Tokyo?

"Yo! On the roof!" someone called.

Yamazaki turned, saw a thin black man atop the tangle of girders that braced the upper end of Skinner's lift. He wore a thick tweed overcoat and a crocheted cap.

"You okay up there? How 'bout Skinner?"

Yamazaki hesitated, remembering Loveless. If Skinner or the girl had enemies, how could he recognize them?

"Name's Fontaine," the man said. "Chevette called me, told me to get over here and see if Skinner got through the blow all right. I take care of the wiring up here, make sure his lift's running and all."

"He's bathing now," Yamazaki said. "In the storm, he became ... confused. He doesn't seem to remember."

"Have some power for you in about another half an hour," the man said. "Wish I could say the same for over my end. Lost four transformers. Got us five dead bodies, twenty injured that I know of. Skinner got coffee on?"

"Yes," Yamazaki said.

"Do with a cup about now."

"Yes, please," Yamazaki said, and bowed. The black man smiled. Yamazaki scrambled down through the hatch. "Skinner-san! A man named Fontaine, he is your friend?"

Skinner was struggling into yellowed thermal underwear. "Useless bastard. Still don't have any power..."

Yamazaki unlatched the hatch in the floor and hauled it open. Fontaine eventually appeared at the bottom of the ladder, a battered canvas tool-bag in either hand. Putting one down and slinging the other over his shoulder, he began to climb.

Yamazaki poured the remaining coffee into the cleanest cup.

"Fuel-cell's buggered," Skinner said, as Fontaine pushed his bag ahead of him, through the opening. Skinner was layered now in at least three threadbare flannel shirts, their tails pushed unevenly into the waistband of an ancient pair of woolen Army trousers.

"We're working on it, boss," Fontaine said, standing up and smoothing his overcoat. "Had us a big old storm here."

"What Scooter says," Skinner said.

"Well, he's not shittin' you, Skinner. Thanks." Fontaine accepted the steaming cup of black coffee and blew on it. He looked at Yamazaki. "Chevette said she might not get back here for a while. Know anything about that?"

Yamazaki looked at Skinner.

"Useless," Skinner said. "Gone off with that shithead again."

"Didn't say anything about that," Fontaine said. "Didn't say much at all. But if she's not going to be around, you're going to need somebody take care of things for you."

"Take care of myself," Skinner said.

"I know that, boss," Fontaine assured, "but we got a couple of fried servos in your lift down there. Take a few days get that going for you, the kind of backlog we're looking at. Need you somebody go up and down the rungs. Bring you food and all."

"Scooter can do it," Skinner said.

Yamazaki blinked.

"That right?" Fontaine raised his eyebrows at Yamazaki. "You stay up here and take care of Mr. Skinner?"

Yamazaki thought of his borrowed flat in the tall Victorian house, its black marble bathroom larger than his bachelor apartment in Osaka. He looked from Fontaine to Skinner, then back. "I would be honored, to stay with Skinner-san, if he wishes."

"Do what you like," Skinner said, and began laboriously stripping the sheets from his mattress.

"Chevette told me you might be up here," Fontaine said. "Some kind of university guy..." He put his cup down on the table, bent to swing his tool-bag up beside it. "Said maybe you people worried about uninvited guests." He undid the bag's two buckles and opened it. Tools gleamed there, rolls of insulated wire. He took out something wrapped in an oily rag, looked to see that Skinner wasn't observing him, and tucked the thing behind the glass jars on the shelf above the table.

"We can pretty much make sure nobody you don't know will get up here for the next couple days," he said to Yamazaki, lowering his voice. "But that's a .38 Special, six rounds of hollow-point. You use it, do me a big favor and toss it off the side, okay? It's of, uh," Fontaine grinned, " 'dubious provenance.' "

Yamazaki thought of Loveless. Swallowed.

"You gonna be okay up here?" Fontaine asked.

"Yes," Yamazaki said, "yes, thank you."

It was ten-thirty before they finally had to hit the street, and then only because Laurie, who Chevette knew from that first day she'd ever come in here, said that the manager, Benny Singh, was going to be showing up and they couldn't stay in there anymore, particularly not with her friend asleep like that, like he was passed out or something. Chevette said she understood, and thanked her.

"You see Sammy Sal," Laurie said, "you say hi for me."

Chevette nodded, sad, and started shaking the guy's shoulder. He grunted and tried to brush her hand away. "Wake up. We gotta go."

She couldn't believe she'd told him all that stuff, but she'd just had to tell somebody or she'd go crazy. Not that telling it had made it make any more sense than it did before, and with this Rydell's side of it added on, it sort of made even less. The news that somebody had gone and murdered the asshole just didn't seem real, but if it was, she supposed, she was in deeper shit than ever.

"Wake up!"

"Jesus . . ." He sat up, knuckling his eyes.

"We gotta go. Manager'll be in soon. My friend let you sleep a while."

"Go where?"

Chevette had been thinking about that. "Cole, over by the Panhandle, there's places rent rooms by the hour."

"Hotels?"

"Not exactly," she said. "For people just need the bed for a little while."

He dug behind the couch for his jacket. "Look at that," he said, sticking his fingers into the rip in the shoulder. "Brand new last night."

<hr>

Neighborhoods that mainly operated at night had a way of looking a lot worse in the morning. Even the beggars looked worse off this time of day, like that guy there with those sores, the one trying to sell half a can of spaghetti sauce. She stepped around him. Another block or two and they'd start to hit the early crowd of day-trippers headed for Skywalker Park; more cover in the crowd but more cops, too. She tried to remember if Skywalker's rentacops were IntenSecure, that company Rydell talked about.

She wondered if Fontaine had gone to Skinner's like he'd said he would. She hadn't wanted to say too much over the phone, so at first she'd just said she was going away for a while, and would Fontaine go over and see how Skinner was doing, and maybe this Japanese student guy who'd been hanging around lately. But Fontaine could tell she sounded worried, so he'd sort of pushed her about it, and she'd told him she was worried about Skinner, how maybe there were some people gonna go up there and hassle him.

"You don't mean bridge people," he'd said, and she'd said no, she didn't, but that was all she could say about it. The line went quiet for a few seconds and she could hear one of Fontaine's kids singing in the background, one of those African songs with the weird throat-clicks. "Okay," Fontaine finally said, "I'll look into that for you." And Chevette said thanks, fast, and clicked off. Fontaine did a lot of favors for Skinner. He'd never talked to Chevette about it, but he seemed to have known Skinner all his life, or anyway as long as he'd been on the bridge. There were a lot of people like that, and Chevette knew Fontaine could fix it so people would watch the tower there, and the lift. Watch for strangers. People did that for each other, on the bridge, and Fontaine was always owed a lot of favors, because he was one of the main electricity men.

Now they were walking past this bagel place had a sort of iron cage outside, welded out of junk, where you could sit in there at little tables and have coffee and eat bagels, and the smell of the morning's baking about made her faint from hunger. She was thinking maybe they'd better go in there and get a dozen in a bag, maybe some cream cheese, take it with them, when Rydell put his hand on her shoulder.

She turned her head and saw this big shiny white RV had just turned onto Haight in front of them, headed their way. Like you'd see rich old people driving back in Oregon, whole convoys of them, pulling boats on trailers, little jeeps, motorcycles hanging off the backs like lifeboats. They'd stop for the night in these special camps had razor-wire around them, dogs, NO TRESSPASSING signs that really meant it.

Rydell was staring at this RV like he couldn't believe it, and now it was pulling up right beside them, this gray-haired old lady powering down the window and leaning out the driver's side, saying "Young man! Excuse me, but I'm Danica Elliott and I believe we met yesterday on the plane from Burbank."

Danica Elliott was this retired lady from Altadena, that was down in SoCal, and she'd flown up to San Francisco, she said on the same plane as Rydell, to get her husband moved to a different cryogenic facility. Well, not her husband, exactly, but his brain, which he'd had frozen when he died.

Chevette had heard about people doing that, but she hadn't ever understood why they did it, and evidently Danica Elliott didn't understand it either. But she'd come up here to throw good money after bad, she said, and get her husband David's brain moved to this more expensive place that would keep it on ice in its own private little tank, and not just tumbling around in a big tank with a bunch of other people's frozen brains, which was where it had been before.

She seemed like a really nice lady to Chevette, but she sure could go on about this stuff, so that after a while Rydell was just driving and nodding his head like he was listening, and Chevette, who was navigating, was mostly paying attention to the map-display on the RV's dash, plus keeping a lookout for police cars.

Mrs. Elliott had taken care of getting her husband's brain relocated the night before, and she said it had made her kind of emotional, so she'd decided to rent this RV and drive it back to Altadena, just take her time and enjoy the trip. Trouble was, she didn't know San Francisco, and she'd picked it up that morning at this rental place on sixth and gotten lost looking for a freeway. Wound up driving around in the Haight, which she said did not look at all like a safe neighborhood but was certainly very interesting.

The loose handcuff kept falling out of the sleeve of Skinner's jacket, but Mrs. Elliott was too busy talking to notice. Rydell was driving, Chevette was in the middle, and Mrs. Elliot was on the passenger side. The RV was Japanese, and had these three power-adjustable buckets up front, with headrests with speakers built in.

Mrs. Elliot had told Rydell she was lost and did he know the city and could he drive her to where she could get on the highway to Los Angeles? Rydell had sort of gawked at her for a minute, then shook himself and said he'd be glad to, and this was his friend Chevette, who knew the city, and he was Berry Rydell.

Mrs. Elliot said Chevette was a pretty name.

So here they were, headed out of San Francisco, and Chevette had a pretty good idea that Rydell was going to try to talk Mrs. Elliott into letting them go along with her. That was all she could think of to do, herself, and here they were off the street and headed away from the guy who'd shot Sammy and from that Warbaby and those Russian cops, which seemed like a good idea to her, and aside from her stomach feeling like it was starting to eat itself, she felt a little better.

Rydell drove past an In-and-Out Burger place and she remembered how this boy she knew called Franklin, up in Oregon, had taken a pellet-gun over to an In-and-Out and shot out the *B* and the

R, so it just said IN-AND-OUT URGE. She'd told Lowell about that, but he hadn't thought it was funny. Now she thought about how she'd told Rydell stuff about Lowell that Lowell would go ballistic if he ever found out about, and here Rydell was the next thing to a cop. But it bothered her how Lowell had been, the night before. There he was, all cool and heavy with his connections and everything, and she tells him she's in trouble and somebody's just shot Sammy Sal and they're gonna be after her for sure, and him and Codes just sit there, giving each other these looks, like they like this story less by the minute, and then the big motherfucker cop in the raincoat walks in and they're about to shit themselves.

Served her right. She hadn't had a single friend liked Lowell much, and Skinner had hated him on sight. Said Lowell had his head so far up his ass, he might as well just climb in after it and disappear. But she just hadn't ever really had a boyfriend before, not like that, and he'd been so nice to her at first. If he just hadn't started in doing that dancer, because that brought the asshole out in him real fast, and then Codes, who hadn't ever liked her, could get him going about how she was just a country girl. Fuck that.

"You know," she said, "I don't get something to eat soon, I think I'll die."

And Mrs. Elliott started making a fuss about how Rydell should stop immediately and get something for Chevette, and how sorry she was she hadn't thought to ask if they'd had breakfast.

"Well," Rydell said, frowning into the rear-view, "I really would like to miss the, uh, lunch-hour traffic here..."

"Oh," Mrs. Elliott said. Then she brightened. "Chevette, dear, if you'll just go in the back, you'll find a fridge there. I'm sure the rental people have put a snack basket in there. They almost always do."

Sounded fine to Chevette. She undid her harness and edged back between her seat and Mrs. Elliott's. There was a little door there and when she went through it the lights came on. "Hey," she said, "it's a whole little house back here..."

"Enjoy!" said Mrs. Elliott.

The light stayed on when she closed the door behind her. She hadn't ever seen the inside of one of these things before, and the first thing she thought of was that it had nearly as much space as Skinner's room, plus it was about ten times more comfortable. Everything was gray, gray carpet and gray plastic and gray imitation leather. And the fridge turned out to be this cute little thing built into a counter, with this basket in there, wrapped up in plastic with a ribbon on it. She got the plastic off and there was some wine, little cheeses, an apple, a pear, crackers, and a couple of chocolate bars. There was Coke in the fridge, too, and bottled water. She sat on the bed and ate a cheese, a bunch of crackers, a chocolate bar that was made in France, and drank a bottle of water. Then she tried out the tv, which had twenty-three channels on downlink.

When she was done, she put the empty bottle and the torn paper and stuff in a little wastebasket built into the wall, cut the tv off, took off her shoes, and lay back on the bed.

It was strange, to stretch out on a bed in a little room that was moving, she didn't know where, and she wondered where she'd be tomorrow.

Just before she fell asleep, she remembered that she still had Codes' bag of dancer stuck down in her pants. She'd better get rid of that. She figured there was enough there to go to jail for.

She thought about how it made you feel, and how weird it was that people spent all that money to feel that way.

She sure wished Lowell hadn't liked to feel that way.

———— • ———— • ———— • ————

She woke up when he lay down beside her, the RV moving but she knew it must've stopped before. The lights were off.

"Whose driving?" she said.

"Mrs. Armbruster."

"Who?"

"Mrs. Elliott. Mrs. Armbruster was this teacher I had, looked like her."

"Where's she driving to?"

"Los Angeles. Told her I'd take over when she got tired. Told her not to bother waking us up when she goes through at the state line. Lady like that, if she tells 'em she's not carrying any agricultural products, they'll probably let her through without checking back here."

"What if they do?"

He was close enough to her on the narrow bed that she could feel it when he shrugged.

"Rydell?"

"Huh?"

"How come there's Russian cops?"

"How do you mean?"

"You watch on tv, like a cop show, about half the big cops are always Russian. Or those guys back there on the bridge. How come Russian?"

"Well," he said, "they kind of exaggerate that on tv, 'cause of the Organizatsiya thing, how people like to see shows about that. But the truth is, you get a situation where there's Russians running most of your mob action, you'll want to get you some Russian cops..." She heard him yawn. Felt him stretch.

"Are they all like those two came to Dissidents?"

"No," he said. "There's always some crooked cops, but that's just the way it is..."

"What'll we do, when we get to Los Angeles?"

But he didn't answer, and after a while he started to snore.

29

dead

mall

Rydell opened his eyes.

Vehicle not moving.

He held his Timex up in front of his face and used the dial-light. 3:15 PM. Chevette Washington was curled up beside him in her biker jacket. Felt like sleeping next to a piece of old luggage.

He rolled over until he could find the shade over the window beside him and raise it a little. As dark out there as it was in here.

He'd been dreaming about Mrs. Armbruster's class, fifth grade at Oliver North Elementary. They were about to be let out because LearningNet said there was too much Kansas City flu around to keep the kids in Virginia and Tennessee in school that week. They were all wearing these molded white paper masks the nurses had left on their seats that morning. Mrs. Armbruster had just explained the meaning of the word *pandemic*. Poppy Markoff, who sat next to him and already had tits out to here, had told Mrs. Armbruster that her daddy said the KC flu could kill you in the time it took to walk out to the bus. Mrs. Armbruster, wearing her own mask, the micropore kind from the drugstore, started in about the word *panic*, tying that into *pandemic* because of the root, but that was where Rydell woke up.

He sat up on the bed. He had a headache and the start of a cold. Kansas City flu. Maybe Mokola fever.

"Don't panic," he said, under his breath.

But he sort of had this feeling.

He got up and felt his way to the front. A little bit of light there, coming from under the door. He found the handle. Eased it open a crack.

"Hey there." Gold at the edges of a smile. Square little automatic pointing at Rydell's eye. He'd swung the passenger-side bucket around and tilted it back. Had his boots up on the middle seat. Had the dome-light turned down low.

"Where's Mrs. Elliott?"

"Mrs. Elliott is gone."

Rydell opened the door the rest of the way. "She work for you?"

"No," the man said. "She's IntenSecure."

"They put her on that plane to keep track of me?"

The man shrugged. Rydell noticed that the gun didn't move at all when he did that. He was wearing surgical gloves, and that same long coat he'd had on when he'd gotten out of the Russians' car, like an Australian duster made out of black micropore.

"How'd she know to pick us up by that tattoo parlor?"

"Warbaby had to be good for something. He had a couple of people on you for backup."

"Didn't see anybody," Rydell said.

"Weren't supposed to."

"Tell me something," Rydell said. "You the one did that Blix guy, up in the hotel?"

The man looked at him over the barrel of the gun. That small a bore, ordinarily, wouldn't mean much damage, so Rydell figured the ammunition would be doctored some way. "I don't see what it's got to do with you," he said.

Rydell thought about it. "I saw a picture of it. You just don't look that crazy."

"It's my *job*," he said.

Uh-huh, Rydell thought, just like running a french-fry computer. There was a fridge and sink on the right side of the door, so he knew he couldn't move that way. If he went left, he figured the guy'd just stitch through the bulkhead, probably get the girl, too.

"Don't even think about it."

"About what?"

"The hero thing. The cop shit." He took his feet off the center bucket. "Just do this. Slowly. Very. Get into the driver's seat and put your hands on the wheel. Nine o'clock and two o'clock. Keep them there. If you don't keep them there, I'll shoot you behind your right ear. But you won't hear it." He had this kind of slow, even tone, reminded Rydell of a vet talking to a horse.

Rydell did like he was told. He couldn't see anything outside. Just dark, and the reflections from the dome light. "Where are we?" he asked.

"You like malls, Rydell? You got malls back in Knoxville?"

Rydell looked at him sideways.

"Eyes front, please."

"Yeah, we got malls."

"This one didn't do so well."

Rydell squeezed the foam padding on the wheel.

"Relax."

Rydell heard him give the bulkhead a kick with the heel of one boot. "Miss Washington! Rise and shine, Miss Washington! Do us the favor of your presence."

Rydell heard the double thump as she startled from sleep, tried to jump up, hit her head, fell off the bed. Then he saw her white face reflected in the windshield, there in the doorway. Saw her see the man, the gun.

Not the screaming kind. "You shot Sammy Sal," she said.

"You tried to electrocute me," the man said, like he could afford to see the humor in it now. "Come out here, turn around, and straddle the central console. Very slowly. That's right. Now lean forward and brace your hands on the seat."

She wound up next to Rydell, her legs on either side of the instrument console, facing backward. Like she was riding some cafe-racer.

Gave him about a two-inch difference of arc between shooting either one of them in the head.

"I want you to take your jacket off," he said to her, "so you'll have to take your hands off the seat to do that. See if you can manage to keep at least one hand on the seat at all times. Take plenty of time."

When she'd gotten it to where she could shrug it off her left shoulder, it fell over against the man's legs.

"Are there any hypodermic needles in here," he said, "any blades, dangerous objects of any kind?"

"No," she said.

"How about electrical charges? You don't have a great record for that."

"Just the asshole's glasses and a phone."

"See, Rydell," he said, " 'the asshole.' How he'll be remembered. Nameless. Another nameless asshole ..." He was going through the jacket's pockets with his free hand. Came up with the case and the phone and put them on the RV's deep, padded dashpanel. Rydell had his head turned now and was watching him, even though he'd been told not to. He watched the gloved hand open the case by feel, take out the black glasses. That was the only time those eyes left him, to check those glasses, and that took about a second.

"That's them," Rydell said. "You got 'em now."

The hand put them back in their case, closed it. "Yes."

"Now what?"

The smile went away. When it did, it looked like he didn't have any lips. Then it came back, wider and steeper.

"You think you could get me a Coke out of the fridge? All the windows, the door back there, are sealed."

"You want a *Coke*?" Like she didn't believe him. "You're gonna shoot me. When I get up."

"No," he said, "not necessarily. Because I want a Coke. My throat's a little dry."

She turned her head to look at Rydell, eyes big with fear.

"Get him his Coke," Rydell said.

She got off the console and edged through, into the back, there, but just by the door, where the fridge was.

"Look out the front," he reminded Rydell. Rydell saw the fridge-light come on, reflected there, caught a glimpse of her squatting down.

"D-diet or regular?" she said.

"Diet," he said, "please."

"Classic or decaf?"

"Classic." He made a little sound that Rydell thought might be a laugh.

"There's no glasses."

He made the sound again. "Can."

"K-kinda messy," she said, "m-my hand's shakin'—"

Rydell looked sideways, saw him take the red can, some brown cola dripping off the side. "Thank you. You can take your pants off now."

"What?"

"Those black ones you're wearing. Just peel them down, slow. But I like the socks. Say we'll keep the socks."

Rydell caught the expression on her face, reflected in the black windshield, then saw how it went sort of blank. She bent, working the tight pants down.

"Now get back on the console. That's right. Just like you were. Let me look at you. You want to look too, Rydell?"

Rydell turned, saw her squatting there, her bare legs smooth and muscular, dead white in the glow of the dome-light. The man took a long swallow of Coke, watching Rydell around the rim. He put the can down on the dash-panel and wiped his mouth with the back of his gloved hand. "Not bad, huh, Rydell?" with a nod toward Chevette Washington. "Some potential there, I'd say."

Rydell looked at him.

"Is this bothering you, Rydell?"

Rydell didn't answer.

The man made the sound that might've been a laugh. Drank

some Coke. "You think I enjoyed having to mess that shitbag up the way I did, Rydell?"

"I don't know."

"But you think I did. I know you think I enjoyed it. And I did, I *did* enjoy it. But you know what the difference is?"

"The difference?"

"I didn't have a hard on when I did it. That's the difference."

"Did you know him?"

"What?"

"I mean like was it personal, why you did that?"

"Oh, I guess you could say I knew him. I knew him. I knew him like you shouldn't have to know anyone, Rydell. I knew everything he did. I'd go to sleep, nights, listening to the sound of him breathing. It got so I could judge how many he'd had, just by his breathing."

"He'd had?"

"He drank. Serbian. You were a policeman, weren't you?"

"Yeah."

"Ever have to watch anybody, Rydell?"

"I never got that far."

"It's a funny thing, watching someone. Traveling with them. They don't know you. They don't know you're there. Oh, they guess. They assume you're there. But they don't know who you are. Sometimes you catch them looking at someone, in the lobby of the hotel, say, and you know they think it's you, the one who's watching. But it never is. And as you watch them, Rydell, over a period of months, you start to *love* them."

Rydell saw a shiver go through Chevette Washington's tensed white thigh.

"But then, after a few more months, twenty flights, two dozen hotels, well, it starts to turn itself around..."

"You don't love them?"

"No. You don't. You start to wait for them to fuck up, Rydell. You start to wait for them to betray the trust. Because a courier's trust is a terrible thing. A terrible thing."

"Courier?"

"Look at her, Rydell. She knows. Even if she's just riding confidential papers around San Francisco, she's a courier. She's *entrusted*, Rydell. The data becomes a physical thing. She carries it. Don't you carry it, baby?"

She was still as some sphinx, white fingers deep in the gray fabric of the center bucket.

"That's what I do, Rydell. I watch them carry it. I watch them. Sometimes people try to take it from them." He finished the Coke. "I kill those people. Actually that's the best part of the job. Ever been to San Jose, Rydell?"

"Costa Rica?"

"That's right."

"Never have."

"People know how to live, there."

"You work for those data havens," Rydell said.

"I didn't say that. Somebody else must've said that."

"So did he," Rydell said. "He was carrying those glasses to somebody, up from Costa Rica, and she took 'em."

"And I was glad she did. So glad. I was in the room next to his. I let myself in through the connecting door. I *introduced* myself. He met Loveless. First time. Last time." The gun never wavered, but he began to scratch his head with his hand in the surgical glove. Scratch it like he had fleas or something.

"Loveless?"

"My *nom. Nom de thing.*" Then a long rattle of what Rydell took to be Spanish, but he only caught *nombre de* something. "Think she's tight, Rydell? I like it tight, myself."

"You American?"

His head sort of whipped sideways, a little, when Rydell said that, and his eyes unfocused for a second, but then they came back, clear as the chromed rim around the muzzle of his gun. "You know who started the havens, Rydell?"

"Cartels," Rydell said, "the Colombians."

"That's right. They brought the first expert systems into Cen-

tral America, nineteen-eighties, to coordinate their shipping. Somebody had to go down there and install those systems. War on drugs,
Rydell. Lot of Americans on either side, down there."

"Well," Rydell said, "now we just make our own drugs up
here, don't we?"

"But they've got the havens, down there. They don't even
need that drug business. They've got what Switzerland used to have.
They've got the one place in the world to keep what people can't
afford to keep anywhere else."

"You look a little young to have helped put that together."

"My father. You *know* your father, Rydell?"

"Sure." Sort of, anyway.

"I never did. I had to have a lot of *therapy*, over that."

Sure glad it worked, Rydell thought. "Warbaby, he work for
the havens?"

A sweat had broken out on the man's forehead. Now he
wiped it with the back of the hand that held the gun, but Rydell saw
the gun click back into position like it was held by a magnet.

"Turn on the headlights, Rydell. It's okay. Left hand off the
wheel."

"Why?"

" 'Cause you're dead if you don't."

"Well, why?"

"Just do it, okay?" Sweat running into his eyes.

Rydell took his left hand off the wheel, clicked the lights,
double-clicked them to high beams. Two cones of light bit into a wall
of dead shops, dead signs, dust on plastic. The one in front of the
left beam said THE GAP.

"Why'd anybody ever call a store that?" Rydell said.

"Trying to fuck with my head, Rydell?"

"No," Rydell said, "it's just a weird name. Like *all* those
places look like gaps, now..."

"Warbaby's just hired help, Rydell. IntenSecure brings him
in when things get too sloppy. And they do, they always do."

They were parked in a sort of plaza, in a mall, the stores all boarded or their windows whitewashed. Either underground or else it was roofed over. "So she stole the glasses out of a hotel had IntenSecure security, they brought in Warbaby?" Rydell looked at Chevette Washington. She looked like one of those chrome things on the nose of an antique car, except she was getting goosebumps down her thigh. Not exactly warm in here, which made Rydell think it might be underground after all.

"Know what, Rydell?"

"What?"

"You don't know shit about shit. As much as I tell you, you'll never understand the situation. It's just too *big* for someone like you to understand. You don't know how to think in those terms. Inten-Secure *belongs* to the company that owns the information in those glasses."

"Singapore," Rydell said. "Singapore own DatAmerica, too?"

"You can't prove it, Rydell. Neither could Congress."

"Look at those rats over there..."

"Fucking with my *head*..."

Rydell watched the last of the three rats vanish into the place that had been called The Gap. In through a loose vent or something. A gap. "Nope. Saw 'em."

"Has it occurred to you that you wouldn't *be* here right now if Lucius fucking Warbaby hadn't taken up rollerblading last month?"

"How's that?"

"He wrecked his knee. Warbaby wrecks his knee, can't drive, *you* wind up *here.* Think about it. What does *that* tell you about late-stage capitalism?"

"Tell me about what?"

"Don't they teach you anything in that police academy?"

"Sure," Rydell said, "lots of stuff." Thinking: how to talk to crazy fuckers when you're being held hostage, except he was having a hard time remembering what they'd said. Keep 'em talking and don't argue too much, something like that. "How come the stuff in those glasses has everybody's tail in a twist, anyway?"

"They're going to rebuild San Francisco. From the ground

up, basically. Like they're doing to Tokyo. They'll start by layering a grid of seventeen complexes into the existing infrastructure. Eighty-story office/residential, retail/residence in the base. Completely self-sufficient. Variable-pitch parabolic reflectors, steam-generators. *New* buildings, man; they'll eat their own sewage."

"Who'll eat sewage?"

"The *buildings.* They're going to *grow* them, Rydell. Like they're doing now in Tokyo. Like the maglev tunnel."

"Sunflower," Chevette Washington said, then looked like she regretted it.

"Somebody's been *look-ing...*" Gold teeth flashing.

"Uh, hey..." Go for that talking-to-the-armed-insane mode. "Yes?"

"So what's the problem? They wanna *do* that, let 'em."

"The problem," this Loveless said, starting to unbutton his shirt, "is that a city like San Francisco has about as much sense of *where* it wants to go, of where it *should* go, as *you* do. Which is to say, very little. There are people, millions of them, who would *object* to the fact that this sort of plan even exists. Then there's the business of real estate..."

"Real estate?"

"Know the three most important considerations in any purchase of real estate, Rydell?" Loveless's chest, hairless and artificially pigmented, was gleaming with sweat.

"Three?"

"Location," Loveless said, "location, and *location.*"

"I don't get it."

"You never will. But the people who know where to buy, the people who've seen where the footprints of the towers fall, they *will,* Rydell. They'll get it *all.*"

Rydell thought about it. "You looked, huh?"

Loveless nodded. "In Mexico City. He *left* them in his room. He was never, *ever* supposed to do that."

"But you weren't supposed to look either?" It just slipped out.

Loveless's skin was running with sweat now, in spite of the

cool. It was like his whole lymbic system or whatever had just let loose. Kept blinking and wiping it back from his eyes. "I've done *my* job. *Did* my job. Jobs. Years. My father, too. You haven't seen how they *live,* down there. The compounds. People up here have no idea what *money* can do, Rydell. They don't know what real money *is.* They live like *gods,* in the compounds. Some of them are over a hundred years *old,* Rydell. . ." There were flecks of white stuff at the corners of Loveless' smile, and Rydell was back in Turvey's girlfriend's apartment, looking into Turvey's eyes, and it just clicked, what she'd done.

Dumped that whole bag of dancer into the Coke she'd brought him. She hadn't been able to pour it all in, so she'd sloshed the Coke out onto the top of the can to wash it down, mix it around.

He had his shirt undone all the way now, the dark fabric darker with sweat, and his face was turning red.

"Loveless—" Rydell started, no idea what he was about to say, but Loveless screamed then, a high thin inhuman sound like a rabbit with its leg caught in a wire, and started pounding the butt of his pistol into the tight crotch of his jeans like there was something terrible fastened on him there, something he had to kill. Each time the gun came down, it fired, blowing holes in the carpeted floorboard the size of five-dollar pieces.

Chevette Washington came off that console like she was on rubber bands, right over the top of the center bucket and into the cabin in back.

Loveless froze, quivering, like every atom in him had locked down all at once, spinning in some tight emergency orbit. Then he smiled, like maybe he'd killed the thing that was after his crotch, screamed again, and started firing out through the windshield. All Rydell could remember was some instructor telling them that an overdose of dancer made too much PCP look like putting aspirin in a Coke. In a Coke.

And Chevette Washington, she was going just about that crazy herself, by the sound of it, trying to beat her way out the back of the RV.

"Hundred years old, those fuckers," Loveless said, and sort of sobbed, ejecting the empty magazine and snapping a fresh one in, "and they're *still* getting it..."

"Out there," Rydell said. "By The Gap—"

"Who?"

"Svobodov," Rydell said, guessing that might do it.

The bullets came out of the little gun like the rubber cubes out of a chunker. By the third one, Rydell had reached over, deactivated the door-lock, and just sort of fallen out. Landed on his back on some cans and what felt like foam cups. Rolled. Kept rolling 'til he hit something.

Those little bullets blowing big holes in the whitewashed glass of the dead stores. A whole section fell away with a crash.

He could hear Chevette Washington pounding on the back door of the RV and he wished he could get her to stop.

"Hey! Loveless!"

The shooting stopped.

"Svobodov's down, man!"

Chevette still pounding. Jesus.

"He needs an ambulance!"

On his hands and knees, up against some low tiled fountain smelled of chlorine and dust, he saw Loveless scramble down from the driver's side, his face and chest slick and shining. The man had been trained so deeply, it occurred to Rydell, that it even cut through whatever the dancer was doing to him. Because he still moved the way they taught you to move in FATSS, the pistol out in both hands, the half-crouch, the smooth swings through potential arcs of fire.

And Chevette, she was still trying to kick her way out through the hexcel or whatever the back of the RV was made of. Then Loveless put a couple of bullets into it and she all of a sudden stopped.

carnival

of souls

At four o'clock Yamazaki descended the rungs he'd climbed with Loveless, in the dark, the night before.

Fontaine had gone, twenty minutes before the power returned, taking with him, against Skinner's protests, an enormous bundle of washing. Skinner had spent the day sorting and re-sorting the contents of the green toolkit, the one he'd overturned in his bid for the bolt-cutters.

Yamazaki had watched the old man's hands as they touched each tool in turn, imagining he saw some momentary strength or purpose flow into them there, or perhaps only memories of tasks undertaken, abandoned, completed. "You can always sell tools," Skinner had mused, perhaps to Yamazaki, perhaps to himself. "Somebody'll always buy 'em. But then you always need 'em again, exactly the one you sold." Yamazaki didn't know the English words for most of the tools there, and many were completely unfamiliar. "T-reamer," Skinner said, holding up his fist, a rust-brown, machined spike of steel protruding menacingly between his second and third fingers. "Now that's about as handy a thing as you can have, Scooter, but most people never seen one."

"Its purpose, Skinner-san?"

"Makes a round hole bigger. Keeps it round, too, you use it right. Sheet-metal, mostly, but it'll do plastic, synthetics. Anything thin, fairly rigid. Short of glass."

"You have many tools, Skinner-san."

"Never learned how to really use 'em, though."

"But you built this room?"

"You ever watch a real carpenter work, Scooter?"

"Once, yes," Yamazaki said, remembering a demonstration at a festival, the black blades flying, the smell of cut cedar. He remembered the look of the lumber, creamy and flawless. A tea-house was being erected, to stand for the duration of the festival. "Wood is very scarce in Tokyo, Skinner-san. You would not see it thrown away, not even small scraps."

"Not that easy to come by here," Skinner said, rubbing the ball of his thumb with the edge of a chisel. Did he mean in America, San Francisco, on the bridge? "We used to burn our scrap, before we got the power in. City didn't like that at all. Bad for the air, Scooter. Don't do that as much, now."

"This is by consensus?"

"Just common sense ..." Skinner put the chisel into a greasy canvas case and tucked it carefully away in the green box.

A procession was making its way toward San Francisco, along the upper deck, and Yamazaki instantly regretted having left his notebook in Skinner's room. This was the first evidence he had seen here of public ritual.

In the narrow, enclosed space, it was impossible to view the procession as anything other than a succession of participants, in their ones and twos, but it was a procession nonetheless, and clearly funereal, perhaps memorial, in its purpose. First came children, seven by his hasty count, one behind the other, in ragged, ash-dusted clothing. Each child wore a mask of painted plaster, clearly intended to represent Shapely. But there was nothing funereal in their progress; several were skipping, delighted with the attention they were receiving.

Yamazaki, on his way to purchase hot soup, had halted between a bookseller's wagon and a stall hung with caged birds. He felt awkward there, very much out of place, with the unaccustomed shape of the insulated canister under his arm. If this was a funeral, perhaps there was some required gesture, some attitude he might be expected to assume? He glanced at the bookseller, a tall woman in a greasy sheepskin vest, her gray hair bound back into a knot transfixed by two pink plastic chopsticks.

Her stock, which consisted primarily of yellowing paperbacks in various stages of disintegration, each in a clear plastic bag, was stacked before her on her wagon. She had been crying her wares, when she saw the children masked as Shapely; she'd been calling out strange phrases that he supposed were titles: "Valley of the dolls, blood meridian, chainsaw savvy..." Yamazaki, struck by the queer American poetry, had been on the verge of asking after *Chainsaw Savvy*. Then she'd fallen silent, and he too had seen the children.

But there was nothing in her manner now that indicated the procession required anything more of her than whatever degree of her attention she might choose to afford it. She was automatically counting her stock, he saw, as she watched the children pass, her hands moving over the bagged books.

The keeper of the bird stall, a pale man with a carefully groomed black mustache, was scratching his stomach, his expression mild and blank.

After the children came five dancers in the skeleton-suits of La Noche de Muerte, though Yamazaki saw that several of the masks were only half-masks, micropore respirators molded to resemble the grinning jaws of skulls. These were teenagers, evidently, and shaking to some inner music of plague and chaos. There was a strong erotic undercurrent, a violence, to the black, bone-painted thighs, the white cartoon pelvises daubed on narrow denimed buttocks. As the bone-dancers passed, one fixed Yamazaki with a sharp stare, blue adolescent eyes above the black, molded nostrils of the white respirator.

Then two tall figures, black men in an ugly beige face-paint, costumed as surgeons, in pale green gowns and long gloves of scarlet latex. Were they the doctors, predominantly white, who had failed to rescue so many, prior to Shapely's advent, or did they somehow represent the Brazilian biomedical firms who had so successfully and lucratively overseen Shapely's transformation, the illiterate prostitute become the splendid source? And after them, the first of the bodies, wrapped and bound in layers of milky plastic, each one riding a two-wheeled cart of the kind manufactured here to transport baggage or bulk foodstuffs. The carts, temporarily equipped with narrow pallets of plywood, were steered along, front and back, by men and women of no special costume or demeanor, though Yamazaki noted that they looked neither to the right nor left, and seemed to make no eye-contact with the onlookers.

"There's Nigel," the bookseller said, "and probably built the cart they're taking him off on."

"These are the victims of the storm?" Yamazaki ventured.

"Not Nigel," the woman said, narrowing her eyes as she saw that he was a stranger. "Not with those holes in him..."

Seven in all, each to its cart, and then a man and a woman, in identical paper coveralls, carrying between them a laminated lithograph of Shapely, one of those saccharine portraits, large of eye and hollow of cheek, that invariably left Yamazaki feeling slightly queasy.

But then a small, red, capering figure. A tailless, hornless devil, perhaps, dancing with an enormous gun, an ancient AK-47, its bolt long gone, the curved magazine carved from wood, and all of it dipped, once, into red enamel, worn now by hands, by processions.

And Yamazaki knew, without asking, that the red dancer represented the way of Shapely's going, like some terrible base stupidity waiting at the core of things.

"Skinner-san?" The notebook ready. "I saw a procession today. Bodies being taken from the bridge. The dead from the storm."

"Can't keep 'em out here. Can't throw 'em in the water. City sticks on that. We pass 'em over for cremation. Some people, they don't hold with fire, they bury 'em over on Treasure. Kind of people live out on Treasure, you kind of wonder if that makes much sense."

"In the procession there were many references to Shapely, to his story."

Skinner nodded over his little television.

"Children masked as J. D. Shapely, two black men painted as white doctors, Shapely's portrait..."

Skinner grunted. Then, distantly: "While since I saw one of those."

"And at the end, a small figure, red. Dancing. With an assault rifle."

"Uh-huh." Skinner nodded.

Yamazaki activated the notebook's transcription function.

Me, you know, I never even got it. Off him, I mean. That piece of him in everybody now. Couldn't see the point at my age and anyway I never held with medicine. Happened I never got the other kind either, not that I didn't have plenty of chances. You're too young to remember how it felt, though. Oh, I know, I know you all think you live in all the times at once, everything recorded for you, it's all there to play back. Digital. That's all that is, though: playback. You still don't remember what it felt like, watching them pile up like that. Not here so much, bad as it was, but Thailand, Africa, Brazil. Jesus, Scooter. That thing was just romping on us. But slow, slow, slow-motion thing. Those retroviruses are. One man told me once, and he had the old kind, and died of it, how we'd lived in this funny little pocket of time when a lot of people got to feel like a piece of ass wasn't going to kill anybody, not even a woman. See, they always had to worry anyway, every time it's a chance, get knocked up and maybe die in childbirth, die getting rid of it, or anyway your life's not gonna be the same. But in that pocket, there, there were pills for that, whatnot, shots for the other things, even the ones had killed people all over hell, before. That was a time, Scooter. So here this thing comes along, changes it back. And we're sliding up on 2000, shit's changing all over, got civil wars in Europe already and this AIDS thing just kicking along. You know they tried to say it was the gays, said it was the CIA, said it was the U.S. Army in some fort in Maryland. Said it was people cornholing green monkeys. I swear to God. You know what it was? People. Just too goddamn many of 'em, Scooter. Flying all the fuck over everywhere and walking around back in there. Bet your ass somebody's gonna pick up a bug or two. Every place on the damn planet just a couple of hours from any other place. So here's poor fucking Shapely comes along, he's got this mutant strain won't kill you. Won't do shit to you at all, 'cept it eats the old kind for breakfast. And I don't buy any of that bullshit he was Jesus, Scooter. Didn't think Jesus was, either.

"Any coffee left?"

"I will pump stove."

"Put a little drop of Three-in-One in that hole by the piston-arm, Scooter. Leather gasket in there. Keeps it soft."

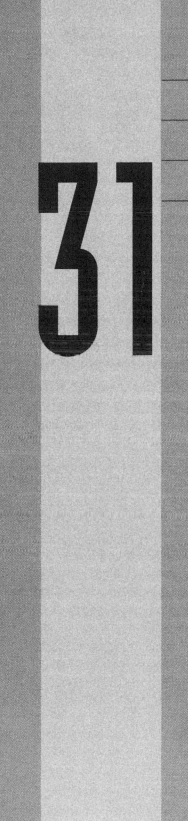

31

driver

side

She didn't see that first bullet, but it must have hit a wire or something, coming through, because the lights came on. She did see the second one, or anyway the hole it blew in the leather-grain plastic. Something inside her stopped, learning this about bullets: that one second there isn't any hole, the next second there is. Nothing in between. You see it happen, but you can't watch it happening.

Then she got down on her hands and her knees and started crawling. Because she couldn't just stand there and wait for the next one. When she got up by the door, she could see her black pants crumpled up on the floor there, beside a set of keys on a gray, leather-grain plastic tab. There was this smell from when he'd shot the gun into the floor. Maybe from the carpet burning, too, because she could see that the edges of the holes were scorched and sort of melted.

Now she could hear him yelling, somewhere outside, hoarse and hollow and chased by echoes. Held her breath. Yelling how they (who?) did the best PR in the world, how they'd sold Hunnis Millbank, now they'd sell Sunflower. If she heard it right.

"Down by the door, here. Driver side."

It was Rydell, the door on that side standing open.

"He left the keys in here," she said.

"Think he's gone down there where the Dream Walls franchise used to be."

"What if he comes back?"

"Probably come back anyway, we stick around here. You crawl up there and toss me those?"

She edged through the door and between the buckets. Saw Rydell's head there, by the open door. Grabbed the keys and threw them sideways, without looking. Snatched her pants and scooted backward, wondering could she maybe fit in the fridge, if she folded her legs up?

"Why don't you lie down flat on the floor back there..." His voice from the driver's seat.

"Lie down?"

"Minimum silhouette."

"Huh?"

"He's going to start shooting. When I do *this*—" Ignition-sound. Glass flying from fresh holes in the windshield and she threw herself flat. The RV lurched backward, turning tight, and she could hear him slapping the console, trying to find some function he needed, as more bullets came, each one distinct, a blow, like someone was swinging an invisible hammer, taking care to keep the rhythm.

Rydell must've gotten it lined up how he needed it, then, because he did that thing boys did, up in Oregon, with their brakes and the transmission.

She realized then that she was screaming. Not words or anything, just screaming.

Then they were in a turn that almost took them over, and she thought how these RV's probably weren't meant to move very fast. Now they were moving even faster, it felt like, uphill.

"Well fuck," she heard Rydell say, in this weirdly ordinary kind of voice, and then they hit the door, or the gate, or whatever, and it was like the time she tried to pull this radical bongo over in Lafayette Park and they'd had to keep explaining to her how'd she'd come down on her head, and each time they did, she'd forget.

She was back in Skinner's room, reading *National Geographic,* about how Canada split itself into five countries. Drinking cold milk out of the carton and eating saltines. Skinner in bed with the tv, watching one of those shows he liked about history. He was talking about how all his life these movies of history had been getting better and better looking. How they'd started out jumpy and black and white, with the soldiers running around like they had ants in their pants, and this terrible grain to them, and the sky all full of scratches. How gradually they'd slowed down to how people really moved, and then they'd been colorized, the grain getting finer and finer, and even the scratches went away. And it was bullshit, he said, because every other bit of it was an approximation, somebody's idea of how it might have looked, the result of a particular decision, a particular button being pushed. But it was still a hit, he said, like the first time you heard Billy Holiday without all that crackle and tin.

Billy Holiday was probably a guy like Elvis, Chevette thought, with spangles on his suit, but like when he was younger and not all fat.

Skinner had this thing he got on about history. How it was turning into plastic. But she liked to show him she was listening when he told her something, because otherwise he could go for days without saying anything. So she looked up now, from her magazine and the picture of girls waving blue and white flags in the Republic of Quebec, and it was her mother sitting there, on the edge of Skinner's bed, looking beautiful and sad and kind of tired, the way she could look after she got off work and still had all her make-up on.

"He's right," Chevette's mother said.

"Mom?"

"About history, how they change it."

"Mom, you—"

"Everybody does that anyway, honey. Isn't any new thing. Just the movies have caught up with memory, is all."

Chevette started to cry.

"Chevette-Marie," her mother said, in that singsong out of so far back, "you've gone and hurt your head."

fallonville

H ow well you say you know this guy?" she asked.

Rydell's SWAT shoe crunched on little squares of safety-glass every time he used the brake. If he'd had time and a broom, he'd have swept it all out. As it was, he'd had to bash out what was left of the windshield with a piece of rusty re-bar he found beside the road, otherwise Highway Patrol would've seen the holes and hauled them over. Anyway, he had those insoles. "I worked with him in L.A.," he said, braking to steer around shreds of truck-trailer tires that lay on the two-lane blacktop like the moulted skin of monsters.

"I was just wondering if he'll turn out like Mrs. Elliott did. Said you knew her too."

"Didn't know her," Rydell said, "I met her, on the plane. If Sublett's some kind of plant, then the whole *world's* a plot." He shrugged. "Then I could start worrying about *you*, say." As opposed, say, to worrying about whether or not Loveless or Mrs. Elliot had bothered to plant a locator-bug in this motorhome, or whether the Death Star was watching for them, right now, and could it pick them up, out here? They said the Death Star could read the headlines on a newspaper, or what brand and size of shoes you wore, from a decent footprint.

Then this wooden cross seemed to pop up, in the headlights, about twelve feet high, with TUNE IN across the horizontal and TO HIS

IMMORTAL DOWNLINK coming down the upright, and this dusty old portable tv nailed up where Jesus' head ought to have been. Somebody'd taken a .22 to the screen, it looked like.

"Must be getting closer," Rydell said.

Chevette Washington sort of grunted. Then she drank some of the water they'd gotten at the Shell station, and offered the bottle to him.

When he'd crashed out of that mall, he'd felt like they were sure to be right by a major highway. From the outside, the mall was just this low tumble of tan brick, windows boarded up with sheets of that really ugly hot-pressed recyc they ran off from chopped scrap, the color of day-old vomit. He'd gone screeching around this big empty parking lot, just a few dead clunkers and old mattresses to get in the way, until he'd found a way out through the chain link.

But there wasn't any highway there, just some deserted four-lane feeder, and it looked like Loveless had put a bullet into the navigation hardware, because the map was locked on downtown Santa Ana and just sat there, sort of flickering. Where he was had the feel of one of those fallen-in edge-cities, the kind of place that went down when the Euro-money imploded.

Chevette Washington was curled up by the fridge with her eyes closed, and she wouldn't answer him. He was scared Loveless had put one through her, too, but he knew he couldn't afford to stop until he'd put at least a little distance between them and the mall. And he couldn't see any blood on her or anything.

Finally he'd come to this Shell station. You could tell it had been Shell because of the shape of the metal things up on the poles that had supported the signs. The men's room door was ripped off the hinges; the women's chained and padlocked. Somebody had taken an automatic weapon to the pop machine, it looked like. He swung the RV around to the back and saw this real old Airstream trailer there, the same kind a neighbor of his father's had lived in down in Tampa. There was a man there kneeling beside a hibachi, doing something with a pot, and these two black Labradors watching him.

Rydell parked, checked to see Chevette Washington was breathing, and got down out of the cab. He walked over to the man beside the hibachi, who'd gotten up now and was wiping the palms of his hands on the thighs of his red coveralls. He had on an old khaki fishing cap with about a nine-inch bill sticking straight out. The threads on the embroidered Shell patch on his coveralls had sort of frayed and fuzzed-out.

"You just lost," the man said, "or is there some kind of problem?" Rydell figured him to be at least seventy.

"No sir, no problem, but I'm definitely lost." Rydell looked at the black Labs. They looked right back. "Those dogs of yours there, they don't look too happy to see me."

"Don't see a lot of strangers," the man said.

"No sir," Rydell said, "I don't imagine they do."

"Got a couple of cats, too. Right now I'm feeding 'em all on dry kibble. The cats get a bird sometimes, maybe mice. Say you're lost?"

"Yes sir, I am. I couldn't even tell you what state we're in, right now."

The man spat on the ground. "Welcome to the goddamn club, son. I was your age, it was all of this California, just like God meant it to be. Now it's Southern, so they tell me, but you know what it really is?"

"No sir. What?"

"A lot of that same happy horseshit. Like that woman camping in the goddamn White House." He took the fishing cap off, exposing a couple of silver-white cancer-scars, wiped his brow with a grease-stained handkerchief, then pulled the cap back on. "Say you're lost, are you?"

"Yes sir. My map's broken."

"Know how to read a paper one?"

"Yes sir, I do."

"What the hell'd she do to her head?" Looking past Rydell.

Rydell turned and saw Chevette Washington leaning over the driver's bucket, looking out at them.

"How she cuts her hair," Rydell said.

"I'll be damned," the man said. "Might be sort of good-looking, otherwise."

"Yes sir," Rydell said.

"See that box of Cream o' Wheat there? Think you can stir me up a cup of that into this water when it boils?"

"Yes sir."

"Well, I'll go find you a map to look at. Skeeter and Whitey here, they'll just keep you company."

"Yes sir..."

PARADISE, SO. CALIFORNIA

A CHRISTIAN COMMUNITY

THREE MILES

NO CAMPING

CONCRETE PADS

FULL HOOKUPS

ELECTRIFIED SECURITY PERIMETER

FREE SWIMMING

LICENSED CHRISTIAN DAYCARE (STATE OF SO. CAL.)

327 CHANNELS ON DOWNLINK

And a taller cross rising beyond that, this one welded from rusty railroad track, a sort of framework stuck full of old televisions, their dead screens all looking out toward the road there.

Chevette Washington was asleep now, so she missed that.

Rydell thought about how he'd used Codes's phone to get through to Sublett's number in L.A., and gotten this funny ring, which had nearly made him hang up right then, but it had turned out to be call-forwarding, because Sublett had this leave to go and stay with his mother, who was feeling kind of sick.

"You mean you're in Texas?"

"Paradise, Berry. Mom's sick 'cause she 'n' a bunch of others got moved up here to SoCal."

"Paradise?"

Sublett had explained where it was while Rydell looked at the Shell man's map.

"Hey," Rydell had said, when he had a general idea where it was, "how about I drive over and see you?"

"Thought you had you a job up in San Francisco."

"Well, I'll tell you about that when I get there."

"You know they're saying I'm an apostate here?" Sublett hadn't sounded happy about that.

"A what?"

"An apostate. 'Cause I showed my mom this Cronenberg film, Berry? This *Videodrome*? And they said it was from the Devil."

"I thought all those movies were supposed to have God in 'em."

"There's movies that are clearly of the Devil, Berry. Or anyway that's what Reverend Fallon says. Says all of Cronenberg's are."

"He in Paradise, too?"

"Lord no," Sublett had said, "he's in these tunnels out on the Channel Islands, between England and France. Can't leave there, either, because he needs the shelter."

"From what?"

"Taxes. You know who dug those same tunnels, Berry?"

"Who?"

"Hitler did, with slave labor."

"I didn't know that," Rydell had said, imagining this scary little guy with a black mustache, standing up on a rock and cracking a big whip.

Now here came another sign, this one not nearly as professional as the first one, just black spraypaint letters on a couple of boards.

R.U. READY FOR ETERNITY?
HE LIVES! WILL YOU?
WATCH TELEVISION!

"Watch television?" She was awake now.

"Well," Rydell said, "Fallonites believe God's sort of just *there*. On television, I mean."

"God's on television?"

"Yeah. Kind of like in the background or something. Sublett's mother, she's in the church herself, but Sublett's kind of lapsed."

"So they watch tv and pray, or what?"

"Well, I think it's more like kind of a meditation, you know? What they mostly watch is all these old movies, and they figure if they watch enough of them, long enough, the spirit will sort of enter into them."

"We had Revealed Aryan Nazarenes, up in Oregon," she said. "First Church of Jesus, Survivalist. As soon shoot you as look at you."

"Bad news," Rydell agreed, the RV cresting a little ridge there, "those kind of Christians..." Then he saw Paradise, down there, all lit up with these lights on poles.

The security perimeter they advertised was just coils of razor-wire circling maybe an acre and a half. Rydell doubted if it actually was electrified, but he could see screamers hanging on it, every ten feet or so, so it would be pretty effective anyway. There was a sort of blockhouse-and-gate set-up where the road ran in, but all it seemed to be protecting were about a dozen campers, trailers, and semi-rigs, parked on cement beds around what looked like an old-fashioned radio tower they'd topped with a whole cluster of satellite dishes, those little expensive ones that looked sort of like giant gray plastic marshmallows. Somebody had dammed a creek, to make a sort of pond for swimming, but the creek itself looked like the kind of industrial runoff you wouldn't even find bugs around, let alone birds.

Sure had the whole place lit up, though. He could hear the drumming of big generators as they drove down the incline.

"Jesus," Chevette Washington said.

Rydell pulled up by the blockhouse and powered his window down, glad it still worked. A man in a blaze-orange fleece jacket and a matching cap came out, carrying some kind of shotgun with a skeletal metal stock. "Private property," he said, looking at where the windshield should've been. "What happened to your windshield there, mister?"

"Deer," Chevette Washington said.

"Here to visit our friends, the Subletts?" Rydell said, hoping he could distract the guard before he'd notice the bullet holes or anything. "Expecting us, if you wanna go call 'em."

"Can't say you much look like Christians."

Chevette Washington sort of leaned across Rydell and gave the guard this stare. "I don't know about *you*, brother, but we're Aryan Nazarene, out of Eugene. We wouldn't want to even come *in* there, say you got any mud people, *any* kind of race-mixing. Race-traitors all *over*, these days."

The guard looked at her. "You Nazarene, how come you ain't skins?"

She touched the front of her crazy haircut, the short spikey part. "Next thing you're gonna tell me, Jesus was a Jew. Don't know what *this* means?"

He looked more than maybe just a little worried, now.

"Got us some sanctified nails in the back, here. Maybe that gives you some idea."

Rydell saw the guard hesitate, swallow.

"Hey, good buddy," Rydell said, "you gonna call up ol' Sublett for us, or what?"

The man went back into the blockhouse.

"What's that about nails?" Rydell asked.

"Something Skinner told me about once," she said. "Scared me."

Dora, Sublett's mother, drank Coke and Mexican vodka. Rydell had seen people drink that before, but never at room temperature. And the Coke was flat, because she bought it and the vodka in these big plastic supermarket bottles, and they looked as though they'd already lasted her a while. Rydell decided he didn't feel like drinking anyway.

The living room of Dora's trailer had a matching couch and reclining lounger. Dora lay back in the lounger with her feet up, for her circulation she said, Rydell and Chevette Washington sat side by side on the couch, which was more a loveseat, and Sublett sat on the floor, his knees drawn up almost under his chin. There was a lot of stuff on the walls, and on little ornamental shelves, but it was all very clean. Rydell figured that was because of Sublett's allergies. There sure was a lot of it, though: plaques and pictures and figurines and things Rydell figured had to be those prayer hankies. There was a flat type of hologram of Rev. Fallon, looking as much like a possum as ever, but a possum that had gotten a tan and maybe had plastic surgery. There was a life-size head of J. D. Shapely that Rydell didn't like because the eyes seemed to follow you. Most of the good stuff was sort of grouped around the television, which was big and shiny but the old kind from before they started to get real big and flat. It was on now, showing this black and white movie, but the sound was off.

"You're sure you won't have a drink, Mr. Rydell?"

"No ma'am, thank you," Rydell said.

"Joel doesn't drink. He has allergies, you know."

"Yes ma'am." Rydell hadn't ever known Sublett's first name before.

Sublett was wearing brand-new white denim jeans, a white t-shirt, white cotton socks, and disposable white paper hospital slippers.

"He was always a sensitive boy, Mr. Rydell. I remember one

time he sucked on the handle of this other boy's Big Wheel. Well, his mouth like to turned inside-out."

"Momma," Sublett said, "you know the doctor said you ought to get more sleep than you been getting."

Mrs. Sublett sighed. "Yes, well, Joel, I know you young people want a chance to talk." She peered at Chevette Washington. "That's a shame about your hair, honey. You're just as pretty as can be, though, and you know it'll just grow in so nice. I tried to light the broiler on this gas range we had, down in Galveston, that was when Joel was just a baby, he was so sensitive, and that stove about blew up. I just had had this perm, dear and, well..."

Chevette Washington didn't say anything.

"Momma," Sublett said, "now you know you've had your nice drink..."

Rydell watched Sublett lead the old woman off to bed.

"Jesus Christ," Chevette Washington said, "what's wrong with his eyes?"

"Just light-sensitive," Rydell said.

"It's spooky, is what it is."

"He wouldn't hurt a fly," Rydell said.

Sublett came back, looked at the picture on the tv, then sighed and shut it off. "You know I'm not supposed to leave the trailer, Berry?"

"How's that?"

"It's a condition of my apostasy. They say I might corrupt the congregation by contact." He perched on the edge of the recliner so he wouldn't have to actually recline in it.

"I thought you'd blown Fallon off when you came out to L.A."

Sublett looked embarrassed. "Well, she's been sick, Berry, so when I came here I told 'em I was here to reconsider. Meditate on the box 'n' all." He wrung his long pale hands. "Then they caught me watching *Videodrome*. You ever see, uh, Deborah Harry, Rydell?" Sublett sighed and sort of quivered.

"How'd they catch you?"

"They've got it set up so they can monitor what you're watching."

"How come they're out here anyway?"

Sublett ran his fingers back through his dry, straw-colored hair. "Hard to say, but I'd figure it's got something to do with Reverend Fallon's tax problems. Most of what he does, lately, it's about that. Didn't your job in San Francisco work out, Berry?"

"No," Rydell said, "it didn't."

"You want to tell me about it?"

Rydell said he did.

"I think he shot through something to do with the damned heater, too," Rydell said. They were back in the RV, outside the perimeter.

"I like your friend," she said.

"I do too."

"No, I mean he really cares about what's going to happen to you. He really does."

"You take the bed," he said. "I'll sleep up front."

"There's no windshield. You'll freeze."

"I'll be okay."

"Sleep back here. We did before. It's okay."

He woke in the dark and listened to the sound of her breathing, to the creak of stiff old leather from the jacket spread over her shoulder.

Sublett had listened to his story, nodding sometimes, asking a question here and there, his mirrored contacts reflecting tiny convex images of them sitting there on that loveseat. In the end he'd just whistled softly and said, "Berry, it sounds to me like you're really in trouble now. Bad trouble."

Really in trouble now.

Rydell slid his hand down, brushing one of hers by accident

as he did it, and touched the bulge of his wallet in his back pocket. What money he had was in there, but Wellington Ma's card was in there, too. Or what was left of it. The last time he'd looked, it had broken into three pieces.

"*Big* trouble," he said to the dark, and Chevette Washington lifted the edge of her jacket and sort of snuggled in closer, her breathing never changing, so he knew she was still asleep.

He lay there, thinking, and after a while he started to get this idea. About the craziest idea he'd ever had.

———————————————

"That boyfriend of yours," he said to her, in the tiny kitchen of Sublett's mother's trailer, "that Lowell?"

"What about him?"

"Got a number we could reach him at?"

She poured milk on her cornflakes. It was the kind you mixed up from powder. Had that thin chalky look. The only kind Sublett's mother had. Sublett was allergic to milk. "Why?"

"I think maybe I want to talk to him about something."

"About what?"

"Something I think maybe he could help me with."

"Lowell? Lowell's not gonna help you. Lowell doesn't give a rat's ass for anybody."

"Well," Rydell said, "why don't you just let me talk to him."

"If you tell him where we are, or he has it traced back through the cel-net, he'll turn us in. Or he would if he knew anybody was after us."

"Why?"

"He's just *like* that." But then she gave Rydell the phone and the number.

———————————————

"Hey, Lowell?"

"Who the fuck is this?"

"How you doin'?"

"Who gave you—"

"Don't hang up."

"Listen, motherf—"

"SFPD Homicide."

He could hear Lowell draw on a cigarette. "What did you say?" Lowell said.

"Orlovsky. SFPD Homicide, Lowell. That big fucker with the great big fucking gun? Came in the bar there? You remember. Just before the lights went out. I was over there by the bar, talking with Eddie the Shit."

Lowell took another drag, shallower by the sound of it. "Look, I don't know what you—"

"You don't have to. You can just hang up right now, Lowell. But if you do, boy, you just better kiss your ass goodbye. Because you saw Orlovsky come in there for the girl, Lowell, didn't you? You saw him. He didn't want you to. He wasn't in there on any SFPD business, Lowell. He was there on his own stick. And that's one serious bad officer, Lowell. Serious as cancer."

Silence. "I don't know what you're talking about."

"Then you just listen, Lowell. Listen up. You don't listen, I'll tell Orlovsky you *saw* him. I'll give him this number. I'll give him your description, and that skinhead's, too. Tell him you been talking about him. And you know what he'll do, Lowell? He'll come out there and shoot your ass dead, that's what he'll do. And nobody to stop him. Homicide, Lowell. Then he can investigate it *himself*, he wants to. Man's heavy, Lowell, I gotta tell ya."

Lowell coughed, a couple of times. Cleared his throat. "This is a joke, right?"

"I don't hear you laughing."

"Okay," Lowell said, "say it's for real. Then what? What're you after?"

"I hear you know people can get things done. With computers and things." He could hear Lowell lighting a fresh cigarette.

"Well," Lowell said, "sort of."

"Republic of Desire," Rydell said. "I need you to get them to do me a favor."

"No *names*," Lowell said, fast. "There's scans set to pick things out of traffic—"

"'Them.' 'Them' okay? Need *you* to get *them* to do something for *me*."

"It'll cost you," Lowell said, "and it won't be cheap."

"No," Rydell said, "it'll cost *you*."

He pressed the button that broke the connection. Give old Lowell a little time to think about it; maybe look Orlovsky up on the Civil List, see he was there and he was Homicide. He flipped the little phone shut and went back into the trailer. Sublett's mother kept the air-conditioning up about two clicks too high.

Sublett was sitting on the loveseat. His white clothes made him look sort of like a painter, a plasterer or something, except he was too clean. "You know, Berry, I'm thinking maybe I better get back to Los Angeles."

"What about your mother?"

"Well, Mrs. Baker's here now, from Galveston? They been neighbors for years. Mrs. Baker can watch out for her."

"That apostate crap getting to you?"

"Sure is," Sublett said, turning to look at the hologram of Fallon. "I still believe in the Lord, Berry, and I know I've seen His face in the media, just like Reverend Fallon teaches. I have. But the rest of it, I swear, it might as well be just a flat-out hustle." Sublett almost looked like he might be about to cry. The silver eyes swung around, met Rydell's. "And I been thinking about IntenSecure, Berry. What you told me last night. I don't see how I can go back there and work, knowing the kinds of things they'll condone. I thought I was at least helping to protect people from a few of the evils in this world, Berry, but now I know I'd just be working for a company with no morals at all."

Rydell walked over and had a closer look at the prayer-hankies. He wondered which one of them was supposed to keep the

AIDS off. "No," he said, finally, "you go back to work. You *are* protecting people. That part's real. You got to make a living, Sublett."

"What about you?"

"Well, what about me?"

"They'll just find you and kill you, Berry. You and her."

"You, too, probably, if they knew what I'd told you. I shouldn't ought've done that, Sublett. That's one reason Chevette and I have to get out of here. So there won't be any hassle for you and your mom."

"Well," Sublett said, "I'm not working for them anymore, Berry. But I'm leaving here, too. I just have to."

Rydell looked at Sublett, seeing him, somehow, in his full IntenSecure outfit, Glock and all, and suddenly that big crazy idea-thing sort of up and shook itself, and rolled over, revealing all these new angles. *But you can't get him involved,* Rydell told himself, *it just wouldn't be fair.*

"Sublett," Rydell heard himself saying, about a minute later, "I bet I got a career-option here you haven't ever even considered."

"What's that?" Sublett said.

"Getting in trouble," Rydell said.

notebook

33

rice
scouring pads
broom
detergent liquid
sleeping bag
stove fuel
oil/gasket

He sleeps now. Rice with the curry from the Thai wagon. Asks where the girl has gone. Tell him Fontaine has heard from her but does not know where she is or why. The pistol on the shelf. Reluctant to touch it (cold, heavy, smelling of oil, the dark blue finish worn to silver-gray down the sides of its muzzle, around the fluted segments of the cylinder. "SMITH & WESSON." Thomasson). Tonight he spoke again of Shapely.

How they did him like that, Scooter, that's just some sorry shit. Same shit all over. Always some of 'em, anyway, makes you wonder how these damn religions last so long or what started it in the first place. Could be he'll be that himself one day, crazy fuckers out killing people for him, or they'll say it's for him. Used to be these Crucified Jesus people, they wouldn't talk at all except on Mondays, and that was the day they'd go and dig one spadeful of dirt out of their grave, Scooter. Every little while they'd get one of them thought he'd got the spirit in

him and they'd just do it, do it with these special chrome nails they
all carried, leather neck-pouch, see, it had to be unborn lambskin.
Hell, you'd have to say they were crazier than the ones got him,
Scooter. Put 'em all away, finally. Weren't any left at all, after about
1998.

34

punching
out of
paradise

Inner Tube, honey," Mrs. Sublett said, "Talitha Morrow, Todd Probert, Gary Underwood. 1996." She was leaning back in the recliner with a damp washcloth folded across her forehead. It was the same color blue as her slippers, and they were terrycloth, too.

"I never saw that," Chevette said, flipping through the pages of a magazine all about Reverend Fallon. There was this has-been actress, Gudrun Weaver, and she was up there hugging Fallon on a stage somewhere. If he'd turned around, Chevette thought, his nose would've barely come up to her breastbone. Looked like he'd had some kind of pink wax injected, all under his skin; had the creepiest-looking hair she'd ever seen, like a really short wig but it sort of looked like it might get up and walk off by itself.

"All about television," Mrs. Sublett said, "so naturally it's of special significance to the Church."

"What's it about?"

"Talitha Morrow is this newswoman, and Todd Probert is a bank robber. But he's a *good* bank robber, because he only needs the money to pay for a heart-transplant for his wife. Carrie Lee. Remember her? In a mature role, honey. More like a cameo. Well, Gary Underwood is Talitha's ex, but he's still got it for her, bad. In fact he's got—whatcha callit?—erotomania, like it's all he ever thinks about and, honey, it's turned pure evil. First he's sending her these chopped up Barbie dolls; sends her a dead white rabbit, then all this fancy underwear with blood on it..."

Chevette let the old lady talk. She could just sort of tune her out, the way she used to do with her own mother, sometimes. She wondered what it was Rydell and Sublett were so worked up about. Up to something; whispering in the kitchen.

She watched a fly buzz around the stuff on Mrs. Sublett's shelves. It looked slow, like maybe the air-conditioning was too much for it.

She wondered if maybe she wasn't starting to fall for Rydell. Maybe it was just that he'd showered and shaved and put on clean clothes from his stupid-looking suitcase. The clothes were exactly the same as the ones he'd been wearing before. Maybe he never wore anything else. But she had to admit he had a cute butt in those jeans. Sublett's mother said he looked like a young Tommy Lee Jones. Who was Tommy Lee Jones? Or maybe it was because she had the idea somehow he was going to do something mean to Lowell. She'd thought she was still in love with Lowell, or something anyway, but now she didn't think so, not at all. If Lowell just hadn't started doing dancer. She'd thought about how that Loveless had got when she'd dumped all that dancer in his Coke. She'd asked Rydell if that was enough to have killed him, and Rydell had said no. Said it was enough to keep him stone crazy for a while, and when he got back together, he was going to be hurting. Then she'd asked Rydell why Loveless had done that, banging his gun into his crotch that way. Rydell had sort of scratched his head and said he wasn't sure, but he thought it had something to do with what it did to your nervous system. Said he'd heard it induced priapism, for one thing. She'd asked him what that was. Well, he'd said, it's when the man is, like, overstimulated. She didn't know about that, but it had given Lowell these total brickbat boners that just didn't want to go away. And that would've been just fine, or anyway okay, except he got all mean with it, too, so she'd wind up all sore and then he'd be badmouthing her in front of these people he hung out with, like Codes. Anyway, she wasn't going to waste any time worrying about what Rydell might have in mind for Lowell, no way.

What she did worry about was Skinner, whether he was okay, whether he was being taken care of. She was kind of scared to try phoning Fontaine now; every time Rydell made a call out, she worried it might get traced back or something. And it made her sad to think about her bike. She was sure somebody would've gotten it by now. She kind of hated to admit it, but that was starting to make her nearly as sad as Sammy getting killed that way. And Rydell had said he thought maybe Nigel had gotten shot, too.

"And then," Sublett's mother was saying, "Gary Underwood goes through this window. And he falls on one of those fences? Kind with spikes on top."

"Hey, Mom," Sublett said, "you're bending Chevette's ear."

"Just telling her about *Inner Tube*," Mrs. Sublett said, from under the washcloth.

"1996," Sublett said. "Well, Rydell and I, we need her for something." Sublett gestured for her to follow him back into the kitchen.

"I don't think it's a real good idea for her to go outside, Berry," he said to Rydell. "Not in the daytime."

Chevette looked down at the cuff around her wrist. Rydell had sawed the other one off and the chain with it, with a ceramic hacksaw he'd borrowed from somebody down the way. Took about two hours.

Rydell was sitting at the little plastic table where she'd had breakfast. "Well, you can't go, Sublett, because of your apostasy. And I don't want to be in there by myself, not with my head stuck in one of those eyephone things. His parents could walk in. He might listen."

"Can't you just call them on the regular phone, Berry?" Sublett sounded unhappy.

"No." Rydell said, "I can't. They just don't like that. He says they'll at least talk to me if I call them on an eyephone rig."

"What's the problem?" Chevette said.

"Sublett's got a friend here who's got a pair of eyephones."

"Buddy," Sublett said.

"Your buddy?" she asked.

"Name's Buddy," Sublett said, "but that VR, eyephones 'n'

stuff, it's against Church law. It's been revealed to Reverend Fallon that virtual reality's a medium of Satan, 'cause you don't watch enough tv after you start doing it..."

"You don't believe that," Rydell said.

"Neither does Buddy," Sublett said, "but his daddy'll whip his head around if he finds that VR stuff he's got under the bed."

"Just call him up," Rydell said, "tell him what I told you. Two hundred dollars cash, plus the time and charges."

"People'll *see* her," Sublett said, his shy silver gaze bouncing in Chevette's direction, then back to Rydell.

"What do you mean, 'see' me?"

"Well, it's your haircut," Sublett said. "It's too unusual for 'em, I can tell you that."

"Now, Buddy," Rydell said to the boy, "I'm going to give you these two hundred-dollar bills here. Now when'd you say your father's due back?"

"Not for another two hours," Buddy said, his voice cracking with nervousness. He took the money like it might have something on it. "He's helping pour a new pad for the fuel cells they're bringing from Phoenix on the Church's bulk-lifter." Buddy kept looking at Chevette. She had on a straw sun-hat that belonged to Sublett's mother, with a big floppy brim, and a pair of these really strange old-lady sunglasses with lemon-yellow frames and lenses that sort of swooped up at the side. Chevette tried smiling at him, but it didn't seem to help.

"You're friends of Joel's, right?" Buddy had a haircut that wasn't quite skin, some kind of gadget in his mouth to straighten his teeth, and an Adam's apple about a third the size of his head. She watched it bob up and down. "From L.A.?"

"That's right," Rydell said.

"I...I wanna g-go there," Buddy said.

"Good," Rydell said. "This is a step in the right direction, you just believe it. Now you wait out there like I said, and tell Chevette here if anybody's coming."

Buddy went out of his tiny bedroom, closing the door behind him. It didn't look to Chevette like anybody Buddy's age lived there at all. Too neat, with these posters of Jesus and Fallon. She felt sorry for him. It was close and hot and she missed Sublett's mother's air-conditioning. She took off that hat.

"Okay," Rydell said, picking up the plastic helmet, "you sit on the bed here and pull the plug if we get interrupted." Buddy had already hooked up the jack for them. Rydell sat down on the floor and put the helmet on, so she couldn't see his eyes. Then he pulled on one of those gloves you use to dial with and move stuff around in there.

She watched his index finger, in that glove, peck out something on a pad that wasn't there. Then she listened to him talking to the telephone company's computer about getting the time and charges after he was done.

Then his hand came up again. "Here goes," he said, and started punching out this number he said Lowell had given him, his finger coming down on the empty air. When he was done, he made a fist, sort of wiggled it around, then lowered the gloved hand to his lap.

He just sat there for a few seconds, the helmet kind of swiveling around like he was looking at stuff, then it stopped moving.

"Okay," he said, his voice kind of funny, but not to her, "but is there anybody *here*?"

Chevette felt the hair on the back of her neck stand up.

"Oh," he said, the helmet turning, "Jesus—"

35

the
republic
of desire

Rydell had liked doing Dream Walls, when he was a kid in high school. It was this Japanese franchise operation they set up in different kinds of spaces, mostly in older malls; some were in places that had been movie theaters, some were in old department stores. He'd gone to one once that they'd put into an old bowling alley; made it real long and narrow and the stuff sort of distorted on you if you tried to move it too fast.

There were a lot of different ways you could play with it, the most popular one in Knoxville being gunfights, where you got these guns and shot at all kinds of bad guys, and they shot back and then you got the score. Sort of like FATSS at the Academy, but only about half the rez. And none of the, well, color.

But the one Rydell had liked most was where you just went in and sort of sculpted things out of nothing, out of that cloud of pixels or polygons or whatever they were, and you could see what other people were doing at the same time, and maybe even put your stuff together with theirs, if you both wanted to. He'd been kind of self-conscious about it, because it seemed like something that mostly girls did. And the girls were always doing these unicorns and rainbows and things, and Rydell liked to do cars, kind of dream-cars, like he was some designer in Japan somewhere and he could build anything he wanted. You could get these full-color printouts when you were done, or a cassette, if you'd animated it. There'd always be a couple of girls down at the far end, doing plastic surgery on pictures of themselves, fiddling around with their faces and hair, and they'd get printouts of those if they did one they really liked.

Rydell would be up closer to the entrance, molding these grids of green light around a frame he'd drawn, and laying color and texture over that to see how different ones looked.

But what he remembered when he clicked into the Republic of Desire's eyephone-space was the sense you got, doing that, of what the space *around* Dream Walls was like. And it was a weird thing, because if you looked up from what you were doing, there really wasn't anything there; nothing in particular, anyway. But when you were doing it, designing your car or whatever, you could get this funny sense that you were leaning out, over the edge of the world, and the space beyond that sort of fell away, forever.

And you felt like you weren't standing on the floor of an old movie theater or a bowling alley, but on some kind of plain, or maybe a pane of glass, and you felt like it just stretched away behind you, miles and miles, with no real end.

So when he went from looking at the phone company's logo to being right out there on that glassy plain, he just said "Oh," because he could see its edges, and see that it hung there, level, and around and above it this cloud or fog or sky that was no color and every color at once, just sort of seething.

And then these figures were there, bigger than skyscrapers, bigger than anything, their chests about even with the edges of the plain, so that Rydell got to feel like a bug, or a little toy.

One of them was a dinosaur, this sort of T. Rex job with the short front legs, except they ended in something a lot more like hands. One was a sort of statue, it looked like, or more like some freak natural formation, all shot through with cracks and fissures, but it was shaped like a wide-faced man with dreadlocks, the face relaxed and the lids half-closed. But all stone and moss, the dreadlocks somehow stacked from whole mountains of shale.

Then he looked and saw the third one there, and just said "Jesus."

This was a figure, too, and just as big, but all made up of television, these moving images winding and writhing together, and barely, it seemed, able to hold the form they took: something that might either have been a man or a woman. It hurt his eyes, to try to look too close at any one part of it. It was like trying to watch a million channels at once, and this noise was rushing off it like a waterfall off rocks, a sort of hiss that somehow wasn't a sound at all.

"Welcome to the Republic," said the dinosaur, its voice the voice of some beautiful woman. It smiled, the ivory of its teeth carved into whole temples. Rydell tried to look at the carvings; they got really clear for a second, and then something happened.

"You don't have a third the bandwidth you need," the dreadlocked mountain said, its voice about what you'd expect from a mountain. "You're in K-Tel space . . ."

"We could turn off the emulator," the thing made of television suggested, its voice modulating up out of the waterfall-hiss.

"Don't bother," said the dinosaur. "I don't think this is going to be much of a conversation."

"Your name," said the mountain.

Rydell hesitated.

"Social Security," said the dinosaur, sounding bored, and for some reason Rydell thought about his father, how he'd always gone on about what that had used to mean, and what it meant now.

"Name and number," said the mountain, "or we're gone."

"Rydell, Stephen Berry," and then the string of digits. He'd barely gotten the last one out when the dinosaur said "Former policeman, I see."

"Oh dear," said the mountain, who kept reminding Rydell of something.

"Well," said the dinosaur, "pretty permanently former, by the look of it. Worked for IntenSecure after that."

"A sting," said the mountain, and brought a hand up to point at Rydell, except it was this giant granite lobster-claw, crusted with lichen. It seemed to fill half the sky, like the side of a space ship. "The *narrow* end of the wedge?"

"They don't come much narrower, if you ask me," the storm of television said. "You seem to have gotten our Lowell's undivided attention, Rydell. And *he* wouldn't even tell us what your name was."

"Doesn't know it," Rydell said.

"Don't know his ass from a hole in the ground, hee haw," said the mountain, lowering the claw, its voice a sampled parody of Rydell's. Rydell tried to get a good look at its eyes; got a flash of still blue pools, waving ferns, some kind of tan rodent hopping away, before the focus slipped. "People like Lowell imagine we need them more than they need us."

"State your business, Stephen Berry," said the dinosaur.

"There was something happened, up Benedict Canyon—"

"Yes, yes," said the dinosaur, "you were the driver. What does it have to do with *us*?"

That was when it dawned on Rydell that the dinosaur, or all of them, could probably see all the records there were on him, right then, anywhere. It gave him a funny feeling. "You're looking at all my stuff," he said.

"And it's *not* very interesting," said the dinosaur. "Benedict Canyon?"

"You *did* that," Rydell said.

The mountain raised its eyebrows. Windblown scrub shifting, rocks tumbling down. But just on the edge of Rydell's vision. "For what it's worth, that was not *us*, not exactly. We would've gone a more elegant route."

"But why did you do it?"

"Well," said the dinosaur, "to the extent that anyone did it, or caused it to be done, I imagine you might look to the lady's husband, who I see has since filed for divorce. On very solid grounds, it seems."

"Like he set her up? With the gardener and everything?"

"Lowell has some serious explaining to do, I think," the mountain said.

"You haven't told us what it is you want, Mr. Rydell." This from the television-thing.

"A job like that. Done. I need you to *do* one of those. For me."

"Lowell," the mountain said, and shook its dreadlocked head. Cascades of shale in Rydell's peripheral vision. Dust rising on a distant slope.

"That sort of thing is *dangerous*," the dinosaur said. "Dangerous things are very *expensive.* You don't have *any* money, Rydell."

"How about if Lowell pays you for it?"

"Lowell," from that vast blank face twisting with images, "owes *us.*"

"Okay," Rydell said, "I hear you. And I think I know somebody else might pay you." He wasn't even sure if that was bullshit or not. "But you're going to have to listen to me. Hear the story."

"No," the mountain said, and Rydell remembered who it was he figured the thing was supposed to look like, that guy you saw on the history shows sometimes, the one who'd invented eyephones or something, "and if Lowell thinks he's the only pimp out there, he might have to think again."

And then they were fading, breaking up into those paisley fractal things, and Rydell knew he was losing them.

"Wait," he said. "Any of you live in San Francisco?"

The dinosaur came flickering back. "What if we did?"

"Well," Rydell said, "do you *like* it?"

"Why do you ask?"

"Because it's *all* going to change. They're going to do it like they're doing Tokyo."

"Tokyo?" The television-storm, coming back now as this big ball, like that hologram in Cognitive Dissidents. "Who told you that?"

Now the mountain was back, too. "There's not a lot of *slack*, for us, in Tokyo, now..."

"Tell us," the dinosaur said.

So Rydell did.

She had the hat back on, when he took the helmet off, but she was holding those sunglasses in her hand. Just looking at him.

"I don't think I made sense of much of that," she said. She'd only been able to hear his side of it, but it had been mostly him talking, there at the end. "But I think you're flat fucking crazy."

"I probably am," he said.

Then he got the time and charges on the call. It came to just about all the money he had left.

"I don't see why they had to put the damn thing through Paris," he said.

She just put those glasses back on and slowly shook her head.

notebook

(2)

The city in sunlight, from the roof of this box atop the tower. The hatch open. Sound of Skinner sorting and re-sorting his belongings. A cardboard box, slowly filling with objects I will take below, to the sellers of things, their goods spread on blankets, on greasy squares of ancient canvas. Osaka far away. The wind brings sounds of hammering, song. Skinner, this morning, asking if I had seen the pike in the Steiner Aquarium.

—No.

—He doesn't move, Scooter.

Sure that's all Fontaine said? But he'd found her bike? That's no good. Wouldn't go this long without that. Cost an arm and a fucking leg, that thing. Made of paper, inside. Japanese construction-paper, what's it called? Useless, Scooter. Shit, it's your language. Forgetting it faster than we are . . . Tube of that paper, then they wrap it with aramyd or something. No, she wouldn't leave that. Day she brought it home, three hours down there spraying this fake rust on it, believe that? Fake rust, Scooter. And wrapping it with old rags, innertubes, anything. So it wouldn't look new. Well, it makes more sense than just locking it, it really does. Know how you break a Kryptonite lock, Scooter? With a Volvo jack. Volvo jack fits right in there, like it was made for it. Give it a shove or two, zingo. But they never use 'em anymore, those locks. Some people still carry 'em, though. One of those up 'side the head, you'll notice it . . . I just found her one day. They wanted to cart her down to the end, let the city have her. Said she'd be dead before they got her off anyway. Told 'em they could fuck off into the air. Got her up here. I could still do that. Why? Hell. Because. See people dying, you just walk by like it was television?

century

city

37

Chevette didn't know what to think about Los Angeles.

She thought those palm trees were weird, though.

On the way in, Sublett's electric car had pulled up behind this big white trailer-rig with A-LIFE INSTALLATIONS, NANOTRONIC VEGE-TATION across the back of it, and the heads of these fake palm trees sticking out, all wrapped in plastic.

She'd seen it all on tv once, with Skinner, how they were putting in these trees to replace the ones the virus had killed, some Mexican virus. They were kind of like the Bay maglev, or like what Rydell and Sublett said that that Sunflower company was going to do in San Francisco; these things that kind of *grew*, but only because they were made up of all these little tiny machines. One show she'd seen with Skinner, they'd talked about how these new trees were designed so that all kinds of birds and rats and things could nest in them, just like the ones that had died. Skinner told her that he'd run a Jeep into a real palm tree, in L.A., once, and about ten rats had fallen out, landed on the hood and just sort of stood there, until they got scared and ran away.

It sure didn't feel like San Francisco. She felt kind of two ways about it. Like it was just this bunch of *stuff*, all spread out pretty much at random, and then like it was this really *big* place, with mountains somewhere back there, and all this energy flowing around in it, lighting things up. Maybe that was because they'd got there at night.

Sublett had this little white Eurocar called a Montxo. She knew that because she'd had to look at the logo on the dash all the way from Paradise. Sublett said it rhymed with poncho. It was built in Barcelona and you just plugged it into the house-current and left it until it was charged. It wouldn't do much more than forty on a highway, but Sublett didn't like to drive anything else because of his allergies. She said he was lucky they had electric cars; he'd told her all about how he was worried about the electromagnetic fields and cancer and stuff.

They'd left his mother with this Mrs. Baker, watching *Space-hunter* on the tv. They were both real excited about that because they said it was Molly Ringwald's first film. They'd get excited about just about anything, like that, and Chevette never had any idea who they were talking about.

She looked at the handcuff. She'd covered it over with black epoxy goop and a bunch of pink and blue beads she'd got off Sublett's mother; basically it looked like shit, but then again it didn't look all that much like a handcuff.

Rydell was just spending more and more time on the phone, and they'd had to stop and buy fresh batteries twice, Sublett paying.

It kind of bothered her that he didn't give her any more attention. And they'd slept on the same bed again, in the room at the motel, but nothing had happened, even though Sublett had slept out in the Montxo, with the seats tilted back.

All Rydell ever did now was talk to those Republic of Desire people Lowell knew, but on the regular phone, and try to leave messages on somebody's voicemail. Mr. Mom or something. Ma. But he didn't think anybody was getting them, so he'd called up the Desire people and gone on and on about the whole story, everything that happened to them, and they'd recorded it and they were supposed to put it in this Mr. Ma's voicemail. Rydell said they were going to stuff it there, so there wasn't any other mail. Said that ought to get his attention.

When they'd got to L.A. and got a room in a motel, Chevette had been kind of excited, because she'd always wanted to do that. Because her mother had always seemed to have real good times when she went to motels. Well, it had turned out to be sort of like a trailer camp without the trailers, with these little concrete buildings divided up into smaller rooms, and there were foreign people cooking barbecues down in what had been the swimming pool. Sublett had gotten really upset about that, how he couldn't handle the hydrocarbons and everything, but Rydell had said it was just for the one night. Then Rydell had gone over to the foreign people and talked to them a little, and came back and said they were Tibetans. They made a good barbecue, too, but Sublett just ate this drugstore food he'd brought with him, bottled water and these yellow bars looked like soap, and went out to sleep in his Montxo.

Now here she was, walking into this place called Century City II, and trying to look like she was there to pull a tag. It was this kind of green, tit-shaped thing up on these three legs that ran up through it. You could see where they went because the walls were some kind of glass, mostly, and you could see through. It was about the biggest thing around; you could see it forever. Rydell called it the Blob.

It was real upscale, too, kind of like China Basin, with those same kind of people, like you mostly saw in the financial district, or in malls, or when you were pulling tags.

Well, she had her badges on, and she'd had a good shower at the motel, but the place was starting to creep her out anyway. All these trees in there, up all through this sort of giant, hollow leg, and everything under this weird filtered light came in through the sides. And here she was standing on this escalator, about a mile long, just going up and up, and around her all these people who must've belonged there. There were elevators, Rydell said, up the other two legs, and they ran at an angle, like the lift up to Skinner's. But Sublett's friend had said there were more IntenSecure people watching those, usually.

She knew that Sublett was behind her, somewhere, or anyway that was how they'd worked it out before Rydell dropped them off at the entrance. She'd asked him where he was going then, and he'd just said he had to go and borrow a flashlight. She was starting to really like him. It sort of bothered her. She wondered what he'd be like if he wasn't in a situation like this. She wondered what *she'd* be like if she wasn't in a situation like this.

He and Sublett had both worked for the company that did security for this building, IntenSecure, and Sublett had called up a friend of his and asked him questions about how tight it was. The way he'd put it, it was like he wanted a new job with the company. But he and Rydell had worked it out that she could get in, particularly if he was following her to keep track.

What bothered her about Sublett was that he was acting sort of like he was committing suicide or something. Once he'd gotten with the program, Rydell's plan, it was like he felt cut loose from things. Kept talking about his apostasy and these movies he liked, and somebody called Cronenberg. Had this weird calm like somebody who knew for sure he was going to die; like he'd sort of made peace with it, except he'd still get upset about his allergies.

Green light. Rising up through it.

They'd made her up this package at the motel. What it had in it was the glasses. Addressed to Karen Mendelsohn.

She closed her eyes, told herself Bunny Malatesta would bongo on her head if she didn't make the tag, and pushed the button.

"Yes?" It was one of those computers.

"Allied Messenger, for Karen Mendelsohn."

"A delivery?"

"She's gotta sign for it."

"Authorized to barcode—"

"Her hand. Gotta see her *hand.* Do it. You know?"

Silence. "Nature of delivery?"

"You think I open them or what?"

"Nature of delivery?"

"Well," Chevette said, "it says 'Probate Court,' it's from San

Francisco, and you don't open the door, Mr. Wizard, it's on the next plane back."

"Wait, please," said the computer.

Chevette looked at the potted plants beside the door. They were big, looked real, and she knew Sublett was standing behind them, but she couldn't see him. Somebody had put a cigarette out on one, between its roots.

The door open, a crack. "Yes?"

"Karen Mendelsohn?"

"What is it?"

"Allied Messenger, San Francisco. You wanna sign for this?" Except there was nothing, no tag, to sign.

"San Francisco?"

"What it says."

The door opened a little more. Dark-haired woman in a long pale terrycloth robe. Chevette saw her check the badges on Skinner's jacket. "I don't understand," Karen Medelsohn said. "We do everything via GlobEx."

"They're too slow," Chevette said, as Sublett stepped around the plant, wearing this black uniform. Chevette saw herself reflected in his contacts, sort of bent out at the middle.

"Ms. Mendelsohn," he said, "afraid we've got us a security emergency, here."

Karen Mendelsohn was looking at him. "Emergency?"

"Nothing to worry about," Sublett said. He put his hand on Chevette's shoulder and guided her in, past Karen Mendelsohn. "Situation's under control. Appreciate your cooperation."

38 miracle mile

"Wally" Divac, Rydell's Serbian landlord, hadn't really wanted to loan Rydell his flashlight, but Rydell had lied and promised he'd get him something a lot better, over at IntenSecure, and bring it along when he brought the flashlight back. Maybe one of those telescoping batons with the wireless taser-tips, he said; something serious, anyway, professional and maybe quasi-illegal. Wally was sort of a cop-groupie. Liked to feel he was in with the force. Like a lot of people, he didn't much distinguish between the real PD and a company like IntenSecure. He had one of those armed response signs in his front yard, too, but Rydell was glad to see it wasn't IntenSecure. Wally couldn't quite afford that kind of service, just like his car was second-hand, though he would've told you it was *previously owned*, like the first guy was just some flunky who'd had the job of breaking it in for him.

But he owned this house, where he lived, with the baby-blue plastic siding that looked sort of like painted wood, and one of those fake lawns that looked realer than AstroTurf. And he had the house in Mar Vista and a couple of others. His sister had come over here in 1994, and then he'd come himself, to get away from all the trouble over there. Never regretted it. Said this was a fine country except they let in too many immigrants.

"What's that you're driving?" he'd asked, from the steps of the renovated Craftsman two blocks above Melrose.

"A Montxo," Rydell said. "From Barcelona. Electric."

"You live in America," he'd said, his gray hair plastered neatly back from his pitted forehead. "Why you drive that?" His BMW, immaculate, reposed in the driveway; he'd had to spend five minutes disarming it to get the flashlight out for Rydell. Rydell had remembered the time in Knoxville, Christmas day, when the Narcotics team's new walkie-talkies had triggered every car-alarm in a ten-mile radius.

"Well," Rydell said, "it's real good for the environment."

"It's bad for your country," Wally said. "Image thing. An American should drive some car to feel proud of. Bavarian car. At least Japanese."

"I'll get this back to you, Wally." Holding up the big black flashlight.

"And something else. You said."

"Don't worry about it."

"When you pay rent on Mar Vista?"

"Kevin'll take care of it." Getting into the tiny Montxo and starting up the flywheel. It sat there, rocking slightly on its shocks, while the wheel got up to speed.

Wally waved, shrugged, then backed into his house and closed the door. Rydell hadn't ever seen him not wear that Tyrolean hat before.

Rydell looked at the flashlight, figuring out where the safety was. It wasn't much, but he felt like he had to have something. And it was nonlethal. Guns weren't that hard to buy, on the street, but he didn't really want to have to have one around today. You did a different kind of time, if there was a gun involved.

Then he'd driven back toward the Blob, taking it real easy at intersections and trying to keep to the streets that had designated lanes for electric vehicles. He got Chevette's phone out and hit redial for the node-number in Utah, the one God-eater had given him, back in Paradise. God-eater was the one who looked like the mountain, or so he said. Rydell had asked him what kind of a name that was. He'd said he was a full-blood Blood Indian. Rydell sort of doubted it.

None of their voices were real, even; it was all digital stuff. God-eater could just as well be a woman, or three different people, or all three of the ones he'd seen there might've been just one person. He thought about the woman in the wheelchair in Cognitive Dissidents. It could be her. It could be anybody. That was the spooky thing about these hackers. He heard the node-number ringing, in Utah. God-eater always picked up on five, in mid-ring.

"Yes?"

"Paradise," Rydell said.

"Richard?"

"Nixon."

"We have your goods in place, Richard. One little whoops and a push."

"You get me a price yet?" The light changed. Somebody was honking, pissed-off at the Montxo's inability to do anything like accelerate.

"Fifty," God-eater said.

Fifty thousand dollars. Rydell winced. "Okay," he said, "fair enough."

"Better be," God-eater said. "We can make you pretty miserable in prison, even. In fact, we can make you *really* miserable in prison. The baseline starts *lower*, in there."

I'll bet you got lots of friends there, too, Rydell thought. "How long you estimate the response-time, from when I call?"

God-eater burped, long and deliberate. "Quick. Ten, fifteen max. We've got it slotted the way we talked about. Your friends're gonna shit themselves. But really, you don't wanna be in the way. This'll be like something you never saw before. This new unit they just got set up."

"I hope so," Rydell said, and broke the connection.

He gave the parking-attendant Karen's apartment number. After this, it really wasn't going to matter much. He had the flashlight stuck down in the back of his jeans, under the denim jacket Buddy had loaned him. It was probably Buddy's father's. He'd told Buddy he'd help him find a place when he got to L.A. He sort of hoped Buddy never did try that, because he imagined kids like Buddy made it about a block from the bus station before some really fast urban predator got them, just a blur of wheels and teeth and no more Buddy to speak of. But then again you had to think about what it would be like to be him, Buddy, back there in his three-by six-foot bedroom in that trailer, with those posters of Fallon and Jesus, sneaking that VR when his daddy wasn't looking. If you didn't at least try to get out, what would you wind up feeling like? And that was why you had to give it to Sublett, because he'd gotten out of that, allergies and all.

But he was worried about Sublett. Pretty crazy to be worried about anybody, in a situation like this, but Sublett acted like he was already dead or something. Just moving from one thing to the next, like it didn't matter. The only thing that got any kind of rise out of him was his allergies.

And Chevette, too, Chevette Washington, except what worried him there was the white skin of her back, just above the waist of those black bike-pants, when she was curled on the bed beside him. How he kept wanting to touch it. And how her tits stuck out against her t-shirt when she'd sit up in the morning, and those little dark twists of hair under her arms. And right now, walking up to this terracotta coffee-module near the base of the escalator, the rectangular head of Wally's pepper-spray flashlight digging into his spine, he knew he might never get another chance. He could be dead, in half an hour, or on his way to prison.

He ordered a latte with a double shot, paid for it with just about the last of his money, and looked at his Timex. Ten 'til three. When he'd called Warbaby's personal portable from the motel, the night before, he'd told him three.

God-eater had gotten him that number. God-eater could get you any number at all.

Warbaby had sounded really sad to hear from him. Disappointed, like. "We never expected this of you, Rydell."

"Sorry, Mr. Warbaby. Those fucking Russians. And that cowboy fucker, that Loveless. Got on my case."

"There's no need for obscenity. Who gave you this number?"

"I had it from Hernandez, before."

Silence.

"I got the glasses, Mr. Warbaby."

"Where are you?"

Chevette Washington watching him, from the bed. "In Los Angeles. I figured I'd better get as far away from those Russians as I could."

A pause. Maybe Warbaby had put his hand over the phone. Then, "Well, I suppose I can understand your behavior, although I can't say I approve..."

"Can you come down here and get them, Mr. Warbaby? And just sort of call it even?"

A longer pause. "Well, Rydell," sadly, "I wouldn't want you to forget how disappointed I am in you, but, yes, I could do that."

"But just you and Freddie, right? Nobody else."

"Of course," Warbaby had said. Rydell imagined him looking at Freddie, who'd be tap-tapping away on some new laptop, getting the call traced. To a cell-node in Oakland, and then to a tumbled number.

"You be down here tomorrow, Mr. Warbaby. I'll call you at your same number, tell you where to come. Three o'clock. Sharp."

"I think you've made the right decision, Rydell," Warbaby had said.

"I hope so," Rydell had said, then clicked off.

Now he looked at his Timex. Took a sip of coffee. Three o'clock. Sharp. He put the coffee down on the counter and got the phone out. Started punching in Warbaby's number.

It took them twenty minutes to get there. They came in two cars, from opposite directions; Warbaby and Freddie in a black Lincoln with a white satellite-dish on top, Freddie driving it, then Svobodov and Orlovsky in a metallic-gray Lada sedan that Rydell took for a rental.

He watched them meet up, the four of them, then walk in, onto the plaza under the Blob, past those kinetic sculptures, heading for the nearest elevator, Warbaby looking sad as ever and leaning on that cane. Warbaby had his same olive coat on, his Stetson, Freddie was wearing a big shirt with a lot of pink in it, had a laptop under his arm, and the Russians from Homicide had these gray suits on, about the color and texture of the Lada they were driving.

He gave it a while to see if Loveless was going to turn up, then started keying in that number in Utah.

"Please, Jesus," he said, counting the rings.

"Your latte okay?" The Central Asian kid in the coffee-module, looking at him.

"It's fine," Rydell said, as God-eater picked up.

"Yes?"

"Paradise."

"This Richard?"

"Nixon. They're here. Four but not Smiley."

"Your two Russians, Warbaby, and his jockey?"

"Got 'em."

"But not the other one?"

"Don't see him..."

"His description's in the package anyway. Okay, Rydell. Let's do it." Click.

Rydell stuck the phone in his jacket pocket, turned, and headed, walking fast, for the escalator. The boy in the coffee-module probably thought there was something wrong with that latte.

God-eater and his friends, if they weren't just one person, say some demented old lady up in the Oakland hills with a couple of million dollars' worth of equipment and a terminally bad attitude, had struck Rydell as being almost uniquely full of shit. There was nothing, if you believed them, they couldn't do. But if they were all that powerful, how come they had to hide that way, and make money doing crimes?

Rydell had gotten a couple of lectures on computer crime at the Academy, but it had been pretty dry. The history of it, how hackers used to be just these smart-ass kids dicking with the phone companies. Basically, the visiting Fed had said, any crime that was what once had been called white-collar was going to be computer crime anyway, now, because people in offices did everything with computers. But there were other crimes you could still call computer crimes in the old sense, because they usually involved professional criminals, and these criminals still thought of themselves as hackers. The public, the Fed had told them, still tended to think of hackers as some kind of romantic bullshit thing, sort of like kids moving the outhouse. Merry pranksters. In the old days, he said, lots of people still didn't know there *was* an outhouse there to be moved, not until they wound up in the shit. Rydell's class laughed dutifully. But not today, the Fed said; your modern hacker was about as romantic as a hit man from some ice posse or an enforcer with a dancer combine. And a lot harder to catch, although if you could get one and lean on him, you could usually count on landing a few more. But they were set up mostly in these cells, the cells building up larger groups, so that the most you could ever pop, usually, were the members of a single cell; they just didn't know who the members of the other cells were, and they made a point of not finding out.

God-eater and his friends, however many of them there were or weren't, must've been a cell like that, one of however many units in what they called the Republic of Desire. And if they were really going to go ahead and do the thing for him, he figured there were three reasons: they hated the idea of San Francisco getting rebuilt because they liked an infrastructure with a lot of holes in it, they were charging him good money—money he didn't have—and they'd figured out a way to do something that nobody had ever done before. And it was that last one that had really seemed to get them going, once they'd decided to help him out.

And now, climbing the escalator, up through all these kinds

of people who lived or worked up here, forcing himself not to break into a run, Rydell found it hard to believe that God-eater and them were doing what they'd said they could do. And if they weren't, well, he was just fucked.

No, he told himself, they were. They had to be. Somewhere in Utah a dish was turning, targeted out toward the coast, toward the California sky. And out of it, fed in from wherever God-eater and his friends were, were coming these packages, no, packets, of signals. Packets, God-eater called them.

And somewhere, high above the Blob, up over the whole L.A. Basin, was the Death Star.

Rydell dodged past a silver-haired man in tennis whites and ran up the escalator. Came out under the copper tit. People going in and out of that little mall there. A fountain with water sliding down big ragged sheets of green glass. And there went the Russians, their wide gray backs heading toward the white walls of the complex where Karen's apartment was. He couldn't see Warbaby or Freddie.

3:32. "Shit," he said, knowing it hadn't worked, that God-eater had fucked him, that he'd doomed Chevette Washington and Sublett and even Karen Mendelsohn and it was one more time he'd just gone for it, been wrong, and the last fucking time at that.

And then these *things* came through a long gap in the glass, just south of where the handball-courts were, and he hadn't ever seen anything like them. There were a bunch of them, maybe ten or a dozen, and they were black. They hardly made any sound at all, and they were sort of floating. Just skimming along. The players on the courts stopped to watch them.

They were helicopters, but too small to carry anybody. Smaller than the smallest micro-light. Kind of dish-shaped. French Aerospatiale gun-platforms, the kind you saw on the news from Mexico City, and he guessed they were under the control of ECCCS, the Emergency Command Control Communications System, who ran the Death Star. One of them swung by, about twenty feet over his head, and he saw the clustered tubes of some kind of gun or rocket-launcher.

"Damn," Rydell said, looking up at the future of armed response.

"POLICE EMERGENCY. REMAIN CALM."

A woman started screaming, from somewhere over by the mall, over and over, like something mechanical.

"REMAIN CALM."

And mostly they did, all those faces; faces of the residents of this high country, their jawlines firm, their soft clothes fluttering in the dancing downdrafts.

Rydell started running.

He ran past Svobodov and Orlovsky, who were looking at the three helicopters that were much lower now, and so clearly edging in on them. The Russians' mouths were open and Orlovsky's half-frame glasses looked like they were about to fall off.

"ON YOUR FACES. NOW. OR WE FIRE."

But the residents, slender and mainly blond, stood unmoved, watching, with racquets in their hands, or dark glossy paper bags from the mall. Watching the helicopters. Watching Rydell as he ran past them, their eyes mildly curious and curiously hard.

He ran past Freddie, who was flat down on the granite pavers, doing what the helicopters said, his hands above his head and his laptop between them.

"REMAIN CALM."

Then he saw Warbaby, slouched back on a cast-iron bench like he'd been sitting there forever, just watching life go by. Warbaby saw him, too.

"POLICE EMERGENCY."

His cane was beside him, propped on the bench. He picked it up, lazy and deliberate, and Rydell was sure he was about to get blown away.

"REMAIN CALM."

But Warbaby, looking sad as ever, just brought the cane up to the brim of his Stetson, like some kind of salute.

"DROP THAT CANE."

The amplified voice of a SWAT cop, bunkered down in the

hardened sublevels of City Hall East, working his little Aerospatiale through a telepresence rig. Warbaby shrugged, slowly, and tossed the cane away.

Rydell kept running, right through the open gates and up to Karen Mendelsohn's door. Which was half-open, Karen and Chevette Washington both there, their eyes about to pop out of their heads.

"Inside!" he yelled.

They just gaped at him.

"Get inside!"

There were a bunch of big plants beside the door, in a ter-racotta pot about as high as his waist. He saw Loveless step around it, raising his little gun; Loveless had on a silvery sportscoat and his left arm was in a sling; his face was studded with micropore dressings that weren't quite the right shade, so he looked like he had leprosy or something. He was smiling that smile.

"No!" Chevette Washington screamed, "you murdering little *fuck*!"

Loveless brought the gun around, about a foot from her head, and Rydell saw the smile vanish. Without it, he noticed, Love-less sort of looked like he didn't have any lips.

"REMAIN CALM," the helicopters reminded them all, as Ry-dell brought up Wally's flashlight.

Loveless never even managed to pull the trigger, which you had to admit was kind of impressive. What that capsicum did, it was kind of like when Sublett got an allergic reaction, but a lot worse, and a lot quicker.

"You crazy, *crazy* motherfucker," Karen Mendelsohn kept saying, her eyes swollen up like she'd walked through a swarm of hornets. She and Chevette had both caught the edges of that pepper-spray, and Sublett was so worried about the residue that he'd gone into a closet in Karen's bedroom and wouldn't come out. "You crazy, outrageous motherfucker. Do you know what you've *done*?"

Rydell just sat there, in one of her white Retro Aggressive

armchairs, listening to those helicopters yelling outside. Later on, when it all came out, they'd find out that the Republic of Desire had set Warbaby and them up as these bomb-building mercenaries working for the Sonoran Separatist Front, with enough high explosives stored in Karen's place to blow that nipple off the tit and clear to Malibu. And they'd also worked in this hostage-taking scenario, to guarantee the SWAT guys made a soft entry, if they had to. But when the real live Counterterrorism Squad got in there, it would've been pretty hairy, at least if Karen hadn't been a lawyer for *Cops in Trouble*. Those were some angry cops, and getting angrier, at first, but then Pursley's people seemed to have their ways to calm them down.

But the funny thing was, they, the LAPD, never would, ever, admit to it that anybody had hacked the Death Star. They kept saying it had been phoned in. And they stuck to that, too; it was so important to them, evidently, that they were willing, finally, to let a lot of the rest of it just go.

But when he was sitting there, listening to Karen, and gradually getting the idea that, yeah, he was the kind of crazy motherfucker she *liked,* he kept thinking about Nightmare Folk Art, and whatever that woman's name was, over there, and hoping she was coping okay, because God-eater had needed an L.A. number to stick into his fake data-packet, a number where the tip-off was supposed to have come from. And Rydell hadn't wanted to give them Kevin's number, and then he'd found the Nightmare number in his wallet, on part of a *People* cover, so he'd given God-eater that.

And then Chevette came over, with her face all swollen from the capsicum, and asked him if it was working or were they totally fucked? And he said it was, and they weren't, and then the cops came in and it *wasn't* okay, but then Aaron Pursley turned up with about as many other lawyers as there were cops, and then Wellington Ma, in a navy blazer with gold buttons.

So Rydell finally got to meet him.

"Always a pleasure to meet a client in person," Wellington Ma said, shaking his hand.

"Pleased to meet you, Mr. Ma," Rydell said.

"I won't ask you what you did to my voicemail," Wellington Ma said, "but I hope you won't do it again. Your story, though, is fascinating."

Rydell remembered God-eater and that fifty thousand, and hoped Ma and Karen and them weren't going to be pissed about that. But he didn't think so, because Aaron Pursley had already said, twice, how it was going to be bigger than the Pookey Bear thing, and Karen kept saying how telegenic Chevette was, and about the youth angle, and how Chrome Koran would fall all over themselves to do the music.

And Wellington Ma had signed up Chevette, and Sublett, too, but he'd had to pass the papers back into that closet because Sublett still wouldn't come out.

Rydell could tell from what Karen said that Chevette had told her pretty much the whole story while she and Sublett had kept her there, and kept her from hitting any IntenSecure panic-buttons. And Karen, evidently, knew all about those VL glasses and how to get them to play things back, so she'd spent most of the time doing that, and now she knew all about Sunflower or whatever it was called. And she kept telling Pursley that there was a dynamite angle here because they could implicate Cody fucking Harwood, if they played their cards right, and was he ever due for it, the bastard.

Rydell hadn't ever even had a chance to see that stuff, on the glasses.

"Mr. Pursley?" Rydell kind of edged over to him.

"Yes, Berry?"

"What happens now?"

"Well," Pursley said, tugging at the skin beneath his nose, "you and your two friends here are about to be arrested and taken into custody."

"We are?"

Pursley looked at his big gold watch. It was set with diamonds around the dial, and had a big lump of turquoise on either side. "In about five minutes. We're arranging to have the first press-conference around six. That suit you, or would you rather eat first? We can have the caterers bring you something in."

"But we're being arrested."

"Bail, Berry. You've heard of bail? You'll all be out tomorrow morning." Pursley beamed at him.

"Are we going to be okay, Mr. Pursley?"

"Berry," Pursley said, "you're in trouble, son. A cop. And an honest one. In trouble. In deep, spectacular, and, please, I *have* to say this, clearly *heroic* shit." He clapped Rydell on the shoulder. "*Cops in Trouble* is *here* for you, boy, and, let me assure you, we are all of us going to make out just *fine* on this."

Chevette said jail sounded just fine to her, but please could she call somebody in San Francisco named Fontaine?

"You can call anybody you want, honey," Karen said, dabbing at Chevette's eyes with a tissue. "They'll record it all, but we'll get a copy, too. What was the name of your friend, the black man, the one who was shot?"

"Sammy Sal," Chevette said.

Karen looked at Pursley. "We'd better get Jackson Cale," she said. Rydell wondered what for, because Jackson Cale was this new young black guy who acted in made-for-tv movies.

Then Chevette came over and hugged him, all of her pressing up against him, and just sort of looking up at him from under that crazy-ass haircut. And he liked that, even if her eyes were all red and her nose was running.

39

celebration

on a

gray day

O n Saturday, the fifteenth of November, the morning after his fourth night with Skinner, Yamazaki, wearing an enormous, cape-like plaid jacket, much mended and smelling of candle-grease, descended in the yellow lift to do business with the dealers in artifacts. He brought with him a cardboard carton containing several large fragments of petrified wood, the left antler of a buck deer, fifteen compact discs, a Victorian promotional novelty in the shape of a fluted china mug, embossed with the letters "OXO," and a damp-swollen copy of *The Columbia Literary History of the United States*.

The sellers were laying out their goods, the morning iron-gray and clammy, and he was grateful for the borrowed jacket, its pockets silted with ancient sawdust and tiny, nameless bits of hard-ware. He had been curious about the correct manner in which to approach them, but they took the initiative, clustering around him, Skinner's name on their lips.

The petrified wood brought the best price, then the mug, then eight of the compact discs. It all went, finally, except for the literary history, which was badly mildewed. He placed this, its blue boards warping in the salt air, atop a mound of trash. With the money folded in his hand, he went looking for the old woman who sold eggs. Also, they needed coffee.

He was in sight of the place that roasted and ground coffee

when he saw Fontaine coming through the morning bustle, the collar
of his long tweed coat turned up against the fog.

"How's the old man doing, Scooter?"

"He asks more frequently after the girl..."

"She's in jail down in L.A.," Fontaine said.

"Jail?"

"Out on bail this morning, or that's what she said last night.
I was on my way over to bring you this." He took a phone from his
pocket and handed it to Yamazaki. "She has that number. Just don't
go making too many calls home, you hear?"

"Home?"

"Japan."

Yamazaki blinked. "No. I understand..."

"I don't know what she's been up to since that storm hit, but
I've been too busy to bother thinking about it. We got the power back
but I've still got an injury case nobody's bothered to claim yet. Fished
him out of what was left of somebody's greenhouse, Wednesday
morning. Sort of down under your place, there, actually. Don't know if
he hit his head or what, but he just keeps coming around a little, then
fading off. Vital signs okay, no broken bones. Got a burn along his side
could be from a bullet, some kind of hot-shoe load..."

"You would not take him to a hospital?"

"No," Fontaine said, "we don't do that unless they ask us to,
or unless they're gonna die otherwise. Lot of us have good reason
not to go to places like that, get checked out on computers and all."

"Ah," Yamazaki said, with what he hoped was tact.

"'Ah' so," Fontaine said. "Some kids probably found him
first, took his wallet if he had one. But he's a big healthy brother and
somebody'll recognize him eventually. Hard not to, with that bolt
through his johnson."

"Yes," Yamazaki said, failing to understand this last, "and I
still have your pistol."

Fontaine looked around. "Well, if you feel like you don't need
it, just chuck it for me. But I'll need that phone back, sometime. How
long you gonna be staying out here, anyway?"

"I . . . I do not know." And it was true.

"You be down here this afternoon, see the parade?"

"Parade?"

"November fifteenth. It's Shapely's birthday. Something to see. Sort of Mardi Gras feel to it. Lot of the younger people take their clothes off, but I don't know about this weather. Well, see you around. Say hi to Skinner."

"Hi, yes," Yamazaki said, smiling, as Fontaine went on his way, the rainbow of his crocheted cap bobbing above the heads of the crowd.

Yamazaki walked toward the coffee-vendor, remembering the funeral procession, the dancing scarlet figure with its red-painted rifle. The symbol of Shapely's going.

Shapely's murder, some said sacrifice, had taken place in Salt Lake City. His seven killers, heavily armed fundamentalists, members of a white racist sect driven underground in the months following the assault on the airport, were still imprisoned in Utah, though two of them had subsequently died of AIDS, possibly contracted in prison, steadfastly refusing the viral strain patented in Shapely's name.

They had remained silent during the trial, their leader stating only that the disease was God's vengeance on sinners and the unclean. Lean men with shaven heads and blank, implacable eyes, they were God's gunmen, and would stare, as such, from all the tapes of history, forever.

But Shapely had been very wealthy when he had died, Yamazaki thought, joining the line for coffee. Perhaps he had even been happy. He had seen the product of his blood reverse the course of darkness. There were other plagues abroad now, but the live vaccine bred from Shapely's variant had saved uncounted millions.

Yamazaki promised himself that he would observe Shapely's birthday parade. He would remember to bring his notebook.

He stood in the smell of fresh-ground coffee, awaiting his turn.

acknowledgments

This book owes a very special debt to Paolo Polledri, founding Curator of Architecture and Design, the San Francisco Museum of Modern Art. Mr. Polledri commissioned, for the 1990 exhibition *Visionary San Francisco*, a work of fiction which became the short story "Skinner's Room," and also arranged for me to collaborate with the architects Ming Fung and Craig Hodgetts, whose redrawn map of the city (though I redrew it once again) provided me with Skywalker Park, the Trap, and the Sunflower towers. (From another work commissioned for this exhibition, Richard Rodriguez's powerful "Sodom: Reflections on a Stereotype," I appropriated Yamazaki's borrowed Victorian and the sense of its melancholy.)

The term Virtual Light was coined by scientist Stephen Beck to describe a form of instrumentation that produces "optical sensations directly in the eye without the use of photons" (*Mondo 2000*).

Rydell's Los Angeles owes much to my reading of Mike Davis's *City of Quartz*, perhaps most particularly in his observations regarding the privatization of public space.

I am indebted to Markus, aka Fur, one of the editors of *Mercury Rising*, published by and for the San Francisco Bike Messenger Association, who kindly provided a complete file of back issues and then didn't hear from me for a year or so (sorry). *Mercury Rising* exists "to inform, amuse, piss off, and otherwise reinforce" the messenger community. It provided me with Chevette Washington's workplace and a good deal of her character. Proj on!

Thanks, too, to the following, all of whom provided crucial assistance, the right fragment at the right time, or artistic support: Laurie Anderson, Cotty Chubb, Samuel Delany, Richard Dorsett, Brian Eno, Deborah Harry, Richard Kadrey, Mark Laidlaw, Tom Maddox,

Pat Murphy, Richard Piellisch, John Shirley, Chris Stein, Bruce Sterling, Roger Trilling, Bruce Wagner, Jack Womack.

Special thanks to Martha Millard, my literary agent, ever understanding of the long haul.

And to Deb, Graeme, and Claire, with love, for putting up with the time I spent in the basement.

Vancouver, B.C.
January 1993

A
C
K
N
O
W
L
E
D
G
E
M
E
N
T
S
•